M

Sandom, J. G.
The hunting club

M

Sandom, J. G.
The hunting club

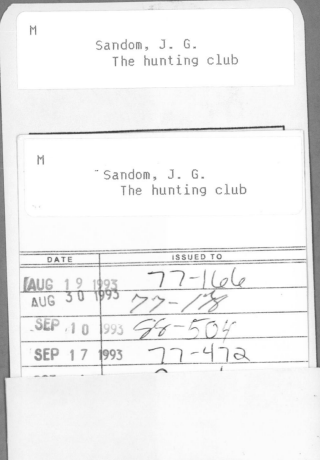

DATE	ISSUED TO
AUG 1 9 1993	77-166
AUG 3 0 1993	77-178
SEP 1 0 1993	88-504
SEP 17 1993	77-472

MYNDERSE LIBRARY

Seneca Falls, N.Y.

The
Hunting
Club

BY THE SAME AUTHOR

Gospel Truths

The Hunting Club

J. G. Sandom

A PERFECT CRIME BOOK
DOUBLEDAY
NEW YORK   LONDON   TORONTO   SYDNEY   AUCKLAND

A PERFECT CRIME BOOK
PUBLISHED BY DOUBLEDAY
a division of Bantam Doubleday Dell Publishing Group, Inc.
1540 Broadway, New York, New York, 10036

DOUBLEDAY is a trademark of Doubleday, a division
of Bantam Doubleday Dell Publishing Group, Inc.

Grateful acknowledgment is made for permission to reprint lyrics from:

"TUNNEL OF LOVE." Words and music by Bruce Springsteen.
Used by permission.

"JOSIE." Words and Music by WALTER and DONALD FAGEN. © Copyright 1977 by
MCA MUSIC PUBLISHING, A Division of MCA INC., New York, NY 10019. USED BY
PERMISSION. ALL RIGHTS RESERVED.

"CAN'T BUY ME LOVE." Words and Music by JOHN LENNON and PAUL MCCARTNEY.
© Copyright 1964 by NORTHERN SONGS LIMITED. All rights administered by MCA
MUSIC PUBLISHING, A Division of MCA INC. Under license from ATV MUSIC, New
York, NY 10019. USED BY PERMISSION. ALL RIGHTS RESERVED.

Book design by Tasha Hall

Library of Congress Cataloging-in-Publication Data

Sandom, J. G., 1956–
    The hunting club / J. G. Sandom. — 1st ed.
        p.   cm.
    "A Perfect crime book."
    I. Title.
PS3569.A51945H8   1993
813'.54—dc20   92-41066
                                                      CIP

M

ISBN 0-385-46778-8
Copyright © 1993 by J. G. Sandom
All Rights Reserved
Printed in the United States of America
July 1993
First Edition
1   3   5   7   9   10   8   6   4   2

Let us swear an oath, and keep it with an equal mind,
In the hollow Lotos-land to live and lie reclined
On the hills like Gods together, careless of mankind.

—Alfred, Lord Tennyson
"The Lotos-Eaters"

The
Hunting
Club

Part 1

I

Thump. Thump. Thump. Across the wetlands of New Jersey, the two
Bell helicopters fly, across the Hudson River to the city. Manhattan
claws the morning sky, the ethereal blueness of another day thrown
up by the Atlantic. The helicopters swoop, Glen Morrow in the
lead, with John Payne riding on his heels, across the leaden winter
water, across the broken wooden docks, the shattered warehouses
and empty lots. *Thump, thump,* the rotors spin, each with the ca-
dence of a beating heart, the gush of unseen thermals, and Morrow
swings his craft across the silver skyline, skidding on the air. The
two ships tilt and slide. Payne feels the blood rush to his head as he
strains against the force of gravity. His body presses at the door,
against the Plexiglas and steel, a thousand feet of air and then the
distant city streets below.

"How'm I doing?" Morrow says, into his headset microphone.

"Okay, but don't get too close to the buildings, or they'll
pull your license, Glen. I mean it. And keep your damn tail
steady."

Glen Morrow's helicopter falls, swoops down along the West
Side Highway by the river. "Jesus Christ," says Payne. He trims his
cyclic stick and follows. They skirt the river at a hundred knots,
past Houston and TriBeCa, skimming the patchwork quilt of
brownstone roofs, riding the shimmer of a thousand cars, the glimmer of Christmas lights and neon, to the south. The financial dis-

trict looms ahead, a stand of crystals, black on blue. The spires of
the World Trade Towers lift the morning sun.

"I told you not to get so close," says Payne, but Morrow does
not hear him. He is trying out his brand new speaker airphone. His
helicopter pulls up to a hover, against the black face of a skyscraper.
Payne shimmies in beside him.

"Pull back," says Payne. "You're still within five hundred
feet." He can clearly see a line of curious faces, gaping out at him
from windows in the building. "Stop showing off."

"Are you ready, John?" says Morrow on the radio.

The words reverberate inside Payne's headset. He turns the
volume down. "For what?"

Thump. Thump. "Tonight. Tom's bachelor party."

"I guess so," Payne replies, but Morrow is already on the
phone with someone else. The bachelor party. It's all they've been
talking about all week.

Payne shakes his head. He pulls up his collective and the helicopter rises slowly. Morrow is talking to a woman. The voice seems
familiar, but Payne can barely hear her, when the knowledge comes
to him from nowhere, and he understands why Glen is hovering so
close. This is Bob Litchfield's building.

"What do you mean he's on the line," says Morrow with disgust. "Tell him it's me, Jill. And look out the window, behind
you."

"I'm sorry, Mr. Morrow. I can't hear you. There's a . . ."

"Just turn around," says Morrow. "That's right. Hello."

Payne sees the telltale hourglass shape of Litchfield's secretary
behind the tinted glass, can almost feel her catch her breath and
pull away.

"Is that you, Mr. Morrow? You're awful close," she says.

"Tell Bobby I'm on the line, Jill."

There is a click and Payne can hear Bobby's high-pitched nasal voice. "I've got Rick on hold, Glen. Let me call you back."

"Did you confirm the reservation?"

"That's what we're talking about. The Quonset Hut, right?
Tom said he'd meet us there at eight."

"Look out your window, Bobby."

There is a gasp, and arms swing wildly in the window next to Jill's.

"You're nuts, Glen," Litchfield says.

"Pull up, Glen, dammit," Payne says, but his words echo in his head. Morrow is talking to the Teterboro tower. Someone has lodged a complaint.

The helicopters drop away, across the pyramids of glass, across the West Side Highway and out into the bay. The Statue of Liberty glows green against the inky water. Morrow is still talking to Mildred in the Teterboro tower. He is explaining that he pulled in close to Litchfield's building because he thought he saw a jumper on the roof, and for some strange reason she believes him, for some uncanny reason she accepts each word without a moment's hesitation, as if there is something in Glen's voice so genuine and clear, so naturally persuasive that to dispute it would seem petty, insincere.

How does he always do it? wonders Payne. Mildred signs off with a word of thanks, and Morrow's laugh resounds across the airwaves.

"I'm telling you, Glen. They're going to yank your license." Payne tries to sound responsible, but he knows that chiding him is useless. It is so hard to be mad at Morrow. It is like being mad at a tree, or the tide.

"They can try," says Morrow, and his ship dives forward suddenly, banking toward the Statue of Liberty, cutting at the air. *Thump. Thump.* Payne starts to follow, but Morrow's A-Star is too fast. Payne pulls up his collective. He flares his ship into a hover, and strains to watch as Morrow's silver helicopter hurtles toward the sea, like Icarus descending. A laugh rolls through his headset. The distant ship banks steeply round the statue, almost crashing through the giant torch. Payne holds his breath. The helicopter falls and falls, and disappears behind the crown, a single rotor disk from Liberty, only to reappear unscathed, skimming the waves across the bay, like a bird of prey, churning up whitecaps, the sound of laughter trailing.

II

He can't hear what the world is saying with the water rushing round his ears, only the music pounding through the white enamel, the rumble of a distant subway, timed to the pulsing of his heart. Payne lifts his face out of the sink and blows a pearl of water from his lips.

His eyes are half closed. He reaches for a paper towel and rips it from the chrome dispenser gleaming on the wall. He wipes his face, and there he is, in the mirror, the hair disheveled, dark and wet along the brow. There is the thin peak of a nose, the hazel deep-set eyes, the wide mouth and high forehead. He crumples the paper towel in his fist and runs a hand back through his dark brown hair. Then he straightens his tie. He is prepared now. He is ready for the world, he tells himself. He spins on his heel and heads out through the men's room door.

A jumble of tables, orange birds of paradise in square terra-cotta pots, a waiter with a tray of sky blue frozen daiquiris— The Quonset Hut is packed tonight, the tables dressed in starched white tablecloths, resplendent with heaped plates of fish and fowl, blackened Cajun blues and Cornish hen, the curve of ribs, *radicchio* salad, crab and shrimp. Countless fluted glasses spill their light across the eager faces of the crowd. Payne looks down at his watch. I have to pace myself. It's early still. Across the room, the background hum of conversation is punctured by Glen Morrow's seductive laugh. There, past the tall blonde with the cinder cocktail dress, beyond her black companion in the double-breasted navy suit. There's Morrow with his Caribbean tan and wide disarming smile, with faithful Bobby Litchfield at his side. And there's Tom Demarest. Poor Demarest. Trying to make a go of it, trying to forget the seconds ticking, ticking slowly toward the moment when he'd finally turn and say, "I do." Somewhere there is the sound of breaking glass. Somewhere a knife slips on a plate and a woman in a chartreuse miniskirt picks up her napkin from the floor, her silver earrings dangling. Payne weaves his way between the tables, drawing the bands of conversation to him, a disappointment here, a compliment, a lie, a curse. He ambles casually around a wide stone pillar and skillfully avoids the waitress—*Hi, I'm Tiffany*—porting yet another bottle of champagne to table twenty-seven.

"What happened? You get lost?" says Avery, as Payne sits down beside him.

"The place is packed. For a Wednesday."

Rick Avery grins and looks around. "The Babylon of our millennium. The overfed and undernourished jetsam of our self-indulgent culture."

"You should have been a copywriter, Avery, instead of an art director," Payne replies. The waitress pops the cork on the champagne.

"A morass of mindless mediocrity, mooning mawkishly," adds Avery.

"Malcontents."

"Misfits."

"Misanthropes."

"Plenty of babes, though," Avery says.

"That, too."

Rick Avery is dressed as always in a pair of black jeans, a black turtleneck, and an umber jacket. His dark brown hair is long and straight, and falls constantly across his bright, black-plastic-rimmed glasses. He smiles and says, "Speaking only as a disinterested observer, I'm sure, Mr. Payne. How is Jan, anyway? Still vomiting when she sees you in the morning? Not that I blame her, mind you."

"She's home." Payne lifts his glass up toward the waitress. "Weaving a tapestry."

"Oh, you guys," says Bobby Litchfield. "You ought to be setting an example for Demarest here."

"Don't look at me," says Avery. "I have yet to fall. I'm the last of the Watusi, the only warrior left."

"The only one not guaranteed to get laid on a Friday night," says Morrow. He looks up at the waitress. "Right, Tiffany?" Glen's tanned face lights up with a smile. He has just returned from another weekend in the Caribbean and his skin is cocoa brown.

"Hey, you missed me," Tom Demarest complains, pointing at his empty glass.

The waitress frowns and pulls the bottle of champagne out of the standing wine bucket. "He thirsts for you," Morrow tells her. "In seventy-two hours he'll be a married man."

Tiffany is a gaunt, red-haired giant from Michigan, looking for a speaking part. "My heartiest congratulations," she says flatly.

She is wearing false eyelashes, Payne notices. Her pink taffeta dress is tight across the chest. "You mean condolences?" he says.

"What's that?" says Morrow. "Trouble in paradise?"

Tiffany empties the champagne bottle into Demarest's glass, and slips it back into the silver wine bucket, neck down through the ice.

"Take it from me, Tom," Morrow adds. "Marriage is a wondrous, sacred act. The union of two people. The sharing of two lives, ideas, ambitions. I should know," he says to Tiffany. "I'm on my third." He reaches out and takes her by the hand. "Pay no attention to these barbarians."

"Let go of me, mister."

"How about another bottle?" Morrow says, releasing her.

She pulls her arm away. "Haven't you guys had enough?"

"Enough!" says Avery indignantly. "Have we had enough, boys?"

"No!" they answer.

Tiffany shakes her head and walks away. They all stare at her as she wiggles in between the tables.

Demarest sighs. "I've never had a redhead," he admits. He is a large man, with the rounded shoulders of a former weight lifter, and light brown thinning hair, combed with aplomb across his bald spot. His eyes are a gravy brown, oxlike, set close together, linked by a tuft of light brown hair at the bridge of his short flat nose.

"What about that girl, Beth Cohen, from Mount Holyoke? She had red hair," says Payne.

"Oh, sure! That was only for a month, fifteen years ago. And it came out of a bottle, so it doesn't count."

"You should see this redhead we just cast for Jackson's Wax," says Avery. "Unbelievable. She plays the girlfriend of a guy who wakes up from a nap in a complete panic when he realizes that he's only got . . ." His face contorts in horror. ". . . *ten* minutes to clean up his apartment before this heavy date. We see the redhead walking down the city streets, dressed in her office clothes, stepping out of a florist with a huge bouquet, thoughtfully examining the label of a California cabernet in a dusty wine store, waving at the old *guido* who works at the corner newsstand. Meanwhile, as she strolls, we keep cutting back to the apartment where this guy is running around like a wild man, spraying and polishing everything in sight with his Original Jackson's Wax. You know. He sprays the kitchen counter and a roast chicken—no red meat, of course—appears out of nowhere, steaming with baby carrots. Spray and puff . . . like magic. The redhead arrives at the front door and we get her view of things: the perfect living room, with everything agleam; the seductive music; the table set for dinner in the background, candlelit; and our handsome hero, twitching his tail like a hungry cat."

"A true man of the eighties," Payne says.

"Right. Sensitive yet strong."

"Bread winner *and* bread baker."

"You taking notes?" says Morrow, jabbing Demarest in the ribs. "We're warning you. It's not too late."

"Prepare to dive," cries Avery. "Whoop, whoop. Dive! Dive!"

"Oh, come on, you guys." Bobby Litchfield takes his wire-rimmed glasses off and begins to wipe them with his kerchief. His eyes are large and wet, the corners red from drinking. His receding hair is short and curly. He is wearing a red silk bow tie and a russet

Gieves tweed jacket. "Don't let them kid you, Tom. I've been married for twelve years and I've never regretted it. Well, practically never." He smiles.

"That's because she doesn't give you enough free time for you to realize you regret it," Morrow says.

"And before you know it you'll have kids. Right, John?" adds Litchfield, with a wink at Payne. He replaces his glasses and pushes them deftly up the snub curve of his nose. "Don't listen to these jerks. Having a kid is really great. It's why we're on this planet in the first place. It's what really counts."

"Tick, tick, tick," says Avery. "Each second brings you closer to the altar." He spreads his hands out on the tablecloth. "Well, I'm happy being free. And I'm the only member of The Hunting Club who can say that now, and really mean it." He lifts his champagne glass. "To Tom and Anna Demarest. May they rest in peace."

Demarest smiles. It is the smile of an idiot, thinks Payne, the smile of a man who hasn't got a clue.

He remembers the day of his own wedding. Four years ago, he had worn the same flat open face. The world had been so full of promise then, of things to come, of possibility. Except the possibility of failure, failure by forgetfulness, dissolution by neglect. It wasn't that he didn't love Jan anymore. It was love itself that seemed to have changed. It had been homogenized by time, made dull by repetition, until the feelings had retreated into background hum, like the constant scratching of cicadas, like the drumming of chopper blades.

"I thought you guys might want to order now." Tiffany has returned, Payne notices, with a handful of menus and another bottle of champagne. She slips the fresh champagne into the wine bucket, and hands the menus to them one by one. "We also have some specials. For appetizers we have fresh chanterelle mushrooms cooked in olive oil with a hint of garlic . . ." Payne watches her mouth as she drones on, the way her lips come together in the corners, the slight overbite, the curve of her nostrils, the pink tenderness where her bright red plastic earrings hang. He takes his menu and drops it on the table. She delivers her lines precisely, smiles, and glides away.

They study their menus for a moment without speaking. Then Avery turns to Morrow. "I have a bone to pick with you," he says.

"Pick away, lad."

"It's about that gaming stock."

"Which one?"

"The one you told me about. The Shangri-la Casino. The one with all the bowling lanes."

"No, that's the Showboat."

"You know the one I mean. In Atlantic City. I did exactly what you told me. I bought the stock at seventeen."

"And?"

"And disaster, man. It dropped to fourteen when I finally sold."

"That was yesterday. I told everyone to sell last week. If you'd come out with us last Wednesday—"

"I did," says Litchfield. "At nineteen fifty. Two thousand shares. Let's see, that's five K if you don't count taxes or commissions." He grins at Morrow. "Thanks, Glen."

"Yeah, thanks a lot." Avery's dark face is bitter.

Morrow hunches over the table. "How many times do I have to tell you guys? If you're going to play this game, you have to have the stomach for it. You have to be able to lose. If you can't afford it, don't take the risk." He fixes a cold stare on Avery. "And the next time I say sell, Rick, sell. Don't fuck around. Don't go up to Vermont for the weekend and forget about it. Don't wait until after lunch. If I tell you to do something, *do* it." He smiles and his face abruptly changes. The blue eyes soften. The lines about his mouth relax. It is the face of a petulant god, thinks Payne. One minute it holds the wrath of thunder under a dark and furrowed brow, the next it lights up like a fissure in the clouds. The deep-set ice blue eyes grow bright. The golden head tilts back. The famous Morrow smile expands across the tanned and noble face, at once both artfully bemused and natural: the proud grin of an older brother watching you at plate; a father looking through a lighted doorway at his sleeping child.

"Ready to order?" Tiffany's Midwestern accent lifts a corner of the conversation.

"Yeah, we're ready," Morrow says.

Payne settles on Atlantic salmon broiled with dill, served with asparagus and new potatoes. He can see the woman at the next table chewing contentedly on the light pink flesh.

As soon as Tiffany departs, the conversation turns to Anna, Tom Demarest's fiancée. Demarest sings her praises. She is the most beautiful, the most understanding, the most impeccable family. . . .

Payne finds himself staring at the woman at the next table. She is eating asparagus with her fingers, gliding the green buds through Hollandaise, biting off the dark tips with white teeth. The woman is about Jan's age, with the same brown hair, the same highlights of red copper even, spilling over her bare shoulder. Her skin is very fair, her features delicate and small. So much like his wife, except, of course, without the bold bow of Jan's pregnant stomach.

The food comes and Payne finds himself drawn into conversation with Avery about his search for an apartment in New York. Now that Demarest is getting married and moving out, Avery can no longer afford the house they've been sharing in Connecticut. It's time to find a loft or a one-bedroom in the city. "It's got to have a lot of light," he says, chewing his mushroom ravioli. "Big windows. I've got to get back to my work. You know I haven't painted in six months."

"I haven't had sex in two."

Avery snorts and turns away. Then he glances back at Payne and says, "You're kidding, right?"

"I wish I were."

"What are you two talking about?" Morrow leans across the table for the champagne bottle.

"Nothing."

"About my apartment. Or lack thereof," says Avery. "How about it, Bobby? I thought you said you knew a lot of landlords."

"If you want to spend two hundred thousand, I can get you a place on Park."

"Actually, I was thinking about Soho or TriBeCa."

"Who wants more wine?" Morrow waves the bottle in the air. "It's still half full."

Payne offers up his glass. "Thanks."

"So, what did you think, John? How'd I do? Today, I mean," says Morrow casually.

"Fine. Just fine," says Payne.

Litchfield knocks Payne's glass out of the way, and replaces it with his own. Morrow keeps pouring the champagne.

"You know you gave Jill a heart attack this morning," adds Litchfield with a giggle. "When your helicopter came whipping up like that, I swear, she almost had a cow."

"Trying to get me fired," Payne replies. "You're crazy, Glen."

"Was that your final class?" says Litchfield.

Morrow nods. He is gazing into space, absent.

"It was with me," says Payne. "I'm a traffic reporter, not a fucking stunt pilot."

"You see. And you were so reluctant to give lessons. I told you so."

"Was I?" Payne says. "I don't remember that."

"I do," Morrow says.

Payne sips his champagne. "You did all right today," he says. "You're a very capable pilot, Glen."

The words have their desired effect. Morrow smiles privately and leans back in his chair.

Why was it so hard to say? Payne wonders. Morrow was a good pilot. More than that, he was a natural. Perhaps that was the reason. Morrow was a natural at so many things. He always had been.

Payne feels the champagne bubbles sting his tongue. Morrow already had so much. Did he really need to fly down to his farm in Pennsylvania? Why couldn't he drive, or take a train like everybody else? When the engine caught and the helicopter shuddered into life, when the steel blades pulled him from the power of the earth, Payne wished to be there by himself. It was his world. It was his city from the air, the towering stone, the metal and the glass, the mile on mile of highway, street, and road. He closes his eyes and rises higher, above the silver Hudson River, above the urban lots, the oily stream of traffic, trimming the bottom of the clouds, suspended, like the baby in Jan's uterus, curled up and all alone in his Plexiglas balloon.

Somewhere a woman laughs. He turns to see if he can spot her in the crowd. Hands rise to gesture or to eat. Someone is pointing.

Someone waves over at the door. Payne sees the crowd reflected in the mirror behind the bar. It shifts and undulates. It seethes and eddies. The woman laughs again but he can't see her.

He turns back to the table. Avery is telling a story about a junior account executive at McQuaid, Delaway and Scoosi, the ad agency where he works. "I've fallen in love," he admits. "She has the face of a Venus. Long blond hair. Green eyes. Curves that don't quit. I'm talking parabolic."

"Why don't you ask her out?" says Morrow.

"I did."

"And?"

"She told me she doesn't date guys she's working with. It's against her code."

"She couldn't say it was your hairy nostrils. Dear John," says Payne, falling in.

"Wait, it gets worse. About two weeks ago I'm working late on the Goldcrest account when I realize I need confirmation on a board change. So I take the stairs up to the A.E.'s office to see if he has sign-off from the client. There's nobody around. It must be nearly nine o'clock. I hear Michael—that's the account exec's name —in his office. It sounds like he's on the phone, because I can only hear one voice. So I knock on the door and poke my head in." Avery pauses for effect. "There's Michael behind his desk, leaning back in his chair, his eyes closed and his hands locked together behind his head. He hears me coming in. 'Yeah, what's up?' he asks me, casual-like, not even opening his eyes. I tell him what I need. He thinks about it for a moment, and then says, 'Go ahead.' So I split."

"That's it?" says Demarest. "What about the blonde?"

Avery smiles. "At first I didn't see them."

"What?"

"Her shoes, man. I was looking up at Michael. He sat there so nonchalant. It was only when I was about to leave that I looked down and saw the bottom of these green pumps poking out from under the desk."

"You gotta be kidding," Payne says.

"An hour later, I'm standing by the elevator to leave when the door opens and there's Michael and the junior A.E. They're all bundled up in their coats. I look down and, sure enough, there are the green pumps."

"So much for her code," says Morrow. He pushes his empty plate away.

"Are we finished here?" Tiffany has returned. "How about some dessert?" She waves at a Puerto Rican busboy, and he starts to take their plates away.

Payne reaches into his jacket and fishes out his Marlboros.

"Are you on the menu too?" says Demarest.

The waitress straightens, arms akimbo, one fist on her hip. "What's that?"

"You heard him," Morrow says. "He's getting desperate as the hour draws near."

"With whipped cream," Demarest continues. "I like whipped cream."

"Now, now, boys, simmer down." Tiffany wags a finger at them. "You want dessert, or not?"

"And hot fudge topping," Demarest says, "dripping down the side."

"You're terrible," she says and laughs. "Well, here, if you don't want anything else." She drops their tab on the table. Litchfield picks it up. He glances at it for a second and hands her his American Express card.

"What about my dessert?" says Demarest.

"Now look what you've done," says Morrow. "He's heart-broken."

The waitress smiles uncertainly.

"Cold, heartless woman, you've destroyed him," Morrow says. Demarest looks crushed. He takes his napkin and dabs the corners of his oxlike eyes.

"Oh, poor baby," she replies. Demarest reaches out for her but she slips gingerly away. "Okay, that's it," she says, no longer smiling. "I don't want to have to call the manager."

"Oohh," says Demarest, with mock terror. "Not the manager. Please, God, not him!"

"Come on, you guys," says Payne. "Cut it out. Thanks for your help, miss."

Everyone laughs. Tiffany shakes her head and strides away.

"No sense of humor," Morrow says.

"Uptight," says Demarest. "Frigid."

"This is an outrage to The Hunting Club," says Morrow. "Our guest of honor has been slighted."

"Insulted," Avery says.

"Spurned, I would say."

"Is it my nose, my breath?" whines Demarest.

"Or both," says Payne. He plucks a book of matches from the ashtray and lights his cigarette.

"I move we adjourn immediately—" says Morrow.

"Seconded," Demarest says.

"—and reconvene in more suitable surroundings."

"Whereto?" says Litchfield, perking up.

"Where the women are easy and the drinks flow free."

"A land just beyond the horizon, a fat country," adds Avery. "Where the deer and the antelope play."

"The Party Girl Lounge," says Morrow. "Six blocks up."

"What's that, a strip joint?" Litchfield crinkles his nose.

"I believe the correct term is exotic dancers," Morrow says.

"I'm game. But only if we take the cars. It's fucking cold out there." Demarest pushes his chair back from the table. "What's the matter, BB? Got something against naked women?"

"Very funny." The busboy returns with Litchfield's credit card. "If you guys want to," he says absently, adding up the figures. "I guess one drink won't kill me."

"No, but the view might," Avery says.

Demarest laughs. It is a forced and stuttering laugh, choked off by a cough. The laugh of a drunk, Payne thinks.

"Give her a fat tip," says Avery.

Payne stares at Demarest struggling with his coat. She earned it, he thinks. And then he wonders, do I look like that? A red-eyed, pale accountant. Once tall and trim, now bulging at the middle. A bald spot yawning on my head. Not as bad, perhaps, but close to it. The same theme. Two thirty-six-year-olds rushing headlong into middle age. And he remembers Demarest from another time, another winter day, his long legs pounding down the football field, the Hadley-Williams game, his arms outstretched, and Morrow's perfect pass descending. They had been 13 and 0 that year, 13 and 0 thanks to Tom Demarest and Morrow. And to think the coach had almost cut Tom from the team, until Glen had intervened.

"Here, Tom," Payne says, stepping in. He slips the coat over Demarest's broad sloping shoulders. Until Glen had practiced with him every day, every rainy afternoon for hours, pass and receive, pass and receive, until Tom could catch them in his sleep, and Morrow pleaded with Coach Dunbar, and Demarest was lifted from the fire, like a moth on Morrow's fingers.

"Thanks, buddy."

They file out through the narrow central aisle between the dining tables. Morrow nods at the maître d' and drives through the brass revolving door, and they gather in the silent street, the night wind nibbling at their skin.

"Nervous, Tom?" says Payne. Demarest shudders from the cold. They both look up, up past the outline of the art gallery across the street, beyond the World Trade towers, where a distant 747 slips into view and is gone.

"I guess a little," Demarest says.

Payne clasps him by the shoulder. Avery and Morrow are walking up the block, with Litchfield at their heels. "That's only natural," Payne says quietly. "Don't worry about it."

"But are you happy, John? In your marriage, I mean. I guess you must be since you're having a kid."

What could he say? "Of course, I am, Tom. You will be too. Anna's a fine girl. I mean that."

They turn quickly from the Quonset Hut and make their way up the street. Payne lifts the collar of his leather jacket up against the icy wind gusting from the river. His words have fallen to the ground, it seems, blown off into the night. They mingle with the echoes of their footsteps, rise up against the brick walls running down the street, and disappear. What business did he have to give advice? He'd known Demarest for fifteen years. Payne flicks his cigarette into the gutter. Too long to tell him the truth.

III

The Party Girl Lounge winks on the corner of White and Church, next to a bodega and the SoHo Neon Gallery. There is a window with a row of blinking lights. The words GIRLS, GIRLS, GIRLS gleam underneath. There is a recessed entrance, with a pay phone by the door.

Payne parks his red Accord beside the curb, right behind Litchfield's Continental. Avery has already found a tight spot for his Supra, next to Morrow's precious BMW across the street. The cars pant in the cold night air. Avery and Morrow jump out. They wave at Payne, then turn and disappear into the Continental.

Payne cuts his engine. He's been to most of Morrow's hangouts in TriBeCa but he's never been to this one. Church Street is almost empty. Low brick buildings line the street, the storefronts shuttered tight. An office tower glimmers in the distance. Night shift, Payne thinks.

He gets out of his Accord, locks the doors, and walks over toward Litchfield's Continental. Despite his quilted leather jacket, the mincing wind cuts through him like a shard of ice. Litchfield's tinted rear window falls. "What's up?" says Payne.

Avery grins, his thin dark face framed by the open window. He spins a joint between two fingers.

Payne shakes his head. He opens the door and ducks inside, slamming the door behind him.

"Don't get any burning seeds on the upholstery," says Litchfield from behind the wheel. His voice barely resounds in the tight space.

Morrow is sitting in the front seat beside him. He rolls his eyes and says, "Liz may find them."

"Or Sally. I don't want my daughter to know my friends are all drug addicts. Is that a lot to ask? Is that so strange? Anyway, I thought you'd quit."

"Except for special occasions," Avery says. "Remember?"

"Perhaps this isn't special enough," Morrow says.

"Just be careful, is all I'm saying."

Avery slips the joint between his lips. "You should learn to relax, Bobby. You've been working too hard lately. All that litigation. All those co-op deals. I think they're getting to you." He turns to Payne. "Got a light?"

Payne pats his coat. He pulls the Quonset Hut matches from his pocket, tears one off, and strikes it against the cover.

Avery leans into the flame. "So, Tom," he says, inhaling. "Where are you and Anna going for your honeymoon?" He passes the joint to Demarest beside him.

Demarest takes a long hit. He squints his large brown oxlike eyes, and his eyebrows knit together. "Secret," he says, without exhaling. He shakes his head. "Good try."

"Oh, right, I forgot. He thinks it's bad luck to tell."

Demarest exhales and passes the joint to Morrow in the front seat. "Rick's been trying to find out for weeks. To no avail."

The ash from the joint falls off as Morrow brings it to his lips.

"God dammit, Glen," spits Litchfield. He wipes the seat off furiously. "I asked you to be careful."

"You're such a superstitious fuck, Tom," Morrow says. He takes a drag off the joint. "It's no big secret, anyway. I know where you're going."

"Where? Who told you? Cindy, right?"

"Maybe. Does it begin with A?"

"All right, all right!" says Demarest. "We're going to Antigua."

"Don't you mean Anguilla?" Avery says.

Demarest elbows Avery in the ribs. "Antigua, Anguilla. What's the difference, you asshole? If you already knew, why were you bugging me all week?"

Everybody laughs. Morrow passes the joint to Payne. He looks at it for a moment, trying to decide. It's been over a year since he last smoked, over a year since he and Jan decided to try to have a baby. It doesn't seem that long. Not really. It seems like only yesterday. He can still remember their lovemaking the night the baby was conceived. Jan lying on the bed with the pillow underneath her. The warm scent of her hair. The rain falling in white sheets against the skylight. He slips the joint between his lips and inhales deeply. The smoke curls up inside his head. He feels it building, building until the back of his skull lifts off and the blood starts pumping through his face. He starts to cough. "Jesus," he says, handing the joint back to Avery. He coughs again. "Nice stuff."

"So what's in Anguilla, Tom?" says Litchfield. He purses his lips, shakes his head. His fat face glimmers in the half-light. "I've never heard of it."

"Nothing. That's it. No big hotels. No casinos. No fancy cruise ships in the harbor. There's absolutely nothing to do except eat, swim in the Caribbean, and make love."

"Boy, is Anna going to be disappointed," Morrow says.

The windows of the Continental are smeared with condensation from their breath. Payne watches the smoke billow in the air. His head begins to throb. He cracks the window open with a slight push of his finger against the panel in the door. The night air slaps his face. He looks outside; a pair of eyes look back. "Hey, Glen," he says. The sound of his voice seems to come from far away. "We've got company."

Everyone looks up. Payne closes the window and the stranger disappears.

"Let's get out of here," says Morrow. He opens the door. The overhead light comes on, and then goes off as suddenly.

They struggle out of Litchfield's Continental. Payne shuts the door behind him and Litchfield locks it from the other side. Morrow is standing beside a man in a long black coat. Payne can see that he's a vagrant. The tattered coat. The rough wool hat. The white eyes glowing in the dark, unshaven face. The man says something and Morrow shakes his head.

The Party Girl Lounge winks on the corner. Demarest and Morrow start to walk toward the entrance, with Litchfield and Avery right behind. Only Payne hangs back. The vagrant has picked him from the crowd. It is always this way, he thinks. There's something about my face. Patsy, it says. Soft touch. The vagrant stops a few feet from the car.

"Got a cigarette?" he says. His voice has the timbre of shifting gravel. Even in the blinking half-light of the street, Payne can see that he's a drunk. The vagrant lifts his hand up slowly, as if in benediction. His fingers are black and swollen. A filthy cuff of thermal underwear pokes from his ragged sleeve.

"Yeah, sure," says Payne. Without even thinking he reaches into his leather jacket and pulls out his pack of Marlboros. "Help yourself." He shakes the pack. A solitary cigarette appears. The vagrant's eyes focus on the filter. It takes him only a moment to take the cigarette from the pack, but it is long enough. Lights flash and Payne can see the vagrant's face, a spider web of capillaries, the broken nose, the sores about the mouth. "Got a light too, mister?" He stabs the cigarette into his mouth.

Payne takes his matches out and hands them to the vagrant. For a moment their fingers touch and Payne recoils instinctively, surprised and something more—disgusted by the stranger's touch, the steely feel, the weathered texture of the skin, the street person. "Here you go, pal. Keep 'em."

Payne turns and walks away. Red lights blink on the corner. He can see Litchfield and Avery disappearing into the open darkness of the entrance to the Lounge. "Wait up," he shouts.

"Thanks, mister," the vagrant says behind him. Payne puts his hands into his pockets. The cold wind gnaws his face. A few more steps and he can hear the sound of music pumping. The lights blink on the corner. The music stops as the door swings closed. "Thanks a lot," he hears again, a little closer now. He reaches for the door within the darkened entrance. He pulls it open and the music slams against him, carried on the warm and smoky air. The lights entice. He hears a woman laugh, the sound of glasses striking, and then the door shuts noiselessly behind him.

. . .

Payne sighs. The jukebox is playing Steely Dan. *When Josie comes home, so good. She's the pride of the neighborhood.* His eyes are drawn to a dance stage to his right. A girl with long black curly hair is lying on her stomach on the stage. She is naked except for a G-string running down between her buttocks. Her legs are bent at the knee, and she is waving her feet back and forth to the beat of the music.

Payne feels himself staring and turns away. The lounge is no more than forty feet long. A bar runs along the wall on one side of the room. Ten or twelve patrons are slumped on bar stools by the bar, or leaning against it. Most are staring at the girl on the first stage by the entrance, but some sit facing the bar, nursing their drinks, talking to the barmaids or each other. Morrow, Litchfield, and Avery are discussing where they should sit. Tom Demarest is staring at the girl on the stage. She is drinking out of a cocktail glass, sipping through a thin red plastic straw. "John. John, over here."

Payne looks up. Avery is calling to him. Morrow and Litchfield have already taken their coats off and are sitting halfway down the bar. Payne settles in beside them. He turns to see the girl flip over on her back. She swings her legs around until her feet face the audience. Then she picks herself up on her elbows and for the first time Payne can see her clearly. She's young, no more than twenty, Puerto Rican. Her hair is dark and curled. Her nose is small and somewhat flat against the face, the nostrils flaring as she breathes. Her eyes are large and almond-shaped, deep brown, unfathomable, distracted, the corners darted with mascara, the eyelids blushed with orange powder. The lips are full, pomegranate red and pouting, soft and wet. She's just a little fat, thinks Payne, as his eyes play over her, the perfect light brown shoulders, the roundness of her upper arm. Puppy fat. He watches her glide her hands along her thighs, across the soft curve of her stomach, up to her breasts. She squeezes her thick brown nipples in her fingers, each digit tipped in red. Then she laughs. She is staring directly at Payne. With a sudden motion, she throws her legs into the air, curling them backward over her head, and cartwheels to her feet.

"Jesus, did you see that?" Demarest says. "She's a fucking gymnast. A pretzel."

Payne takes his leather jacket off and stuffs it in his lap. He turns to order a drink but Morrow is already talking to the barmaid. There is a mirror running the entire length of the room behind the bar. Bottles of liquor crowd the shelf. Balloons dangle from the wall, festooned with tinsel. There is another barmaid, a Vietnamese or Thai girl at the far end of the bar. She is laughing with a customer, engaged, a million miles away.

"Drinks or more champagne?" Morrow shouts above the din.

Payne shrugs. "Whatever Tom wants, I guess."

"Drinks," Demarest decides. "Bring on the hard stuff."

Morrow smiles and hands the barmaid a one-hundred-dollar bill. She is dressed in a black bodysuit and fishnet stockings. Her hair is blond and teased. A diamond stud winks in her nose. "Thanks," she says with a bold smile. Her teeth are bad, but it doesn't matter. She takes a glass and drags it through the ice sink behind the bar, bending over in front of Morrow to let her cleavage show.

Morrow laughs.

"What'll it be, gentlemen?" They order their drinks and she sets them up before them.

Payne scans the lounge. Most of the patrons are men in suits, Wall Street types, young professionals like him. There are a couple of thin black men in T-shirts sitting at a table below the second stage near the back of the room. A heavy metal rocker guards his beer beside them. And to his right, a thin bald man sits quietly with his hands around his Perrier, mesmerized by the Puerto Rican dancer on the first stage near the door. He looks like a bank teller, Payne thinks absently. A computer programmer.

"Do you dance, too?" says Morrow to the barmaid.

She shakes her head. "Tend bar. Though I don't know how much more naked I could get. You know what I mean?" She laughs, then looks up at the mirror on the wall. Something has caught her eye. A rouge line out of place. She smooths it with the palm of her hand.

"Yeah, sure," says Morrow, turning round. "What do you say we grab that table, guys? It looks like the last one." He spins away from the bar without waiting for an answer.

The table is situated directly below the second stage at the rear of the room. They settle down beside it. The jukebox is playing Madonna's "Like a Virgin." On the first stage by the entrance, the Puerto Rican girl is dancing by the mirror on the wall behind the stage. She is facing the glass, watching herself as she moves her ass backward and forward in time with the music. Madonna whines. The dancer leans against the mirror with one hand, as she runs the other over her buttocks.

A door to the right of the second stage opens onto the main floor and two new girls appear. One is black and painfully thin, with smooth coffee brown skin and high cheekbones. She is wearing a tight blue miniskirt and turquoise halter top.

The other girl catches Payne by surprise. She has dark brown hair, pinned loosely at the top of her head in a knot. She is wearing glasses which appear too big for her face. Her skin is milky white in the hot glow of the track lights. The girls walk directly beside their table, and Payne can smell their perfume as they pass. It is sweet and floral. The second girl looks down. Payne feels her gaze upon him like a gust of wind off the sea. Her eyes are round and dark behind the lenses of her glasses. Her lips are glossy pink. She looks Irish, Payne thinks, like Jan. She smiles and he feels a stirring deep inside him. He is embarrassed at the candor of her gaze. The innocence is gone. The lips part and he can see her small white even teeth. There is something about her, he thinks, something wounded and vulnerable. No, more than that. Something available. It is a look which belies her glasses and the schoolmarm hair. She is wearing a white blouse buttoned at the throat. Suddenly she looks up, then turns away. Payne watches her retreat across the lounge. Her miniskirt rides high along her thighs, drum tight across her buttocks. Her legs are long, well-shaped and lean, alabastrine on stiletto heels. She stops at the end of the bar beside a forty-five-year-old suit with a mustache. They obviously know each other. He kisses her on the cheek. She says something and the man laughs, but the sound is drowned out by the music.

"Hey, Payne. Payne?" says Avery.

"Hey what?"

"Put your tongue back in your head. Someone may trip on it."

Payne reaches for his gin and tonic and turns casually away. On the stage by the entrance, the Puerto Rican dancer has dropped down to her knees. She slips off the stage to the floor of the bar. Then she gathers up her tips, her outer clothes, and her drink, and makes her way across the lounge to the second stage. Payne feels as though he's watching her through a window. Her movements are strangely natural, unplanned and unrehearsed. She might be dressing in the morning in her room, or stepping from a bath. She is completely alone. She takes another sip from her drink, and parks it at the rear of the second stage beside her clothes and money. Then she smiles at Morrow and swings up on the stage. Everyone at the table looks up. She crawls forward on her hands and knees to the edge of the stage before them. Her thick pink tongue plays once across her teeth. A faint blue vein runs from the corner of her mouth, like a trail of wine to her chin. She lies down on her stomach, props herself up with her elbows, and slides a finger into her mouth. It disappears with excruciating slowness between red lips. She repeats the movement over and over, staring down at Morrow. Her hips begin to rise and fall in time with the music. The jukebox blares "The Boys of Summer," by Don Henley. The dancer pulls her finger from her lips and licks the red tip of her fingernail. Morrow rises. He reaches for the stage. There is a twenty-dollar bill, folded lengthways, in his fingertips. The girl smiles, leans over for the note, but he ignores her. He pokes the bill between her breasts. It sticks to the sweat on her skin. She squeezes her breasts together so that the bill won't fall, and lifts herself to her knees. She grins at Morrow. Her teeth are large and white, unnaturally bright against the light brown skin. Her black almond-shaped eyes widen as she glances at the note for the first time. Then she throws it over her shoulder without looking, and it lands at the rear of the stage, only inches from her drink.

"Big spender," Tom Demarest roars as Morrow slips back to his seat.

"She's working hard. She deserves it."

"I bet that's not the only thing that's hard around here," Avery says. "So how did you hear about this place? Your mother tell you?"

"It's been here for years," says Morrow with a laugh. "Ted from the office brought me here last month, after the Equus deal."

Payne looks over and notices the black dancer has taken the

first stage near the entrance. She is wearing light blue three-inch heels. She rocks back and forth to the music, spins and leans against the mirror on the wall. She turns her head, so that her face is flush to the glass. She reaches behind her. Her purple fingernails are long and curled. They ride along the back of her black thighs, catch on the hem of her miniskirt, and slowly roll the blue material up. Her buttocks quiver as she stamps her feet. She leans a little farther forward and slips a hand into the front flap of her G-string.

"Captain, Captain," Avery says with a thick Scottish brogue. "The engines can't take any more. The dilithium crystals are going to blow."

They all laugh. The biker at the next table looks over for an instant and they all laugh again. Morrow leans his head toward Avery. "What do you mean you think all bikers have small dicks?" He speaks in a stage whisper. Avery kicks him underneath the table.

"Grow up, you guys," says Litchfield.

The girl begins to rub herself between her legs.

"Grow up! Is that what you said? Did you hear that?" Avery says to Payne. "Don't you realize, Litchfield, that my very livelihood depends upon my ability to intuit the eighteen-to-thirty-five-year-old? Do you know how big that market segment is? Do you realize how much money they spend?"

"A lot of taxes," Demarest says. He finishes his drink and slams it on the table. "Billions. Man, it's hot in here."

"Billions and billions of particles," says Avery.

"Googols," Payne replies.

"Oh, God, let's not talk taxes," Morrow says. "It's almost the fifteenth. Time for the quarterly bloodletting."

Payne laughs. Morrow always complained about taxes. It was his litany, his theme song. But then, of course, Morrow paid more taxes every quarter than Payne made the entire year.

The barmaid with the black bodysuit appears beside them with a tray. "How about another round, boys?" she asks, taking up their empty glasses.

"Thanks," says Morrow. "Are you sure you're not a dancer?"

"Sorry to disappoint you." She starts to turn away.

"Never?"

She stops, hesitates as if to listen to a distant sound, then looks down in his face. "Do I know you, mister?"

Morrow smiles. He has the countenance of a priest, a counselor or confessor, Payne thinks.

"No, I don't think so."

She parks the corner of her tray on her hip. "I used to dance. In Jersey."

"Why did you stop?"

"I got tired."

Morrow reaches into his Armani jacket and removes his crocodile wallet. "Here. Buy yourself an alarm clock." Another one hundred dollar bill appears, like sleight of hand.

She laughs and shakes her head. "I don't think so. But I'll get your drinks," she says, and walks away.

Litchfield shoves Morrow by the shoulder.

"Can't buy me love, love, everybody tells me so," sings Avery.

"Fuck you," says Morrow with a smile.

"Ah, who can fathom the wiles of women?" Avery says. "Mysterious as the East."

"Where men are king," says Demarest.

"King Tom, God help us," Payne says. "Is that what Anna calls you?"

"Come here, King," Avery says, as if he's calling a Great Dane. "A little harder, King."

"Oh, shut up."

"Don't listen to him, Tom. Rick's just jealous," Litchfield says. "Believe it or not, even sex gets better when you're married."

"Yeah, right," says Avery sarcastically. "If better is the same thing every night for the rest of your life."

"Every night, if you're lucky," Payne says.

"Right."

"What's better, Glen," asks Litchfield, "sex when you're single, or when you're married? Honestly."

"Honestly?" Morrow ponders for a second. "Sex out of marriage."

"That's not what I meant."

"You asked the question. Tell me if I'm wrong. Go ahead, tell me the sex you had in Atlanta last year wasn't the best you ever had."

"Shut up, Glen. You're just drunk."

"I'm not drunk," says Morrow.

"Aha," says Avery with relish. "Atlanta, did you say? No, wait, I remember. That real estate junket, last September. Come to think of it, he did seem particularly frisky after that trip."

Litchfield shakes his head, glancing first at Morrow, then at Avery. "You're wrong."

"And what about that time in New Orleans?" says Avery. "You notice, members of the jury, it's always the hot climates. Humidity. That's the catalyst."

"That's not what I meant. It's still better with Liz."

Morrow smiles. "Yeah, I guess you're right," he says. "I guess it is."

"What do you mean by that?"

"Nothing." Morrow stands up suddenly. "Got to pee." He pats Avery on the shoulder.

Avery looks up. Morrow smiles at him and Avery starts to rise. "Me, too," he says. "Back in a minute." They head toward the men's room at the rear of the bar.

"What did he mean by that?" says Litchfield once again.

He is like a dog with a bone, thinks Payne. He just won't put it down. "Nothing," he says. "You know Glen."

"Yeah, that's the problem."

"Hey, check it out, Tom," Payne says, trying to change the subject. "I think you've got a fan."

Demarest looks up. At the rear of the stage the Puerto Rican girl is leaning over with her hands around her ankles, looking through her legs at Demarest, her long dark curly hair hanging down. She is mouthing the words of Billy Idol's "Rebel Yell" thumping from the jukebox. She stands and spins around. Her breasts bounce as she shimmies to the lip of the stage. Demarest leans back with surprise. The girl is dancing right above him. He grins and she smiles back, then drops down to her knees. Her tongue slides hastily across her teeth and disappears. Payne reaches for his drink, but it's no longer there. The girl continues to smile at Demarest as she strokes her open thighs before him with her nails. She takes one of her breasts up in her hand and squeezes it to her lips. Her tongue darts at the black nipple. Her impenetrable gaze drifts from her breast to Demarest and back again. Suddenly, a hand appears above them. It is Morrow. He and Avery have returned. A twenty-dollar bill pokes out from Morrow's fingers. "Go ahead," he tells Demarest. "Give it to her."

"No, thanks." Demarest shakes his head, still grinning.

"Go ahead, man," Avery says, as he sits down. His face is flushed and gleaming in the light.

Demarest looks back at the dancer. She is squeezing her breasts, trying to push both of her dark nipples into her mouth at the same time. Her black eyes are barely open. She sways to the charged beat of the music. Demarest takes the money from Morrow's fingers. He stands clumsily against the table, reaches forward, tilting. The note falls from his fingers but it never hits the stage. In a flash, the girl has snatched the paper from the air. She leans back on her haunches. "Thanks," she says to Demarest. She smiles and slips the note into her G-string. As she plucks the narrow waistband, she shifts the black material to the side, exposing herself before them for an instant. Then with a laugh she throws her head back suddenly and somersaults across the stage.

"Damn," says Demarest. He looks at Morrow with a grin and falls back in his chair. "Damn! I thought that was illegal."

"Take it easy, Tom. Haven't you ever been to a strip joint before?"

"Sure, I have. Don't you remember? That time in Springfield, back in college. It was you and me and Rick and that guy Stephen from Gamma Psi."

"Oh, God. I'd hoped never to remember that night." Avery groans and covers his face with his hands.

"That's it?" says Morrow. "That was the only time?"

"I think so. I mean, come on, let's face it, Glen. Who goes to strip joints, anyway?"

"I see mostly men in suits."

"What I don't understand," says Litchfield, "is why—just because it's a bachelor party—we all feel obligated to go to a place like this. This whole thing is from another era."

"And this from a man who has more bow ties than I have socks," says Morrow.

"It's retro," Avery says. "Like taffeta and tie-dyed T-shirts. It's today. It's now. It's happening."

"Man, you're fucked up," says Payne.

"But not fucked up enough. Not nearly. The world is changing too fast." Avery waves his hand. "The city is crumbling around us. Look at the crime. The street people. In two days I will lose my roommate." He grabs Demarest by the scruff of the neck and shakes him. "I've known this guy for twenty years. Since Hadley. Twenty years, man."

"Nineteen," says Demarest, correcting him.

"Whatever. This is my maudlin speech. Don't interfere when I'm singing your feeble praises."

"Sorry."

"Almost a quarter of a century. He's known every girl I've ever loved. He's stayed up with me, comforted me, yelled at me, cried with me. He was there when I got my first real job." He shakes his head. "You all were. And when I got fired. Through all of it. Through three cars and a hundred girls. Too many years."

"Who ordered Bombay Gin and tonic?" The Asian bar girl shows up out of nowhere with a tray.

"I did," answers Payne.

"What happened to the other girl?" says Morrow, looking round.

"She's busy. Who gets J and B on the rocks?"

"Does she ever dance?" says Morrow.

"No, I don't think so. What's the matter, mister? I don't make you happy?" She laughs and squeezes up against him. She is only about five feet tall, with long black hair, and a pronounced spoon-like jaw. Her smile is far too wide. Her ears poke out from underneath her hair. But her eyes shine brightly and her laugh is bubble-light, infectious.

"You make me *very* happy," says Morrow, taking up his drink.

"I dance," she says. "You come back Monday. I'm very good dancer."

"I bet you are."

She begins to sway to the song on the jukebox. She is wearing a leopard leotard and a pleated black miniskirt. Payne can see the garters holding up her nylons. Her heels are at least three inches tall and yet she still seems tiny next to Morrow.

"Where are you from?" says Morrow.

"Thailand."

"You're a long way from home."

She laughs again. "This is my home now. You like my dancing?"

"Sure," says Morrow. He reaches into his jacket and pulls out his wallet. "How much do I owe you for the drinks?"

"You already pay before."

"Then why don't you keep this," he answers, handing her a twenty. "For your dancing."

She snatches up the bill. "Thank you! You're so handsome too." She stuffs the bill into her skirt, drops down suddenly into his lap and kisses him on the cheek. "You come back Monday. I do a dance just for you."

Morrow starts bouncing her on his knee. "Promise?" he says.

She buries her hand between his legs. "Promise," she answers with a grin.

Morrow continues to bounce her in his lap. Litchfield asks her something about Thailand but Payne can't hear what she is saying. The jukebox is playing "Beast of Burden." The bass line pounds the room as Jagger remonstrates. Payne closes his eyes. It is suddenly unbearably hot in the room. He can feel the sweat running down his sides under his jacket and shirt. He takes another sip from his drink and it occurs to him that he can barely taste the tonic. It is pure gin. The bar girl laughs the same balloon-light laugh. Payne opens his eyes. She has wrapped her arms around Rick Avery's neck. Her long dark Oriental hair cascades across her leotard. Payne sees her lean forward to nibble on Avery's ear. Her wide mouth opens, the white teeth gnash against the skin, and she looks up at him, at Payne, and winks. Payne smiles and suddenly he thinks about his brother, Sam. The music lifts him over time, across the years, and he can see the paper in his hand, the airmail envelope, the funny foreign stamp. Sam's last letter to him. His parents had received one more, and then, of course, the one sent on by Colonel Phillip Jones, the company commander. Sam had just come back from a week of R&R in Thailand. He had gone to this little bar somewhere in Bangkok. Payne had been too young then to understand all of the jokes and innuendos. But years later, when he had found the letter and reread it, the same words had revealed new meaning and it had seemed as though his brother were alive still somewhere else, still telling jokes, still laughing.

Payne opens his eyes as the bartender jumps to her feet. She pulls her leotard aside and one of her breasts pokes free. It's small and pale, capped with a tiny dark nipple. "We're closing soon," she says. "But come back Monday. Special dance for you. Remember. Just for you."

Litchfield is grinning now. His bow tie is crooked and Payne can see a smudge of lipstick on his cheek.

"Time for another pee," says Morrow, rising to his feet. "How about it, Tom?" He taps his jacket pocket.

"Don't mind if I do." Demarest stands uncertainly. "Back in a minute."

They disappear into the men's room and Avery turns to Payne. "You should check it out, John."

"You guys are terrible," says Payne.

"Lighten up. It's a bachelor party. How often do we get fucked up like this? Maybe once or twice a year. Besides, I told Melissa I'd see her later."

"Good for you."

"Hey, man." Avery wraps his arm around Payne's shoulders. "Did you mean what you said before?"

"Before what?"

"About Jan. About not getting laid. Why didn't you tell me?"

"Forget it. I don't want to talk about it."

"So why'd you bring it up? Are you still mad about last Wednesday? You should have gone out with Melissa and me."

"It was Club night out, Rick. Remember? And I'm not mad."

"Just disappointed. I can tell. Don't you ever get tired of the guys? Jesus Christ, John. I know you do." Avery looks at Litchfield. He is playing with his swizzle stick, staring at the stage.

"Sometimes."

"Things are changing, John. Can't you feel it? It's like the end of an era."

"Come on, Rick. It's Tom's night out. Just leave it alone, okay? Okay?"

"Okay, okay," says Avery. He pulls his arm away. "I didn't mean anything. Look," he says, reaching for his drink. "It's your friend."

Payne turns to follow Avery's gaze. The dancer with the glasses and the dark brown hair is moving toward the stage. She says a few words to the Puerto Rican girl, who points to their table without looking as she gathers up her money. The dancer with the glasses stares at Payne.

"She's got your number, boyo," Avery says. "Look out."

The Puerto Rican dancer disappears through a door to the right of the stage. The jukebox is playing "Tunnel of Love." Bruce Springsteen's voice crackles over the guitar. The girl with the glasses swings easily up onto the stage. She fiddles with her purse and cigarettes and rises slowly to her feet.

Fat man sitting on a little stool. Takes the money from my hand while his eyes take a walk all over you. . . . She starts to move to the music. She glides to the center of the stage. The light picks up the highlights in her hair. *Hands me two tickets, smiles, and whispers good luck.* She stops and plants her feet. She starts to unbutton her shirt. *Cuddle up angel cuddle up my little dove.* Her pink fingernails click on pearl buttons. The material parts. Payne can see the white skin gleaming underneath. *We'll ride down baby into this tunnel of love.*

She pulls her blouse out of her skirt, looks down at Payne, and smiles. He can feel the tension in the moment, the slow aching pace of the second hand as it crawls across the beer clock on the wall. He can see the curve of her breasts where she has pulled her blouse apart. She bends toward him and her breasts swell up against the white material. She rolls her head, the motion carries to her shoulders and her chest, her hips revolve, her thighs part slightly, and she's turned the other way. Her back is to him now. She dances lightly to the far end of the stage and leans against the mirror. With one hand she begins to remove the hairpins from her hair. It falls in waves about her head, across the straight line of her shoulders. It shakes and bounces as she dances. She drops her hands. Her fingers have found the zipper of her skirt, and she is pulling at it gently. *I can feel the soft silk of your blouse, and them soft thrills in our little fun house.* For a moment it appears caught, for a beat only before sliding down. The skirt drops to the floor and she steps free of it with a kick. Her legs look even longer in her light pink G-string. The half moons of her buttocks quiver at the bottom of her blouse. She takes her glasses off, folds them, and drops them on her purse. He can feel the blood rise to his face. The music pounds. Someone is crying in the background, or is it just the juke-box? He reaches for his drink. It is nothing but ice. He sucks a cube into his mouth and cracks it with his teeth. He can hear the clear shards grinding in his head. *Then the lights go out and it's just the three of us, you me and all that stuff we're so scared of.* She turns and stares and suddenly she's there, above him, only feet away. He spins the ice in his drink. She smiles. There is no one else. The room is empty. They are the only ones left, the last two people on earth. *Gotta ride down baby into this tunnel of love.* She turns around. One hand disappears and the blouse falls from her shoulder. Another and it is halfway down her back. She snatches at it, turns and faces him again. The blouse is crumpled in her hands, covering her breasts. Then it is gone. She stands there with her arms crossed vaguely across her chest. Her large brown eyes appear more vulnerable without her glasses. Her hair curls playfully across her collarbones. She drops her hands, and in that instant Payne can feel the room fill up with people. He hears the sound of Avery to his left. The front door closes. The Thai bartender laughs. The music swells around him. The dancer smiles her smile of small white even teeth. Payne feels his heart pound in his chest. Her breasts are right before him. They appear larger now, round white with thick pink nipples poking up. He rises slowly to his feet. There is a ten-dollar bill in his hand. He reaches forward slowly, slowly. She leans a little closer, across the small divide between the table and the stage. The bill comes up. He feels the tendons stretching in his arm. There is a small red heart-shaped birthmark underneath one breast. He tilts against the table and their eyes lock for a moment as the paper brushes up against her fingers and is gone.

Payne rolls back on his feet. The biker and the two black men have disappeared. Avery is grinning right beside him. "Easy, boy," says Avery. "Whoa, there."

Payne feels the blood rush back into his head. He slips into his chair. "I should slow down. Too much to drink," he says.

Demarest and Morrow loom suddenly above him. He pushes them both away. "Give me some air!"

"What's up?" says Avery. "What's the matter?"

"They told us they're closing," Demarest says. His eyes are shiny and huge.

"Yeah, they told us in the bathroom." Morrow glowers under heavy brows. He grinds his jaw.

"What's next?" says Avery.

"Onward and upward."

"Anywhere but here. We're all paid up," says Morrow. With that he turns and walks away.

Litchfield follows in his wake, then Avery and Demarest. Payne slips his jacket on and glances over at the stage. The girl has disappeared. The stage is empty. The music has stopped too. Someone turns a light on by the door. For the first time he notices the duct tape on the floor, holding the carpet to the wall. The ceiling is painted red, the same lush color as the bar.

"Hey, John!" cries Avery from the door. "John, let's go."

There is a rope of flashing Christmas lights behind the stage. The walls are plaster, faux Tudor wood beams showing through. The door is closed beside the stage, dressed with red ribbon and a plastic wreath. "John!"

Payne turns away. The girl is gone. And besides, what was he going to do? He's a married man, for God's sake. And almost thirty-seven. She's just a teenage stripper in a bar. He zips the zipper on his jacket. The whole thing is ridiculous. He starts for the door. He's going to be a father soon. He picks his pace up. Avery is waiting by the exit. Payne is relieved, for this is what his life has come to mean, the daily conquest of the smallest peccadillos, the constant clash and compromise. He has won another victory. He follows Avery through the door. The cold wind catches him. He moves into the night, a step, a measured pace in the lifelong rush from fraudulence.

IV

The moon is a week shy of being full. It hangs above the World Trade towers like a burnt-out neon advertisement. Payne pulls his collar up. A pair of discarded Christmas trees huddle in the street. Moonlight drips from their tinsel. There is a fire burning in a garbage can down by the river. Two shapes dance dreamily around it. Trying to keep warm, Payne thinks. Anything to keep warm.

A car honks. Litchfield is waving to him from the Continental. Payne looks both ways. "What's the plan?" he says, crossing the street, aware of his walk, aware of the liquor in him. Then he realizes he's shouting. The rear door swings agape.

Payne slips inside, the car door slams shut with a thump, and there is Avery beside him, with Demarest on the other side. Litchfield turns the engine over; it shudders and ignites. "What's going on?" says Payne. "What time is it anyway?"

"After three," says Litchfield from behind the wheel. His fat face is puffy with booze.

"Yeah, time for bed," says Avery. He raises his eyebrows twice and laughs. "Hey, Glen. How about a nightcap, buddy?"

"You like that, huh?"

"Very nice."

Morrow reaches into his jacket and pulls out a bullet-shaped vial. He turns the little plastic lever on the side and shakes it briefly. Then he turns the plastic lever back. "Here," he says, and hands it to Avery.

Avery slips the rounded head of the vial into one nostril, closes the other with his finger, and inhales. His dark head swings back. "Yeah," he says, dabbing at his nose. "Melissa will thank you in the morning."

"You know," says Litchfield, "I wish you wouldn't . . ."

"Don't start," says Morrow curtly. He glowers at Litchfield for a moment, and then begins to laugh.

"What? What is it?" Litchfield turns to the rear of the car. Demarest and Avery laugh too. In the flat glow of the streetlight, Payne can see that Litchfield's face is streaked with lipstick.

"Cute," says Morrow.

"You'd make a great transvestite," Avery says.

Litchfield examines his face in the mirror. "Very funny. It was that Thai girl from the bar," he says, wiping his lips. "She couldn't keep her hands off me. What was her name again?"

"I didn't ask," says Morrow.

"She certainly was spritely."

"Spritely! Jesus, Bobby," Morrow says, "she had her hand in your crotch and you call her spritely." He reaches for the vial.

"I liked the Puerto Rican one the best. Did you see the way she moved?" says Demarest. He rolls his eyes. "Man! A fucking contortionist, that's what she was. A yogi. The mind boggles at the possibilities. If I weren't getting married in three days . . ."

"Yeah, sure, sure," says Morrow.

"That's it, I'm out of here," says Avery. "I can't take it any-more. I'm fed up with the way you guys always talk about women. It's degrading. It's sexist. It really makes me sick." He leans over Tom Demarest and unlocks the door. "And besides, I promised Melissa I'd fuck the living hell out of her tonight."

They all laugh. Demarest opens the door and cold air rushes in. He and Rick Avery slide over the seat and slip quietly out the door. "Hey, Rick. See you on Saturday," Payne shouts, but the door slams shut on his words. Out the window, he can see Avery and Demarest on the sidewalk. They are laughing, clasping each other around the shoulders, hugging in the moonlight. Rick's long hair hangs down across his glasses.

Nineteen years, thinks Payne. Avery was right. Everything was changing. Everything was falling apart.

Avery pulls away. He smiles at Demarest, lifts his right hand slowly in a kind of wave, and turns to walk away. The rear door opens. "See you tomorrow," Demarest says.

"Hey, close the door," says Morrow. "It's fucking cold in here."

Demarest ducks inside the Continental, slamming the door behind him.

"Turn the heat up," Morrow says.

"And then there were four," says Payne.

"What's that?"

"Nothing." Payne turns toward Demarest. "Are you all right, Tom?"

"Fine," he answers absently. Then, looking up, he adds, "I could do with another hit, though."

Morrow smiles and reaches once again into his pocket. "Help yourself," he says, handing the vial to Demarest.

Demarest tilts the vial and takes another snort. "That's better." He hands the vial to Payne.

Payne looks at the little bottle in his hand. "No, thanks," he says uncertainly.

"Go ahead, man, it's okay," says Morrow. "There's more where that came from."

"Bad for the ticker."

"Oh, come on, once a year? Besides, after all that drinking, you're going to need a pick-me-up before driving back to Peekskill. How you feeling, anyway? You look a little pale."

"I'm okay."

"You better not be sick in my car," says Litchfield.

"Bobby, you're so sensitive, you amaze me," Morrow says. "Listen, John, if you want to crash at my place, you're welcome to. You can have your old room. It's no big deal."

"No, I told you, I'm okay." Payne looks down at his hand. "Once a year, I guess." He turns the plastic lever on the vial. It is almost full. He can see the cocaine through the smoky glass. He turns the vial upside down and the chamber fills with powder. He brings it to his nose. The rounded plastic head fits snugly in his nostril. He covers the other with a fingertip. He snorts and the cocaine billows through his head, dispersing, shifting from particles to waves, setting off synapses in his brain like Chinese firecrackers. His eyes begin to water. His nostril stings. He feels himself begin to rise, begin to hover on the surface tension, one molecule above the light brown leather seat. His fingers tingle. His head swings on his shoulders. He zooms in on the street. A yellow cab glides by. It shudders to a stop and a tall black man in a long plaid coat ducks into it and is gone. There is a light on by a door. In the incandescent nimbus Payne can clearly see the three girls from the lounge. They are standing very close, their faces inches from each other. They are stamping in the cold, talking, mouthing words that freeze soundlessly in the air above them.

"Hey, look," says Litchfield. "Over there."

For a moment no one speaks. Payne can feel the blood rush through the capillaries on the surface of his face. His heart pounds furiously in his chest. Can they hear that? he thinks. Or just me? Is it just me?

"Looks like they're going home," says Morrow. "Maybe we can give them a ride."

"I'd like to give them a ride, all right," says Demarest.

"Me, too," says Litchfield.

"I'll ask them," Morrow says.

Litchfield grabs Morrow by the arm. "Hey, I thought you were only kidding."

"What do you think they'd say?" Demarest leans closer to Payne, closer to the window. Payne can feel his breath on his neck. It smells of scotch. Somewhere a subway rumbles underneath the street.

Morrow laughs mirthlessly. "Probably how much," he says.

"How much?" says Litchfield.

"Yeah, you know—shekels," Demarest says. "Money."

Morrow laughs again. "You think you could take it, Tom? A last fling. The swan song of your sexual freedom. I don't know, Tom. What would Anna say?"

"What do you mean, I couldn't take it? And who would tell

Anna, anyway? You?" Demarest turns and looks back through the window. "Better to do it now than afterwards, when I'm married. Like you guys."

"Too late," says Litchfield glumly. He wipes the window with his palm. "Looks like they're leaving."

Payne rubs the condensation from the glass. Another cab has pulled up to the curb across the street. The dancer with the glasses opens the door and ducks inside. The black girl follows right behind her. Only the Puerto Rican girl remains under the light. She says something and waves. The car door closes and the yellow cab slides off. Somewhere a distant sledgehammer pounds the street.

"Looks like your favorite, Tom," says Morrow. "I think I'll have a little talk with her."

"About what?" says Demarest.

"About my friend, who's going out of circulation for the rest of his life, in two short days."

"I don't know, Glen," Demarest says.

"What's the matter, Tom?" says Litchfield. Bobby's voice is sweet and goading. "Can't handle it?"

"Fuck you, Bobby."

"Bobby's coming, too, aren't you?" Morrow says.

Litchfield looks up with surprise. "It's not my party."

"No, it's mine," says Demarest. "And I insist. What's the matter, BB? Cat got your schlong?"

"I told you not to call me that."

"Shut up, you guys," says Morrow. "She's leaving." He holds his hand out suddenly toward Payne. "Hold this." Payne feels the vial in his palm.

Morrow turns, the front door opens, the freezing wind cuts in, and he is gone.

They follow Morrow with their eyes as he walks across the empty street. The Puerto Rican dancer is wearing a rabbit fur coat, high heels, and light-colored tights. She is walking slowly up the street, beyond the reclining Christmas trees, the bodega and a stand of garbage cans, beyond the neon gallery, through a cloud of rising steam and stops. She has seen Morrow in the street. She smiles uncertainly and dips her hand into her purse. Morrow approaches and she completely changes. The hand withdraws from the purse. She moves her body sideways, facing him. She turns her head and without warning laughs as Morrow nears her, laughs and laughs, and then steps forward with a smile, turning her ankle out. Morrow comes to a halt a foot away. He has his hands in his pockets. Payne can see the condensation of their breathing reflected in the neon light. And suddenly he is aware of Demarest beside him, of the silence in the tight cab of the Continental, as if he's sitting in a plastic diorama, a globe of water filled with plastic snow, the vial pressed in his sweaty palm.

Morrow leans a little closer. The girl smiles nervously. Morrow reaches into his pocket and she steps back. Payne sees the wallet suddenly appear, the long thin fingers picking, the telling triangle of cash pop up between his fingers. The girl says something with a laugh, and the fingers dip again. She smiles, looks down the street, then covers Morrow's hands with hers.

The window squeaks as Litchfield wipes the moisture from the glass. There is that sound again, Payne hears, the subway local passing, that distant pounding of the street, but it is only his own heart pumping in his chest. Morrow steps back. He turns into the street. He is smiling. He walks briskly to the Continental and pulls the front door open. The light glares overhead, illuminating his golden hair. The cold air rushes in and Morrow reappears, the night still clinging to his clothes. "Listen up," he says. "It's all arranged. She lives right around the corner in a loft. And she loves company. The more the merrier, she said. Those were her exact words. Her name is Yolanda, and she's waiting for you, Tom."

The air is suddenly charged. There is a humming in Payne's head, a frequency transition, a settling of the wave. He leans forward. All their heads seem to fall together, like planets round a common sun. It is Morrow. He has wiped his thick blond hair back from his face, revealing the tanned brow, the deep-set ice blue eyes, the famous Morrow smile. His face is beaming.

"Okay," says Demarest breathlessly. He looks up through the window at the girl retreating down the street. Then he begins to nod. "Okay, I'm in."

"All right," says Morrow with a grin. "The Hunting Club

strikes again." He turns and stares at Payne. "How about it, John? When's the last time you got laid? Don't let us down now."

"I don't know," Payne hears himself reply. He feels the cocaine pumping blood. "I guess so."

They turn and stare at Litchfield.

"Don't look at me," Bobby says. "You guys go on ahead. It's pretty late. I should be getting back."

"To what?" says Payne.

"To the airport for the next flight to Atlanta?" Demarest says.

"Either fish or cut bait, Bobby," Morrow says. "But don't get holier-than-thou."

"I knew he couldn't do it."

"Leave him alone, Tom," Morrow says. "If he's not interested . . ."

"I didn't say I wasn't interested."

"It's up to you, Bobby. Either you're interested or you're not."

Litchfield does not answer. They sit there for a moment in silence, staring through the windshield, looking at the dancer walking slowly up the street. She is only a hundred yards away when she hesitates and stops below a streetlamp. Then, without warning, she props a foot up on the base of the lamppost. The strap of her shoe has slipped. She slides it up around her ankle, glances over her shoulder to make sure they're watching, and slips her hand up underneath her coat between her legs.

"Jesus Christ," says Demarest. "In the fucking street."

"Let's go, Bobby," Morrow says. He grinds his jaw. "Are you in or out?"

They stare at Litchfield. He wipes his mouth, still trying to remove the lipstick. He looks back out the window. The girl has dropped her leg. She straightens her rabbit coat and looks once more in their direction. Then she turns and walks away.

"Okay," he says at last. "I'm in." Litchfield's voice is barely audible. He turns toward Morrow suddenly. A tight, ironic smile plays on his lips. Payne can't be sure if he is angry or excited. He slaps the dashboard and the headlights blaze. "Let's go."

. . .

There is a hole in the metal ceiling. Payne sees the floors unroll as the elevator climbs noisily into the darkness, foot by foot, yard by yard, rising on the slick black cable through the shaft.

"Hey, Glen," says Demarest. "How come she didn't want to ride with us?"

"She said she had to freshen up. Clean up a little, you know."

"Yeah, sure."

The elevator rises. In the distance, Payne can see a solitary light bulb shining like a star. Someone is playing salsa on the floor below. The horns climb through the darkness, congas popping. There is a sprinkling of high notes, a voice, and then it's gone, drowned out by the steady groaning of the elevator. What am I doing here? Payne thinks. What the hell am I doing?

The floor shakes and the elevator grinds to a halt. The door collapses on itself, revealing a gray hall, a single light bulb dangling from the ceiling, a fire hose. Morrow drifts out onto the landing. Litchfield follows, then Demarest and Payne. The elevator door clanks shut behind them.

"Six B," says Morrow flatly. "Bingo." He points at a tall gray metal door in a corner of the landing. "Come on, you guys. Look alive. Jesus, what a sorry bunch." He raps a quarter up against the door. A hollow metal sound resounds.

No one answers and Morrow knocks again. He starts to whistle quietly as if he's waiting for a bus. The tune is the allegro from Mozart's *Eine kleine Nachtmusik.* He knocks once more and Payne can hear a footfall on the other side. The peephole shines and darkens in the door. A moment later there is the sound of a bolt being pulled back, metal against metal, and the door swings open.

Yolanda is standing in the doorway. She is wearing a long silk robe, open in the front. Her hair is brushed. Her cheeks are newly rouged. Her mouth looks wet with lipstick. "I thought you guys were never coming. I thought you got cold feet or something," she says. "Come on, then." She turns and walks away.

They follow her into the loft. The walls of the hall leading from the door are at least ten feet tall. The light is dim. Payne can barely see a closet to one side, a half-built bathroom on the other. He locks the door behind him. They make their way along the corridor. The walls appear brand new, unpainted Sheetrock thrown up yesterday. He can still see nail heads peppering the white. The hall extends into a living room. A stereo glows from a metal bookcase to his left. The shelves are jammed with seashells, stuffed animals, and photographs. A sofa is parked against the wall. The pillows are large and pink, trimmed with small tassels. A small fake Christmas tree strung with tinsel shimmers in the corner. A wicker coffee table squats beside it. There is an ashtray stuffed with burnt-out cigarettes, a small black lacquer box, a single candle glowing. The air is thick with the scent of gardenias. Yolanda waves a hand. "Sit down, don't be shy," she says. She is wearing a bra the color of peacock herl, a garter belt and panties underneath her robe, and Payne can see the deep line of her cleavage, the way her creamy coffee thighs spill over at the top of her dark nylons. She plays with her hair for a moment, then turns to the stereo and says, "You guys like music?"

"Sure," says Morrow. He slips his coat off, folds it neatly, and drops it on the back of a chair. "Especially when you're dancing to it."

She looks up at him and smiles. "You like my dancing, huh?"

"It's great," says Demarest. His gravy brown eyes are bloodshot from drinking. He laughs a belly laugh, rolls his sloping shoulders.

"Really? You're not just saying that?"

"Absolutely," Morrow says.

They take their coats off one by one, and drop them on the Formica table in the corner of the room. Yolanda tunes the radio, crashing through the static until Al Green croons softly from the speakers. "Let's Stay Together." I have this album, Payne thinks suddenly. Yolanda turns away from the stereo. She fiddles with the cord of her robe and says, "Hi, I'm Yolanda."

They introduce themselves. Morrow and Litchfield sit together on the sofa. Demarest flops into an overstuffed green armchair by the doorway leading to the kitchen. "Here," says Yolanda. She pulls a chair out from the Formica table and pushes it toward Payne. He starts to sit down but Yolanda steps in front of him. She is barefoot and seems much smaller now than at the lounge. She smiles and suddenly he feels her hand between his legs. He takes a step back, tripping on the chair. She reaches out for him again. He can feel the softness of her breasts against his chest. "Mmm," she says, looking up into his eyes. "Now I know why she's marrying you."

Payne laughs and shakes his head. "Sorry," he says and steps away. "Wrong one." He points at Demarest.

Suddenly she is gone—the warmth, the softness, the scent of her long dark hair. Yolanda drapes herself across the armchair over Demarest. He laughs and wraps his arms around her. "So you're the lucky one," she says.

"I guess so," Demarest says.

She reaches down between her legs. The robe falls open and Payne can see her fingers grope for Demarest beneath her. "I take it back," she says. "It feels like I'm the lucky one tonight." She looks at Morrow and smiles. "I'm glad you guys waited for me now. How about a drink?" With that she slips out of the armchair and rises to her feet.

They watch her as she glides across the room and disappears into the kitchen. Demarest pulls himself up in the armchair. "Man!" he says, straightening his tie. They all look at one another for a moment, then break into laughter without warning.

"What do you guys want to drink?" Yolanda shouts from the kitchen. "I've got beer, vodka, scotch, and some white Italian stuff that tastes like licorice." She pokes her head out through the door.

"Scotch is fine," says Demarest, shrugging.

"Yeah, sure," says Morrow. "Scotch all around."

They nod. Payne sits on the chair by the Formica table. The surface of the table is lime green, flecked with gold. Payne reaches out unconsciously and picks up a plastic salt shaker beside the pile of coats. It is shaped like a round pink pig. It is wearing a waistcoat and tie.

Yolanda reappears with a tray of glasses filled with ice and a bottle of Johnny Walker Red. She pours them each a drink. Then she sets the tray on the table and measures out three fingers for herself. "Bottoms up," she says. They watch her as she downs the glass.

"Where did you learn to drink like that?" says Morrow.

"I went to night school," she replies, wiping her mouth with the back of her hand.

"I bet you did."

"I'm a fast learner." She pours herself another drink, but before she can bring it to her lips, Morrow grabs her by the arm.

"Hold it," he says. He takes her glass and puts it on the table. "How about a hit of this first?" He slips a hand into his jacket and removes a Ziploc plastic bag, filled with white powder.

Yolanda's almond-shaped eyes grow wide. She reaches for the bag but Morrow pulls it back.

"There must be at least ten grams there, man," she says. "Or more."

Morrow laughs. "Something like that. You want some?"

"Are you kidding?" She steps toward the wall, removes a mirror with a bright chrome frame, and slips it gently on the coffee table. Then she kneels down on the floor beside it and begins to wipe the mirror with a corner of her robe. When she's finished, Morrow pours a pile of cocaine on the glass.

"Fish scale," says Yolanda. "I'm impressed." She opens the black lacquer box on the coffee table and removes a razor blade. "Can I cut it?"

Morrow nods. "Go ahead," he says.

She begins to cut the cocaine into long thin lines. Morrow takes a hundred-dollar bill out of his wallet, rolls it in his fingers, and gives it to Yolanda. "Thanks," she says. She stuffs the end of the bill into her nose and runs the note along the longest line, inhaling the powder as she moves. Payne can see her robe fall open as she leans across the table. He can see her breasts reflected in the glass. He watches as she slips the bill into her other nostril and runs another line. When she's finally finished, she smudges the remnants of the two lines on her fingertip and rubs it on her gums. Then she leans back on her haunches, smiling. "Nice shit. You guys dealers or something?"

"I'm not." Morrow points to Litchfield with his thumb and says, "But he is."

"I am not." Litchfield tugs on his bow tie, visibly embarrassed.

The girl laughs. She picks the mirror up and places it on Morrow's lap. Then she hands him the hundred dollar bill.

"Thanks," he says. He takes the note. She holds the mirror up before him and he snorts two lines of coke, one in each nostril. When he's done, she picks the mirror up and drops it onto Litchfield's lap.

"I wouldn't bother with him. He doesn't snort," says Demarest.

"Is he kidding?"

"He used to smoke pot in high school," Morrow says. "Long before you were born."

"I'm not that old," says Litchfield, squirming.

"I didn't think so," she says. "Come on, then. It's good stuff."

"No, thank you."

She pouts and squeezes in between his legs, kneeling immediately before him. "Don't you want to play?" She dips a fingertip into the pile of coke and rubs it on the inside of her upper lip. "Tastes good," she says. She opens the front of her robe.

Demarest begins to laugh. "Jesus, BB, looks like you're going to faint."

"Shut up, Tom."

Yolanda laughs. She reaches into her robe and starts to fondle her left breast. "Don't you want to play, BB?"

"Don't call me that."

"He doesn't like that name," says Morrow.

Yolanda lifts her breast out in her hand and starts to knead the thick dark nipple in her fingers. "What's your name then, honey?"

"Robert," Litchfield says. "I told you." He stares down at her breast.

"Do you like that, Robert? You like my tits?"

"Yes."

Yolanda reaches out and runs a finger through the pile of cocaine on the mirror. She squeezes her breast with one hand, and starts to rub her nipple with the cocaine on her finger. "Feels good," she says. "You like that, Robert? You want to touch my nipple?"

"Yes."

"Are you sure? I don't think you really want to."

"I do," he answers breathlessly.

She reaches down and pulls her bra cups to the side. Her breasts spill out of the material. They are only inches from his face, supported by the glass. She picks the mirror up. "Go ahead," she says. "You can touch them if you want to . . . as soon as you have a snort." She giggles and leans against him.

"This isn't fair," he says.

She hands him the hundred-dollar bill.

"This isn't fair, I'm telling you. This is outlawed in the Geneva Convention. Torture of any kind. It says so specifically."

She lifts the mirror toward his face. He slips the bill into his nose and takes a short snort from the nearest line.

"Good boy," she says.

Litchfield shakes his head. "That's enough." He pushes the tray away. "You guys are trying to kill me."

Yolanda laughs roundly. She rolls to her feet and carries the mirror over to Payne. He takes a sip of his drink as she kneels on the ground before him. Yolanda gives him the rolled-up hundred-dollar bill, but it slips out of his fingers, dropping onto the floor. She picks it up. "No more drinks for you," she says. Payne clamps the rolled note in his fingers. He cannot concentrate. He looks down at the lines of cocaine on the mirror. Yolanda's breasts are pressed against the glass, one swollen nipple topped with white cocaine. He puts the bill into his nose and leans against the mirror. He can see his own face in the glass, his chin, his mouth, the thin nose with the curled note in one nostril. He runs the bill along a line, inhaling inch by inch, the powder disappearing. The cocaine hits him and he feels the blood flush through his face again, the sudden lift, the buoyancy, and she is gone. He sits back in his chair. His head grows light. He shuts his eyes and in the darkness he can feel the burning in his nose, a flare of pain and he is through the envelope, out of the clouds, his body hums, he hears the whistling of the blades and he can see the city far below, the taillights streaming through the streets, a carnival of incandescent color, the red, the green of traffic lights, the neon stuttering, the buildings bright as icicles, the bridges strung like frozen spider webs. He opens his eyes and there is Demarest in his chair. Yolanda kneels before him. She is holding a breast up to his mouth.

"You want to daisy-chain?" she says. "I could do all of you. I like that. Or one on one?"

Demarest pulls his mouth away.

"What do you want, Tommy?" she says to him. "You want to fuck me? Huh, baby? You want to fuck me hard, is that what you want? I like it rough." She shears the word off with a smile. She pouts. She takes his hand and slips it in between her legs. "That's right, baby," she says. "Right there."

"Let's go. Let's go to your room," he mutters hoarsely.

She takes another snort of cocaine from the mirror and rises to her feet.

"Drive carefully," says Morrow with a laugh.

Yolanda picks up the mirror and lays it tenderly on the table. Demarest staggers to his feet.

"And don't forget your license," Litchfield says.

The girl takes Demarest by the hand. She leads him toward the corridor at the far end of the room. "Don't wait up for me," Demarest tells them. He grins and disappears, his laughter echoing down the shadowed corridor.

Payne takes a sip from his drink. The ice has melted. It tastes warm and weak. He stands uncertainly and reaches for the bottle on the coffee table. "I thought I'd never see the day," says Payne, as he pours himself another drink. "Bobby doing cocaine." He shakes his head. "Incredible."

"I've done it before," says Litchfield casually.

"Oh, sure. When?"

"That time in Florida. After my bar exam."

"I doubt it," Morrow says.

"You don't know everything about me."

They both laugh simultaneously. "We don't?" says Payne. "Move over."

Morrow shifts a little to the side and Payne sits down between them.

"There are a lot of things about me you don't know," says Litchfield.

"Oh, yeah," says Morrow, reaching for the scotch. "Name one."

Litchfield ponders for a moment. "Well, I can't think right now, but I'm sure there are," he says.

Payne laughs again. His head feels light. It is as if the world has all turned treble now; there is no bass. He laughs and laughs. It is the liquor and the drugs. It is the sight of Litchfield in his russet Gieves tweed jacket, the red bow tie, the brushed gray flannel slacks against the bright pink sofa. It is the tinsel in the tassels, the pig salt shaker on the table. He closes his eyes and drifts off for a second, the lifetime of a dream, adrift on Morrow's deep and even voice, until the palm trees hiss above him in the warm wind of the Keys. He sees the bright white streets, the pink and sky blue bungalows, the green line of the sea. After Litchfield's bar exams they'd gone, for just five days, the lot of them. That was the time that he had hooked that bonefish on the flats. The silver bullet, they had called it—have another beer. And on the last night they had gone to Papa's for a drink and Litchfield had insulted that strange guy with the bald head without even knowing how, he couldn't remember what he'd said, but it didn't make a God damn difference, and the crazy guy had waited for them in the street, in the fragrant shadows of a bougainvillea, waited and waited until they'd stumbled out into the night, alive with swirling stars, completely unaware until they heard him scratching up the sidewalk in the darkness, like a palmetto bug, like a crab with that bald head, and Morrow had defended them, had stepped in Litchfield's place to take the punch. It was always Morrow. They would have run if they had been alone, but it was Morrow who just stood there laughing, Morrow glancing off the blows, and Payne had rallied to him like he always did, like they had always done and always would.

"Jesus, that was quick."

Payne opens his eyes and there is Demarest standing in the doorway, a wide smile on his lips. He strides into the room. "Long enough." He sinks into the dark green armchair. "Who's next?" he says, but Morrow is already on his feet, already moving through the doorway, down the dark corridor, already on his way.

Payne notices his drink in his hand. He takes another sip,

leans forward slowly, and puts it on the coffee table. Then he slips back, beneath the sound of Litchfield's distant voice, between the sentences, and he is back in Florida, thigh-deep along the flats, the emerald water shining, the bonefish running for its life. He holds the rod above his head. He hears the black spool spinning, whining as the fish strips off the line.

"Let's go," says Morrow suddenly, and Payne looks up, but it is only Litchfield he is calling, Litchfield lurching to his feet. "I hope you're satisfied," says Litchfield, and he buttons up his jacket. "I hope you're happy, Glen," and he is gone, and Morrow pours another drink, and he and Demarest are kneeling at the table, and they are gone, across the green horizon, on the far shore of the flat, and they are shouting at him in the wind, jumping up and down and waving, shouting as the line strips off the reel, until the spool is empty and the line gives way and he can see it flying through the rod guides one by one, across the sky and it is gone, gone, gone.

"Hey, John." His body shakes. "Hey, John, are you awake?"

He opens his eyes and there is Litchfield looming over him, with Morrow right behind.

"Yeah, I'm awake," he says.

"You're up."

"I don't think I can make it."

"If I could, you can," Bobby Litchfield says, and pulls him to his feet.

He leans against them for a moment, then pushes them away. "Let go of me," he says. "Get off!" He brushes feebly at his clothes. Demarest has passed out in the armchair by the kitchen. Payne takes a step, then two, and he is moving toward the door. The corridor is dark. He puts a hand out to the side. He runs his fingers on the surface of the wall as he walks forward. Three steps, four steps, five. Behind him Morrow laughs. Payne hears the sound of music chiming, the slice of a guitar, the bass line pounding. Another step and he is there.

It is a small room after all, thrown together, like the loft. There are dark posters on the walls, a mirror, a candle burning, a bureau with a boom box and an Indian print. Yolanda lies across a small brass bed. She is fiddling with a piece of paper when she stops, looks up, and sees him in the doorway. "Last but not least," she says. "Well, what's the matter, honey?"

He moves into the room. There is a white fur carpet on the floor, like the skin of a Samoyed. "Well, come on," she says. "I won't bite you. Not hard, anyway." She laughs. She is naked now. He can see her breasts shine in the candlelight, the way they fall off to the side. He can see the triangle of thick black pubic hair. He takes another step and she is at his belt. Payne closes his eyes. The salty smell of sex and sweat lingers in the air. He feels her slipping down his pants. He feels her pulling at his boxers, sliding them across his thighs until he's cold and bare before her, exposed and solitary even as he feels her warm wet mouth envelop him, soft, soft, and he looks down and there she is, her face an inch away, her thick lips wrapped around him, soft, and the condom out of nowhere, glistening. What am I doing here? he thinks. In the candlelight, beneath the hair, her face could be Jan's face, except it's not. It's not. He puts his hands about Yolanda's head and draws her to him. She struggles and is gone. "Come on," she says, reclining on the bed. "You're ready." And then he is. His right knee first, and then the left, he crawls up on the bed. She opens for him and he slides inside her easily, without a moment's pause, without a thought except of Jan, Jan lying in their bed at home, alone and worrying, Jan turning in the darkness yet again, Jan pushing him away. Not now, he thinks. Not now. Always not now.

"Hey, take it easy, will ya?" she says, as her head bumps up against the headboard.

"Sorry," he says, but he is not. He looks down at Yolanda. Her eyes are closed, her full lips barely open. Her breasts bounce up and down as he pounds into her. She cries a tiny sigh, and in a flicker of the candle she is gone and there is Jan, the small familiar mouth, the scented brown hair, open arms, the tension building, building and he falls. His arms collapse. He slips against her chest. He rolls against the cold flat welcome wall, against the shadow, and is gone.

.   .   .

It is a dreamless sleep, the sleep of a child. When he awakes, he gathers up the pieces slowly. The pungent smell. The candle has burned down. The blanket and the bed, the poster on the wall, the sweat-soaked sheets rise up out of the darkness and he remembers where he is. His head is pounding and his mouth is parched. His eyes can barely focus. "Yolanda," he says, and nudges her. She doesn't move.

He rolls a quarter turn. The temperature has fallen. He feels wet and cold, as if he's slept through a long fever. "Yolanda," he says again. In the distance he can hear somebody laugh. It's Demarest's laugh, high-pitched and stuttering. He turns around. Yolanda is lying on her back, sound asleep. He reaches toward the bedside table for the lamp. The candle sputters and goes out. "Dammit, Yolanda, wake up." He feels for the lamp, for the little knob below the shade, and turns it on.

The room unfolds. The pink shade of the lamp gives off a rosy hue and he can see Yolanda lying next to him. He nudges her again. She seems to stir, her head falls to the side, and a drop of dark red liquid spills out of her open mouth, runs down her chin as the jaw drops and the blood pours unabated, pours from her nose and mouth, runs like an open tap and down onto the wet red sheets.

Payne leaps up from the bed. The wet sheets tangle in his ankles and he slips across the floor. His elbow slams against the bureau. The wind is knocked out of his chest. He rises to his feet, his fingers slipping on the wall. The blood still spills out of Yolanda's face. He feels the acid bile rise in his throat. The radio is playing. Someone is singing a song, someone is singing, but it is only him, alone and naked, screaming.

V

"Jesus Christ!" says Morrow from behind.

Payne turns. Their eyes are fixed upon the bloody frieze. "What did you do to her?" cries Morrow. "What the *fuck* did you do?" He rushes over to the bed. "Jesus Christ, John. Jesus, what a fucking mess. I think she's dead."

Payne shakes his head and looks down at Yolanda. He cannot speak. He cannot find the air to fill his lungs. "I don't know . . ."

"What do you mean, you don't know?" says Morrow. He reaches out to touch Yolanda's neck, but hesitates and looks back up at Payne. "She's dead, man. You must have hit her or something."

"Put some clothes on," Litchfield says. Everyone is suddenly aware of Payne's nakedness. He looks down at himself. His thighs are rust red from the drying blood. "I don't know. I just . . ." He cannot finish. He doesn't have the strength. All he can think of is Yolanda's head, bumping up against the metal headboard.

"You just what?" screams Demarest. "You just fucking what?" He pushes Payne against the wall. "Now what are we meant to do?"

"Leave him alone," says Morrow, stepping up. "John. John, get a hold of yourself. Listen to me."

Morrow's tanned face swims into view. "I'm cold, Glen,"

Payne whimpers. He hugs himself and looks down at the bed. Yolanda's head hangs forward, a strand of congealed blood still clinging to her nose. The sheet is soaked flat across her breasts, black-red in the rose light. What is that sound? Payne cannot tear his eyes away. Like the clicking of a clock, the patter of my own heart pumping.

"John, listen to me. You'd better take a shower and wash yourself off. And try not to touch anything. John, are you listening to me?"

Payne follows the white outline of Yolanda's shoulder against the bloody sheets. "I didn't mean it," he says. The soft curve of her upper arm arcs down beneath the sheets, unseen for several inches underneath the wet red cotton, only to reappear, now streaked with crimson threads, a fleshy wrist, a hand, a finger pointing to the floor, a droplet on a polished fingernail, to the gathering pool below. The constant dripping is like the sound of gentle kisses.

"She must have hit her head against the headboard," Litchfield says. "It was an accident."

"Great. An accident," says Demarest. "What the fuck are we going to do now, Glen?" He glowers at Payne. "This is all your fault." He puffs himself up to his full height.

Payne looks up. Demarest is a vague white shape in the corner. "I didn't mean to hurt her," he says.

"Tell that to the cops."

"The cops." Payne shakes his head and the room falls into focus.

"Maybe if he confesses they'll go easy on him," Litchfield says. "He's never been in trouble before. He comes from a good family." He steps forward. His wide face gleams with perspiration. His mouth is grim, his eyes made huge by the magnifying lenses of his glasses. His red bow tie is crooked. "I'll defend you, John, no charge. Don't worry, you can count on me."

"What the hell are you talking about?" snaps Morrow. "Nobody's confessing anything around here. What are you, fucking crazy? How do you think this is going to play at William and Roget? You haven't been a partner there that long. And what the hell do you know about criminal law, anyway? We're not talking about a condo deal here. This is murder."

"Manslaughter," Litchfield says, falling back against the point. "There's no premeditation."

"You think they'll be making that distinction at William and Roget? Will Elizabeth? Or Sally? How old is she now? Will she understand?" Morrow takes a step toward the center of the room. "And what about you, Tom? What will Anna say? If this gets out, do you really think she's going to marry you on Saturday? Is that what you think?" He laughs tightly. "Listen to me. All of you. If one of us goes down, we all fall. We all have families we care about."

"So what are we meant to do?" says Demarest again. He rolls his oxlike eyes. "What? You tell us, Glen. I'm not going to jail for this. I didn't kill her. Forget it. I'm not going to jail. No way."

"Shut up! Stop fucking whining, Tom." Morrow looks down at Yolanda's body in the bed. "We've got to stick together. I know that much. We've got to think."

"I don't want you guys to get in trouble. Not because of me," says Payne. "It's my fault. Maybe Bobby's right. Maybe if I tell them what happened . . ."

"I said shut up," shouts Morrow. "You don't know what you're saying. You want to go to jail? You want your kid born without a father, is that what you want?" He turns his back on them. He looms over the bed. He runs his fingers through his thick blond hair. "We're not telling anyone about this. Do you understand? This is going to be our secret. Just us. Just The Hunting Club. We'll have to . . . get rid of her somehow. Jesus, I never knew there was so much blood. What a fucking mess. We'll have to wrap her up in something, something she won't bleed through." He stands perfectly still. "Something special for her trip. Yeah, that's right. We'll have to pack a suitcase for her. Yolanda's fed up with her job. You know how it is. She needs a break, like everybody else. A vacation. She needs to get away. She's sick and tired of her life."

They move as if they have done it all a hundred times before. Morrow leads them through the process. First the analysis and goal.

This is a woman going on a trip, he tells them. What does she have to take? How should the finished space appear? Payne stands before the mirror over the bathroom sink, sponging off the dried blood from his face, in that slight depression just behind the jaw below the ears. He can hear them cleaning up the bedroom down the hall. They are talking but their words are indistinct. They are talking about him, he is sure. About what he has done. He looks at his face in the mirror. The hazel deep-set eyes are bloodshot, the lips drawn thin, the forehead creased with lines. He feels as though he's looking at himself from far above. It is not him. It is a stranger's face. A shiver latches to his back, crawls up his spine. The nausea follows and he feels the vomit sliding from his mouth as he tips forward to his knees, remembering the salmon and the scotch.

Payne showers slowly, feeling the hot water flush out every pore. He soaps and rinses himself three times. When he's finished, he dries himself with a large pink towel, her towel, and checks himself in the mirror once more. His head is throbbing but at least the nausea is gone. His stomach feels empty. He combs his hair with his fingers, wraps himself up in the towel and heads back down the corridor to the bedroom. The room is freezing. Morrow has opened the window behind the bed and the wind tugs at the curtains, revealing a brick wall and a black cable line across the way.

"Feeling better?" Morrow says.

They are all staring at him. He can feel their eyes upon him and he tightens his hand on the towel. "Yeah, thanks," he says.

He searches the room for his clothes. Everything looks different. They have sponged down the walls. They have soaked up the blood from the floor. He looks up, slowly, tentatively. Yolanda is still lying on the bed, her body wrapped completely in the bloody sheet, like a giant red cocoon. Beside her is an open garment bag, made of clear plastic.

"Don't just stand there," Demarest says. "Help us put her in the bag."

Payne dresses in a corner of the room, embarrassed by his nakedness, turning modestly away. When he's finished, they gather around the bed. Morrow slips his hands beneath Yolanda's dark hair, grabbing a handhold of sheet. The rest follow. On the count of three, they lift the body up and over the garment bag. It is surprisingly light in their hands. They can hear blood pour out from underneath, the sound of passing gas. Morrow slips the plastic casing of the bag around Yolanda's chest. The girl is so small that she fits easily into the bag. He zips it shut. The entire exercise has taken them only a few minutes. Their movements are precise and elegant. Each object seems familiar in their hands. They lift the bag with skill. They hoist it swiftly down onto the floor, and Payne remembers the long warm afternoons at Hadley, the river oxbowing across the valley past the college to the range, and their four out on the silver water. They tipped Yolanda through the air just as they used to lift their boat out of the river years before. She settles on the wooden floor. Mercifully, the rug is untouched by the blood. It lies at the center of the room, a startling white. They flip the mattress over. The other side bears no mark of the carnage. There is a small stash of jewelry and cash underneath—a silver pin, a garnet bracelet, a necklace of coral and gold. Morrow scoops it up. They slip the mattress into place and start to make the bed with fresh sheets.

In another twenty minutes the room is immaculate. Litchfield has already cleaned the living room. No trace remains of the last hours. They have wiped the surfaces for fingerprints. They have checked for hairs and fibers. They have washed the glasses and replaced them in the cupboard by the kitchen sink. They have retraced every step, traveled back in time, removed themselves and introduced another plausible scenario. A large brown plastic suitcase is discovered. They pack it carefully. Three times they are forced to open it to slip in one more item, more evidence to reinforce the story. And then, without warning, they are finished. Nothing remains. The loft is part of the conspiracy. Litchfield takes the suitcase. Morrow, Demarest and Payne lift the garment bag and carry it out into the hall, down the long dark corridor to the front door, where they hesitate, where they put the body down and hover for a moment, each lost in his own thoughts. There is a different world beyond that door, one which they won't be able to tidy up as easily. Payne feels himself recoil, spin, fall. He reaches a hand out toward the wall to steady himself.

"No talking," Morrow says. "Bobby, you go down first with the suitcase. When you know everything's clear, send the elevator back to the sixth floor. We'll follow with . . ." He gestures at the garment bag. "Let's just hope nobody else needs the elevator at this hour. If anyone's on the street, give us a signal before we come out. Make sure not to look in their eyes. We don't want anyone remembering us. Is that clear?"

They nod.

"All right, Bobby. Good luck."

Litchfield throws them a nervous grin. He pushes his glasses up his nose, unlocks the door, and steps out onto the landing. Morrow locks the door behind him.

Don't look anyone in the eyes, thinks Payne. They may see something. They may sense that little dark spot behind the hesitant glance. They may see what you are. Morrow leans into the door, peeping through the viewer, waiting for the elevator. After a while he says, "It's here." He turns the lock. "Let's go."

They lift the garment bag, Morrow opens the door, and they are moving briskly across the landing. Demarest almost loses his grip on the bag as they step into the elevator. He is hunched over, trying to hold the garment bag away from his dark suit. The weight shifts in their hands and they can hear liquid sloshing about in the plastic. The door of the elevator closes. They descend slowly. Floors scratch by. Payne can almost see them as they pass, the darkened landings, the empty ill-lit halls. The same salsa music is playing in the distance. It must be a radio, he thinks. There are the horns again, strident and full. There is the percussion. Another floor and the elevator shudders to a stop.

They hold their breath; they swing the garment bag away. Demarest's face is bone white. The door creaks open slowly.

For a moment, no one moves. The landing is empty. Someone must have pushed the button, and then decided to walk. They can hear the sound of footsteps mounting stairs. Someone is speaking in Spanish. The door just hangs there—open. The three men stand completely still, holding their grisly burden in the cold glare of the landing light. Through the music, Payne can barely hear the sound of a rooster crowing on another floor. The footsteps gradually recede. The door slams shut, the elevator groans and once more they descend into the darkness.

The first floor of the building is empty. They hurry through the hall, their tired fingers slipping on the plastic. Yolanda's body is no longer light. Morrow opens the front door with his foot. He checks the sidewalk. He says, "All clear," and they are in the street, under the night sky. They heave the bag into the trunk. Payne takes a step away. It seems that only moments before they had been careful not to drop the body roughly on the floor, as a mark of reverence, as if Yolanda might wake up. But now it no longer seems to matter. Yolanda has been dead for hours. They have all had time to separate her from the bloody shape curled in the trunk of Litchfield's Continental. The sheet has gradually unraveled and she is visible within the clear garment bag, her breasts pressed up against the plastic, slick with blood. Her hair is tangled round her neck, her head turned off so that her face looks up at them, illuminated by the tiny light bulb in the trunk. Her full lips, cast now with a purple hue, are parted slightly, exposing the very tip of her tongue between her large white teeth. Her eyes are open. They gaze up through the see-through plastic, glazed yet still pugnacious, saying, "Hey, take it easy, will ya? Take it easy. Hey, take it easy will ya . . ." Payne slams the trunk shut with a thud.

They drive aimlessly through the city streets for the next ten minutes, trying to decide what to do. Demarest suggests the wetlands in New Jersey, but Morrow has another idea. "Head up the West Side Highway," he says.

"Where to?" says Litchfield.

"Across the GW Bridge."

"The wetlands?" Demarest asks.

"No, forty-six, to Teterboro."

The words punch into Payne like nails. "The airport? Are you crazy, Glen?"

Morrow turns and stares at Payne. His bright blue eyes seem to glow in the darkened car interior. "It's the only way to be sure."

"But they'll see us, Glen. The line crew—or Cracker or Ted."

"Too early. You know I'm right, John."

The car turns up the West Side Highway. Payne looks out through the window at the river to his left. He can see the George Washington Bridge in the distance. It shivers over the icy Hudson River; it glimmers and winks. He sighs and nods his head.

It takes them just under forty minutes to make the drive out to Teterboro. The West Side Highway is practically deserted. Even the bridge is empty. They glide across the upper level in silence. Route 46 winds west for miles past strip malls and fast food joints, across another bridge, and finally to the cutoff for the airport.

Payne reaches into his jacket and takes out his ID. "Here," he says, handing the card to Litchfield. Litchfield slows the car down as they approach the gate. He opens the window, slips the card into the metal box, and the gate slides open noiselessly.

Hangar twenty-six glows dreamily at the end of the drive. A series of runways stretch beyond it toward the distant spike of the control tower.

Litchfield noses the car toward the pilots' lounge at the far end of the hangar, but Payne drops his hand on his shoulder. "Go round the other side," he says. "We can drive right through into the hangar." The Continental creeps along the drive. When they reach the hangar doors, Litchfield brings the car to a complete stop, and Payne gets out. There is a small portal set within the nearest hangar door. Payne slips his key into the lock and it opens without a fuss.

It is pitch black inside the hangar, but even in the darkness Payne can sense the enormity of the room. He reaches for the light switch on the wall. A moment later the fluorescents sputter and come to life, illuminating three Bell helicopters and a fixed wing corporate jet. Payne flicks the door switch and the electric motor starts to hum. One of the massive hangar doors begins to open, inch by inch. Behind it, he can see the headlights of the Continental. The car is waiting patiently in the night, the engine humming, exhaust fumes steaming into clouds.

The door is still opening as Litchfield pulls the car into the hangar. Morrow jumps out almost immediately. He rushes past the A-Star nearest to the door and heads toward the office at the rear of the hangar. Payne follows close behind.

They reach the gray metal door leading to the pilots' lounge. Everything should be familiar, thinks Payne; he comes here every day. And yet it's not. It is as if he has never been here before. The Ansel Adams photographs. The Cessna calendar. They make their way directly to the High-Way Traffic office.

"Where is it?" Morrow says.

"Where's what?"

"The key to the tug."

"In the desk," says Payne. "Top drawer."

Morrow rifles through the drawer. "You'd better suit up," he says. "It's getting late."

Payne moves into the locker room behind the pilots' lounge. He takes off his jacket and tie and hangs them up in locker number seven. Then he slips on his dark blue one-piece flight suit, with the golden zipper up the front. It's still cold, so he puts his leather jacket back on, checks his pockets for his car keys and ID, and steps in front of the mirror. His hair is a mess. He brushes it back from his face. There is a SAFETY FIRST sticker glued to the concrete wall above the mirror. He looks back at his face, at the puffy hazel eyes, the pallid forehead and blanched cheeks, and remembers Phil Randazzo from the Bridgeport airport: *Eight hours between the bottle and the throttle, kid. Remember that and you'll live longer.*

Payne stands there looking at his face. Is there a difference? he thinks. He studies his eyes carefully. They look flat and dead, like the eyes of a landed fish. Like Yolanda's eyes. He zips his flight suit up and starts back toward the hangar.

Morrow has already hooked the tug to the dolly carrying the Bell 206 helicopter. Litchfield and Demarest are standing by the trunk of the Continental parked adjacent to the dolly. The trunk is open just a crack. Payne can see a line of light slice the air behind them. Morrow is standing on the dolly. He is leaning across the back seat of the helicopter.

"Hurry up, for God's sake," Litchfield says, his fat face shimmering with sweat. He turns and opens the trunk.

The garment bag has shifted during the ride out from Manhattan. Payne can see it as he draws near. Yolanda is curled up now in a kind of fetal position, hugging a large white plastic bag by the spare tire.

"All right," says Litchfield. "On the count of three."

They reach for the garment bag, take hold.

"One, two, three," says Litchfield, and the body swings up from the trunk in one smooth movement. They turn and stagger toward the helicopter. Morrow is sitting in the back seat of the Bell, his arms outstretched to help them lift the body. They feed her in head first, careful to keep her steady so that the blood doesn't shift to one side without warning and tip their burden off balance. Morrow grabs the top of the plastic garment bag and drags the body across the seat. In a moment the entire bloody length has disappeared into the helicopter.

"We'll need some tools," says Morrow. "A chain or something heavy."

Litchfield and Demarest look at one another.

"To weigh her down," says Morrow.

"Her suitcase," Payne says, stepping up.

"I've got some sand, a whole bag full," says Litchfield.

"Great."

Litchfield and Demarest rifle through the trunk of the Continental and hand the items up to Morrow one by one. A plastic bag of sand and salt. A lug wrench and a jack.

Payne curls the plastic corners of the garment bag inside the door and slams it shut. His hands are shaking. He presses them against the fuselage, drawing comfort from the frigid metal, the solid feel of it. He closes his eyes. He grits his teeth, resolved. Then he turns and says, "Take forty-six and go back to Manhattan." He reaches into his jacket pocket. "Tom, you pick up my Accord and drive it back here to the airport. Leave it outside the pilots' lounge with the keys in the exhaust." He hands him his car keys and ID. "Bobby, I guess you follow Tom. You're going to have to come back here to pick him up. Then you can both go home. I'll drive Glen back to his BMW. Don't worry. We won't be long. By the time you're back in Jersey, we should be almost on the ground."

Without waiting for an answer, he jumps into the tug and starts her up. "Open the hangar door," he shouts at Demarest. "Over there." Demarest dashes to the panel on the wall. Hangar door three slides open slowly, unmasking the night sky, the empty open runway. Payne slips the forklift into gear and she jerks forward, the dolly lurching in her wake. He can feel the heavy rotors hanging in the air above him. The tug moves out into the darkness, into the cold, out of the hot air blasting through the tunnel sheets from the heaters in the ceiling. The helicopter on the dolly shakes a little as it crosses the metal runner in the floor. Payne turns the forklift lights on. Far across the runway to his right, he can see the outline of a corporate jet about to taxi home. A line of icy lights, a chain of distant hangars glimmers across the runway like a diamond necklace on black felt. He tugs the dolly out into the open, where he stops.

To the east, mingled with Manhattan's artificial halo, Payne can see the clean wash of the morning sun waiting beneath the horizon. The clouds have almost disappeared. The sky swirls like blood in water. He shivers and looks back at the hangar door. Litchfield and Demarest are standing in the opening. They are staring at him. They are waiting. The whole world is waiting for him.

He climbs into the helicopter, slipping his legs between the cyclic control stick and the front seat. His headset is lying on the empty seat beside him. He slips it on and plugs the cord into the overhead console. Then he turns and looks at Morrow in the back seat. Morrow is already wearing his headset. The garment bag is lying across his lap.

Payne takes a deep breath and straps his seatbelt on. He starts the cockpit check. Beginning at the bottom of the center console beside his left foot, he moves his hand over the switches to check their positions. Then he checks the radio and pushes the igniter circuit breaker in the console overhead. His left hand settles on the collective control stick, and his right hand on the cyclic stick between his legs. He tests the directional control pedals underneath his feet. He turns the throttle open to the indent starting position and squeezes the trigger on the collective. The electric motor whines, the rotors slowly spin. There is a flat hissing noise as the turbine catches. He glances automatically at the exhaust-gas temperature gauge on the console. The needle rushes past the red line as the rotors blur, and then settles back to green.

Thump. Thump. Thump. Payne tunes in the control tower on the radio. Mildred is on duty. He can recognize her silky voice despite the crackling interference. "Chopper eight-six November," he says. "Four two seven niner, requesting clearance for takeoff."

Mildred taps him into her computer and clears a flight path for him out of Teterboro. Payne opens up the throttle. He checks the rotor disk to see that it responds correctly to the cyclic stick. Then he slowly pulls up the collective and the nose of the helicopter rises off the dolly. He corrects for drift. The helicopter stabilizes and he raises the collective further. The ship lifts above the dolly. Payne hovers for a few more seconds at about ten feet, checking the gauges and circuit breakers one more time, before nosing the cyclic forward. The helicopter starts to move across the runway. He twists the throttle slowly. The ship accelerates across the ground, faster and faster until he feels it jump into a climb. It has reached transitional lift, that moment when the rotor system slips into undisturbed air, and all things come together. The forty-eight-foot rotors whirl at more than 300 rpm. The eight-foot tail rotates in perfect unison, correcting for torque. The air. The ship. The will to fly. All things combine to reach perfection.

"Where to?" says Morrow on the intercom.

Payne feels the cyclic kicking in his hand. "Rockaway Point," he says. "Down past the Verrazano Bridge."

They skim across the wetlands of Moonachie, across the turnpike. Dawn is beginning to break and Payne keeps looking to the east, waiting for the copper sun to suddenly reveal itself.

He trims the stick and the helicopter drifts across the Hudson. The river rolls like mercury. He can already see the dark shape of Ellis Island in the frigid waters of the upper bay, and beyond it on a narrow rise, the Statue of Liberty, green against black. He glides east across the water, above the straight-edged streets of Governor's Island, across Gowanus Bay to Brooklyn. There is light traffic on the Queens Expressway and Payne finds himself making mental notes, as if planning his first broadcast of the day. Brooklyn is lit up with the light of a hundred thousand Christmas decorations. He flies past Bensonhurst to Gravesend Bay. The shallow water is littered with abandoned ships, burned out and sea swept. Coney Island toggles into view. Payne looks down at the giant parachute jump, at the jumbled spiral of the roller coaster. A solitary car pulls over onto the side of the road, and turns out its lights. Lovers, Payne thinks absently, and this passing notion crushes down upon him out of nowhere. Lovers. He can feel the pressure of the sea air shift beneath him. He looks down at the lights of Brighton Beach. It is the Brooklyn Aquarium. He sees two giant tanks right next to one another near the beach below. The tanks are open to the sky and Payne can make out movements dimly in the water. The beluga whales. They are swimming slowly round in circles, round and around, floating in the heated waters of the blue aquaria, the slightest distance from the sea.

Payne lowers the collective and the ship drops forward out into the bay. "Get ready," he tells Morrow. A tug is sailing north into the narrows. He can see a tiny seaman within the illuminated wheelhouse. Payne pulls the helicopter up and steers her toward the open ocean. "I'm going to bring her to a hover now. Don't open the door until she's absolutely still. And try to avoid the skids."

"Roger," Morrow says calmly. "Ready when you are."

There is a pink light in the distant sky. The stars are beginning to fade. Payne flies the craft steady for another minute in silence. Then he flares at two hundred feet to slow the helicopter down, and settles into a high hover. They are at least five miles east of Sandy Hook. New York glares to the north. The Atlantic sleeps in the east, deep and forgetful. He lowers the ship toward the ocean. The water is dark and choppy. A January wind blows in from the northeast. He can see whitecaps far below. He can see the water churning, black and forbidding. The cyclic bucks in his hand. "Get ready," he says again.

"Roger."

"Go."

There is a rush of icy air. The helicopter jumps and without thinking Payne adjusts the collective. He looks down at his left hand, through the Plexiglas, catching the movement in the corner of his eye. The suitcase and the garment bag descend into the darkness. There is a soundless splash. He tips the helicopter to the side to see. The water crowns and tumbles back onto itself and disappears. Another wave reclines against the first, and it is lost against another still until the water weaves a tractless sea and all is as it had been.

Payne pulls up the collective. The pitch angle of both rotor blades increases, and the disk climbs high into the sky, dragging the fuselage behind, dragging the seats and straps and instruments, dragging the passenger and pilot too, the whole damn thing into the sky.

"It's over, John. She's gone. We're going to be okay now. Don't worry. It wasn't your fault. It was just an accident. It's up to us now, John. We've got to be strong. Just like in college, remember? Be strong like you were in New Haven. Remember? Bobby and Tom, they're not like us, John. It's up to us to hold it together."

Payne does not turn around. He does not need to. Morrow's voice is in his head. He does not need to see the face, the strong jaw and high cheekbones, the bright blue eyes, the golden hair. He and Morrow are connected now in a way they never were before. All of them are.

"We're going to be okay, John. You hear me? The . . ." Morrow's voice crackles in his headset. "All of us, John. We're going to be okay."

"Yeah, sure, Glen. It's okay. You can say it." He pulls up the collective and the helicopter leaps into the night. "The Hunting Club."

Part 2

Part 2

VI

The sun sets through the trees as Payne drives his red Accord along the highway. To his left, far across the grinding Hudson River, he can see snow still sprinkling the distant palisades. A few fingers of steam scratch the pewter sky above the power plant, drawing red light. A hawk fishes the ice blocks by the railway tracks. The river slithers by, thick and ponderous, cold, like the blue-gray glacier which first carved the valley ten thousand years before.

Payne exits off Route 9, past the strip mall with the pizzeria, past the minimart and then down into the woods, along the narrow country road which cuts behind the Sportsmen's Center on the back way to his house. It has grown dark in the last few minutes. The houses are lit up in the black woods, aglow with Christmas decorations. Green and red light reflects off patches of dirty snow left over from a few days back, a storm that kept him grounded for two hours. People move about in distant windows, carrying on with their lives, talking, eating. They are oblivious, thinks Payne. He turns the corner and his street comes into view. There is the great frosted meadow stretching out beyond his house. There is the white siding, the spiked angles of the Cape Cod nestled in blue spruce. There is the picture window, the Christmas tree, the tinsel and the colored lights. He pulls the car over onto the side of the road. There is the wreath on the front door, the crimson ribbon dripping. His heart is pounding in his chest. He takes a final drag off his cigarette, opens the car window, and throws the butt into the street. He can't put it off anymore. He is already late. He has to go back to his life, as if nothing has occurred, as if he is the same John Payne who left only the day before. For a moment he can see a shadow move across the window in the living room. It pauses by the mirror near the entrance, and is gone. Payne slips the Honda into drive and crawls the last few feet into the driveway.

Jan is a small woman, despite her pregnancy, with serious brown eyes and long brown hair, tinged with red. When she appears at the garage door, Payne can see that she is angry. "You're late," she says. She hasn't smoked in months, and still her voice is husky. "And thanks for calling. Why didn't you tell me you were staying in town?"

Payne appears stunned. "I thought I did," he lies.

Jan rolls her eyes. "Yeah, well, you didn't." She glances at her watch. "You'd better get going and shower," she says, "or we're going to be late."

"Late?"

"For dinner. Ron and Aggie's wedding anniversary. For crying out loud, John. They're your parents. Why do I always have to remember these things."

He pushes past her into the hall. "I'm sorry," he says. "It must have slipped my mind." Then he hesitates and stops. He turns slowly. Jan has never looked more beautiful. She is wearing the red-and-green plaid maternity dress he gave her for Christmas, and her grandmother's ruby earrings. Her cheeks are flushed. Her hair is tied in a loose knot at the top of her head. A wisp, the slightest tress, hangs off to one side. She plays with it and says, "What's the matter? What are you staring at?"

Payne tries to smile, but he feels false, and turns away. "You look good."

"Yeah, right," she says. "To a buffalo, maybe." Then she adds, "What's the matter with you?"

"Me? Nothing, why?"

"You're so pale. You guys were up all night, weren't you?" She shakes her head. "That damn bachelor party. I wish you'd never gone."

"So do I," he answers darkly. For a moment he is perfectly aware of his body, the stubborn motion of his lungs, the rush of blood, the short hair standing on the nape of his neck. "It's cold in here." He taps at the thermostat on the wall. "I guess I should wear a suit. I'm sure Dad will."

He climbs the stairs and undresses in the bedroom in the dark. Then he showers slowly, reveling in the familiarity of his surroundings—the leak from the shower head, the cut in the hot water valve that Jan made with the monkey wrench when she tried to change the washer, the drip drip drip, the way she leaned away, fell over, and the blood began to pour out of her nose, her mouth, running the length of her right arm. Yolanda! Where are you now, Yolanda? Are you drifting in your plastic bubble at the bottom of the cold black sea? Be strong, Glen had said. You've got to be strong. Tom and Bobby aren't up to it. Just like that fall night in New Haven, when they had gone out to see The Doors play at the Coliseum, that dark wet autumn night full of a Cyclops moon, and their shadows slicing through the dead leaves on the square. It was their sophomore year at Hadley. They were sharing a quad at Theta Upsilon—Morrow and Litchfield, Demarest and Payne. Avery hadn't joined the frat yet. And they had driven down in Demarest's old Chevy Biscayne with the mottled top, and parked on a side street because they refused to pay the fee at the garage. Slam went the door. Slam, slam. And they were idling up the street in the glow of streetlights and the creamy moon. Litchfield was dressed in a long blue coat his mother had bought for him, and he was worried that it made him look too short. Morrow wore his sheepskin jacket, Demarest his football colors with the elbow pads, and Payne his brother Sam's old bomber jacket. They had been smoking Marlboros and drinking Rolling Rocks on the drive down from Massachusetts, and they were laughing and making fun of Litchfield's coat, hooting and dancing around him, pounding up the sidewalk on their way to the concert hall when it happened.

The gang seemed to materialize out of nowhere. One minute the sidewalk was empty, then suddenly the shapes converged, across the street, just up ahead, out of the darkest stoops and storefronts. "Suck it up," said Morrow, and the air of indomitable good-heartedness that had filled them all a moment earlier was blown out like a birthday candle. A silence followed, a silence magnified by the squeak of sneakers and the rasp of leather on the street. And then it started, "Where you goin', white boy?" But they didn't turn around. They kept on walking faster up the street, the circle tightening. "Ain't seen no white boys up here fo' a looong time."

And then someone appeared on the path. He was a skinny black kid, about their age. He stood at the center of the sidewalk with his arms crossed, wearing a long black coat with large shiny buttons. He wore bell bottoms and leather boots. "What you lookin' at," he said to Demarest. He had a scar over his left eye.

"We're not looking for trouble," Morrow said. He started to walk around him but the black kid raised his hand.

"This is our turf, man. No one aksed you here."

"We're leaving," Morrow said.

"No one said nothin' bout leavin' neitha."

"Look, we don't want any trouble," Demarest said.

"Then you come to the wrong place. Look around you, college boy. This is Trouble, USA."

They looked about. Two other black kids stood in the street, and another one behind them. Leaning on cars, on lampposts, they were smiling at them. They were laughing. "Tha's right."

"With a capital T, that rhymes with mon-eey! You dig? You boys looked tired."

"We're not tired," Demarest said.

"Well, you look mighty tired, carrying those big fat wallets around all day. Maybe we can help you eeease the weight off."

"You want money," Litchfield said. "Here!" He reached into his brand-new coat, pulled out his wallet. "Take it. Go on. Just don't hurt us, okay?"

"No one said nothin' bout hurtin'," someone said, and in a second Demarest was buckled at the waist. Someone had punched him in the stomach. A sucker punch. Tom was spitting up beer. He was fighting for his breath.

"How old are you?" said Morrow.

The skinny kid with the long black coat looked surprised. "Twenty," he said.

"Nineteen. How much do you weigh?"

"Just take the money," Litchfield said, throwing the wallet to the ground. In a second it was gone.

"One eighty. Why you askin', faggot?"

"You and me," said Morrow.

"Let's get out of here," Demarest urged. "Glen, they're too many of them."

"One seventy-five," said Morrow. "So, I'll give you the five pounds."

And everyone turned and looked at Morrow, and Bobby Litchfield started up the street, walking at first, then at a trot, then running at full tilt, with Demarest behind, Demarest throwing his big fat wallet under a parked car. They ran and ran, shouting a rallying cry, shouting for Payne to run, but he could feel his feet stuck to the concrete. He wanted to run. He tried to. But he was looking at this one big black kid with an Afro and an orange baseball cap who was smiling at him from the street. There was something about his face. Payne was mesmerized by the dark eyes in the shadow of the orange visor, the faint mustache, the toothy grin.

Morrow began to stretch his arms, keeping an eye on the black kid in the long black coat. They circled one another slowly, like wrestlers in a ring, searching for openings. The black kid feinted to the left and started to laugh. "White pussy. Faggot," he kept saying, over and over, while Morrow just kept circling.

"No knives," said Morrow. Payne looked at him, at the kid with the long black coat, and suddenly he felt like he was in some black-and-white TV clip, one of those old science fiction shows where the astronaut gets stuck in time, and everything begins to happen in slow motion. He saw the black kid lunge, and Morrow stepping back. He saw an arm swing round, a great black fist, and the way that Morrow caught it in midair, seemed to pull it forward suddenly, tilting the balance, tilting and rolling until the black kid was suddenly flying forward through the air, snapping at the wrist, and crashing to the sidewalk on his back.

The smack on the concrete, the sharp echo of the air punched from the black kid's lungs brought Payne out of his reverie. The kid with the baseball cap was closing in. He was moving up, when Payne felt the punch—before he even saw it. He felt another on his face, and he was suddenly punching back, and hitting with his head down, punching and kicking and yelling something that he did not even understand. Just yelling as the siren boomed, as he felt his collar jerked back from behind. It was the cops. And there was Litchfield getting out the back door of the black-and-white. They had run for help. They had gone on to get reinforcements, they kept saying afterwards. They kept on saying it. But Morrow knew. "I owe you now," he told Payne later at the frat. "You kept your head. Unlike those crybabies." And within a week the story had made its way around the campus, and the older boys began to treat Payne differently, with the kind of grudging admiration they normally reserved for Glen.

Be strong, thinks Payne, as the hot water washes over him. How could he ever tell Morrow that he hadn't had the strength to move, much less to run away that night, like Demarest and Litchfield—but he had wanted to. He had wanted to flee as much as any of them. Except for Morrow. To run away, to hide. *Like you were in New Haven.*

Payne turns up the hot water. He tilts his head back, letting the spray splash his face, his forehead, and his eyes, the water growing hotter by the second. *Be strong.* The water starts to sting. *Be strong. Be strong. Be strong.*

He turns the water off. Then he steps out of the shower and dries himself with his old towel. It is beginning to fray, and this imperfection gnashes at his heart. The same old feel. The tumble-dry smell. When he's finished, he pulls a pair of gray flannel trousers and a blue blazer from his closet and starts to dress. The bedroom is at the top of the house, and he can see gray clouds in the night sky through the skylight in the roof as he picks out a tie. "Which one?" he says to Jan.

She is standing in the doorway, her arms crossed above her swollen belly, waiting. "The striped one, I guess. Either one. We're going to be late."

"I know. I know." He looks down at the silk tie in his left hand. It is the most ordinary object he has ever seen. "Thanks," he says, throwing it around his neck. It slides smoothly underneath his collar. He fashions the knot carefully, checking it in the mirror. He slips on his blazer. The knot is perfect. He can barely feel it riding on his Adam's apple. "Okay. All set," he says.

They decide on taking the Subaru wagon instead of the Accord because the clouds look threatening. Payne drives in silence, intent on the tunnel of country road illuminated by the headlights of the car. Occasionally, the clouds part and the country is exposed, blanched by milky moonlight—a stand of ghostly barren trees, the frozen surface of the Croton reservoir, slicing the black horizon.

Jan relates a story about a fellow marketing executive at IBM who is going off to Cayman Brac for two weeks with her husband. "Two weeks in the hot sun," she repeats like a mantra.

"Tom and Anna will be going to the Caribbean after the wedding," says Payne. "If everything goes okay."

"Well, they deserve it. And what do you mean, if everything goes okay? Why wouldn't it?"

"No reason. When do we pick up the Merritt Parkway?"

"We're not even in Connecticut yet." Jan shifts uncomfortably in her seat. "He's kicking again. Want to feel?"

Payne reaches out and places his hand on Jan's stomach. There. And there again. He can feel the movement within. He is amazed. He imagines the baby wrapped in its placenta, breathing liquid, listening to the echoes of the world.

"I think Melanie and Ken may get divorced."

Payne pulls his hand away. "What's that?" Jan is talking about their next-door neighbors.

"She came over after work today and we had a long talk. Poor kid. She says he's been cheating on her for over a year. She doesn't know what to do. She says she still loves him." Jan sighs. "You still love me, don't you?"

He looks at her beside him. Her profile is only dimly visible in the darkened car interior. "Of course I love you. What do you mean?" He feels his heart jump.

"I'm sorry about the other night. I know I haven't felt much like it lately. It isn't you. It's me. I don't know. I don't feel very attractive." Suddenly her face slips into view, caught in a plane of light shot through the windshield. There are tears in her eyes. Payne turns. The light dims as a passing car drives by.

"But you are," he says. "You've never looked more beautiful to me. I mean that. I love you, Jan."

"There's the exit," she answers, pointing vaguely to the right. He can hear her crying softly. He tries to think of something to say. He searches for the few right words he is convinced exist for this occasion, for every occasion, if only he could find them. If only he were glib, like Avery or Morrow. But he is not. He must be content to wrap himself up in the darkness of the car, in the silence, like Yolanda in her bloody sheet.

In a few minutes Jan starts to talk again, but she no longer tries for conversation. She complains about the sound of gunfire coming from the nearby Sportsmen's Center. She rails against the price of baby furniture. She decries the pains of pregnancy, the suffering of women, the plain unfairness of it all.

He has never loved or needed her more than he does now, and he has never felt more distant. "Jan," he says.

Her story falters. "What is it?"

"I . . ." He cannot even begin.

"I know," she says.

"You do?"

"I knew you wouldn't remember. Don't worry, I found one in my desk at work. You can sign it in the car when we get there. It's that Klimt, the one we picked up at the Met. "The Kiss." Aggie will love it. It's sooo romantic."

He stares for a moment at the gauges, dials, and censors glowing on the dashboard. "Thanks," he says. "You always know what I'm thinking."

There seems to be more snow here in Connecticut than there was in Westchester. The house Payne's father built is situated on four acres in the eastern part of New Canaan, adjacent to the Silvermine River. It sits on a sandstone bluff overlooking a pond; a bulky Norman-style stone house, with massive chimneys, a tennis court, a pool, and a host of smaller outer houses running to the river. The pond is dammed off at one end, tailing into a narrow ravine which carries the Silvermine eastward. The house dominates the ravine like a fortress. It towers at the end of the driveway, flanked by snow-splashed oaks and maples, great stands of white birch blazing in the glare of hidden spotlights.

The yellow Subaru chugs up the hill. Payne parks the car in the gravel circle directly in front of the house. Jan gives him the card and he signs it furiously on the dashboard in the moon-light.

It's grown colder, Payne thinks, as he climbs the front steps of the house. Jan rings the doorbell. The door opens with a sudden rush, and there is Ronald, Payne's father, as if he's been standing there the whole time.

He is a tall man with a slight stoop, dressed in a dark twill suit, with a white shirt pinned at the collar, and a dark green tie. His face is ashen and long. Nests of broken capillaries lend the cheeks a false hint of color. His hair is gray, his eyes deep-set, the honest blue of a mountain sky. "Good to see you, John," he says. "We were worried. And how's my girl? Beautiful as ever." He ushers them into the entrance hall, closing the door behind them. "Looks like snow again. Let me help you with your coats."

"Really? I think it's too cold for snow," says Payne. "Where's Mother?"

"In the kitchen."

"Giving Mrs. Hathaway some cooking lessons. I'll see if I can trip her up," says Jan. She hands her coat to Ronald and waddles up the corridor.

"Is she still suffering from morning sickness?" Ronald whis-pers, as soon as Jan has disappeared.

"All gone. She still cries a lot, though. I need a drink."

Payne heads into the study. It is a large paneled room. A stained glass window overlooks the great lawn on the south side of the house. The walls are decorated with antique maps. Africa. The early Americas. The archipelago of Indonesia. Exotic imaginary creatures swim in paper seas, scaled dragons and seasnakes, water-spouts and whales, and Payne remembers how forbidding they seemed when he was a child.

"Gin and tonic?" Ronald asks. He is standing at the wet bar in the corner.

"Thanks." Payne looks about the room, scanning the table by the bookshelves. "Did you get the evening paper?"

"Never read it," Ronald says. "Not since that Australian fellow bought it. Nothing but sex and murder now."

"Great."

"I've still got the *Times*, though, if you're interested." He pours out a generous tumbler of gin. "How's the flying game?"

"Why do you always insist on calling it a game, Dad? Have you ever noticed that? It's always *the flying game*. Never my job, or my career. Why is that, do you think?"

"I think I'd better make it a double."

"I mean I know it isn't high finance. I know I don't work for the third largest bank in the world. That's very clear to me."

"John, you look terrible!"

Payne's mother stands in the doorway, her arms outstretched, her golden charm bracelet dripping from her wrist. She is wearing a long silk dress, sky blue and aquamarine. "Come here, you. Why is your face so red? Are you burned?"

Payne walks over and kisses his mother on the cheek. "Is Ronald making cocktails?" She pokes at her silver hair. "He's such a gracious host, isn't he, Jan? Come on, darling. Make us a scotch. And don't be shy with the scotch. He always makes them so weak."

"Here, John." Ronald hands Payne his drink.

In a few moments they move into the living room where Agnes pulls Jan down onto the love seat by the fireplace. Payne takes the club chair while Ronald stokes the blazing fire. "Well," says Jan, "if I may do the honors." She raises her glass of Perrier. "To Agnes and Ronald. Happy wedding anniversary." They sip their drinks in silence. "How many is that, twenty-nine?"

"She's so kind," says Ronald. "Actually, it's forty-eight."

"Ronald!" Aggie cries.

"Well, it is."

"Oh, I almost forgot," says Jan, rifling through her purse. "Here." She hands Agnes the card.

"How thoughtful of you."

Mrs. Hathaway appears out of nowhere. She is a blue-haired

stocky woman in her sixties, wearing a starched white cotton apron over her black uniform. She's worn the same damn thing for thirty years, thinks Payne. As long as he can remember.

Agnes rips into the card. "Oh, look," she says, flashing it before her. "A Klimt. It's sooo romantic. See, Mrs. Hathaway."

"Yes, Mrs. Payne. Dinner is served."

They move into the dining room. Mrs. Hathaway has spared no effort, Payne can see. The finest linen is on the table. A pair of silver candelabra glow with the light of a dozen long-stemmed ivory candles. The dining room fire has been lit, a rarity since the days when he and Sam had come home for the Christmas holidays.

They chat on about the wedding anniversary as Mrs. Hathaway serves oysters and a Veuve Clicquot. Payne can barely focus on the conversation. The gin has made him light-headed, and he realizes that he hasn't eaten since the salmon the night before. The oysters are ice cold and delicious. He consumes them without looking. The champagne sizzles on his tongue. He could be a million miles from New York City, insulated by the rich wood paneling, the parquet floors, and Persian rugs, crowned by the shimmering chandelier, protected by the mantle of his father's deep and even voice, an oyster in an oyster shell.

There had been a time once, years before, when he had asked —with all the seriousness of adolescence—how many third-world dictators had brokered their countries' future to pay for all of this? He had made so many protests then, so many stands on principle. He had refused to attend his brother's military funeral. He had sabotaged the internship his father had arranged for him at the bank. He had always known what *not* to do.

Unlike Litchfield, who had gone to Yale Law, or Morrow who had earned his MBA at Harvard, Payne had never felt the urge to stay in school after college. Instead he had drifted from one job to another. First a DJ for a small rock-and-roll radio station near Scranton, Pennsylvania. Then a sales position for a cable franchise. Nothing had worked. The truth was that all he had ever wanted to do was fly. He had earned his pilot's license before he could even drive, and—like his older brother, Sam—was soloing in helicopters before he was eighteen. Flying was the only thing that worked. It was the only place where he could be alone, in control yet free, always ahead of the craft.

Payne looks over at the wall above the carving table. Aggie has been tending the shrine. A half dozen crimson gladioli, out of season, stand in a tall blue Lalique crystal vase below the portrait of his brother. Sam is looking out across a distant space, his young face tanned and beaming, his shirt collar open, his hair a little long. He had been twenty-one then, on the eve of leaving college, in the middle of exams, and yet Agnes had insisted on the portrait. It was the proper thing to do, she claimed, but it was as if she had known even then that he would soon be gone, to Vietnam, to *that place over there*, as she called it, as if by failing to remember the name she would somehow make the ending less conclusive.

Mrs. Hathaway floats into view, carrying a carving board with a standing prime rib roast. Ronald rises to meet her. "It's about time," he says. "I'm starved." He picks up the carving knife and fork, and Payne admires the way the two prongs slip so easily into the roast, the way the blade comes down, glides through the meat, flips the neat flap of beef onto the plate.

"How's your friend Glen, John?" Ronald asks.

"He's all right."

"Seen much of him lately?"

"Just last night."

"What's he up to these days?"

"Same old thing at ZBJ."

"Really. Anyone like it well-done? You do, don't you, Jan?"

"Sure, Ron."

"She likes it medium, Dad. Remember?"

"I'm sure it's fine," says Jan.

Ronald stabs a pair of pieces with the fork and drops them on a plate. "That's for Jan," he says to Mrs. Hathaway. "Still fooling around with those gaming stocks?"

"He's not fooling around, Dad. He made close to a million dollars last year, before taxes."

"John, please," says Agnes. She leans back with a sigh as Mrs. Hathaway serves her.

"Oh, I'm sure he's very successful," Ronald adds. "I'm not disputing that. It's the manner of his success I question."

"Glen Morrow has always been a perfect gentleman," says Agnes.

"Thank you, Mother."

"Well, it's true. From the very first time I saw him at that horrible Pound Ridge reservoir. They'd just taken you away, John, in that ambulance. Ronald, you remember? You and Sam went with him."

"I remember. Sitter's Point."

"And there was Glen, just standing there, shivering in that towel, soaking wet. He was looking at the ambulance as it pulled away, and then he turned and saw me sitting there, and he came right up to me, just like that. 'Are you all right, Mrs. Payne?' he asked me. Somehow he knew my name. 'You look a little pale,' he said. And then he said, 'He'll be okay. John's a tough kid, and a good swimmer.' And I don't know why, perhaps it was his face, or the way he stood there shivering like that with his jaw out, perhaps I was worried about him, but I suddenly felt better. I no longer felt faint." She turns toward Payne and smiles. "And I realized then that just because Sam was captain of the swimming team didn't mean you weren't a good swimmer too." She laughs a high thin laugh. "It seems like such a long time ago now, doesn't it? You were at St. Mark's then, John, remember? And you were so mad because you wanted to go to Choke, like your friends, but a certain individual—who shall remain nameless—insisted it would be better if you went to *his* old school."

Ronald Payne coughs.

"Yes, Mother."

"And then when Sam . . ." She hesitates. She takes a long sip of her wine. "I'll never forget the way Glen helped you, John. You were so sad and angry then, we didn't know what to do. You didn't even want to go to college. We'd given up. Hadn't we, Ronald? You were so wild."

"I wasn't wild."

"But Glen knew. Can John play tennis? Can John go fishing? Can John drive into town? Oh, he knew exactly what to do. The way he picked your spirits up . . . Glen Morrow will always be a perfect gentleman to me."

"Yes, well," says Ronald with another cough. "I'm sure he

knows what you like, dear. He usually makes it his business to know what people like, what they need. Or think they need. Personally, I distrust perfection, especially when it appears in people. Seems to me Glen has always relied too much on his good looks, his charm, and that damn smile of his. There are no shortcuts in life. It's brick by brick, step by step. I know that's not a particularly fashionable thing to say these days, but that's the way it is."

"Oh, Ronald!" Agnes says.

"Who put you up to this?" says Payne. "Is this you or Charlie Morrow talking?"

"You make it sound as if a father shouldn't worry about his son's interests. I'll concede Charles is concerned. What's wrong with that? He feels Glen takes too many risks. Unnecessary risks. And so do I. Look at that Equus deal. Completely over-leveraged. Those bonds are worthless. That debt will bankrupt the company within five years, you mark my words."

"I don't know anything about it. I fly helicopters for a living, remember? You can hear me on the radio."

"Yes, I know." Ron hands Mrs. Hathaway a plate. "For John," he says.

She brings the plate over, and drops it on the tablecloth before him. She does not approve of these debates. Payne can see it in her churlish eyes, the purse of her lips. Mrs. Hathaway is of the old school. Children are not meant to contradict.

He studies his plate. Brussels sprouts cooked with bacon. A heap of scalloped potato. The steaming slab of prime rib roast. There is so much food. Once this too would have disturbed him. The opulence. The plenitude. But now he finds it comforting. How can he fault his father, or his success? Who is he to debate the ethics of usury when he can still feel the wetness of Yolanda's blood between his legs? He stabs his fork into the prime rib on his plate. The meat is rare. He can see the blood collect around the tines. It seems to bubble up, to gather force and spill over the fatty skin. It pools around his Brussels sprouts. It laps against the lip of the bone white china plate. "Excuse me," he says, pushing his chair away from the table. "I'm sorry . . ."

"What is it, John?" says Jan.

"Too much champagne. I'm sorry." He rises to his feet. "A little air, I think. I'll be right back."

He drops his napkin on the chair and heads out toward the living room. The fire is still burning. The room feels unbearably hot. He dashes toward the French doors at the south side of the room. He wrestles with the handles. They feel ice cold in his hands. He pulls them open and the night wind rushes in, riding on the vast silence of the winter night. He stumbles forward onto the empty brick patio. There is a thin sprinkling of snow on everything in sight. It stretches all the way to the distant woods, across the great south lawn, a field of white in the cold moonlight, immaculate and undisturbed, save by his looming shadow. He leans forward, bracing himself against the freezing wind. It tears at him. It seems to cut against his face.

"Are you all right, honey?"

It is Jan. She stands in the open doorway leading to the living room, the warm light streaming out behind her. "You'll catch your death of cold out there. What's the matter with you? Do you feel sick?"

"Jan, I have to tell you something."

"You know you're going to ruin your shoes."

"I don't care about my fucking shoes. Will you listen to me?"

"What is it?" she cries. "What's the matter with you today?"

He tries but the words don't come. They settle in his throat like stones. He cannot tell her anything. He shakes his head. He looks up at the night sky. The clouds have parted and he can see Orion flashing, Betelgeuse and Bellatrix and all the other countless stars above him, swirling, weighing in upon him, until he feels crushed and suffocated, as if he is standing at the bottom of a lake. It is the secret lying over him like the wide sky. I am a murderer, he thinks. You're married to a murderer. I can still taste the blood in my mouth.

"What's going on out here?" Ronald appears in the living room behind Jan. "You've insulted your mother, you know. She spent hours on that roast. Is everything all right?"

"It's fine," Payne answers. His voice is thin and strained. "Too much champagne. Not enough sleep. Don't worry about me. I'm fine now." He starts back toward the house. "Sorry, Dad. I hope I haven't ruined your anniversary."

Jan says, "Maybe we should go home. John's been working extra hours lately. What with the baby and everything, and my stopping work soon."

"No, I feel better now. Really, I do." He steps into the living room, and his voice resounds in the enclosed space. "Everything's just fine."

That night, Payne lies awake in bed. His eyes are open. He is listening to the sound of the alarm clock ticking. He can hear Jan breathing next to him. She is awake too. He can sense her eyes upon him. He can feel her breath on his neck. He would give anything to be able to turn, to take her in his arms, to press her close to him. But he cannot. It has started to snow. He can see the flakes through the skylight, falling, covering the glass, weighing in upon him from above. And if he turned and took her in his arms, whose face would he see?

The night descends. He tries to sleep but it is useless. The sweat pours off his body underneath the goose down comforter. He can feel it running down his neck, into the hollow below his ear. There is too much. It pools around his hips. The sheets are soaking wet. It's Jan, he thinks. It must be Jan. He tries to turn. I must have . . . in my sleep. The sheets are wound about his legs. He kicks and feels a soft wet shape beside him. Jan moans. He can hear liquid pouring out, the constant drip, drip, drip. A cord is wrapped about his legs. He feels it tightening as he kicks. He rips the wet sheet from his chest, throws back the comforter and there it is, still pulsing at his feet, the head discernible within the blue placenta, the half-formed lips entreating. Payne screams. The sound reverberates inside his skull, a rooster cry, and he is screaming to the sound of the alarm clock by his head. He slams his hand down on it, turns it off. He takes a breath. He turns and looks at Jan. She is sleeping soundlessly beside him.

He rises from the bed, cold and naked in the darkness. The dream still presses down upon him, and he finds himself in the nursery down the hall, standing by the walnut chest of drawers, the piece that for three months he'd promised Jan he would remove. A cold sweat chills his bare shoulders. He can feel the moonlight struggling to get in, struggling to reach across the floor and touch his feet, crawl up his legs. He finds his fingers on the handle of the drawer and pulls it open.

Sam's .45 lies in a nest of socks, still holstered, still waiting for him after all these years. He takes it from the holster. *Go on and take it*, Sam had said, on his first and only stateside leave. *Go on. You can keep it. I brought it home just for you.* It still feels surprisingly heavy in his hand. It still smells of oil and Sam and Vietnam, and he cocks it without thinking, without feeling the resistance of the trigger on his finger. Go on. The same familiar Cyclops eye. Old friend. They had spent a lot of afternoons together, a lot of nights, keeping each other company, waiting for the dawn. For all those months after Sam's death. Go on. He feels his finger tighten on the trigger. He puts the barrel in his mouth. The dark familiar smoky taste. Go on. Go on. Save everyone else the trouble.

"Honey?"

It is Jan. Payne slips the gun back in the holster. He closes the drawer.

"What are you doing?"

"It's four o'clock," he says, staring out the window. He turns around. "Time to get up."

Jan is standing in the doorway, rubbing her eyes. She is wearing her pale pink flannel nightgown.

Payne gestures with his hand. "Why don't you try and go back to sleep?"

"I had a bad dream." She yawns. She combs the hair back from her face with her white fingers. "But I can't remember what it was."

"Go back to sleep. I'm sorry. I didn't mean to wake you."

It takes Payne twenty minutes to shower, dress, and make a breakfast which he doesn't eat. There is a stillness in the air. He can feel it even before he opens the garage door. It is the snow. An inch or two has fallen, no more. It covers the lawn, the lilac bushes, the boughs of evergreens. He can feel it crunching underneath his tires as he backs the red Accord out onto the driveway, and down into the street.

Traffic is still light on Route 9. Everything is dusted with a thin layer of snow, and Payne imagines it from the air, the slow stream of lights through the trees, the arteries of traffic, pumping toward the city. He flicks the radio on. It is just before five, time for the headline news. He feels his pulse quicken. Until now, he has never noticed the lisp in the announcer's voice, the buzz in the dashboard, the way the car pulls off to the left. He strains to concentrate, but there is nothing but the usual fare. Corrupt politicians. The budget deficit. He turns the radio off. It is only a matter of time, he thinks, before someone discovers she's missing. A friend, a relative. Her boss at the Party Girl Lounge. Someone will notice. Her landlord, when she fails to pay the rent. Her mother. And then what? They'd track The Hunting Club down, through the lounge, the Quonset Hut. He'd be exposed. It wouldn't matter that it was an accident. Morrow was right. Who would make the distinction? Jan would still know. His parents. His friends at work. His unborn child. He remembers his nightmare and his fingers tighten round the steering wheel. All of that blood, he thinks. He stares out at the dark road, at the taillights of the car ahead of him, red in the reflecting snow, blooming like the gladioli underneath Sam's portrait.

This letter is for you, kid, and just for you, so you'll know what it's really like. He can still remember the handwriting, the slant of the blue lines on weightless blue paper. Sitting on the patio, after three hard sets of tennis with the Taylor kid. Drinking an iced tea in the shade. *Don't give it to Mom or the Old Man. This is just you and me and what happened today, my first real day in the field, although I've been in this fucking place for more than three weeks already. . . .*

Sam had been flying his B-model Huey gunship low across a line of trees, mortars popping all around him. He was going in with a squad of slicks—troop carriers—to pick up three platoons that had just spent two weeks in the bush, and he could see the soldiers coming, waving, helping each other on, carrying their wounded. He could see the flash of small arms fire in the trees behind their line.

They were terrified. Even from a hundred feet, Sam could feel it—the desperation, the adrenaline. He hovered by a set of dykes which stretched out from the jungle. The grunts were running, but it seemed to take forever, exposed as they were on the open dykes. He watched them stumble, dance and fall. Exposed as they were. That's when he opened up. He saw the rockets flare and arc away, blasting the jungle skyward. He watched the tracers from his flex gun stream into the woods, watched the green pulp fry under the fire, the branches flying, and at the center of his sights was this one VC in black. The VC turned to flee but there was nothing he could do. Sam trimmed the cyclic stick and watched the bullets stumble through the grass, slither like a fire snake across the distant back, popping off the head.

It was so easy, Sam wrote. *And it felt so good, it scared me. The power of it all. You move a finger and it's done. It's so easy, John. It's like a drug. I can't stop thinking about it. Forget what I said before. Don't ever come to this place. You're too alive when everything else is dead.*

For years Payne had never understood those words. But now, as he sits in his dark car, they rattle in his head like a refrain. It is as if he has been asleep his whole life, and then suddenly awakened. He is aware of everything around him. The feel of the steering wheel in his hands, humming with the engine. The buzzing in the dashboard. The smell of cigarettes. The whining of a distant siren. His eyes flash to the mirror. There it is, the blue light of the state police. He's coming down the Saw Mill fast, passing heedlessly, ignoring the snow and the black ice on the roadway. Payne feels his stomach clench. The noise of the siren is deafening. The police car appears huge in the mirror, lunging past him up the road, kicking up slush in its wake, Dopplering out of sight.

Is this what it will be like my whole life? he thinks. Waiting for a car to pull me over? Is that it? Too alive? He reaches into his jacket for a cigarette and flicks the windshield wipers on.

In a few minutes Payne turns off the Henry Hudson Highway, onto the ramp for the George Washington Bridge. Traffic is heavier now. Soon there will be ten- to fifteen-minute delays coming into the city. But the road to Teterboro is clear. He can see a single-engine Mooney climbing high into the night sky to the west. It banks slowly and the light of the rising sun reflects for a moment on its wings. It climbs and climbs, the red and green lights on the wing tips fading, rising, free.

The airport is practically deserted. He parks in the lot next to the chain link fence and heads for hangar twenty-six. The pilots' lounge is a small room, decorated with hotel lobby furniture—overstuffed pastel chairs, a badly stained wooden coffee table, a desk, a Georgia O'Keeffe print on the wall. Suddenly the phone rings on the desk. It seems unnaturally loud. Payne walks over to pick it up but it stops ringing only inches from his hand. He hesitates. He stops. There are the morning papers, in a pile. He picks up the *Daily News*. He flips through the pages, slowly at first, then more quickly. Nothing. Nothing.

"John!"

A hand falls on his shoulder. He jumps, he turns, but it is only Cracker. "Morning," Payne says casually.

Cracker is forty, with the deeply tanned face and lined forehead of a Midwest farmer. He's flown everything from corporate to sea rescue in his thirty-five hundred hours in the air. "Got a call," he says with a grin. "Sounds important." He stands there in his blue windbreaker and jeans, smiling, as if he knows it all already, as if he's just too good a sport to tell. Then he shrugs and smiles and simply moves away.

"Thanks," says Payne. He picks up the telephone.

"John?"

It is Morrow. Payne sits down on the desk.

"Have you seen the morning papers?" Morrow says.

"Yeah, I've seen them."

"Nothing, right?"

"Plenty of murders, but not mine."

"Snap out of it, John. Everything's going to work out fine if we just keep our heads and stick together."

"Okay, Glen."

"Look, who's going to care, John? She was just a stripper, just a part-time hooker who got in over her head. It was an accident," says Morrow. "I'm sorry it happened. I feel bad for her. But I feel worse for you. She's dead, and there's nothing in the world we can do to bring her back. Nothing. You and the rest of the Club are all that matter now. Do you hear me? How did you sleep?"

Payne doesn't relate his nightmare. It would seem like a weakness to Morrow. "All right, I guess. How about you?"

"At first I couldn't," Morrow says. "Then Cindy woke up. I don't know why or how, but I was so excited. Usually I'm dead after doing so much coke. I guess after everything that happened . . . I don't know. The whole night long, I felt so alive," says Morrow. "Isn't that weird? John? John, are you there?"

"Yeah, I'm here. Look, Glen, I've got to take off. It's almost six-fifteen."

There is another long pause. "Are you going to be okay, John? Maybe we should have lunch, talk things over."

"No, I can't. I'll see you at the rehearsal. I've got to go. I'm fine." Payne hangs up. He leans against the desk. All he can think of is his brother Sam, smiling, like the portrait in his parents' dining room, squeezing off that last round through the trees.

VII

Morrow hangs up the telephone. He leans back in his chair and shudders. It is clear now. Payne is going to be trouble. He feels the knowledge settle on his heart like a great stone. After all these years. An impenetrable sorrow fills him, and he wonders, with all his powers of analysis, with all his research skills and logic, what it means about himself that he cares more about the loss of trust, than he cares about losing Payne. But they are all counting on him now. They need him.

A shadow falls across the door. Damage control. That is the issue at hand. He will schedule a time for his sorrow.

"Mr. Morrow."

Morrow looks up. It is Pete Buchanan, EVP and lord chamberlain of research. He was in early. "Mr. Buchanan," Morrow says cordially. "Come in. Come in, have a seat."

"Can't stay. I'm flying off to Tokyo at eight. I have a nagging suspicion that the Japanese CMO market is about to heat up." Buchanan hovers in the doorway. He is a lanky gray-haired man in his fifties, gold-wire-rimmed and tall, in a blue serge suit and red suspenders. "But I wanted to congratulate you. Your report on Shangri-la. You are dancing in step with the mistress."

Buchanan's metaphors were always sexual. The market had been his mistress for more than thirty years. "Thank you," Morrow says.

"First the Equus deal, now this. The client sleeps more peacefully. He dreams of flower beds and spacious well-kept lawns, of fountains whispering, of warm winds blowing through the elms across the river. You've kept the contract with the franchise, Glen." Buchanan nods. "You and Cindy should come out to Kent again. Next Saturday. When I get back from Japan. The Chestertons will be there, and Monsieur Lazarre. You remember Philippe, don't you?"

"Of course. We'd love to."

"How is your beautiful wife?"

"Fine, fine."

"Mm, yes, well." Buchanan pinches the bridge of his nose. His wire-rimmed glasses slip into place, and his eyes fall into focus. They are penetrating, diamond-tipped. They seem to cut right into Morrow. "Until next Saturday."

"Have a good flight."

Buchanan vanishes as suddenly as he arrived. The doorway is empty. Morrow looks down at his walnut desk, at the Mont Blanc pen set, the golden letter opener with the ZBJ seal on the handle. Cindy is smiling at him from her malachite frame. It is a new photograph, taken just before Christmas in Rome. She is wearing the sable coat he'd given her. She is standing on the Spanish Steps, her long blond hair held back by a dark blue Hermès scarf, the color of her eyes, a single earring flashing gold, and her smile of perfect teeth. She is perfect. Perfect. And his eyes fold through the photograph, blend with the malachite, and he's kneeling on the marble floor of the great hall in his father's house, bending over with his arms out, encircling a spinning metal top. His mother, the ice queen, is playing abroad, busy, no doubt, with another Latin diplomat. His hands are the hands of a five-year-old, the tiny fingers reaching for the silver top, steadying the air as it spins along the baseboard toward his father's wing-tipped shoes. His father laughs, and dances up the hall, trying to avoid the spinning top, his cashmere topcoat billowing, his hat and scarf revolving. He was always dressed to go. The top spins down the marble hall, faster and faster, in time with his father's laughter, in time with the turning of the earth, the circumnavigation of the sun, the spinning of the galaxy itself.

One hundred institutional investors control forty percent of all the free capital in the country, and Morrow knows each one of them. He's made billions for ZBJ. At seven hundred base, with bonuses and perks, he earns a princely sum each year. Almost a million when times are good. And they are good.

His eyes focus on the photograph. Cindy's mouth is partly open and he finds himself drawn into it, remembering the night before, her startled kisses as he entered her again. All night they had made love. He could not stop himself. He had been charged with energy, the drugs, and more than that. He cannot hide it from himself. Yolanda dancing in his head. Yolanda kneeling at his feet, the mirror in her hands.

He leans back in his chair. His eyelids close and there she is again. Just like the dream he'd had the night before. He sees Yolanda lying on the bed. He stands above her as she takes him in her mouth. He sees her watching him with her black, almond-shaped eyes. He feels the tumid softness of her tongue, the agonizing rasp of her lower lip against his skin. He hovers on the moment, spinning, traveling down across the marble floor, in step. And then, all of that blood. He turns his head away. He reaches back to scratch his neck. It is sunburnt where the lanyard of his sunglasses was rubbing on his neck, rubbing off the sunblock. He feels the skin unroll. He plucks the epidermis and feels a patch peel from his neck. He pulls it and the skin gives way, tearing, ripping off in his hand.

The phone begins to purr. Morrow opens his eyes, leans forward, and picks up the receiver. It is the security guard in the lobby downstairs. "What is it, Max?"

"Mr. Litchfield's on his way up. I asked him to wait for just a minute while I called you, Mr. Morrow—you know the procedure —but he just breezed right by me. Didn't sign in. Didn't even stop when I called his name. Now, I could have stopped him, Mr. Morrow, physically, if you know what I mean, but seeing he's your friend . . ."

"It's all right, Max. Thank you."

Morrow hangs up the receiver. He leans back in his chair, spins about, and stares out through the window at Manhattan. His office is on the thirty-fifth floor. He can see dozens of little dots, tiny ants, scurrying about in overcoats below, marching to work, or home, with glances at the clock. The Myrmidons, as Chazz, his classics don at Choke, had called the masses. The foot soldiers of Achilles. Mindless and meaningless. He looks uptown across the island, across a glade of smaller office buildings, the low-slung roofs of Chinatown, past sooty water towers, past SoHo to the tall stone splinter of the Empire State, and north to Rockefeller Center. This was his aerie, and from it he could weigh and measure all the commerce of the entertainment world. That was his job. He studied what he saw and put it all on two typed pages every fortnight, and a major study six times yearly. He traveled constantly, at least one month each quarter, preparing his reports, interviewing studio heads, captains of the gaming industry, looking for things you couldn't read between the columns of a Lotus spreadsheet. Eighty percent of his time was spent summarizing research, doing the maintenance, issuing action paths to buy or sell. The balance was spent on the Big Deals—mergers and acquisitions, capital needs. And all of it flowed through here, from across the country, across the oceans to New York, under the sea and through the sky by satellite and cable, under the pounding city streets, condensing in the basement of the ZBJ skyscraper, and welling up right here, beneath his feet, in a rush of fiber optic light, through his telephone and modem, into *him*.

The telephone purrs. He picks it up. Litchfield has arrived at the reception area. "Send him right in," Morrow says, but he's already there. "How you doing, Bobby?"

Litchfield slams the door behind him. "How do you think I'm doing?" He shrugs his coat off and throws it on the walnut coat rack in the corner of the room. His fat face is chalky white; his bow tie is askew. "I'm going crazy, that's how I'm doing." He begins to sit down, but changes his mind and starts to pace the office. "How am I doing?" He laughs bitterly. "How the hell are *you* doing?"

"I'm fine."

Litchfield comes to a sudden stop. "I bet you are," he says, looking down at Morrow. "You're amazing, Glen. How can you be so calm?"

"Because I understand the way things work. That's my job."

"What the hell are you talking about?"

"Sit down, Bobby."

"I'd rather stand."

"Sit down!"

Litchfield pulls up. He hesitates, then takes the chair in front of Morrow's desk.

Morrow leans forward on his elbows, weaving his fingers together. He smiles at Litchfield. He shakes his head, just so, the slightest hint of a rebuke. *Enough.* Litchfield settles in his chair, drawn by the intimacy of Morrow's gestures. "Listen to me, Bobby," Morrow says. "I've always taken care of you, haven't I?"

Litchfield simply turns away.

"Nothing is going to happen to us. I'm going to see to that. The Hunting Club is safe."

"How can you be so sure? What if they find her?"

"They'll never find her, Bobby. Never. No one saw us. No one saw anything. She was the only one, and now she's gone. No one can connect us to what happened."

"But someone's bound to miss her—"

"No one will know. Her suitcase is packed and gone. They'll think she took a trip, left town. No one will want to know the truth. She was just a hooker, Bobby, a tramp. Don't you get it? Nothing's going to happen to us."

He raises his head and smiles at Litchfield. The morning winter sun reflects across his face. "As long as we stick together, right? One for all, and all for one. Like always, Bobby, right?"

"What about Tom?"

"We'll see him tonight at the rehearsal. Don't worry about Tom. He'll be all right. I'll make sure of that." He rocks gently in his chair. "He's not the one I'm worried about."

"What do you mean? Who? Payne?"

Morrow nods. He swivels in his chair and looks out through the window at the sawtooth skyline of Manhattan. Then he turns and smiles at Litchfield, saying, "How would you feel if you knew you were a murderer?"

.   .   .

Litchfield walks along the sidewalk briskly, feeling the eyes of Morrow on his back, the thick nape of his neck, thirty-five stories away. He turns the corner of the street and leans against the building, cheek pressed against the stone. His heart is banging. He hovers in the shadows. A drop of sweat begins to wind its way across his shoulder blade, around the fleshy hollow of his armpit, and down along his side.

The sidewalk is filling up. Litchfield closes his eyes. He gulps for air. He loosens his crimson bow tie and opens the top two buttons of his shirt. A girl with teased hair and blue makeup passes by. She smells of lemon soap. A pair of messengers in spandex pants, a brace of businessmen. An old Korean man approaches, hugging the building, trying to push him out into the sidewalk traffic, but Litchfield holds his ground. He pulls himself up to his full height. He sucks his belly in. He scowls and the Korean man looks up, and hesitates, and finally edges around him. Litchfield stands firm. Relax, he tells himself. Take it easy. His heart begins to slow, his breath returns. For God's sake, man, relax. You're going to give yourself a heart attack. Act normal. He turns and looks in through the storefront window. He is standing by a gift shop. The store is closed, and he remembers it is early still. His wife Elizabeth is probably still asleep. And Sally too, still lying there, the ruffle of her cotton nightgown bunched about her throat, her mouth half open, breathing, completely unaware, surrounded by down pillows, her light pink comforter, the poster of George Michael, the vanity, the jewelry box, the rose wallpaper, and the ivory trim. He tries to focus on the objects in the store. Take it easy, he repeats. Breathe deep. He fumbles for the words which Morrow spoke to him before, but they no longer seem to work. Stripped of the resonance of Morrow's voice, they bob about inside him, unmoored and drifting, a blouse, a skirt, a suitcase on the surface of the sea.

Stop it! Stop it! An object in the window grabs his eye. He has yet to buy a wedding present for the Demarests, and he finds himself line-sighting the display, searching for anything to disconnect him from his memory. There is a tall transparent vase, fake Orrefors. There is a shelf of Royal Copenhagen plates, a phalanx of salt shakers, paintings, statuettes, stone eggs and amulets, and at the center, fixed by light, a hand-carved crystal of the palest iceberg blue. The light is dim, but he can just make out a host of ghostly shapes carved on the glacial surface. It looks a little . . . yes, a reindeer running on the icy tundra, her feet dragged down by wolves, her neck turned from their snapping jaws, horns pitched, eyes rolled and staring at the starless sky.

VIII

The Reverend Gregory Periwinkle presides over the rehearsal with the patience of Job. He is a large round man in his early forties, with a dark unruly mop of hair, an outpouring of chins, a sonorous deep voice. He stands at the head of the aisle, his back to the green marble altar, his hands uplifted like an orchestra conductor. "First the right foot, stop. The left foot, stop. The right foot, stop . . ."

Demarest, dressed in a camel hair jacket and gray trousers, jerks like a puppet up the aisle.

"See how easy?" Periwinkle says. "All right, now. Maid of honor and best man. And then the rest of you as well."

The two lines of the wedding party start to move. First Avery and Mary Beth O'Connell, who works with Anna at *Sight* magazine. Morrow and Cindy follow. Then Litchfield and Elizabeth, and at the end of the procession, Payne. Jan sits and watches from a nearby pew. Right, stop. Left, stop. They shuffle up the aisle, across the ochre tiles, their footsteps echoing through the vastness of the Romanesque church, the shallow transept arms, around the great square piers, the barrel vaulting, the tower, and the dome.

After a brief dramatic pause, Anna Leuthold and her father, Dick, appear at the entrance to the nave. She is a slight woman, with short blond hair and a pug nose. Her face is round as a salad plate. She is wearing a royal blue silk suit with padded shoulders and navy pumps. Dick is holding her by the arm. He has a startled expression, like an animal spooked by a loud noise. He is the president of one of the country's most successful discount brokerage firms, and he still looks helpless and confused. His eyes beseech the Reverend Periwinkle for direction. Right, stop. Left, stop. They shuffle up the aisle.

"That's right now," Periwinkle says. "Tom takes her by the hand—take her by the hand, Tom—and you step back, Dick, and sit down in the front row there, that's right." Dick Leuthold flops down in the pew, a blank expression on his face.

He is no longer needed, Payne thinks bitterly. He's obsolete, redundant. An appendix of love.

The Reverend Periwinkle lectures for another fifteen minutes, sonorously instructing them, cajoling, blocking out their entrances and exits. Finally, it's over. Tom and Anna thank the wedding party, and remind them that the dinner reservation at the Palm Court is for eight o'clock—sharp. They put their coats on in the narthex. Morrow is laughing at a private joke. Cindy is standing right beside him. There's Avery and Mary Beth, and Litchfield talking to Elizabeth, and Jan, Tom Demarest, and Anna, too.

Payne hangs back in the warm glow of the nave, observing all the dark familiar faces as if this is the first time he has ever seen them. There's Morrow, chatting amiably with Dick, his face almost hidden in the shadows. He smiles the famous Morrow smile, and Dick's round shoulders drop and roll and shiver with a laugh. There's Litchfield, trying to make a point, gesticulating in a grim determined way, his crimson bow tie crooked, shaking his head at someone out of sight. "Who are you?" Payne says softly to himself. He hasn't had a full night's sleep since Tuesday, and he can feel his mind begin to wander. The crowd disbands. It squeezes through the carved brass portal, out into the cold. He follows, stops, and sees the avenue, the flat face of the Helmsley Building, peaked with gold, the way the Pan Am Building rolls and rises, dressed in light, flanked by the tunnels of Park Avenue, up, up and skyward to the glowing snow clouds far above.

"Are you all right?" says Jan.

He jumps and turns and says, "A little tired. How about you?" He lays a hand across her stomach.

"Okay, I guess. Come on. Anna will kill us if we're late." She takes him by the hand and leads him down the steps. A cab is waiting for them by the curb.

It takes them only a few minutes to reach the Plaza Hotel. The doorman, trimmed with gold brocade, escorts them up the stairs and glides away, his fingers bristling with green bills. They are all waiting in the foyer, caught by the maelstrom of the bold red carpet at the center of the room. Under the crystal chandelier, a massive floral decoration blooms like a firework behind them.

The dining room is all but empty. A line of potted palms extends along the side facing the foyer. Peter Demarest, Tom's father, postures at the entrance, arms akimbo, attended by the maître d'. Two sides of the room are ringed with arched glass doors that face the central hallway of the great hotel. A bald violinist dressed in an ill-fitting black tuxedo pivots before the mirrors on the west wall, playing a nameless show tune. Somewhere a piano answers back and they are moving through the room, first Anna, Dick and Peter too, between the stone stands topped with yet more palms, then Demarest and his mother, Pat, between the marble capitals, the electric candelabra, when Morrow suddenly appears from nowhere, dressed in a navy double-breasted suit with a red rose on his lapel. "Hey, John," he says. "John, hold on a minute."

Payne motions Jan to follow Avery. Then he turns toward Morrow, saying, "What do you want, Glen?"

"Take it easy. Jesus Christ! I was just wondering how you are."

"I'm here, aren't I?"

"So I see." Morrow shakes his head reprovingly, and takes Payne by the arm. "Look, I just wanted to tell you that we're all behind you, John. All of us. We're on your side."

"What side is that, Glen?" He pulls away. He bites his lower lip and says, "Forget it, Glen, okay? Just forget what I said. I know you're trying to help. And I appreciate it, I really do. I'm just really confused right now."

Morrow smiles warmly. He lays a hand across Payne's shoulder. "It's important to know who your friends are, John. Especially at a time like this. It's important to know who you can count on. You know what I mean?"

"Yeah. Yeah, sure, Glen." Payne shakes off Morrow's hand. He starts across the dining room. Jan is seated at the same table as Mary Beth and Avery, Cindy and the Litchfields. A pair of candles glimmer on the bone white tablecloth, reflecting in the water glasses, reflecting in the wine and cocktail glasses, too.

There is a large bouquet of baby's breath and yellow roses at the center of the table.

There is the lulling hum of conversation.

Payne smiles and sits down next to Jan. She is talking with the Litchfields about Elizabeth's parents, who are moving soon to North Carolina.

Payne glances over at the next table. Morrow is standing between Demarest and Dick Leuthold, telling a story. Payne can't hear what he is saying, but it is clear that Demarest is not amused. He is staring at his drink, not even listening.

"Excuse me, sir," a waiter says, as he drops a plate before him. Payne eyes the food suspiciously. Brazilian hearts of palm, rolled in smoked salmon, topped with parsley and the tiny crimson roe of flying fish.

He should eat. But it has become impossible.

"They're finally leaving Greenwich in the spring." Elizabeth leans forward, pouting. Litchfield's wife is a soft, expansive woman with a widow's peak, and large deep-set dark eyes. "It took Mom twelve years and two bypass operations to get him to retire." She throws a glance at Litchfield. "I wish Robert would slow down. He's turned into a nervous wreck."

Litchfield looks up with a liquid smile. "She thinks I work too hard," he says. He stares at Payne over his snub nose. He shrugs and stabs at his smoked salmon.

"That's what I say to Glen," adds Cindy with disgust. "But does he care? Does he even pay attention?" She fiddles with her pearls like worry beads.

"Well, at least you've got that tan," says Jan. "Where did you go this time?"

"The Bahamas."

"Must be nice."

"They're all like that," says Elizabeth. She shakes her head.

"Who?"

"Men. These men, at least. The Hunting Club. I can't speak for the rest of the subspecies."

"What is this Hunting Club?" asks Mary Beth. "Anna's mentioned it before, too." She turns to Avery beside her. "Do all you guys belong? What is it, anyway, a gun club or something? Some kind of secret society?" She looks about the room suspiciously. "I promise, I won't tell."

"You could say that," Jan says.

Avery shakes his head. He starts to laugh. "Off the record, right? I wouldn't want this ending up in *Sight.*"

"Off the record. Scout's honor," says Mary Beth. She looks so earnest with her glasses and her long red hair. She is wearing a white silk blouse with a brooch encrusted with false gemstones. When she lifts her hand up in a kind of scout salute, Payne is convinced that he can see the blue veins pumping in her wrist, just underneath the skin. Her fingers are so thin. They look as though they could snap off with just the slightest provocation.

"It's nothing, really. We're just good friends," says Payne. "That's all. Old friends."

"John's known Glen since New Canaan Country Day. Glen met Bobby and Tom at Choke," says Avery. "John and I went to St. Mark's, to maintain that religious upbringing." He laughs. "Then we all went to Hadley College together."

"And there you have it," says Payne.

"Glen and Tom were on the football team together, first at Choke, then Hadley. Little Three Champions two years running. John and I were on the swim team. Infinitely more sophisticated."

"And we all did crew," says Litchfield.

"Why do you call yourself The Hunting Club?"

"It's just an old joke," says Avery.

"At Choke we called ourselves The Club," says Litchfield distantly. "But when we got to Hadley it all changed." He fiddles with his bow tie.

"That's not it. Tell her about the Quabbin trip," says Avery. He swallows a piece of salmon. When Litchfield does not respond, he says, "We went on a hunting trip near Quabbin Reservoir. It was during the fall semester, our junior year. We were all living in this beat-up old house on the road to Somerville. Anyway, one day I got this yearning to go camping in the woods. You know—back to nature. This is nineteen seventy, mind you, seventy-one. Well, before I know it everyone is talking about pitting themselves against the elements, fishing with bare hands, building snares. My little nature trip had turned into a safari. Glen had gone hunting with his father once or twice, when he was a kid, but I had never even touched a gun. None of us had, really, except for Bobby here. Bobby's a crack shot. He won all kinds of prizes at Choke." He takes a sip of his white wine. "Anyway, we rented this cabin up in the woods and took off for a long weekend. It was autumn and the leaves were changing. I don't know if you've ever been to western Massachusetts in the fall, but it was just incredible. Peak season. The oaks and maples were like brass, brushed brass, like flames of fire on the branches. We sat around for three days and did nothing but drink and play poker and eat. And hunt, of course." He laughs. "We did plenty of that. We hunted all day long, carrying these heavy guns around on our shoulders like something out of *Combat*. Or maybe I should say *F-Troop*. We even saw some deer."

"Wait a minute. Glen told me . . ." Cindy hesitates. "I thought you got at least one deer."

Avery laughs. He pushes his long dark hair back from his gaunt face. "Are you kidding? We didn't hit a thing the whole weekend. Someone would always take a shot, and then the deer would run away, and we would end up chasing it across the whole damn country for the next two hours. Up this hill. Down that one. Into bramble thickets. Jesus, what a nightmare. We had a lot of fun, though, didn't we? Didn't we, boys?" He looks at Litchfield first, and then at Payne. Neither will look at him. "Well, we did. And that's when we changed the name. Instead of The Club, we called ourselves The Hunting Club. You know. It was a kind of inside joke."

There is the sound of cutlery on plates, of water glasses chiming. For a moment no one speaks. Then Mary Beth says, "I've only known Anna for two years. I used to be at *Vogue*, but *Sight* is much more fun. It takes more risks."

Payne feels a hand drop on his shoulder and Morrow slips into the empty seat by Cindy. He looks at her. He smiles affectionately, but she just frowns and turns away.

"Want your salmon?" Jan says.

Payne shakes his head. "No, thanks. Go ahead though, if you want it." He passes her his plate.

"You've hardly eaten anything for days. What's wrong with you?"

"Must be the flu or something. My stomach," he replies. He tries to sound sincere. He shrugs. "One of those twenty-four hour things."

"Now take, for instance," says Mary Beth, "the article I'm working on this week."

"What's it about?" Avery reaches for his wine glass.

"Pollution and the ecomovement."

"Oh, God," says Morrow. His eyes roll in his head.

"Shut up, Glen," Avery says. "Go on. I'm fascinated."

"Well, I don't know, but have you noticed what's been going on the last few years?"

"What do you mean?"

"I mean with the environment." She waves her long thin fingers in the air. "The shrinking of the world. The way all things affect the rest. Connected. Like global warming and the ozone layer."

"Oh, please." Morrow sighs. "I've yet to see the slightest evidence, real evidence, that the so-called hole in the ozone layer is anything but natural."

"Let her finish, Glen," says Cindy.

"The world is upside down. Rain used to bring life," persists Mary Beth, "but now it's full of acid. The sea was once a symbol of boundless plenty; now it's choked with hospital waste and pesticides. Even sex, which used to mean love and procreation, now—in this age of AIDS—means death, pain, suffering. And what are we doing about it? Nothing. We just sit back and watch. We never get close. We never connect. We're guilty by neglect, voyeurs. We're murderers by extension."

Payne glances up at Morrow, who smiles tightly, turns away. Litchfield reaches for his drink.

Avery is the first to speak. "You're married, aren't you? I thought you had a husband somewhere. A doctor, right, Mary Beth?"

"Divorced," she says with a coy smile.

"Right. Right."

An olive-skinned waiter with a pencil-thin mustache approaches with a tray.

"Beef tournedos?" he says. He smiles and tips the tray and Payne can see the red medallions. They are splayed out like a fan of meat. "No, thank you," he replies.

Jan sighs beside him. "Yes, please," she says, and then, "You have to eat, John. Something."

"Maybe some potatoes."

"Is that all?" She cuts a piece of tournedos. "How about a bite? Just one?" She lifts the piece of meat up to his face.

Payne recoils. "No, thanks."

"Just like Robert," says Elizabeth. "He was hung over all day yesterday from that dumb bachelor party. What did you guys do, anyway?"

Morrow looks at Litchfield. Then he looks at Payne. "Boy stuff, you know," he says. "We had dinner at the Quonset Hut. We had a few drinks."

"A few!" says Cindy.

"You weren't complaining the other night," says Morrow.

"It was just a bachelor party. That's all," Litchfield says. He fixes the arms of his glasses behind his ears. "We had dinner at the Quonset Hut. We had a few drinks."

"That's right," says Payne. He looks around the table. Rick Avery is staring at him curiously.

"What did you girls do for Anna?" Morrow asks.

"Nothing," Jan says.

"I thought you had a bachelorette party for her last weekend."

"Oh, that. That was nothing," says Elizabeth. "We just went out for Thai food."

"Sure," says Morrow.

"What does that mean?" Cindy says.

"Nothing."

Payne pokes at the roasted new potatoes on his plate. He tries to block out all the sounds around him. The words. The sound of silverware. The swallowing of flesh.

"So, Jan," says Morrow. "I hear that IBM is going to launch a new line of PC's for the home market."

Jan puts her fork down on her plate. "Who told you that?"

"I have my spies."

Jan looks at Payne beside her. "Well, it's news to me," she says.

Payne shakes his head. "I didn't say a thing."

"Thanks, John," says Morrow.

"For what?"

Morrow winks at Jan and takes another bite.

"You're a real jerk," says Payne.

"Now, now," says Avery. "This is meant to be a celebration."

"I hate it when you do that," Jan says.

"Do what?" says Morrow.

"Put business over your friends."

"I don't know what you mean."

"Yes, you do. You always do. That's why I hate it."

"Come on, you guys," says Avery. He pushes his plate away. "Here comes Tom."

Demarest slouches over to their table. He is carrying a wine glass in his left hand. He grins at them and says, "How we all doing over here?"

"Fine. The food is great," says Avery. "Just great."

Everyone nods in agreement. "Top drawer," says Litchfield.

"It wasn't my idea. Thank Anna. I hate this dump."

"It's not a dump. I love the Palm Court," Cindy says.

"Yeah, well . . ." Demarest looks across the room. He blinks his eyes. "I guess the wine list isn't bad," he offers up reluctantly.

"Speaking from experience," says Elizabeth. "How's Anna holding up?"

"Fine, I guess. Haven't talked to her all night. Between you and me," he says, leaning forward, leaning, touching the table with his fingertips, "I don't think this has got much to do with Anna and me."

Demarest is so close that Payne can smell the liquor on his breath.

"It's really for the 'rents," says Demarest. "We don't have anything to do with it. We're just . . . icons. Ciphers. Symbols. We're the variables. The rest is a set piece."

"Aren't you excited?" asks Elizabeth.

"I'm terrified," says Demarest, and laughs. It is as if his slack mouth can't contain the sound.

"You'll be all right," says Payne.

Demarest turns and looks at Payne. His eyebrows knit together. The smile fades from his lips. "What did you say?"

"I said you'll be all right."

"Why shouldn't I be?"

Payne looks surprised. "No reason."

"What do you mean by that?"

"Nothing. I didn't mean a thing."

"Yes, you did." He leans closer to Payne. "I know you did."

"Take it easy, Tom," says Morrow.

"Don't tell me what to do. It's my wedding."

"He didn't mean anything, Tom," says Avery. He smiles, and Payne can feel the room relax.

"Why don't you join us for a bit?" says Jan. "Leave the old folks. Pull up a chair."

"Can't stay," says Demarest. He pushes himself back from the table. "Being a bad son. Hope you liked the food. It cost Dad a fortune." He laughs again. "And we haven't even had the crème brûlée." He turns and walks back toward his table.

"Boy, he's polluted," says Elizabeth. "Must be the wedding jitters. Robert was like that too."

"I was?" says Litchfield. "I don't remember that."

"Of course you don't," she answers, patting his hand. "You've blocked it completely from your mind."

"Excuse me," Payne says, pushing back his chair.

"Where are you going?" Jan grabs him by the sleeve. "Aren't you having coffee? Don't pay any attention to Tom, John. He isn't himself."

Payne nods. "I know. It isn't Tom. I just don't feel good."

"If this keeps up—promise me—you'll go and see Doctor Simpson." She takes him by the hand. "Promise."

"I'll be all right. Why don't we just go home?" He pushes himself to his feet.

"Now? We can't leave yet. I promised to help Anna with the arrangements. It won't take long."

Payne stands there looking at the table. They are all staring at him, but he has forgotten what Jan said, just now, a moment ago. He tries to remember. What were they talking about? What am I doing here?

"Let's get a nightcap," Avery says. He rises to his feet. "Come on, John. Let's check out Trader Vic's."

"I'll join you," Morrow says.

"No!" Payne takes a step back from the table. "I'll be okay," he says. "Really. Keep Cindy company."

Morrow drops back in his chair.

"We'll see you later." Avery looks at Jan and smiles. "Don't worry."

He takes Payne by the elbow. They move across the Palm Court carefully, weaving in between the tables. Avery waves at Demarest as they pass by, but he doesn't respond. He simply stares at them with glassy bovine eyes, then turns away.

"What's going on?" Avery demands, as they move into the hall.

"What do you mean?"

"Between you and Tom."

Payne glances at the twenty-thousand-dollar watch in the window in the wall. It is glistening with diamonds, like tears, like dewdrops in a spider web, like the Brooklyn Bridge at a thousand feet. "Nothing," he says. "Nothing at all."

"Don't bullshit me, John."

They turn the corner by the Oak Room and descend the dark red stairs toward Trader Vic's. There is a long outrigger canoe at the foot of the stairs. It is covered with dead palm fronds. There is a paddle in the bow, and Payne wonders for a moment how an open craft as small as this could sail across the South Pacific, across miles of tractless water, from Micronesia to Hawaii, with only the stars to guide her.

"Are you listening to me? John?"

"Yeah, I'm listening."

They move into the bar. It's dark and intimate. A few small tables line the walls. The place is almost empty. Only a few couples whisper to each other over frozen daiquiris and mai tais served in pineapples. A solitary Asian bartender stands behind the bamboo bar, shaking a tumbler with precision. Avery slides against a rattan stool. "What do you want to drink?"

"What are you having?"

"Rum swizzle."

"Okay," says Payne. He sits down at the bar. "If you're having one."

The bartender smiles and sets to work.

"So, what's going on, John?"

"What do you mean?"

"Don't give me that shit. Who do you think you're talking to?"

"It's nothing. Really."

Avery settles on his stool and looks at Payne. "Yeah, right," he says, sarcastically.

"Just forget it. Okay, Rick? It's got nothing to do with you."

"If you say so."

The bartender parks the drinks before them on the bar, and Avery hands him a twenty-dollar bill.

"Look, I'm sorry, Rick. It's just . . ." Payne hesitates. "Let me ask you something," he continues.

"What?"

"Do you remember that time near Amherst, back at Hadley, on the road out to U Mass?"

"There were a lot of times at Hadley," Avery says.

"You know, our senior year. When we followed that woman in the white Toyota. Remember? We thought we saw gas or something leaking out the back, and we followed her through those back roads for miles and miles, honking our horn at her, remember?"

"Yeah. Yeah, I remember." Avery laughs nervously. "She thought we were nuts."

"She wouldn't stop. She kept on driving and we kept on getting closer and closer, yelling at her out the windows."

"I thought she did stop."

"Eventually."

"That was fifteen years ago. What made you think of her?"

"I never asked you before, but was there a moment when you

knew, when it was obvious that she couldn't understand what we were doing?"

"What do you mean?" says Avery.

"I mean, she didn't know about the leak. She couldn't see it. Was there a time then, when it was suddenly clear that she was simply scared?"

"We told her about the gas."

"It was just water leaking out her bumper, Rick."

"We didn't know that—not when we were chasing her. We thought it was gas or something."

"When?"

"What do you mean, when?"

"When did you know? I mean, when did you first realize that it wasn't gas or anything dangerous?"

Avery shrugs and sips his drink. "I don't know. That was a long time ago, man. I don't remember."

"Well, I do. I remember exactly. One minute we were chasing her to warn her, to let her know about the leak. Morrow was driving, remember? We were right on her tail. And the next we were just chasing her. Just *chasing* her. She was terrified, and we knew it. She thought we were going to . . . I don't know. But that's why she kept on driving. And then she stopped, remember? She pulled up by those cattails on the side of the road and she got out and came at us, and she was crying, 'Leave me alone. Leave me alone.' Remember? And Bobby said, 'You've got a leak, miss,' but we all knew that it wasn't true. We all *knew*, Rick."

"What's your point, man? That was fifteen years ago. So she got upset. Big deal. Nothing happened. She just got into her car and drove away."

Payne looks at Avery. There is a cold gleam in his eye. "I still remember, Rick. Like it was yesterday."

"What's going on, John?" Avery asks. "Talk to me, man. Did something happen the other night?"

"What do you mean? Why do you say that?"

"Because of what Bobby said."

"What did Bobby tell you?"

" 'We had dinner at the Quonset Hut. We had a few drinks.' "

"Well, we did, didn't we?"

"Come on, man. Those were the same words Glen used. The exact same words."

Payne shakes his head.

"John, talk to me. I'm your friend."

"I know you are." He looks at Avery's thin dark face and says, "Don't you think I know that? Jesus Christ. Don't you think I want to talk to you? You're my only friend these days." Payne takes a long sip from his drink. He can taste nutmeg clinging to the rum. He can taste lime. "You were right, Rick, what you said the other night. It is all changing. It's all falling apart."

"Come on, John . . ."

"Sometimes I wonder what it means. It's funny, but I've never really felt like I belong. And not just to The Club. To anything. Maybe that's why it was always so important to me."

"Jesus Christ, John. What's gotten into you?"

"Why did you join, Rick?"

"What?"

"The Club."

"I don't know, John. I didn't really join. I just hung out. I liked you guys, I guess. You were crazy. And I always liked you, even back at St. Mark's. You know that."

"It was Morrow, wasn't it?"

"Maybe. I don't know, John. In part, I guess." Avery sighs. "Look, Glen was a star. Class president. Big man on campus. Quarterback. I guess I felt a little flattered when he asked me to join. Didn't you? And then there were the girls, of course. Let's not forget the girls." He laughs and tips his drink toward Payne.

"No, it was Morrow, Rick. Morrow and all he represents. We all wanted to be part of him, to get a piece. You and Tom, and Bobby too. We all wanted to *be* Glen Morrow. Everything comes so easy to Glen. Everybody loves him. He has that incredible ability to make whoever he's talking to feel like they're the most important person on earth." He gulps his drink. Then he smiles and says, "Did I ever tell you about my job, Rick?"

"What about it?"

"No, of course I didn't. I never even told Jan. Why am I pretending?"

"What about your job?"

"Do you remember after college when I was wandering around trying to figure out what to do with my life? First Dad's bank. Then that DJ gig in Scranton. Then that sales job for New Jersey Cable."

"Yeah, I remember. You and me both, pal. I've always felt that the real benefit of a liberal arts education is that you're expertly trained to do nothing."

"After I came back up to New York," insists Payne, "I stayed with Glen for a few months at his brownstone. This was when he was married to Yvette. He'd graduated from Yale and was working for ZBJ, and he'd just bought that incredible projection TV system so he could research the entertainment industry. We'd stay up all night watching old movies, talking and talking, drinking beer, and he knew how crazy I was about flying, and how Aggie used to send me money just so I could keep my license current. Anyway, one day I'm flying out of Teterboro, and I meet this guy named Jack Murphy who happens to work for High-Way Traffic. And he tells me that they're looking for new pilots for the network, and would I like to try out. 'Where do I sign?' I tell him. Two weeks later I've got the job of my dreams."

"That's the story?"

"No!" says Payne. "That's just it. Not the whole story, anyway. For years I thought it was just a coincidence. You know. You hang around pilots, you hear about flying jobs. But at the Christmas party this year, this pilot I work with named Cracker gets a little tight and we end up arguing about something really stupid, and he tells me, 'You only got this job because your friend pulled some long strings.' "

"What do you mean—Glen?"

"He apparently did some kind of financing favor for the chairman of Metrox Corporation. They own High-Way Traffic. And as part of the deal he had the chairman call up the president of High-Way Traffic to make an opening for me in the New York office."

"That's so typical. And he never told you, right?"

"Never. Not a peep."

"That's just what he did with me and Mary Decker."

"Who?"

"At Hadley. You remember Mary. She was the one who always wore that gold heart with the diamond in it, dangling over her sweater fronts."

"You've got strange taste, Rick."

"Yeah, you noticed, huh? Now they have to have tattoos."

Payne laughs and sips his drink. "What about Mary?"

"I had the hots for her. I mean real bad. I couldn't stop thinking about her. I'd be doing the strangest things, like working on a paper, or doing laps, and I'd see her lying there, naked, at the bottom of the pool. Weird. But she wouldn't take me seriously. She was crazy about Glen. He'd once taken her to some stupid ice hockey match or something and it must have been the high point of her life because she never stopped talking about it. I would have given my left nut for a night with her, and he was throwing her away."

"If you had a left nut. Anyway, I thought you did go out with Mary Decker for a while."

"I did. That's what I mean. I'd just about given up when she finally started noticing me. At first I thought it was my magnetic personality, my charm, my poise—"

"Yeah, right!"

"It was Glen. He told her he'd take her to the Snow Ball if she went out with me. And she did. And we even slept together, and it was great, for about two weeks. Man! Didn't everything seem compressed back then, kind of jammed together?"

"We lived in smaller rooms."

"I guess so." He smiles ruefully. "Anyway, it didn't last. She turned out to be a big fat bore. And the irony is that Glen actually took her to the Snow Ball, and they both said they had a great time. Go figure."

"What is it about Morrow and his favors?"

"That's how he gets you in his clutches."

"No, seriously."

"He's helped everybody in the Club at one time or another. You remember how he worked so hard to keep Tom on the football team. And getting Bobby in the frat. And Mary Decker. And what he did at Sitter's Point. Too much of a favor, that one. Like those

Indian tribes in the northwest, where the chiefs are always giving gifts. The more extravagant the gift, the more important you become. Potlatch. That's what it's called. That's his thing. Glen has to give."

"But why?"

"Because that's what makes him tick. Do you remember when Bobby tried to pledge T.U., and no one wanted him?"

"What about it?"

"Glen used his influence and persuaded everyone to let him in, and Litchfield was so grateful he wouldn't stop thanking him. Day and night, for weeks, until Glen finally got fed up, and he turned to Bobby one day in class—I remember—and with this cold expression said, 'I didn't do it for you, BB. So stop thanking me. Okay? I didn't do it for you.' And he was serious." Avery takes another sip. "See what I mean? Potlatch. It's time to grow up and leave the nest, man. It's time to move on, or you're always going to be in Morrow's shadow. Look at Bobby. He'll never stop being the fat kid, running hard to keep up."

"Excellent toady, though. Makes a great martini."

"Excellent. And Tom . . . Well, the best thing I can say about Tom is that he's getting married. I love that guy, but let's face it, he'd probably bankrupt Saudi Arabia if he were finance minister. Not exactly Hadley's brightest star. How do you think he got his job?"

"Glen?"

"Actually it was Litchfield, but only because Glen told him to."

Payne laughs flatly. He shakes his head. "Poor Bobby. It must be so hard being The Club clown. The fool. Do you think people are born that way? The butt of everybody's jokes. I guess that's why Glen let him in. He needed somebody to laugh at. I always wondered about that. Glen and Bobby. They seemed like such unlikely friends at Hadley, except for the fact that they had gone to Choke together. Even so."

"I heard a rumor once," says Avery, and looks down at his drink. He starts to fiddle with his swizzle stick. "Tom told me. A long, long time ago."

"What?"

"It's probably bullshit. I mean, I know it is. It's one of those stories people start just to be mean, you know? Just to kick dirt up because they're jealous."

"What are you talking about?"

"About Glen and Bobby at Choke. They say that they were pretty close. Real close, you know? Choke was an all-boys school then. You remember the King kid at St. Mark's? You always hear those kinds of rumors."

"What are you saying? Glen and Bobby? You're kidding, right?"

"That's what Tom told me. But you know it isn't true. I mean, look at them. Look at Cindy, for Christ's sake. She's a knockout." He swirls his drink. He glances at Payne, then turns away. "One thing I do know for a fact, though. I heard this from both Tom and Steven Bennett at T.U. He went to Choke as well."

"What?"

"I don't know all of the details." Avery shakes his head. "But I heard that Glen got into trouble a lot for breaking out of school his senior year. He had some babe in town—you know Glen—and he was sneaking out after curfew to see her every Thursday night. They'd already caught him twice before, but he just kept on doing it. Anyway, the dean of students finally got fed up and set a trap for him. He'd been trying to expel Glen the whole year, but the head-master wouldn't hear of it. Glen was captain of the football team. He was untouchable. So the dean devised this trap, but somehow or other word got out about it, and when the lights came on, it wasn't Glen they found with one leg sticking out the pantry win-dow. It was Bobby. The dean was furious. He felt that Glen had set him up, had made a fool of him in front of the whole school. And he had, I guess. Poor Bobby. He really took the rap for Glen. They gave him twenty licks with a birch cane." He sips his drink. "Ah, yes," he says, "the days of corporal punishment. When men were men."

Payne shakes his head. He swigs his drink. The story had the ring of truth to it. It was just like Morrow to create a lifelong friend-ship to reward a single act of bravery. Morrow hated owing favors.

Give him a gift and he gave you five, just not to be outdone. Pot-latch.

Avery starts laughing. "What is it?" Payne says. "What's so funny?"

"Some sacrifice! I bet you Bobby loved it. For some people, the only pleasure in life is when they finally get to throw themselves on a hand grenade to save someone. But they can't do it to save themselves; they're not worth it. They have to do it for a guy like Glen."

Payne looks at Avery, a sad smile tugging at his lips. "Thanks, Rick."

"For what?"

"For the drink," says Payne. "And for the company."

"We should do this more often. Just the two of us. Forget about what the other guys say."

"We should. I'd like that. Soon, I hope . . ." Payne cannot finish. He takes a final sip from his drink. He turns away. "Soon."

IX

The right foot, stop. The left foot, stop. The left foot, stop. They stumble up the aisle, trying to keep in time with the Schubert. The pews are packed with glowing faces, heads turned and leering at the groom. The sexes split apart: the women, dressed in rich silk evening gowns of the deepest emerald green, to the left; the men, in tails, to the right. And Tom, poor Tom, a solitary in between, his head down and his feet apart, watching the far end of the aisle like a child standing on the seashore, bracing for a wave. The organ music swells. The trumpets sound. The crowd stirs in a flash of light as the camera crew reveals itself, and there—at last—is the bride. Dick holds her by the arm. They move into the nave, and Payne is taken by the music, lifted by the great sigh of the crowd, the impossible whiteness of the dress which seems to carry Anna down the aisle. He feels a hot familiar breath against his face. It is Jan. She smiles and he smiles back, and in the space of understanding what a smile is Payne is standing in a world four years less jaded, with Jan beside him once again, the wedding band still sliding up her finger, fitting just so.

The ceremony gradually unrolls. He finds his eyes ascending, past the altar to the gradine topped with roses, past the amber marble of the lower apse, the great cream marble cross, and to the half-dome far above, sprinkled with colored glass and gold. The mosaic settles in his eyes, Christ with His arms outstretched, the moment of Transfiguration, surrounded on both sides by Moses and Elijah, astride a mountaintop, and out of the bare ground beneath His feet flow streams of bright blue glass, that boil and froth and bubble up, that snake back on themselves, that spill incessantly.

There is the kiss, the trumpet fanfare, and Tom and Anna Demarest release each other for the first time. They sail along the aisle. Illicit flashbulbs pop, film whirs in the obligatory winding-up of memories. The great crowd seethes forward, hungry to catch a close-up of the bride; that smile, so freshly minted. The wedding party follows. Payne can feel Jan's hand in his. Her fingers scratch playfully at his palm. She smiles at him again, a smile so burdened down with love that he feels empty in response, as if to open a great clearing for her in his heart. The organ music swells. He pulls her close to him, so close that he can almost feel the warm familiar plains and contours of her shape without even touching her. The baby turns inside her. He looks up at the great rose window in the southern transept, red seraphim, blue cherubim, Saint Michael with his cross and globe. The stained glass seems to throb with light as they walk by, a fire wheel, and Jan withdraws her hand. He turns and looks at her again, caught in the crimson light descending from the rose, the cobalt blue, one hand across her pregnant stomach. He has never seen her look more captivating, more balanced, more serene.

The trumpets sound a final strain. The carved bronze portals open. The half-light of the January dusk unravels through the entrance and Anna dashes down the steps, with Tom immediately behind her. The Demarests skip across the sidewalk. They disappear into the open door of the longest of the eight black limousines parked trimly by the curb. The wedding party follows down the steps. Each couple has a car at their disposal, and Jan and John slide swiftly into theirs. In a moment they are gliding into traffic up Park Avenue.

"My feet are killing me." Jan kicks her shoes off with disgust. "God, what a nightmare! And did you see that kiss? She practically had to force him. I can't believe it. To screw her name up! Her name! I swear he's drunk."

"I didn't think it went so badly. And he's not drunk. He's just nervous. He only had one tiny little drink to help him loosen up."

"I knew it. And you guys encouraged him, I bet."

"Jan, let's not fight. Let's just get through this, okay?"

She purses her lips. She looks at him out of the corner of her eye.

"Okay?" he repeats, tilting his head.

"Okay. Okay," she answers wearily. "I don't want to fight either. It's just that he makes me so mad. Anna's been looking forward to this for—gee, let me see now—her whole life. I mean, come on!"

The limousine has climbed the last few blocks with the steady movement of a blue-chip bond. They make the turn at Sixty-fifth, and swing back east again. "I'm sure Tom's doing the best he can," says Payne. "Under the circumstances."

"Under the circumstances! They've been planning this wedding for months. How much time does it take? Either you're ready to get married, or you're not. What's he worried about, anyway? He won't lose his precious Hunting Club, if that's what he's afraid of. That comes with a lifetime membership. He can even have a baby. Look at Bobby."

The marquee of the Mayfair Hotel floats into view through the glass. They have arrived. The limousine coasts to a stop. Payne helps Jan out of the car and they make their way through the glass-and-brass revolving door into the lobby of the hotel.

Tom and Anna Demarest are standing by the front desk. In the close confines of the lobby, offset by the mirrors and the painted paneled ceiling, the bride looks even more radiant. She is the center of attention. The events coordinator from the hotel has found his way beside her. Glen and Cindy hover just behind. There is Dick Leuthold and Pat Demarest, and a pair of German businessmen observing from afar. And then she's gone. The events coordinator, a thin man with a pale mustache, has whisked her off to the Park Avenue Room at the far end of the lobby. A bar has been prepared, the rumor circulates. A bar, a bar. The word swims idly through the crowd, from lip to ear. Coats are discarded into strangers' arms. The guests coast up the stairs, along the corridor and to the back, to the Park Avenue—no, not the Mayfair Room—on the other side.

. . .

The room extends past three tall windows looking out onto Park Avenue. A bar has been set up at the far end, manned by a bartender in a bright gold jacket, and already some of the guests are lining up for service. A waitress shuffles by. Her tray is bubbling with champagne. Payne snatches up two glasses without thinking, until he sees Jan frowning at him, and remembers she is pregnant. "Soda?" he asks the waitress.

"At the bar," she answers with exaggerated slowness, as if he is a foreigner.

There is a pile of presents on a low round table near the wall. Never in his life has Payne seen such elaborate wrapping. The paper alone must have cost a small fortune. There are bows of every color and design, blue silk the shape of peonies, red roses, burnt orange origami tags.

"It was beautiful," says Liz Litchfield at his side. Her arm is wrapped around Jan's wrist. "The whole thing. Magical. That's what it was. And the music. Don't you think?"

"I think it went pretty well. I liked the French horns."

"Pretty well! Listen to him. Five- to ten-minute delays in the back pews. Honestly! Anna looked fabulous, absolutely fabulous. I've never seen a more radiant bride. With the exception of you, Jan, of course," she adds with a laugh.

"You're right," says Jan. "She does look wonderful. It's a fabulous dress."

"Fabulous."

"I helped her pick it out."

"I thought I heard you did."

"I guess there are always a few glitches at every wedding. Remember the florist, John? What a scene that was. And somehow we survived."

Payne looks at Jan with a smile. Already it is undergoing its rewriting—the past, the last scene, with the curtain still descending. Now, suddenly, the Demarests' wedding is a great success. It's all in the perspective, in the head. Like a great switch. You only have to find the switch, and it will go away. All of it.

The guests have all arrived, and all who want to drink are drinking. Then the events coordinator with the pale mustache announces dinner, and there is a general swelling toward the door.

Empty champagne glasses, soiled napkins, and half-eaten canapés on plates are strewn about the room. Someone is laughing wildly, a woman with a purple dress, with a big black bow in her hair. Peter Demarest is holding her by the arm. Payne starts to follow Jan and Elizabeth, when Morrow suddenly appears.

"A word, please, John. Alone."

Jan frowns and says, "We'll meet you in the dining room. Don't be long, honey." With that she's swallowed by the crowd.

"What is it now?" says Payne.

"I wanted to talk to you. To all of you, before Tom leaves."

They stand off to the side, watching the chamber empty out. Eventually only Demarest and Litchfield remain. A busboy enters with a tray, but Morrow intercepts him in the open doorway, and ushers him away. As Morrow draws the busboy out into the hall, Demarest and Bobby Litchfield sidle up to Payne.

"Great wedding, Tom," says Payne, immediately regretting his remark. Of course it had been great. How flip of him to say so.

"Yeah, right." Demarest slips his hands into his trouser pockets. He rolls his oxlike eyes. He looks away.

"I mean it. Anna looks beautiful, man. The music was great. Everything worked out fine."

"Are you making fun of me?"

"What are you talking about? Jesus Christ, Tom."

"You're making fun of me."

"It was a compliment," says Litchfield. "Take it easy, Tom."

"No, it wasn't. It's because I messed her name up, right? You couldn't let it go, could you? You just couldn't resist."

"You don't know what you're talking about," snaps Payne. "You can take it any way you want, Tom. Frankly, I don't give a damn. I know how I meant it." He pokes a finger into Demarest's chest. "And if you've got something to say to me, I wish you'd just come out and say it."

"All right," says Demarest. "I'll say it. You better keep your mouth shut, John. You better be quiet, or so help me . . ."

"So help you what, Tom?"

"This is our secret. And you know what a tough time you have with secrets."

"What does that mean?"

"You know what it means."

And he does. Payne pushes Demarest away. Even after all these years, they haul the memory behind them. It was sophomore year, and Payne and Avery were celebrating a stellar swim meet against Brown, and Payne had broken the fifty-meter freestyle record set back in '62. They were partying at Boltwood House in Tony Boswell's room, and smoking bongs and drinking a nameless thundering punch. And somehow or other the subject came up about frats, and Avery had laughed at Payne for joining T.U., and said that frats were square, and chauvinistic too, and that he'd never join one. And Payne had agreed, claiming he didn't really care about frats, only his friends, only the living accommodations, and they had smoked another bong and Avery had said, "Like, what is that weird thing you do with your hands?"

"The T.U. handshake. It identifies you as a brother."

"Well, it's the queerest thing I've ever seen. Let's see it up close."

"You're not a brother."

"Come on," Avery kept whining. "I've known you since you were thirteen. You said you didn't give a shit about frats. And I won't tell."

And Payne had finally shown him. And they had laughed about it for the next two days, and made a lot of fun, except that Avery was indiscreet, and someone overheard, an offhand word, a joke, and they had told somebody else, and so on down the line. Until one night, at two A.M.—it was a Wednesday—when they came and wrestled Payne out of his bed, and propped him up in his pajamas before the assembled frat, and in the candlelight accused him of betrayal. That's what Tom Demarest was saying. That's what he meant now eighteen years after the fact. "Yeah, I know what it means," says Payne. "I fucking know."

And if it hadn't been for Morrow, they would have thrown him out. All for that stupid handshake. Depledged him, or whatever. Another unrequested favor. And the solution so typically Morrow. Instead of kicking Payne out for revealing T.U. secrets, Glen had persuaded Rick to join the frat, thereby unhinging the betrayal.

Demarest grabs Payne by the wrist. "You better keep your mouth shut, John," he says. His face is flushed with anger. Beads of sweat gleam on his brow. "I swear. You're the one who did it. You fucking killed her, John. The blood is on your hands." They both look down at Payne's white fingers as if they can still see it on his flesh. Payne struggles to get free. They wrestle for a moment longer, and Payne leans forward suddenly, and Demarest slips back, he takes a step, then two, and trips against a low round table by the wall. He stumbles trying to rise, and reaches for support, but there is nothing but the pile of presents on the table. They slip under his hand, they spin out of control and tumble with a great noise to the floor.

Payne reaches out to help him up, but Demarest slaps his hand aside. Then he rises awkwardly to his feet. Scattering the gleaming packages, he steps, in one uninterrupted movement, drawing his fist up in an uppercut that catches Payne completely by surprise.

Payne's head flies back. There is a brittle crack, and he falls backwards, trying to balance on his feet, just trying to clear his head.

Morrow grabs Demarest from behind, clenching him in his powerful arms. "That's enough," he says.

"Let go of me. Get off," cries Demarest, but there is nothing he can do in Morrow's grasp.

Payne opens his mouth and tries to move his jaw. A stabbing pain cuts through him. "Jesus Christ, Tommy." He palms his jaw. "You can still hit, though."

"You idiot," Litchfield says. He gathers himself to his full height, leaning close to Demarest. "What are you trying to do? Who needs the cops when we've got you two?"

"Fuck you, BB," Demarest spits. "You're just as bad as he is."

"What did you call me?"

"You heard me, Baby Balls."

"I told you not to call me that."

"Go fuck yourself."

For a moment the words seem to hang in the air. They watch as Litchfield's body starts to turn, the unfamiliar spiraling of the hips, the hand first opening, then winding back, the slow imponderable movement forward. The palm strikes Demarest across the open cheek. There is a loud slap, eons after the act, and Demarest falls back in Morrow's arms.

Payne starts to laugh. The sight of Litchfield striking Demarest, the way the arm moves in a kind of feeble arc, the open palm, is so preposterous that he cannot help himself. The sheer improbability of Litchfield striking anyone . . . He laughs again, ignoring the pain in his jaw. He looks at Morrow holding Demarest. Morrow is now laughing too. He is staring at Litchfield, staring at Payne. Demarest laughs hoarsely, and Morrow releases him and steps away.

"All right, you guys," says Morrow. "I want you to shake hands. Go on. It's over, don't you get it? That's what I've been trying to tell you." He pushes Demarest forward. "Go on, both of you," he says. His voice is tempered with such natural authority that they find themselves moving together. "Everything's going to be okay. I told you it would be, didn't I? While you guys have been freaking out, I've been doing some research. There were no reported homicides from the Church Street precinct last Wednesday night, or any other night since then. No missing persons. No rapes or major larceny. No fraud," he says and smiles. "Nothing to link us to the scene of the crime, because as far as they're concerned, there hasn't been a crime." He pauses for effect. "Most murders are solved within the first seventy-two hours. If they're not, the chances of the murderer being found fall practically to zero. To zero. I bet you didn't know that. But I've done the research. I know the numbers." He turns toward Demarest. "It's over, Tom. It's finished, and look at you. My God! After everything that's happened. Doesn't that girl Yolanda mean anything to you? Doesn't she? Listen to me. If her death is to have any kind of meaning, it's to help us appreciate what we almost lost. All of us. You, Bobby—Elizabeth and Sally. You, John—in three months you're going to be a father. And you, Tom. You, most of all. It's over. Over! You can go on your honeymoon without worrying about it. You can breathe now," he says to Payne. "We can all breathe." He pauses. His smile sets in his face. "Unless one of us makes a mistake." He looks at each of them in turn. "Unless one of us gets cold feet and decides to try to save his own neck at the expense of the others."

He steps up with his arms extended, his hands cupped like a

beggar. "Let's make a promise to each other, an oath, just like at Sitter's Point, that no matter what happens, no matter what, we're going to stick together, okay?"

Litchfield takes Morrow by the hand.

"We're all in this together," Morrow adds. "We've got to do whatever it takes to protect The Hunting Club. Promise. And no one will be blamed for anything." He looks at Demarest with his bright blue eyes, but Demarest stands firm. Then he smiles, and Morrow takes his hand. They look at Payne in turn. He feels them staring at him.

"I'm sorry, John," says Demarest.

Payne nods. He reaches out, he wraps his hand around Glen Morrow's fingers, around Tom Demarest's and Litchfield's too. He feels the digits wriggling in his palm, writhing, until he cannot tell where one ends and the next begins.

"I guess I lost my head a little." Demarest glances up at Payne. "It's just that I love Anna so much. I don't know. I want to be worthy of her."

"All right, you guys," says Morrow. He pulls his hands away. "I don't know about you, but I'm starved. And Anna's waiting." He smiles his smile at Demarest. "Obviously, a man who's never been married. A neophyte. A virgin, practically. Lesson number one, Tom. Never ignore a young wife. She doesn't stay that way very long."

Demarest shakes his head and laughs. They stand together by the door. Payne stretches his jaw, and even that feels better now. He looks up at his friends. How could he have been so wrong? They were all willing to put themselves at risk for him, for him! After what he'd done. After everything . . .

They descend the stairs into the hotel lobby. It is busy and bright, full of bellhops and hotel guests, people checking in with suitcases, people with plans. The air seems suddenly charged. Perhaps it is the champagne, or the shot in the chin. The crowd undulates as they pass by, parting to give them room, turning to look at the four young men dressed in tails with creamy orchids pinned to their lapels. They turn the corner and the doors to the L'Orangerie swing open.

A small ensemble in the corner plays Cole Porter's "I've Got You Under My Skin," and Payne can feel the music buoy him as he passes through the door. The noise of conversation throbs about him. They stride into the room, air-light, and Anna smiles and waves at Demarest and he splits off and rushes up to kiss her. Payne searches for his table. A waiter almost bumps right into him. He turns and turns but he can't see Jan in the crowd. The walls of the room are covered with stenciled paneling and mirrors, and the tables seem to multiply before him. There's Morrow kissing Cindy. There's Avery and Mary Beth. There's Bobby and Elizabeth. There's Demarest and Anna, at the center of this bright and shiny world, unburdened by the secret of Yolanda's death. Payne spins and turns and there she is, his Jan, beyond the swan ice sculpture, waving at him with her tiny hand, waving just at him. He can hear her wrist joint swivel with the slightest click, like the flipping of a switch. He takes a step and it occurs to him that after all this time, after everything that's happened, he's suddenly very hungry.

X

The black stretch limousine ascends I-95, rooting up the miles with an understated growl. The highway winds and eddies, climbs and descends past Larchmont and White Plains, where the limousine cuts over to 287 West. It is two o'clock in the morning. There is little traffic on the road, only a truck or two, crawling their way across America.

Inside the limousine, Payne leans back in his padded seat, watching Jan's silhouette against the night. She is staring out the window as the slumbering, half-lit towns of Westchester slide by. Her hair has fallen. A wisp hangs down along her cheek. He can just make out the ruby earring in her ear. He can see her chest rise slowly as she breathes, rise and descend, as the blood pumps through her heart, as the engine throbs beneath them.

She looks just as she did some fourteen years before, when he had come upon her quite by accident, lost on his way from the bathroom in Betsy Bradhurst's house. She was sitting in a stuffed gingham chair with both her legs drawn up beneath her, wearing a white cotton tennis dress and a red pullover, reading a book. It was a perfect Fire Island twilight, with a sultry breeze blowing up the beach through Point o' Woods, and a hint of starlight cutting through the sky. And he had introduced himself, a friend of the Averys visiting, old school chums, and she had put the book down and scrutinized him with the kind of languorous gaze that—in a few years, he would learn—she normally reserved for paintings.

That weekend, as Avery and The Club tried in succession to cajole and sweet-talk every girl in Point o' Woods, Payne found himself alone with Jan, bike riding to the general store, meeting behind the tennis courts, at the Club House, at parties and then walking on the beach, walking and walking and talking about nothing in particular, listening to the pounding of the waves. She had seen him at Point o' Woods before, she confessed. He was a friend of the Averys and Morrows. Yes, she knew Glen. She had gone out with Glen once, long ago, but only once, and never again. There was something about Morrow. . . . And the first time Payne had kissed her, Jan's passion overwhelmed him, riding her thighs up on his leg as they embraced, giddy from the whirling stars. He had told her everything without reserve, for she had never seemed to judge him. She was so damned practical. Even things that he had found impossible to talk about with Glen or Rick, he found himself revealing to Jan.

He had spent the summer after graduation at his father's bank, crawling through an internship that he had promised two years earlier he would try. But he knew that he would never be a banker. The war was a grinding numbness on TV. Each evening Uncle Walter counted off the dead. Everything had changed. College was over. Everyone was going off to law school or to business school. Everyone was going to be a doctor . . . except John Payne. He didn't know what he wanted. Sam was dead. So he had finally acquiesced and gone to New York for the summer, riding the 6:07 every morning to the city, pretending to be an adult. He struggled with government reports on interest rates. He learned regression analysis. He played the well-bred unctuous intern so well that everyone began to look upon him as a double of his father. They expected him to hang around forever . . . while everything was changing. And on one dark and wind-swept night on Fire Island, he felt as if the sea itself was neither large nor deep enough to hide the horror that he felt whenever he imagined himself riding on that train to New York for the next thirty-five years. The waves, the waves were pounding on the beach as he and Jan walked toward the Pines along the dunes, and he had thrown her to the sand and in the moonlight they had made love. And after, he had told her about everything, about his fears, the internship, the gnawing dread he felt each morning as he climbed the marble steps which isolated the bank from the rest of the world. Jan sat there without speaking, with her dress up, her tousled hair, her blouse open at the throat. And with a sigh she seemed to snatch him from the undertow. "Well, obviously," she said. "You'll have to get another job." For months he had been looking on the bank internship as something of a prelude to a long, premeditated pattern in his life, something defined and preordained, as certain as the turning of the earth. And with a few words she had liberated him. He wasn't quitting the internship; he was getting another job. That's all. How easily, how smoothly she had drawn him down and into her again, alive and wondering, like a man in a new country who stares across a wild horizon, and in an instant has no past.

He had moved to Pennsylvania, and found a job as a replacement DJ at a tiny rock-and-roll radio station near Scranton. The people were fun and suitably irreverent. He lived in a run-down old farmhouse by a pond, and Jan drove down most weekends from New York. It was a great year, but the economy grew soft, inflation soared, and one day all the people he had come to trust as family revealed together, at the weekly meeting, that he was being fired— laid off, they said. There is a difference, really. Blame Nixon.

He had cast about for several months after that, living on savings, living on handouts from his mother, afraid his father would find out, when Rick Avery had told him about this cable company in Newark where his sister worked, at a time when few people even knew what cable was. And Payne had gone and interviewed, and they had offered him a real job for real money as a sales rep. And though Jan was against it, he took the job, and they were married a year later. They bought a condo out by Hopewell in New Jersey. Within six months they had found the cheapest gas station, the most comfortable cinema, and the friendliest supermarket in the county. They plumbed the fastest back roads to the train station. Jan snagged a job with a pharmaceutical company, working in marketing, while Payne continued to cultivate his territory. But even then he knew that it would never last. For some reason, try as he might to emulate his fellow reps, to laugh at their jokes, to dress like them, he simply couldn't get excited selling time slots to car dealers. Within a year he was fired. They lived on Jan's small salary. It wasn't much, but it was enough to keep them going until he heard about that job at High-Way Traffic. She kept him going. She always had.

He looks at Jan beside him on the seat of the limousine. From that first night on Fire Island, she had been there to set him right. How could he have nearly sacrificed everything he had for a few short minutes of madness? He was going to be a father. He had to start acting more responsibly. This had been a lesson, a terrible lesson to be sure, but a lesson nonetheless. It was like having a second chance. He owed it to Yolanda to try and rebuild his marriage and his life. He had to give her death some meaning. From now on, it would all be different. He and Jan would start afresh.

Jan turns and looks at him. "Are you awake?" she says.

"Yes."

"I can't see your eyes. It's too dark."

"I'm awake."

"I'm happy you're feeling better."

"Thanks."

Jan slides across the seat and leans her head against his shoulder. "I like the way you look in tails. You ought to get dressed up more often."

"Didn't you know? This is what I wear under my flight suit every day."

Jan nuzzles up against him. "Stop making fun of me."

"I'm not." He strokes her face. "I'm serious."

"Oh, pooh!"

"Pooh? What does that mean, pooh?"

"Stop it."

He looks down at her face only a few inches away. Her eyes are closed. In the shadows her mouth seems to be trembling. He leans a little closer, tasting her breath, the familiar scent of her. He feels the heat rise off her face. Her lips part slightly. He feels her draw him close and they are kissing suddenly, first softly like a morning kiss, still tentative, and then with greater force, as if the long weeks of denial have only been a preparation for this moment. He reaches out and pulls her tight against his chest. He buries his face against her neck. He cannot let her go, not now, not after almost losing her. She is his only lifeline to his one true self. Even more than Glen or Rick, she is the only one who knows when to forgive him, when to accept his moods, his dissembling and white lies, and when to stand against his falseness. He would give almost anything if only he could tell her, if only he could make her understand that it was just a moment of weakness, a terrible misjudgment. *It was just an accident,* he'd say. He knows she would forgive him, that despite everything she would see it from his side, would understand, but the words don't form. They gather in his throat, stunted, misshaped. Their bitterness is just for him, just for the members of The Hunting Club.

"A penny for your thoughts," she says.

"Is that all they're worth?" He squeezes her gently. "I was thinking how lucky I am."

"I've been saying that for years."

"Well, you were right."

She touches his face with her hand. "Ssh," she whispers in his ear. "Don't talk. Just kiss me."

He presses her against him. He hears her moan, feels the vibration through her lips. The green silk barely covers up the softness of her thighs. He feels her warm hand on his leg. He feels her reaching for him and his eyes slit open and he sees Yolanda lying there beside him, her mouth half open, her eyes glazed over by the thought of one more man inside her.

"What is it?"

Payne sits up in his seat. He turns away. His eyes fall on the rearview mirror in the front. The driver's eyes are staring back. "We're almost there," Payne says. The driver does not look away. He simply stares, his dark narrowed eyes framed by the mirror, laughing.

Jan sits up with a sigh. She pats her dress down, starts to fiddle with her hair. "Where are we?"

"Near Croton."

"Already? It looked so different for a minute." She turns away and yawns.

Soon the limousine swings off 9A to Peekskill. The streets are empty at this hour, completely desolate. Only the wind cuts through the barren trees, blown down the distant rib line of the Hudson palisades, along the black vein of the river. The car slides past the Sportsmen's Center, past the middle school, and up into their street.

Payne stands shakily in the driveway, groping for his wallet, as Jan unlocks the front door of the house. He tips the driver, and the limousine backs out of the small driveway, almost clipping the stone wall. It is a cold, uncompromising night. The stars gleam down relentlessly. Payne tilts his head, their light spills deep into his eyes, and suddenly he's flying right beside them in the sky, untethered by the earth, unbounded, free.

The light on the front stoop flicks on. Payne looks up and there is Jan in the window of the living room. She is staring down at him. The Christmas tree is glowing right behind her. She appears to shimmer on its nimbus in green light—the emerald of her evening dress. He mounts the front stairs two at a time. He pushes at the door and it opens with a bang as the knocker bounces on itself. He slams the door shut. Jan is gone. He can see the rustling edge of her hemline floating up the stairs. He follows right behind her, taken by the gentle sloping of her shoe, the heel, the way she holds her dress up in her hands so that it doesn't drag across the steps. And then they're in the bedroom, and he can see her sitting on the bed, her legs crossed at the knee, her calf hidden in the billows of her slip. She is leaning back against the bed, looking down, waiting for him, holding the posture for him, teasing.

He walks up to the bed. She leans across to touch him but he pushes her away; she falls, supine, her hair splayed out behind her on her pillow. There is a rectangle of starlight on the sheet, a pillar of milky sky thrust through the skylight. Her head lolls to the side, so that her face cuts through the starlight, and he can see that she is looking up at him through half-closed eyes. She reaches up behind her with one hand, trying to unzip her dress. "Help me," she says.

He takes the zipper in his fingertips. It slithers down her back, unfolding, revealing her white skin, the lacy slip beneath. She wriggles and the dress falls off her shoulders. She tugs and pulls. He slips it down across her pregnant stomach, across her thighs. She lifts her legs up and the dress pulls free. Jan smiles. She reaches up for him, but he hangs back, unwilling to give up the moment, the sight of her illuminated by the stars above, her white face glowing, the pale curve of her neck, the way her breasts fall softly to the side against her slip, straining the silken straps each time she breathes.

"Come here," she says. "I've been neglecting you."

He takes a small step forward. "I love you, Jan," he says with such conviction that she hesitates, she opens her eyes to fix him in her gaze.

"I love you too," she says.

"Ever since that first night, at Betsy Bradhurst's house. Ever since the first time I saw you, I knew that I would love you, that I could never love anyone else. I knew it, Jan." *It was just an accident, that's all.*

"Come here. Don't talk." She pulls him toward her on the bed. He stretches out beside her, feeling the warmth of her, smelling her hair. "I want you in me."

"I never had a chance."

"Ssh." She whispers in his ear. She bites at him. She reaches down for him exactly as the phone rings by his head. He jumps. The telephone rings again.

"Jesus Christ," he says.

"Who can that be, at this hour?"

"Don't answer it."

She rolls across the bed.

"Just let it ring. Maybe they'll go away."

"What if it's important? What if it's Aggie or Mother?" She reaches for the telephone.

"No, don't!" he shouts, but it's too late. The receiver is in her hand.

"Hello," she says. "Oh, it's you. No, not yet."

Payne sits up on the edge of the bed. Jan looks at him and rolls her eyes. "Now?" she says, after a pause. "Do you know what time it is?" She hands the receiver to Payne. "It's Glen."

He shakes his head. He whispers, "I don't want to talk to him."

"Well, what am I meant to say, John? He knows you're here."

Payne takes the receiver from her hand. "Yeah, Glen. What's up?"

"Brace yourself."

"What is it?" Payne looks over at Jan. She is standing by the bed. He reaches into his pocket for his cigarettes.

"When Bobby got home tonight there were a bunch of hang-ups on his answering machine. No big deal, he thought. So he and Elizabeth went to bed."

Payne hooks the phone under his chin and takes out a cigarette.

"The phone rang ten minutes later. Elizabeth picked it up, but there was no one there. So she hung up. Another ten minutes, and it rang again. This time Bobby picked it up."

Payne lights the cigarette with his lighter. He draws the smoke deep in his lungs.

"Do you have to do that here?" says Jan.

Payne looks up.

"You know I don't like you smoking in the bedroom. It's not good for the baby."

"Just a minute, Glen," he says, and cups the phone. "Look, I'm sorry. This is important. Give me a second, will you, honey?"

"It's three in the morning!"

"Please," he says.

Jan starts to answer, but stops herself. She picks her emerald dress up from the windowseat. She shakes her head, and vanishes out the door.

"John? John, are you there?" says Morrow.

"I'm here. Who was it, Glen?"

"Do you remember that black stripper at the Party Girl Lounge? The skinny one?"

"Yeah, I remember."

"Her name is Candy. She says she knows what we did to Yolanda. She wants forty thousand dollars or she's going to the cops."

Payne lets the words descend upon him one by one, until they fit together, piece to piece, like a mosaic, and the burden of their meaning weighs upon him from above. *It was just an accident, that's all. I promise* . . . "I thought it was over," he says quietly. He feels nothing. He looks down at the patch of icy light washing the sheet. His hand is lit up by the starlight. He can see each curve, each tiny hair, on every finger in detail. "I thought you said that we were in the clear."

"I thought we were."

"Well, that's just fucking great." He curls his hand into a fist. "You said it was over, Glen. But it's not over. It's going to go on and on and on, until we're all in jail, or dead, or on the run."

"Get a hold of yourself, John."

"Well, what are we supposed to do?"

"I think we should take care of her. Permanently."

"What are you saying? Are you crazy, Glen? You're fucking crazy, that's what you are."

"We're going to have to do it in the end."

"You're out of your fucking mind, Glen. We're going to pay her off, that's what we're going to do. We don't have any other choice. What do you care, anyway? It's only money." He laughs grimly. "What did Bobby say?"

"He votes we pay her off."

"And Tom?"

"He's on his way to Anguilla."

"No proxy, no vote. I guess it's two to one."

"All right, John. We'll try it your way—this time. But I'm telling you right now. If it doesn't work, I'm not letting some cheap black stripper ruin my life. You hear me? I've worked too hard for what I have."

"We'll pay her off, Glen. You agreed. We'll pay her off and that will be the end of it." Payne hangs up the phone with a bang. His hand is trembling. He curls his fingers in a fist. He tucks the fist

into his lap. The end of it. The end of it. The more he repeats the
words, the less reliable they seem. Even if they pay her off, it will
not be the end. It will go on and on. . . . He squeezes his fist into
his lap, he curls his body round it. This is the hand, he thinks.
These are the fingers. He presses the fist into his stomach. And this
is the man behind it.

Part 3

Part 3

XI

"Shimp oh pohk," says the Chinese waiter. The dim sum steam in tiny bowls at the center of the tray.

"No, thanks," says Payne. "I'll pass."

Morrow points his chopsticks at a bowl of small white dumplings. He nods his head. He mumbles something as he chews. The waiter drops the dim sum on the table, beside a triangle of empty bowls, beside three cups of steaming tea.

"Did you bring the bag?" says Payne, as the waiter moves away.

Morrow reaches for another dumpling. Chopsticks dance in his hand. The hand of a pianist, thinks Payne, dexterous and strong. The quarterback he once was. The fingers pluck the small white dumpling, lift and carry in a blink. The dumpling disappears into his mouth. It is still hot. Morrow moves it about, he chews, he cracks his lips to let the steam pass. Then he swallows hard and says, "I've got it." He kicks at something underneath the table.

There is a burst of calls and conversation by the door, and Payne looks up to see a long-haired Chinese teenager pose briefly in the entrance. His friends are seated by the window overlooking Mott Street, at a long Formica table. There are five or six of them, dressed in hound's-tooth coats or leather jackets with their collars up. How can they stand it? Payne thinks. The restaurant is steaming hot. The boy at the door begins to saunter over and someone cracks a joke or something in Mandarin or Cantonese, and he stops short and slaps one of his friends across the back.

"What time is it?"

"You just asked me, Bobby," Morrow says.

Litchfield stares at his wrist.

"Relax. We've still got plenty of time."

Litchfield looks up, a blank expression on his face. He seems to freeze, then begins to search the pockets of his russet tweed jacket frantically.

"What is it now?"

"The address. I wrote it on a piece of paper. I put it in my jacket, but now it's gone. I know I had it." He rolls to one side, poking plump fingers in his trouser pockets.

"Don't you remember it?"

"Of course I do."

"So why do you need the paper?"

Litchfield stops squirming. "It's off the West Side Highway. The Hudson Cement Company. On Tenth between Twenty-eighth and Twenty-ninth." He smiles. "Here it is," he says sheepishly, his glasses shining. "I had it all the time."

"Hey, John," says Morrow.

Payne is staring at the Chinese teenager by the door. The boy has taken off his coat. He is frighteningly thin, cadaverous, wearing a shiny black shirt, like silk pajamas. He carries himself with an air of casual sovereignty. He says something, something indiscernible in the noisy restaurant. Then he turns, as if he feels Payne's gaze upon his back. His eyes! Payne cannot move. They are the eyes of a hooked fish, roiling in black waters. They stare, unblinking, a deep relentless black, as if they know. They know. Murderer!

The tracers streamed into the woods, the branches flew apart, and at the center of my sights there was this one VC in black. I trimmed my cyclic stick, and watched the bullets stumble through the grass, slither like a fire snake across the distant back . . . It was so easy, and it felt so good, it scared me. The power of it all. You move a finger and it's done. It's so easy, John. It's like a drug. I can't stop thinking about it. . . .

"John?"

Hey, take it easy, will ya? And her head bumped up against the head-board. Take it easy, mister.

"John!"

"What is it?"

"Remember what you promised," Morrow says.

"What?"

"At the reception. About The Hunting Club."

"I remember."

"John's always been a man of honor," Litchfield says. "Despite that handshake thing."

Payne turns on him. "Honor!" he says. "Jesus Christ, Bobby. We're going to pay off some fucking stripper with a laundry bag full of money and you're talking about honor. That's a laugh."

"You wanted to pay her off," says Morrow. "Don't take it out on Bobby."

"Jesus Christ!" says Payne. He pushes his chair back from the table.

"I haven't done anything wrong," says Litchfield. "It was just an accident."

"And don't make light of your promise, either," Morrow adds. "Because I won't. Because, no matter what you think, I am a man of honor. Where it counts, John. Between us. In this moral universe."

"If you say so, Glen."

"I wish Rick were here," says Litchfield. A hush rolls over the table like a summer mist.

Payne knows exactly what he means. They all do.

Morrow finishes his tea. Payne pushes his plate away. Litchfield pokes at a dumpling on his plate, the shape of a Shar-Pei puppy.

Even at Hadley, Rick had been the peacemaker. It was always Rick, his humor and his irony which made their arguments seem pointless. But this time Avery was not involved. He couldn't be.

Morrow waves the waiter over and pays the bill. As they slip their coats on and hurry out the door, Payne feels the eyes of someone staring at him from somewhere in the crowded restaurant, but he does not turn around. There is no point. He knows whose eyes they are. They have already been inside him, and there is nothing left to see.

The Chelsea plant of the Hudson Cement Company stands by the West Side Highway, immediately adjacent to the Hudson River. It boasts the tallest cement silo in Manhattan, a gravel sorter and a newly paved parking lot for the company's two dozen trucks. The trucks are painted white with pink and light blue polka dots, the whimsy of a bored executive, a vain attempt to make the hulking shapes seem less offensive to the public as they shatter the peace of the loudest street. A couple of decrepit trailers are parked beside the gate. The gate is padlocked shut, but there is an opening in the chain link fence which even Litchfield can fit through.

They make their way along the dusty path. "Where is she?" Litchfield says.

"Don't worry," Morrow answers grimly. "She's here." A bright yellow laundry bag spins in his hand. "She's making sure we're alone."

"I wish we weren't. I don't know, Glen. I've got a bad feeling about this."

"Will you shut up? We've been over this a hundred times. It was your idea to pay her off, John."

"I know, but maybe I was wrong. Maybe we should have told the cops, like Bobby said. A long time ago. That first night. It was an accident . . ."

"There she is."

They turn to follow Morrow's gaze. A black woman in a fake fur coat is standing beside the trailers. "It's her," says Morrow. "I remember her now. It's Candy."

They make their way toward the trailers. Candy spots them coming up the path and waves at them to hurry. "Where you been?" she says as they approach. "I ain't got time to wait 'round all day for you."

"Traffic," Morrow says. He smiles at her, and in the space of just two syllables the temperature seems to drop.

She points an orange fingernail at him. "Don't fuck wit' me. It's cold. Where's the money?"

Morrow holds the laundry bag out by the string.

"Is that it?"

He nods.

She reaches for the bag but Morrow pulls it back. "Just a minute," he says. "How do we know that once we pay you off, you won't come back for more?"

She smiles. It is a beautiful smile, Payne thinks, and for the first time he can see how young she really is. Eighteen or nineteen, maybe. No more. Her hair is straightened in a kind of '60's bob. She is wearing three round silver earrings in one ear. Her full-length fake fox coat is wrapped about her throat, but he can still remember what she looked like on the stage, the way that she leaned against that mirror on the wall, and ran her fingernails across her thighs, lifting her miniskirt.

"Because I told you so," she says at last.

"That isn't good enough."

"Tha's all you gettin'."

In a moment Morrow is on top of her, pushing her back against the trailer wall.

"Get the fuck off me, asshole."

Morrow slams his elbow in her chest and Payne can hear the air knocked out of her. Candy starts to whimper. "Now you listen to me, you little bitch," Morrow says. His voice drills through her like an icicle. "We're going to let you keep this money. Because we told you we would." She struggles underneath him but he shoves her back against the wall. "Because these gentlemen here believe you'll live by your word, Candy. That you won't go to the cops. That you won't ever bother us again. But I know different, and I'm telling you right now that if I ever see you again, if I ever hear your voice, if I so much as hear your fucking name, I'm going to hunt you down like a wild animal. You hear me? If you say one fucking word I'm going pull your fucking tongue right out of your mouth, by the roots, you understand me?" He lays a hand on her face, like a hood on a horse, and she stops struggling. "Do you hear me?"

"Bumper," she cries.

"Glen, cut it out," says Payne. He touches Morrow's shoulder, but Morrow spins away.

"Do you?"

"I hear you jus' fine, homeboy."

The deep voice seems to rise out of the shadows. They turn to see a large black man step out from behind the trailer. There is a gun in his hand. It is pointed at Morrow's chest. "Surprise!" he says. He grins, his eyes grow wide, and then he shakes his hand, waving the .38. His smile collapses. His eyes narrow and he says, "Yo, get off her, man."

"Take it easy, mister," Payne says. "He wasn't going to hurt her."

"Why not? I do all the time." The man laughs at his own joke, and Payne can see that one of his side teeth is capped with gold.

Morrow backs away from Candy. "Don't do anything stupid," he says.

"Who you callin' stupid, stupid. I'm the one with the gun, muthafucka. Looks like you the stupid one to me, ain't that right, Candy?"

"Tha's right, Bumper." Candy straightens her hair.

"Stupid," he says. He nods and leans back on one foot. He crosses his arms. "Now I'll tell you what's stupid, muthafucka. Comin' here is stupid." He laughs.

Bumper is wearing a long black coat, a thick black wool sweater, and jeans. He is around twenty-five years old. His hands are huge, but his head seems small, his ears unnaturally so compared to his great neck, bulging with veins, his shoulders. "Comin' with that bag," he adds slyly. "Now that's real stupid. Give it here."

"What are you going to do to us?" asks Bobby Litchfield. His eyes are bulging in his face. He fiddles with his blue bow tie.

"Well, I don't know yet, do I? That depends."

Morrow hands him the laundry bag.

"On what?" says Litchfield.

He smiles at Morrow and shakes the bag in his face. "Dis is jus' the first installment, homeboy. Like you buying a car. Like you buying a little piece of mind. Street insurance. That's what I'm sellin'."

"What does he mean?" demands Litchfield. "What do you mean, insurance?"

"It's gonna take a lotta years, a lotta yellow bags to help me forget what you did to my poor baby girl, Yolanda. One of my best girls, too. Not like this lying, lazy bitch." He nods at Candy.

"But you agreed," says Litchfield. "Candy promised us . . ."

"Now what did I jus' tell you. Candy's a lying, lazy bitch. She'd fuck her father for a dollar. And you know what? She did!" He begins to laugh.

"Well, we're not going to pay it," Litchfield says.

"The fuck you ain't. 'Cuz if you don't, I'm gonna tell the man." He laughs another belly laugh. He opens the laundry bag with his fingers and peers inside. "Oh, I can see it on the TV now." He looks through the opening as though it were a lens. "Fine up-standing white folk like you caught up in this terrible murder. First you raped her, then you smashed her head in—"

"We didn't rape her," says Payne.

"—and then you dumped her little round body, with those big brown eyes and those big soft tits, and you went back to your skinny white wives you been playin' dirty and your fine cribs and fancy cars and you tried pretendin' it was jus' anotha' day. What's anotha' Puerto Rican? What's anotha' nigger girl, huh?"

"Shut up," says Morrow suddenly.

"You're gonna pay, homeboy, and I'm gonna love it."

"I said shut *up*."

"Or what? What the fuck you gonna do, muthafucka? One call an' you all housebound." He laughs. He swings the bag shut on its string. "How long you think you'd stay alive on the inside?" He points his gun at Litchfield. "You better be a Mormon, homeboy, 'cuz you gonna have a messa husbands. They'll stretch your butt so far, you be hidin' up your own ass."

Candy laughs. "That's a good one, Bumper. Hide up your own ass—"

"You're not going to turn us in," says Morrow flatly.

"What's that?"

"You won't turn us in."

"I'm gonna fuck you up, you keep dissin' me." He takes a step closer to Morrow.

"Just keep the money," Payne says, holding out his hands. "We did what you wanted."

"He's not going to hurt us."

"Shut the fuck up," Bumper shouts. He shoves Morrow back with one hand. "I'm warnin' you, man." He flourishes his gun.

"I know you won't." Morrow does not move. Even as Bumper lifts his gun as if to strike his face, Morrow stands there without flinching, without moving an inch. "And do you know how I know?" His voice is calm.

"I'm warnin' you, muthafucka. Stop dissin' me." He pushes Morrow back against the trailer wall. He sticks the muzzle of the .38 against his neck, puckering the skin.

"Because you're not stupid."

A quizzical expression crosses Bumper's face.

"Because you know that if you tell the police, or if you do anything to hurt us, any one of us, we'll never pay you again. And then where are you, Bumper? You're a man without money. Without power. You're a nobody. You're a two-bit pimp, who once had a chance to make some big money, and he let it slip right through his fingers."

"Yeah," says Bumper. "I'm not fuckin' stupid."

Morrow smiles his warmest smile. His ice blue eyes grow bright. He turns and looks at Candy, and the power of his presence sweeps across her. She starts to laugh. Soon Bumper is laughing too, laughing so loud and full that he can barely hear the sound of his own rib cage blowing open.

One moment Bumper is standing, and the next he is writhing on the ground, five feet away and screaming like a chain saw, screaming as the blood spurts through his fingers from his chest. Morrow steps up, he turns, and in an instant Bumper's screams are cut off in midcry. His head rises off the ground. A hole opens at the center of his forehead, and his head slams back against the frozen earth with a dull crack. A gurgle of blood and brain begins to seep up through the opening.

"Oh, my God," says Candy. "Oh, my God, you killed him." She drops to her knees beside him.

Payne finally sees the smoke, rolling in the cold air, curling from the barrel of the gun in Morrow's hand. There is some kind of silencer on the end. It is elegant and compact. Morrow turns and the gun is gone.

"You had no right to kill him—"

"Shut up," says Morrow.

"Oh, Bumper, Bumper." She strokes his hair, trying to keep the fake fur from the pulpy mass oozing from his head. "Look at you, baby. Look at you—"

"Stand up."

"It was his idea." Candy's voice is shrill. "I told him not to do it. You goin' to kill me now. I know you are. Jus' like Bumper. Oh, Lord, have mercy." She looks up at Payne. "You tell him, mister. You look like a nice man." She turns toward Litchfield. "I'll do anything you want."

"Get up."

"Oh, please don't hurt me." She reaches out toward Morrow with one hand. The other still holds the fur away from the spreading blood. "I'll do anything for you, baby. Anything. Whatever you want. I'm good too, baby. I'm the best. All of you, if you want. All at the same time. I can do it, baby. You know I can. Please let me do it. I really want to."

"I told you to get up."

"Okay, baby. Whatever you want. Jus' tell Candy what to do." She scrambles to her feet.

"What have you done, Glen?" Payne says. Everything seems far away, at the end of a long tunnel: Bumper, lying on the ground, the blood still coursing from his chest, his head; Candy, shivering in her fake fur coat.

"He had his gun at my neck. You saw him," Morrow says. "He was going to kill me."

"No, he wasn't."

"Here. Put these on." Morrow reaches out to Payne. He is holding a pair of latex gloves, flesh-colored, like the ones that surgeons wear. "You, too," he says to Litchfield.

"I'm getting out of here," says Payne. "This is insane, Glen."

He starts to turn away but Morrow jerks him around. He brings his face directly next to Payne's and says, "He stuck a gun in my neck, John, *my* neck, not yours, *mine*. When it's your neck, you can play it any way you want." He pushes Payne away. He runs a hand back through his hair. "Now put those gloves on and shut up. I've got to think." He looks at Candy, like a cat spotting a fly. "I've got to find out the horizons, the parameters of the damage."

"Let's just get out of here," cries Payne.

"Don't turn yellow on me now, John. Not in the middle of it. I'm counting on you, John. Just like in New Haven. Why do you think we're all here, anyway? We came for you, John, for you. To clean up your mess. You're the one who got us into this."

"Don't leave, mister." A weak smile trembles on Candy's lips. "We'll all have a good time."

"Watch the door, John," Morrow says. He leans over the body. He lifts Bumper roughly by the shoulders and drags him down across the path behind the trailer. Then he picks up a length of iron rod from a nearby pile of debris, and slips it into the padlock on the trailer door. There is a loud snap as he rips the lock from the frame. "Let's go," he says to the woman. "You, too, Bobby."

Candy steps up through the door, and with a whimper Litchfield follows. The trailer sways and shakes as Morrow vanishes behind them. The door slams shut. Payne collapses up against the trailer wall. His head feels light. His hands tingle as he slips the rubber gloves on, one finger at a time. His heart is rattling in his chest. *It will go on, and on, and on. . . .* He hears a cry ring out inside the trailer. It is Candy's voice. He palms his latex-covered hands about his ears, forming a seal, trying to keep the sound out, trying to find the switch to turn it off, but it will not go away. He hears her still, he hears her calling out to Morrow to be kind, be nice to her, and his palms slip from his ears and he finds himself, his back pressed up against the trailer wall, he finds himself slide down along the siding toward the window near the door.

"I'll ask you again," says Morrow. "Who else?"

"Tha's it. Jus' me and Susan and Bumper. Look, mister. You can put that gun away. I'll tell you everythin' you want."

"Who's Susan?"

"A dancer at the lounge. She was there that night. She danced the last set."

"I remember her," Payne hears Litchfield say. "A brunette with glasses."

"Tha's right. Tha's Susan. We was worried. Yolanda bein' late

and all, and missin' work. Bumper had me call but she didn't answer her beeper. So me and Susan, we went over. Yolanda and me
was wives-in-law, before she busted on Bumper. Real tight. She
said he was a no good wanna-be, and she was right. Didn't deserve
no choosing cake. I loved that girl. I could tell her anything . . ."

"How did you find out what happened to Yolanda?"

"Like I said, we went over, Susan and me, and we seen the
place was empty. Now the last time Yolanda split on me she went
somewheres in the Caribbean with this real nice older John from
Jersey she been clockin' for three weeks straight. Treated her jus'
fine. Bought her all kinds'a things, like dresses and jewelry . . ."

"Go on."

"Well seein' how I always loved that necklace, and seein' how
she was goin' to be away anyway, I didn' think she'd mind if I
borrowed it for jus' a few days. It was pink coral and real gold."

"You were looking for a necklace?"

"She kept her trap under her mattress. You know. I was there
and we was sisters, man. I didn' think she'd mind. She was gone.
The place was empty. But when I turned the mattress over, saw
that, that stain . . ." The word hangs in her throat, liked a barbed
hook. "Oh, please, mister. I won't say nothin'. I promise."

"How did you track us down?"

"Please, mister." Her voice cracks with fear.

"Just answer the question. How did you find us?"

"All right, don't get mad, mister. I'll tell you. Jus' don't get
mad at me. It's the matches, see? We thought back to the night
Yolanda disappeared. We r'membered your party. It was easy. You
tipped real nice. Then I aksed Jimmy if he seen you."

"Who's Jimmy?"

"Jus' some wino hangs out on Church Street, hangs out right
in front. And he says 'maybe,' which is yeah. 'The nice one give me
a cigarette,' he says, 'give me some matches, too.' The Quonset
Hut. Tha's what they say. The matches. So Bumper sends me over
to check it out and, well, when a man has a secret, look out, if
Candy wants to know, she's goin' to know. Took me five minutes to
get the manager to show me the receipt. Five minutes. I was wearing my leopard outfit with the orange pumps. Some waitress there

remembered you all right. Man, she broke out on you. Table twenty-seven, she says, twenty-seven, and there it was, right on the piece of paper: Robert T. Litchfield."

"And so you called him up."

"Bumper made me. I didn't want to. Not after I saw that stain there. Not me. I'm a girl knows how to keep her mouth shut."

"What are we going to do?" says Litchfield.

"Jus' let me go, mister. You keep the money, I don't want it. I don't want no money."

"What are we going to do, Glen? We can't just let her go."

"Yes, you can, baby. I'll be good. Candy'll be good."

"Glen, tell me what to do." Litchfield's voice is raw.

"Shut up, both of you. I'm trying to think."

"Glen . . ."

"Shutup, Bobby. Shutup. Shutup. Shutup!"

There is an eerie silence in the mobile home. Payne feels himself drawn closer to the window. No one is talking. No one is even breathing.

"What are you going to do, mister, with that gun? Oh, Lord, please, mister. Please don't shoot me."

"You can't just shoot her, Glen."

"Please, mister. Let me make it up to you. I'm better than Yolanda, baby."

"What are you going to do, Glen?"

"Wha's the matter, baby? What is it with you two? Don't you like me, is that it? You want to do me together? Wha's wrong, baby?"

"Shut up," says Morrow.

"Wha's the matter? You two ain't—"

"I'm warning you."

"It's all right, baby. Whatever shakes your tree."

"Get over there. On the counter. No, by the sink."

"Okay, baby. Whatever you want. Jus' put the gun down. You don't need no gun. I ain't goin' noplace."

"Here, take it, Bobby."

"I don't want it."

"Take it."

Payne slumps against the chilly metal siding of the trailer, the window only inches from his face. But he cannot look inside. He closes his eyes. He cannot.

"Take it, I said!"

"All right, all right, Glen."

"Cover her."

"Don't worry, baby. You don't need no gun. Ooh, yeah. Let me pull it up. You like that, don't you? Ooh, yeah. Yeah, tha's right. Let me feel it. Come on, baby. Oww, don't pinch. Oww! Come on, baby, be nice to Candy. Be nice, tha's right."

Payne cups his ears with his palms. His breath congeals in the air. He can smell the sweet aroma of the latex gloves, the newness of them. The sweat is freezing on his skin.

"Come on, baby. Candy wants it. Right there, baby. Come on. Ooh, yeah, baby, tha's right . . ."

Payne looks up at the sky. It is a glaring iceberg blue, criss-crossed by a single jetstream far above, so high he cannot even see the plane. And then it's gone. It's gone.

"All right, Bobby, it's your turn."

"Not me," says Litchfield. "No way."

"What's the matter, Bobby?" Morrow's voice is goading. "Didn't that look fun?"

"I'm not interested. And you don't know where she's been."

"Give me the gun, Bobby. The gun . . . Now, take your pants off."

"Come on, Glen. I said I wasn't interested."

"You heard me."

"Glen, don't do this. You don't have to do this."

"No, but you do. You deserve it, Bobby."

"Come on, baby. Come to Candy."

"All the way off, Bobby."

"Tha's it, Bobby baby. Oh, you're so cute. Come here. Come on, baby, let me get it hard."

Payne can hear the sound of his own heart pumping blood, like the dark red blood which burst from Bumper's chest, pumping to the rocking of the trailer as it shivers on its chassis.

"Tha's right, baby. Tha's it, come on. Come on. Come on—"

There is a crash and Litchfield screams. He is wailing like a baby. Payne spins about. He presses his face against the cold glass of the window. Wailing and gasping for breath, Litchfield crawls across the trailer floor, his trousers snagged about his ankles, his face, his glasses sprayed with blood. Atop the counter, swept with fur, Payne sees Candy's silhouette. Her miniskirt is curled about her waist, her panties torn apart. A garter belt is wrapped about her stomach. She is still wearing her bra. She is still lying there, still motionless, still waiting for him to look at her, or all that's left, the shattered lower jaw, the jagged hole in the skull.

Payne throws the door aside. He leaps into the trailer. The smell of blood blows past his face. Litchfield is still writhing on the floor, still whining.

"What have you done?" Payne's voice is barely audible. He cannot breathe. "For God's sake, what have you done, Glen?"

"I did it for you," says Morrow. "To protect you." He looks up from the bloody sink. "To protect all of us."

"I didn't ask for this. I didn't want this."

"We've got to stick together. They knew about you, John. They knew what you did to Yolanda. They were going to tell the cops. Is that what you wanted?"

"No, but—"

"We've got to dump the bodies."

"You're crazy." Payne reaches out to Litchfield, to help him to his feet. "I'm not having anything to do with this. This is your doing, Glen. Come on, Bobby. Let's get out of here."

"Don't touch me," Litchfield screams.

"Bobby!"

"I mean it, John, don't touch me. Glen's right. You got us into this."

"You're both crazy."

"Grow up, John," Morrow says. "I told you I wouldn't sit still for this. That asshole put a gun to my neck. He threatened to kill me. And that bitch knew about Yolanda. She knew! The secret we've all been trying to protect. Your secret, John. John's dirty little secret. Not just that you killed her, John, but what you felt when you did it. What you felt inside."

"I don't know what you're talking about."

"Yeah, you do. We all do. That's what binds us together. Isn't that right, Bobby?"

"That's right, Glen."

"We all dream about her, John. All of us. Because of you, John. Because of you. Now pick up that piece of garbage. It's beginning to stink in here."

The door swings open and Morrow vanishes, with Litchfield on his heels. They fade into the morning light, they disappear and Payne is suddenly aware of Candy lying there beside him, the stillness of her chest, the reminiscent sound of droplets falling to the floor. He scoops her up in his arms, trying not to look, trying not to see her even in the corner of his eye. He staggers through the open door.

"Glen, wait. Wait! We can't go to the airport. It's too late," says Payne, catching the pleasure in his own voice, nestled underneath the anger. And then he thinks, do I want to get caught, is that it? Just to get back at Glen? "What are we going to do?"

Morrow rounds the corner, dragging Bumper by the collar. "Feel how cold it is," he says.

"Great—so it's cold!" says Payne. "So what?"

"You're a pilot. You know about thermal layers."

"What are you talking about?"

"The river, John. Behind you." Morrow straightens, shakes his head. "This time of year they'll sink like stones into the colder layers, down into the muck. The tide is going out. I checked."

"You checked!"

"This morning. I went on-line. Computers don't sleep, John. Start cleaning up the trailer, Bobby. We'll be right back." He throws Bumper on his shoulder. He leans and staggers down the path. Payne follows, with all that's left of Candy in his arms. It is only twenty feet to the beginning of the wooden dock which stretches out into the river. When they reach the water, Morrow climbs down onto the rocks beneath the wooden planking. They lay the bodies gently on the rocks, the cold black water lapping at their feet. Then Morrow pulls his gun out, saying, "Turn away."

"What are you going to do? Jesus Christ, Glen, they're already dead!"

Morrow fires four quick shots into their chests. "To help them sink," he says.

Payne lets himself slip backward, down onto the dock. He

falls, he lands against the planking, warm and solid underneath his hands. A splinter pierces the latex glove and bites into his palm. He feels a bitter breeze come off the river, the Hudson, the same river as the one which runs only a few miles from his house, where Jan is sitting at this very moment, reading the Sunday *New York Times*, drinking her morning coffee in the sun room; the same river, parting open to admit the small round head, the mighty neck and lifeless shoulders, sliding noiselessly along, discreet more than uncaring, willing to look the other way as the '60's bob uncurls and flutters in the inky current, the fake fur coat, the miniskirt, unfurling in the darkness like a shroud.

XII

The light punctuates the darkness like a revelation, like an epiph-
any, through tangled uprights shadowy with weed, waving to him,
waving him on across the silent muddy flats, alive with cans and
bottles, twinkling back, the more than fifteen feet of muck and
human hair and seaworm eating the decay, a purge of CO_2, a kick
and there she is, the right arm firmly lodged inside a brace, the
body wrapped around a piling, grasping at the pier, holding on as if
for life against the streaming tide.

The diver lifts the elbow out and she pulls free and spins until
her face is caught up in the light beam for a moment before swimming off into the darkness, but it is long enough to set the image in
his mind, the shattered lower jaw, the hole in the skull, the sign of
eels at work along the eyes—in just a day, and it's so fuckin' cold.
He sets the grappling hooks, one underneath each arm, and jerks
the line twice with a firmness that reminds him he is angry, angry at
the early hour and the unrelenting cold. The body lurches forward.
He spins some debris from his face, a piece of plastic, a garbage
bag, and follows in the darkness with a kick, reaching for the
outline of her feet, the high-heel pumps, the solid feel of them
and he is gliding through the water, towed by the body and the
grappling hooks between the pilings. The darkness of the pier
evaporates. He kicks, he rises slowly, breathing out, releasing his
firm grasp around the woman's skinny ankles, breathing out and

upward toward the cluster lights, the surface like a looking glass and through.

Detective Anthony Capozzi of the Thirteenth Precinct, Homicide Division, stands on the deck of the police launch, watching the half-clothed body of the young black woman being hauled across the gunwale.

"Hey, Bill, why don't you just cut her up for me right here, like a tuna. Put her in plastic bags," he says. "Then I can fit her in my Aries." He laughs, slapping his sides to drive away the cold, shifting his weight from one foot to the other, like a boxer. Capozzi is lean and muscular, with thick black hair and black eyes gleaming under his watch cap. He is thirty-six, but he seems much younger in his pea coat and cowboy boots. Only the lines about his eyes reveal the fourteen years he's been with the Thirteenth.

The beefy black man at the winch cuts off the power and the grappling lines relax. "Very fucking funny. You try working this thing. Piece 'a shit . . ."

"What you say?"

"The winch, man. The fucking winch."

Capozzi leans across the body of the girl as Bill removes the grappling hooks. The body starts to bleed out of the openings in her back and underarms; she rolls, revealing what is left of her face, the shattered lower jaw, the blank space where her mouth had been. Water rushes through the opening, snakes across the deck.

Capozzi jumps. "Jesus Christ! You see that? I swear there was something crawling around in there."

"Could 'a been a crab. Found one big as a cat in this guy's rib cage 'bout a year ago. Then you've got your eel family. Sometime it's hard to know where the eel starts and the floater ends."

"Thanks. I get the picture."

"What's the matter, Capozzi? You don't look good." He starts to laugh, a high-pitched wheeze, like the closing of a rusty car door. "Didn't figure you for the squeamish type. Not Detective Anthony Capozzi. Shit, man. Just heard you got another commendation. Too bad about Golden. I heard he—"

"Yeah, too bad."

"I don't pay no attention to rumors. I met your uncle once. Worked on a case together, must be five years now, maybe six years ago. Good cop, Mario. No matter what they say." There is a pause, just long enough to let the cold in. Bill shivers. "Yeah, well. So, what do you think?"

"About what?"

The beefy black man points down at the corpse. "The floater, man."

Capozzi shrugs. "Looks like a gunshot wound. Point-blank range."

Bill tosses the grappling hooks onto the deck. He leans closer to the body to get a better look.

"Nine millimeter, maybe," adds Capozzi. "Broke through the upper jaw."

"Point-blank, all right." Bill straightens, starts to yawn. "Lucky she got her arm jammed in those pilings. Probably never found her otherwise. Maybe in the spring."

At that moment, the diver appears on deck. His face mask is riding on the hood of his dry suit. He is struggling with his gloves. "Time and a half." He spits. "My wife keeps asking me, 'What are they doing to you, what are they saying to make you get up at four-thirty in the morning like this,' and I tell her, 'Time and a half.' It's like a magic spell. Like sayzame. She just rolls over. Hey, Capozzi. You know how friggin' cold it is down there?"

"I don't like this any more than you do."

"And for what? Some fucking hooker."

Bill says, "What are you, an expert? How do you know she's a hooker?"

"It's obvious, man. Look at that fucking outfit. The garter belt. The high-heel shoes."

"Half the kids in my neighborhood look like that. That's the style now—the Madonna look."

"I rest my case."

"Fuck you, asshole."

"Bag her up, Bill," says Capozzi. "Where's the guy who found her?"

Bill hooks his thumb across his shoulder toward the dock. "Couple 'a faggots. Spotted her at low tide couple hours ago. Say they were taking a walk . . ." His eyes roll in his head.

"I hate this case already." Capozzi looks down at the body on the deck. Despite the bony opening where her mouth had been, the shattered nasal cavities, he is still drawn to her eyes, or what is left, the sharp incisions in the lids, the telltale marks of eels. "I hate floaters." He scans the glowing outline of New York, the gray black sky above. "And I hate getting up this early."

"Time and a half," the diver says. "I'm tellin' you. Just keep saying it. It helps."

Bill slips the corpse into a plastic body bag, feet first, and then the rest, the miniskirt, the blouse, the shoulders and the broken head.

Time and a half, Capozzi thinks. Bill zips the bag closed with a deft flip of the wrist.

Time and a half. But no time left for you, girl. Whoever you were.

Capozzi makes his way along the deck to the gangway leading to the pier. Two men in leather jackets are talking to a uniformed policeman at the foot of the gangway. They look up as he approaches.

"Who's the guy found the victim?"

"I did," the older of the two replies. He is in his late thirties with close-cropped hair, pale blue eyes, and a leather jockey cap.

"We both did." The younger man is blond with a mustache and glasses, wire-rimmed.

"What time?"

"About three-thirty or four," the older man replies. "Couple of hours ago."

"How did you spot her in the dark?"

"It was the strangest thing." The young man's voice is thin, with a slight Southern slur. "We were just standing there, when the clouds opened up, all of a sudden, and the moon shone through, just a little mind you, just for a second too, and we looked down, and there she was, looking back at us, her arm pulled back like that around the piling. Then the clouds closed up again and she was gone. We both looked at each other without talking, and we knew exactly, I mean *exactly* what was going on in each other's minds. It was weird. Like we were in sync. It was just for a second, but we knew—*we'd seen a corpse*. We waited for at least ten more minutes before the moon broke through again. And there she was, just hanging there in the current, looking at us, her mouth wide open."

"What were you doing on the waterfront at four A.M.?"

"We were just walkin'," says the older man, defensively.

"You couldn't have seen her from the road. You must have climbed the fence if you were out here on the pier. In the dark," Capozzi says. "What were you doing? Looking for something?"

"We didn't do anything."

"We saw a car," says the younger man.

"That was yesterday."

"Two cars. We were walking by the cement plant after brunch—"

"We didn't see anything," says the older man. "We were just minding our business. What we should be doing now."

"It was a scream, I know it was. A woman's scream," the young man insists. His face colors.

"You don't know that for sure. You didn't know then, and you don't know now."

"We should have looked. We might have saved her life."

"Don't be so melodramatic."

"We heard about the killings at the trailer on TV. At the cement plant, all of that blood. It was on the news. So we came back to check it out. They said they hadn't found a body."

"And that's when you spotted her?"

"It's like we were drawn right to the spot. Like we were caught up in the same current, you know what I mean?"

"What kind of car? At the cement plant, where you heard the scream."

The young man says something but his words are drowned out by the wind.

"What was that?"

"Two cars. A red . . ."

The wind drums round their heads, kicking the spray up from

the river. Capozzi looks up. A helicopter suddenly appears around the masthouse of the police boat. It is flying dangerously low, only a hundred yards or so above the water.

"Fuckin 'a," the uniformed policeman says.

Thump. Thump.

The older man holds on to his dark leather cap. Instinctively they draw together in a circle, ducking their heads. "What did you say?" Capozzi shouts.

Thump. Thump.

The chopper rises without warning, then swings away. "We're on TV," the young man says. He leans back, smiling at the sky.

"It's just a traffic chopper," says Capozzi, as the ship drifts up the West Side Highway. The wind dies down. The urgent pounding of the engine fades.

"Will we be interviewed for this? Tim hates it when I say this, but I've always known that some day I'd be on TV."

"What did you say? What kind of cars?"

"Cars? Oh, yeah. A large black BMW with a telephone antenna. Real leather seats, I noticed that! And a brand-new red Accord."

XIII

Payne trims the cyclic stick and the helicopter veers away. For a moment he feels his hand drawn down, he sees the ship slide toward the surface of the river, shiny and black, like an ancient lava flow, drawn through the shattered surface to the silence and the calm below. But he fights the urge and climbs and lifts, and he is rushing up the West Side Highway, away from the frantic figures, the white police launch hung with lights, the small black body bag spread out across the deck.

A voice crackles in his headset. "High-Way Four, do you read me? This is Chopper Shadow One. John, is that you?"

"Roger, Shadow One."

"Man, I don't know what's gotten into you lately, but you'd better quit joyriding or Kelly's going to pull your license."

"Hit a bird, Jack. Almost burst the bubble. Seagull, I think. Came out of nowhere."

"Roger. Shadow One out."

The connection is gone. The crackle of the radio is replaced by the sound of his own breathing in his headset. In. Out. In. His heart pounds. He stares down at the glossy river, winding across the country at dawn. There is the George Washington Bridge with its illuminated wingspan, like an angel lifting off the water, and he remembers Mrs. Beckman. One day—was it two or three years ago? —on his morning run, a gray Ford station wagon had pulled up to the side of the bridge, midcrossing, and Mrs. Ida Beckman had turned to her three kids and said, "Now you just wait right here." And they had, rapt with attention as they watched their mother get out of the car, lock the doors, walk to the rail, climb up, and step off into nothingness. Payne had arrived upon the scene just in time to see the splash, and he had called it in, but they would never find the body. And he had flown up to the upper level and hovered there until the cops came, watching the traffic slow and stop, watching the children in the station wagon watching him.

The river winds below. Candy's river, down to Yolanda's sea. He hears them calling to him in the space between the thumping of the rotor blades, but he cannot do it. Cool black siren slumber. *Thump, thump.* As tempting as it is. Now you just wait right here, he thinks. He sees Sam's gun inside the walnut drawer. He sees the children in the station wagon once again, their faces pressed against the glass, screaming soundlessly, like the unborn baby in Jan's womb.

And he is standing on the bluff at Sitter's Point, ten and a half and scared, on the top rock where all the high school kids dive off. Below him he can see the slate green water pressing at the earth. Sam and his friends are calling out to him to jump. Jump, they say. Go on and jump. They're laughing, splashing, and the great blue bowl of the sky is spinning overhead. The sky, the sky, above the evergreens. He wants to reach out and embrace it. The distant clouds. To fly. He crouches, leaps and dives. The water rushes up to meet him, the sound of laughter dies and there is nothing but the pumping of his own heart as the water shatters on his face and he is through and spinning down and trying to turn and suddenly the stone, and nothingness. . . . And that's how he met Morrow. Poor Sam was on the other side, too far away to help, to even see the way his body shook and stopped and simply hovered there, suspended in the water column, completely motionless for a full minute. But Morrow saw, and pumped his lungs with air by hyperventilating, and dove and kicked and wrestled to the bottom of the pool, and pulled the white unconscious form up by the arms and rushed him to the surface. That's how they met, although it wasn't until a few days later at the hospital that Payne first shook his hand, and thanked him personally.

"I guess you saved my life," he said, trying to sound tough.

"Someone else was bound to see you," Morrow had said. "It just happened to be me." And then he smiled, the red lips curling upwards in the corners, the light brown suntanned freckled cheeks, the tiny perfect nose of an eleven-year-old in summer, the white teeth and the golden hair. "And you're a good swimmer. I've seen you around Sitter's Point before. You've got an older brother, right? His name is Sam."

"How do you know?"

"I guess I've met just about everyone in the Payne family sometime or other this week. I like your mother."

"You do!"

"I think she's funny. I met her at Sitter's Point. I hardly ever get to see my mother."

"How come?"

"I don't know. She's always traveling."

"Sounds like my father."

"Well," said Morrow, stepping back. "I just came by to see how you were making out. I guess I'll be going." He shuffles over toward the door. "See you around. It's a long summer."

"Yeah, I'll see you." And he had.

They had gone swimming together. They had gone bike riding, and fishing, and hiking, sometimes with a friend of Glen's called Litchfield whom he knew from Choke, sometimes with Rick Avery, and to ball games in the city, and they had built a tree fort by Glen's house in that great oak tree near the shed. He was so good at everything. His father was a successful stockbroker in the city and Glen always had the finest tools, and plentiful supplies to build with. Other kids just slapped a couple of planks together and called it a clubhouse, but Morrow designed his forts before he built them. It took them two months to finish, and Payne was with him every step of the way, each morning and each afternoon that summer, working until dark, hammering nails and hauling, and always that unspoken memory, the dive at Sitter's Point, the moment of blackness. The bond.

And they had gone back once again to Sitter's Point after their sophomore year in college, that summer eight years later when Payne was working as a lifeguard at New Canaan Country Club. It was Glen Morrow's birthday, and it was breathless and hot, and they had bought a couple of six-packs and found themselves on the back roads near the Pound Ridge Reservation. Litchfield was driving his father's new Cadillac. Morrow was beside him, with his elbow hanging out the window, smoking endless Marlboros. The radio was playing The Temptations and all the windows were open so that the wind tugged at their hair. Payne and Avery and Demarest were in the backseat singing with the radio, craning their necks for the access road, looking for the hemlock by the stone.

It was well past three in the afternoon when they finally parked and made it out to Sitter's Point. Morrow carried a kite his mother had just sent him from Nepal. They climbed up onto the warm stones by the edge, above the great pool. They were laughing and drinking, and Morrow unfurled the kite, and it took off with a great whoosh and sailed off far above the evergreens, across the slate green reservoir. And he had suddenly let go, and it had climbed a little higher for a second, before the crush of gravity had made it stumble, stop and fall, until it pierced the surface of the reservoir, crimson and gold. Morrow had just laughed, just laughed and laughed, and turned to them and said, "I have a present for you too."

"But it's *your* birthday," Demarest had said.

"Well, it's a present for all of us," said Morrow. "And besides, I'm fed up hearing you guys bellyache about the frat all the time. Ever since spring."

"What is it?"

"We'll be going back to Hadley soon for junior year, so I asked my father, and he told me I can rent this house I found on the road to Somerville, just south of Hadley. It's got four bedrooms, and each one's got a fireplace. What do you say, guys? What kind of a club are we if we don't have a clubhouse?"

"Off campus?" Litchfield said. Bobby was packing his glasses in his leather case, wrapping them up in his cotton shirt.

"We were friends long before we joined T.U. To hell with the frat." Morrow's smile flashed.

"I don't know if my parents will let me live off campus." Litchfield shook his head.

"Don't be an asshole, you don't have to come. Do us a favor, BB," Demarest said.

"What's it look like, Glen?" said Avery.

"It's that great big yellow house by the trout stream we fished this spring, a mile past Amherst Orchards. We can only have it for a year, though, and it isn't cheap."

"Man, that's great," said Avery. "You're right, Glen. To hell with Theta U. They were a bunch of jerks anyway. I always said so."

Morrow smiled and pulled his T-shirt over his head, and tossed it to the ground. He stripped off his jeans and underwear, revealing the well-toned body underneath, the lean cuts of his naked muscles, the almost hairless chest, the powerful shoulders. Then he turned and stepped up to the edge. "Last one in gets beer."

"You want to dive off here?" said Payne. He looked around. Everyone else was pulling off their clothes. Morrow balanced on the edge. Demarest was still struggling with his socks. Avery was doing his swimmer's stretching exercises, showing off. Even Litchfield teetered on the gray lip of the granite bluff, pasty white and overweight, trying to cover up his naked body with his hands.

"What's the matter, John?" said Litchfield.

"Nothing."

"You look like you've seen a ghost."

"I said it's nothing."

But Morrow had seen it in his eyes, had come on over, saying, "Leave him alone. If he wants to dive off somewhere else . . ."

"I'm fine," said Payne. "I'm a better diver than any one of you jerks. Ask Rick."

"Let's all jump off together," Morrow had said.

"I said I'll be okay. Why do you always have to make everything into such a big deal?"

"Because it is a big deal." And Morrow had taken him by the hand and said, "I'm not going to let anything happen to you."

"You're drunk, Glen. Jesus Christ! How many beers have you had?"

"I'm not drunk. We don't need the frat, John. We've got our

own frat, don't we? We've got The Club," he said. "Come on, you guys. It's my birthday." And Demarest and Avery and Litchfield staggered forward, linking their hands with his, their fingers intertwining.

"Let's make a new pledge, just like at Theta U., but to each other this time, instead of to some stupid frat. To The Club," said Morrow.

"The Club," they all said, all together.

"Are you ready?" Morrow stared across the reservoir, his eyes focusing on something indistinct and distant.

"I don't know, Glen," Payne said.

"It's okay, John. Trust me."

And they had spread out in a line, a human chain along the granite bluff. And they had started running, to gather speed, to scream together in a great balloon of sound as they had rushed out through the emptiness, and they had fallen, fallen, linked against the bright blue sky, into the cold green waters of the reservoir.

Payne turns the ship to starboard and cuts across the promenade to Harlem. The sun is rising. The world is waking up. He flicks the switch and says, "Traffic is light on the Henry Hudson. Twenty- to thirty-minute delays inbound on the GW Bridge due to a stalled tractor trailer on the upper span . . ." *And they've pulled the body of a young black hooker from the Hudson River.* ". . . John Payne, High-Way Four, reporting."

Can they tell, through all those countless car and office radios and Walkmans? Can they hear the difference? What does the voice of a murderer sound like?

That evening, Payne sits in his study alone, watching the local news on TV. There is nothing about Candy. He flicks to another station with his remote. A toddler shot down by stray bullets in the Bronx. A fire in Jersey City. The weather looks like snow. He flicks to another station and the phone rings by his elbow. Payne stares down at the receiver on the table. It rings again. He could rip it from the wall, he speculates, in less than five seconds, and hurl it across the room into the television. It would implode with a blinding light. Glass would fly across the bookshelves, across the carpeting, the pale blue vase his great-grandfather had brought back from Japan. There would be a great noise. . . .

"It's for you," shouts Jan.

He looks up. Jan is standing in the kitchen, the telephone receiver in her hand.

Payne shakes his head.

She says something, hesitates, and puts the phone down on the counter. Then she moves heavily toward the study, toward him, saying, "John, I'm getting sick and tired of this. He's just going to keep on calling 'til you talk to him. What's going on between you, anyway?"

"Nothing."

"I'm not blind, John. I've got a right to know." She stops inside the door. "Are you listening to me?"

"I'm listening."

"Then answer me. If you guys had a fight, I wish you'd just come out and say it. Don't keep me in suspense. Just settle it, will you? I'm fed up being the go-between."

He puts the news on mute. He turns and takes her in—the black stretch leggings, the sweatshirt from Belize.

"What's wrong?" she asks, softening. She leans against the chair, reaches out to stroke his hair. "How can I help you if you won't even let me in?"

He glances up, but he's afraid to meet her eyes, terrified of what she'll see. Instead, he turns and picks up the receiver. He brings it to his ear.

"John? John, is that you?"

"It's me."

"You sound terrible. I've been trying to reach you all day," says Morrow. "Why didn't you take my calls?"

"I was busy."

"It gets easier, doesn't it?"

"What does?"

"Lying. The more you do it, the easier it gets."

"You should know, Glen. You do it for a living."

"Look, John, let's not quarrel. Let's try to stick together."

"They found one, Glen."

There is a silence. Then Morrow says, "What did you say?"

"You heard me."

"I don't know what you mean. You're not yourself, John. You shouldn't be talking with Jan there. You should be lying down, taking it easy."

"I saw it with my own eyes."

"John, why don't you get some rest and I'll come by this evening. We can go out, talk things over in person. You know what I mean? In person. Bobby, too."

"I'm not interested."

"Club night out, John."

"Jesus Christ, Glen. You don't get it, do you? I'm not interested. It's over. Finished."

"You don't mean that, John. You're just upset."

"I mean it, Glen. I've had it. I'm hanging up now, okay? I'm sorry. Don't call me anymore. Don't have Bobby call me. I'm sorry, Glen. Good-bye." Payne hangs up. He looks back at the television. He turns the sound on with the hand remote.

Jan settles on the ottoman before him. She leans forward, trying to block his view, but he just tips the other way. Finally she sighs and says, "Now you're not going to talk to *me?*"

He doesn't answer.

"John, you haven't slept in three days. You're not eating. You look like a wreck. You're arguing with your friends."

"They're not my friends."

"Well, they were your friends. What's gotten into you? It's another one of Glen's stock tips, isn't it? I know it is. Betsy says it's illegal. And it's my money, too. It's *our* money."

"It's nothing like that."

"Then what is it? What have I done?"

"It's nothing you've done. It's got nothing to do with you."

Jan takes him by the hand. Payne does not pull away. He simply sits there. He has no energy. Jan reaches for his face. He looks at her for a moment, and feels enkindled by her eyes. They stare right through him. She kisses him. She leans against his chest. *"Wha's the matter, baby?"*

He starts. "What did you say?" He pushes her away.

"I said, what's the matter?"

"Nothing's the matter."

"John, talk to me—"

"I've got nothing to say."

Suddenly she's gone. She's on her feet. "Fine, be that way. Don't talk to me." She shakes her head and says, "I just don't understand you anymore. What do you want from me, John? What? One minute you complain we're not intimate anymore, we never kiss. Then, when I try and comfort you, all you do is push me away. Well, how do you think I feel?" She storms over to the television, slaps it, missing the controls, slaps it again. The screen goes blank.

"Look at me, John. I look like a God damn whale. How do you think I feel?"

"Stop it, Jan."

"No, why don't *you* stop it? Why don't you say no to Glen, just once, just this one time, and really mean it! You always say you're going to. You always say that you don't need The Club, that you've grown out of it, but in the end you always go back to them. It's like you can't live without each other, like you're not a full person without them."

"Stop it, I said. I'm not seeing them anymore, all right? It's over. The Hunting Club is finished."

"That's what you said when Sam died. When they called him a fool—just for dying! But that wasn't enough, was it, John? Nothing is ever enough."

"Keep Sam out of this."

"Oh, right. God forbid anyone says anything bad about Sam. Except Glen, of course. Glen can say anything."

Payne stands. "You've never liked Glen. Right from the start. Why? What happened between you two?"

"Let's not pick at that old scab. He just doesn't like to hear no."

"You don't know him like I do. He's like my brother, Jan. Do you think this is easy for me?" He turns away. "I remember when Sam died, and I was working at the Bridgeport Airport. Long before I met you. Glen came over to my house. My mother had called him. I had been in my room for more than a week, not eating, not sleeping. Just playing records over and over, looking at photographs, reading Sam's old letters to me, looking at that damn gun. I was numb. The earth could have opened up before me, could have torn the house in half and left me hanging there and I wouldn't have cared. And then Glen came by. He didn't say much. He just kind of hung around. Then he urged me to go out. To see the stars during a special configuration, an interstice, because he knew I liked astronomy. To take a walk, to fish, to hike. It was never anything he said. He knew better than to talk about it, about Sam, I mean. But somehow he made me feel like I mattered, perhaps now more than ever. That it wasn't my fault for surviving. That I didn't have to always compare myself to Sam. Especially now that he was dead, because now, now I could never beat him. And the way Glen talked, the way he made me feel . . . I don't know, Jan. Don't you see it? Don't you sense it when you're with him? He's like a mirror. He holds himself against you, and somehow you can see everything that's best in you, and all you could become."

"Listen to you. Just *listen!* You'll never change, John. You don't care about me. All you care about is your precious Hunting Club." Her voice is thin with anger. She crosses her arms.

He reaches out and takes her by the wrists, pulling her arms away from her swollen belly. "I told you I'm not seeing them anymore . . ."

"Don't lie to me. Let go." She tries to wriggle free but he grips her even tighter. "Let go," she cries. "You're hurting me, John."

"Jan, you've got to believe me. Please believe me. Please!"

She pulls one hand free, shrieking, "Get away from me. Get off me. *Take it easy, will ya?*"

He pushes her away, without even thinking, without even watching as she stumbles backward on the rug and slams against the wall. There is a sickening crack as her head strikes the wall. Her eyes grow wide with fear.

"You're crazy, John," she says. She starts to rub the back side of her head. "You really hurt me." Her eyes begin to tear.

He rushes toward her. "I'm sorry, Jan," he cries, but she holds him back.

"What's gotten into you lately? The way you can just turn off like that. It scares me, John. Sometimes I think you're capable of doing anything."

"I didn't mean it."

"I wish I wasn't pregnant. God help me, but I do."

"Don't say that, Jan."

"But I do. Look at us. It's not even born, and we barely get along. All we do is fight. I'm fed up with fighting. I'm tired of it, John. I'm tired of everything."

"Please don't say that, Jan. . . ."

"You don't love me. Maybe you never did. We should never have had this baby. You were jealous of it the minute I got pregnant."

"That isn't true."

"Yes, it is. Go on, admit it. You don't have to be jealous. You're not the younger brother this time."

"What are you talking about?"

"What am I talking about? Oh, God! *That's* what I'm talking about!" She turns her chin up, and he sees her eyes are filled with tears. "You never have any idea what I'm talking about. I didn't follow you to Nowhere, Pennsylvania, or put up with that stupid cable job for this. I want more for my baby." The tears spill from her eyes. "This is the only club I want you to belong to, John. Me and the baby. This club! Is that so wrong? Is that so much to ask?"

Payne takes her in his arms. He feels her breath on his face. Her eyes glimmer in the light, like molten glass, glistening with tears, and his heart creases. He takes her face between his hands and kisses her, once, twice, hard on the lips.

"I'm sorry," he whispers. He closes his eyes. He hugs her tightly. "You're right, I've been a fool. You're the only thing that matters now. You and the baby. You're all that's left." He buries his face in her hair. "Please don't cry, Jan. Please. I'll take care of it. I promise. Whatever it takes," he says, opening his eyes. "Whatever it takes, I'll do it."

Detective Capozzi stands in the elevator, holding a bouquet of orange tulips wrapped in cellophane, trying hard not to stare at the

Chinese nurse by his side. He stares and she stares back, and smiles, and he tries smiling too but it comes off all wrong, a kind of leer, and she just turns and looks up at the numbers flashing, past geriatrics and oncology. Five, six, seven, and he remembers Jack Wells sitting in the cruiser, smiling through the window, just smiling as the police car drives away.

It had all started two weeks earlier with a Mrs. Mary Wells of Chelsea, who—according to a neighbor—had gone to church one Sunday in her usual way, and then simply disappeared. At first the suspicions seemed too ripe, but after a time Capozzi found himself believing her—this woman in her fifties, fidgeting with her cheap purse, afraid to look at him, but honest, simply terrified at what might have happened to her neighbor. She knew more than she said, that was for sure, so he and his partner Harry Golden had gone downtown to meet the missing woman's husband, a tall good-looking man with dark brown hair in his early forties named Jack Wells.

Wells owned a local fish wholesaler on Ninth Avenue and Eighteenth Street. He seemed genuinely worried by his wife's sudden disappearance. Mary had been having an affair, he suspected, for some time now. No, he didn't know the man. His wife denied it, and he'd never been able to prove or disprove his suspicions. Yes, Mary had taken her makeup and jewelry.

The way he casually revealed his fears set Capozzi on edge. He was too glib, to easy with his feelings. After ten minutes, Wells excused himself. He had to get some sleep, he told them, he had to get up early. So they'd gone downstairs and waited in Capozzi's battered gold Dodge Aries, and sure enough, a half hour later there he was, Jack Wells all right, but now a different Wells, wearing a business suit and coat, a different walk even, flagging a cab and away. They followed him to SoHo, where he got out in front of a seven-story flatiron building on Wooster Street, home to a Ms. Faith Kurrus, herbalist, part-time hair stylist, full-time mistress.

It took them the better part of nine days, steady watching, to finally pin him down, to find the hotel, the desk clerk, and the store where he had bought the trunk and nylon rope. Mary Wells had never made it to the church that Sunday, not once in fact during the past two years. Instead, she had checked in to a small hotel near Bleeker Street and Hudson every week, where she had met the same dark man in his late thirties, *'con ojos como esmeraldas,'* the Honduran maid had said. *With eyes like emeralds.* What they did in that room for three hours was anybody's guess, but it wasn't your average siesta. The manager complained of damage to the bed, deep cuts and scrapes, like the marks of chains or handcuffs—the work of eels.

The green eyes, it turned out, were nonprescription contact lenses, spotted by Golden in the medicine cabinet of the Wells bathroom during an unannounced call. For the last two years, Mary Wells had indeed been having an affair . . . with her own husband, or at least another side of him, the man whom he became when he dressed up and rendezvoused with her at that hotel in the Village every week. But that specific Sunday things got out of hand. Somehow or other—they would never know exactly why—the masquerade had gone awry, and Mary Wells had been garroted with a yard of steel barbed wire. The rest the desk clerk had revealed during a grisly night of questioning, the sawing of the limbs, the plastic bags, the fish parts stuffed inside the trunk around her. The clerk had been more than happy to get it off his chest, as they reviewed his emigration papers from Tobago, but when they went to pick up Wells at work, an employee delayed them long enough for Wells to disappear into the storage rooms beneath the fish wholesaler . . . a maze of cold dark corridors, a turn, and Harry stumbled to the stinking floor, cursing the wind out of his chest, a great curved hook of stainless steel curled right around his shoulder blade, stained crimson with a sudden spurt of blood. Wells just gave up after that, unable to face Capozzi's gun, and smiled as they ducked his head and stuffed him in the back seat of the cruiser, his bright teeth grinning out the window as they drove away, more grease for the machine.

There is the bell, the elevator door swings open, the Chinese nurse looks back at him and exits. Fourth floor—this is it. Capozzi steps out right behind her. "Can I help you," she says, turning. Her uniform is bright white and seems to crackle as she moves.

"Yeah, thanks." He looks down at the piece of paper in his hand. "Room four fifty-six. Recovery."

"Harry Golden?"

"That's right."

"Come on, I'll show you. He's my patient."

He follows her down the hall, through a set of swinging doors to room 456. Golden is watching television, a rerun of *Star Trek*. Captain Kirk is being chased by Klingons.

"Look at this," says Capozzi, storming in. "Lying on his butt, watching TV. Paid vacation. That's all it is."

Golden grins. "Tony!" he says. "What's happenin'?" He appears thinner in the light blue hospital gown. His short red hair sticks up at the back. His mustache needs a trim.

"I'm fine, you lazy bastard." Capozzi shakes his hand. The grip is weak, and Golden winces as he lies back on his pillow.

"Amy, I want you to meet my partner," Golden says. "Amy Choo, Anthony Capozzi. Amy's been taking care of me."

The nurse turns and shakes his hand. "Pleased to meet you," Capozzi says.

"Look out, Tony, she's got a boyfriend. And he's got a real job too, an intern. And he's handsome."

"I'd be surprised if she didn't."

Nurse Choo smiles. "He's not my boyfriend. He's just a friend." She looks up at Capozzi for a moment more, then moves away. "And he's not that handsome. See you later, Captain Golden." And then she's gone, her white shoes squeaking.

Capozzi says, "Captain Golden? Captain, did she say?"

"Who am I to correct her? She tries so hard."

"So, how you feeling . . . Captain?"

"I feel fine. 'Til you came, anyway. What are we working on?"

Capozzi suddenly remembers the flowers. He thrusts them forward. "What should I do with these guys?"

"For me? I'm touched," Golden says sarcastically. He points to a tall white ceramic vase stuffed with fading daisies on the table near the window.

"Aren't these the ones I brought last week?"

"I guess so."

The words cut through Capozzi. Had he been the only visitor all week? The only one? He looks through the window at the red lights of the passing cars below, the snow-dusted rooftops of the Village, draped here and there with cables, the fire escapes, the water towers, the jumble of antennae.

The flowers crumble in his hands. He picks up the vase and dumps the dying blossoms into the garbage can in the bathroom. Then he carefully fills the vase with water.

"So what's our case?" shouts Golden as the faucet runs. "Now that Herr Wells is housebound."

"Your case is to stay in bed until you're better."

"Come on, Tony. It was just a little cut. He caught me by surprise."

Capozzi carries the vase back to the table in the outer room. He slips the cellophane off the tulips and places them one by one into the vase. "He caught *us* by surprise, Harry. Both of us."

"It wasn't your fault, Tony."

"And you lost a lot of blood. You split your shoulder bone. You've got to give yourself time to heal."

"I've been here a whole fucking week. I've got to get out of here. I'm serious, Tony, I'm going stir crazy. Just like Errol. How is Errol, anyway?"

"He's fine."

"Are you walking him enough? I told you, he needs a lot of exercise. Irish terriers were bred for the country, not for this fucking cesspool. I knew I should have found a kennel. I knew it."

"I told you—he's fine. He's not what I'm worried about."

"Then what's our case, Tony? Come on. How else am I going to feel better?"

"Will you shut up if I tell you? Will you promise to get some rest?"

"I'll shut up."

Capozzi sets the orange tulips at the center of the table.

"You should have been a florist, Tony. You've got the gift."

"Fuck you, Golden."

"The case?"

"All right, all right," Capozzi says. He sits down on the end of the bed. He unbuttons his coat. "A floater wrapped herself 'round the Twenty-ninth Street pier, near the Hudson Cement Company early Sunday morning. Pretty sight. Took three slugs at close range. One in the head, two more in the lungs. Nine-millimeter, soft-nosed, too. Entered the skull above her left ear and took the jaw away. Turns out to be a hooker named Carolynn, a.k.a. Candy Simms. Clocked for a pimp named Tommy Albert."

"Bumper Albert. I know him."

"You knew him, probably. Hasn't been seen since Sunday night. Odds are he did Candy and split town, or maybe somebody did him. Hard to tell. Forensics found two blood types in the Hudson parking lot. They think a guy got wacked outside the trailers, and the girl inside, on the counter near the kitchen sink. They found a bullet in the drain. Must have ricocheted off her jaw and washed down when they tried to clean up afterward. She had the semen of two different men inside her. Coroner thinks the shock of being shot may have kind of locked the come inside her. The sample didn't get corrupted by the river. There were traces of cocaine in her blood."

Golden sits up, nursing his right shoulder. "I knew it. I knew it," he says. "Bumper's been dealing coke out of the Party Girl Lounge for years. He's connected. I'm tellin' you, check out his sheet."

"I did."

"Yeah, of course you did." Golden stretches his shoulder. His face glows with relief. "Maybe he got greedy, tried to muscle in. Maybe the family didn't like that."

"What about Candy?"

"She was there. She was a witness."

"And the come?"

"She was entertainment, Tony. Bumper and his friend fucked her for a while. Thanks for the lay, and by the way, you're dead. Bang!"

"Without a raincoat? I doubt it." Capozzi frowns.

"Got a better idea?"

Capozzi shakes his head. "Nope," he says. He ambles over to the window. "Not yet, at least. But it doesn't feel like a hit. It isn't signature." He looks at Golden in the bed, his red hair fluffed against the pillow. "Maybe worth a trip down to the lounge, though, if only for the view."

"You dirty old man."

"Eat your heart out, Harry."

"Go walk my dog."

"Yeah, yeah." Capozzi starts for the door, then stops and turns to speak, but the words are caught up by his partner's stare, his smile.

"What is it?" Golden says.

Capozzi starts to answer, stops.

"It wasn't your fault, Tony."

Capozzi hesitates, then says, "I should have been there, Harry. That's my job. I'm supposed to be there for you. You almost died, and they gave me a fucking commendation."

"I'm tellin' you, it wasn't your fault. Ever since this thing with your uncle, you've been drivin' yourself crazy. Ease up on yourself, Tony. You don't have to prove nothin' to me. Nobody blames you for what your uncle did. You saved my life, Tony. That's what partners do for each other. You stopped me from bleeding to death. And you caught the fucker, didn't you? That's what counts."

"Yeah, I caught him." Capozzi shakes his head. "And he just sat there grinning at me as they drove away."

"Don't worry about it, man. They'll lock his ass up for good soon enough, I'm tellin' you. I've been practicing. Listen: *The seven-and-one-half-inch baling hook entered my right shoulder through the back, Your Honor, when I wasn't looking, when I was turned the other way, splitting the bone and causing massive pain and bleeding. And that's the man who did it, Your Honor. I saw him. I swear, on my mother's grave.* What do you think? Pretty good, huh?"

Capozzi leans against the door. He smiles and says, "I think I'm going to be sick. Where's Nurse Choo?"

"I hate your guts, Capozzi. You keep your hands off my nurse, I'm warnin' you."

"Good-bye, Captain Golden."

"Good-bye, Antonio. And be careful. Without me around, everybody's going to figure out what a fraud you really are, a puppet without strings, a straw man for the mighty Golden. You hear me?"

But the door is closing and Capozzi is already gone.

XIV

Payne wakes automatically, starting in his easy chair. Pitch black, the house is still, the study is completely quiet. The silence weighs upon him, black and cold, weighs on his neck and chest so that he cannot move. There is something out there in the dark, in the great meadow beyond the house. He cannot see it, but he knows it's there. He can feel it twitching its tail. It has been another night of broken sleep, of nightmares. Somewhere, in the distance, in another yard, he can hear a dog howl. He looks down at his watch. It's four A.M. He wipes his eyes. Time to get up and shower. Time to face another day.

An hour later he is standing in the kitchen, eating a bowl of raisin bran, listening to the news on his old transistor radio. This was how he had first heard about the Tonkin resolution, the mining of Haiphong Harbor, the offensive near Da Nang in which his brother had been killed . . . waiting for the school bus in the kitchen with Mrs. Hathaway and his mother, watching her wait and wait until there were no more hopes to cling to, no more telegrams and letters, no more phone calls to Washington, D.C. And Jan was right: They had called Sam a fool—Bobby Litchfield and Tom Demarest—just for dying, just for doing what he thought was his duty. And Payne felt lost for months. What was the point if it could end so quickly, and so much without purpose? His father gardened. His mother wept. Payne used to hear her in her dressing room at night, but no one could give her any comfort. Her son was dead, she kept on saying, as if Payne belonged to someone else. He was just a reminder of her loss, a survivor in an unjust world, an accomplice almost.

". . . Hudson River early this morning. The body was found by a passing jogger who reported it to police."

Payne freezes. He puts his bowl down on the counter and turns up the volume on the radio.

"The victim was identified as Michelle Powell of the Bronx, a prostitute who was known to work in the vicinity of the Jacob Javits Convention Center in Manhattan. She was twenty-one years old."

For a moment Payne feels relieved, then guilty for the feeling. For a moment only, until he hears, "Police speculate Powell may have been the victim of the same killer responsible for another fatal shooting of a prostitute which occurred early Sunday morning near the Twenty-ninth Street pier. According to Captain Peter Hollings of the Thirteenth Precinct, both victims were shot at point-blank range with a nine-millimeter handgun, and then dumped into the near-freezing waters of the Hudson River. Anyone with information about either of the killings is urged to contact the Thirteenth Precinct Homicide Division. And the New Jersey Devils win their third game . . ."

Payne stands there very quietly for the next few minutes. The sound of the announcer fades. His head feels light, as if he's climbing fast, like the moment of transitional lift, and he is through the clouds, into the white light and the blue. What was it Glen had said? "Club night out, John. . . . You know what I mean? Bobby, too."

He looks over at the pale green digits glowing in the microwave. 5:05. It's getting late. There might be traffic, he thinks, trying to fill his head, trying to find the right distracting words to keep him from the speculation. *Club night out.* And then another girl had died. Or was it just coincidence? Is he imagining things? Payne hugs himself. He leans forward over the sink. He feels the nausea rushing through him but he isn't sick. He can't be. He turns the tap on, splashes water on his face. He looks up at the window. There is a face, reflected in the glass, but for a moment it is not his face. He shakes the water from his eyes. His brother's eyes stare back, his brother's chin, and then the steam clears and he sees his own familiar outline in the glass, pale as a new moon in the winter sky.

The drive to Teterboro Airport is somehow reassuring, familiar as it is after all these years. He knows each turn, each blind spot, exactly when to change lanes to avoid the slowest cars. It takes him less than an hour to reach the gate. He is the first to arrive. The pilots' lounge is empty.

Payne suits up in the dressing room, checks the weather, and makes his way along the corridor to the hangar. It is a cold clear morning, straight from Canada. He flicks the hangar lights on and the ships flash into view. Three blue Bell helicopters. A six-seat corporate jet. He can hear the heaters bellowing above.

The tug is a little cranky this morning, but after a moment's hesitation he glides her over to the dolly carrying the Bell 206 traffic helicopter. It takes him almost twenty minutes to check the helicopter—from Jesus nut to sleds. When he's finished, he opens the outer hangar door. An icy wind whistles through the opening. Payne flips the collar of his jacket up and slips into the tug. The sky is glowing to the east. It is New York, and not the sun, that lights the world up at this hour. The air is so clear that he can almost feel the electricity, the humming of a hundred million light bulbs, the pulsing neon, the klieg lights stabbing at the sky. The tug slows to a stop. Payne gets off and walks back to the hangar door. He slips the key into the lock. The door begins to close, and it occurs to him as it groans shut that even now he is concerned about the commonest of courtesies. Cracker would freeze his butt off if he left it open. After three murders, he's worried about being rude. He laughs quietly, pulls a cigarette from his jacket, and lights up. The smoke tastes acrid and delicious, warming the arctic air, making the blood pump through his head. Payne looks up at the sky. The sun is beginning to rise. It is getting lighter by the second. Somewhere a marsh bird sounds a lonely cry. He can see cattails leaning in the dawn, far across the runway to the east. Club night out. The marsh bird cries again. Time to go hunting.

Payne takes another drag. He drops the cigarette to the ground and grinds it under his heel. Then he walks over to the dolly and climbs into the helicopter.

It feels even colder in the confines of the cabin.

This is where she lay in her bloody garment bag.

He settles an icy headset on his head and plugs the cord into the overhead console. Then he straps his seat belt on. Next he checks the switches by his foot. He tests the radio. Everything works. Everything's in place. He punches the ignitor. He checks the pedals underneath his feet, the cyclic and collective sticks. He turns the throttle, pulls the trigger, and the electric motor whines. The turbine catches as the rotors spin. *Thump. Thump. Thump.* He sees a shape, the left door opens, and Morrow swings into the other seat. A cold wind rushes in behind him.

"What are you doing here?"

Morrow doesn't answer. He is already slipping on the belt and headset. He plugs into the console. Then he turns toward Payne and gives him the thumbs up.

"What the hell are you doing here?" says Payne.

"We've got to talk."

"I've got nothing to say to you."

"Maybe not. But I've got something to say to you."

"Get out of here, Glen."

"Not until we've talked."

Payne pushes Morrow up against the door. "I said, get out!"

Morrow simply slaps Payne's hand away. "You'd better take off, or you're going to be late for your broadcast, John. And you know how you hate to be late."

"Get out, I said." Payne pushes Morrow more violently. "Get the fuck out."

Morrow pushes back. "You're wasting fuel."

"Fuck you!" Payne punches Morrow on the arm. "Fuck you!" he says, and punches him again, harder. "This is my ship, Glen, and I told you to get out." And then Payne sees the gun. He hesitates, pulls back. His eyes grow wide. Morrow is pointing it at his heart. They are both breathing heavily. Payne looks up at Morrow's face. He is smiling tightly. His golden hair is out of place. There is a mottled patch of skin on his neck above the collar, a triangle of light pink flesh.

"Go on," says Morrow.

Payne slips his hand back on the cyclic stick.

"Go on," says Morrow once again. "Take it." He turns the gun around, offering the butt to Payne. "What's the matter, John? Isn't that what you want? Go ahead, shoot me." He jabs the butt into Payne's ribs. "Because that's the only way I'm getting out of here until we talk."

Payne looks back at the gun. Morrow's gloved hand is wrapped around the barrel. The butt is lean and black, cold as an adder. Then it is gone, a small bulge underneath his sweater.

"All right," says Payne. "But this is the last time, Glen. Do you understand? The last time."

He adjusts his headset. He requests clearance from the tower. He checks the rotor with the cyclic stick, pulls the collective, and the helicopter rises off the dolly.

Payne hovers for a few more seconds, checking the gauges one more time before nosing the cyclic forward. He twists the throttle slowly as the helicopter moves across the runway, picking up speed, faster and faster until they hit transitional lift and rise and climb into a rush of morning light.

They sweep south across the wetlands, across the turnpike to the river. The Hudson spills out far into the bay, a thousand miles of silt and muck and jetsam, the history of a hundred years from Saratoga to the sea. Below, they can see Liberty, the beacon glaring, no longer bearing a message of hope to Payne, but one simply of irony—or worse, like Tantalus, of vain desire, to be forced to fly so close each day. Not now, he thinks. I will never be free again.

The ship skims east across the bay, past Bensonhurst, still dressed in Christmas decorations, past Gravesend Bay to Coney Island. There's the aquarium, the giant tanks, the white beluga whales still swimming round and round, only a few feet from the open sea. "Say what you came to say," says Payne. "I'll put you down on Twenty-sixth Street, after my morning run."

"Thanks."

"Don't thank me. I don't want your thanks."

"Then you won't have them, John. Believe me."

Payne turns and looks at Morrow. His face is dark and menacing, his eyes mere slits under his headset, his mouth pinched tight. Payne has never seen him look so angry, and he feels the power of his own resentment turn to fear.

Thump. Thump. "Listen, I don't—"

"Just be quiet for a minute, John. Don't say anything. Not a word. Nothing. We've all had it with you, John. You got us into this. Like it or not, you killed that girl. And don't give me any of that shit about an accident. You've been holding that anger up inside you for a long, long time. She just set it off. You killed her, and then you dragged us all in there with you, into your own private hell. You're responsible for this. You're the one who made us who we are. Yes, murderers. Say it, go on. Admit it. You're the one who was covered in blood, and now, when it starts to sting a little, when the going gets tough, you turn on us. Your friends. The ones who backed you up. The ones who risked their lives to try and cover for you. Well, John, if you think it's hard to look at yourself in the mirror, think what it's like for us. Look at what we've had to do. Because of you, John. Because of *you.*"

"You didn't have to kill anybody. They weren't going to go to the police."

"They didn't have to, you fucking idiot. They could have simply called it in—a tip, an anonymous lead. How long do you think Tom will stand up under questioning? Or Bobby? How long before they crack? Look at you. You're already cracking, and no one's even talked to you. You selfish bastard. I *had* to kill them. You forced me to. It was that or go to jail. Is that what you wanted? Is that it? You gave me no choice. None of us would even be here if it weren't for you, John. And you've got the nerve to judge me. Me! After everything I've done. For you, John. For you and The Hunting Club."

"And for yourself."

"Yes. And for myself. It's time you started thinking about *your*self, about your family, your—"

"Don't drag Jan into this. Just keep her out of it."

"If only that were possible."

"What does that mean? Is that a threat? If you lay a hand on her, Glen, I swear, if you lay one finger on her, I'll kill you."

Morrow smiles. "Yes, I'm sure you could. And that's what's bothering you, isn't it? Well, don't blame me for making you see who you really are, John. That's my gift. Some people can play the piano." He shakes his golden head, and says, "We're all capable of murder, John. We all carry the mark. Look at Sam. And you, John.

We're all murderers in our hearts. You taught me that. You proved that to me the night you started this whole thing. Last Wednesday. My God, is that all that it's been? Less than a week! It seems like a lifetime ago. And you know what? It is."

"What do you mean?"

"You know what I mean. Yolanda's dead. You killed her. So are Bumper and Candy. There's only one person left who knows what you did to Yolanda."

"What are you saying? The other stripper?"

"That's right, John. Susan. Candy's friend. The last one. The only one left."

"You're crazy—"

"You started this. It's up to you to finish it."

"You want me to kill her, is that it? Is that what you came here to tell me? You're really insane, Glen, you know that?"

"Listen to me, John. Listen to me carefully, because I'm only going to say this once. We don't have any choice. It's that simple. If you don't take care of her, we're all going to jail. Is that what you want? You're responsible for this, John. When are you going to stop being everyone's younger brother? First it was Sam, then me. When are you going to start taking responsibility for yourself, John, for your own actions? You dragged us into this. You finish it. Then things can go back to normal."

"Normal! That's really funny, Glen. You think it can ever be normal again? You make it sound like I have some kind of moral responsibility to protect The Hunting Club. Protect what? A gang of murderers!" Payne nods his head at the city below, the hundred million light bulbs glowing. "Look around you, man. We're the outsiders now. We're the aberration. We stepped across the line. We don't belong anymore, can't you feel it?"

"Belong to what—the teeming masses, the Myrmidons? Are they more important than Jan?" says Morrow. "Is that what you think? More important than your baby? How will it serve society, your friends, your family, if you punish yourself, if you let yourself be locked away? Is that the kind of father you want to be, John?"

"Shut up."

"You want to leave Jan a widow, is that it? No, worse than a widow, because you won't be dead. It'll just seem that way. Year after year, as she comes to visit you in prison, trying to get by on her salary. Just like before, after you lost your job at the cable company."

"My parents will help."

"Oh, sure. I'm sure they'll be so proud. *How are the children, Aggie?* The dead war hero and the murderer."

Payne pushes the collective and the helicopter veers away. The city angles crazily beneath them. He drives the ship out to sea.

"And for what, John? For a couple of lousy hookers? Because of an accident. You're going to give up everything. Is that what Jan deserves? Is that what your baby deserves? What kind of life will he have? *Look, there's that Payne kid. They say his father's in jail for murder. Killed the hooker he was humping.* Is that what you want, John?"

The sky is growing light. The sun is shining on the water, a pearl gray pink. It calls to him.

"Is that what you really want? I don't think so. You owe me, John. Remember Sitter's Point. I think you know what you have to do. If not for us, if not for me or for yourself, then for Jan. For your baby, John."

"I can't," says Payne. The words choke in his throat. "I can't."

"Yes, you can, John. You can because you have to."

"I can't," he says. He feels Morrow slap his face.

"Yes, you can, John. You know you can. You've done it before." Morrow slaps him again.

"I'm telling you, I can't, Glen."

Morrow grabs Payne by the hand. He wrestles for the controls, the collective dips, the helicopter plummets. "What are you doing?" screams Payne. He pushes Morrow with his shoulder. "Let go."

"No one's taking me to jail, John."

The ship begins to pick up speed. Payne can hear the rotors straining as they hurtle toward the sea. "Let go," he screams, but Morrow keeps on pressing the controls. The ship falls, the black water rushes up to meet them. "You're going to kill us, Glen." *Thump. Thump.* "Let go. We're going to crash!"

Two hundred feet, one hundred, fifty and the water roils below, glistening in the dawn, black as the pupil of an eye, when Morrow suddenly lets go, the ship pulls back, the collective and the cyclic sticks recoil. The skids cut through the whitecaps, catch, cut, rise up as water splashes on the Plexiglas. Payne yanks on the controls and the engine roars. The helicopter kicks and rises, bucks, then begins to climb. Payne's heart pounds in his ears. Sweat trickles down his neck. The helicopter screams. It climbs and climbs and soon the engine's roar returns to normal, the cabin levels off, the waves crawl toward the distant shore.

"You see, John," Morrow says. His voice is low and even. "I told you. Everyone's equipped with an overriding drive to survive. It's part of the genetic makeup. Even you, John." He reaches under his sweater. He takes out the shiny black gun. "That's why you're going to take care of her. For me and the rest of The Hunting Club. For Jan and the baby. And for you, John. For you." He holds the gun out in his hand. "Besides," he says. "Isn't it easier to kill the second time around, now that you know you're a murderer?"

Payne looks down at the gun. It is elegant and compact. It is beautiful. It is perfect. He looks back up at Morrow's face. Then he nods, and smiles and says, "All right, Glen. All right, you win. You always do, don't you? But this is the last time. After this, we're finished. Do you hear me? Just to never see you again. All of you. Just to get there." Payne snatches the gun from his hand. "Whatever it takes, Glen, I'll do it."

Part 4

XV

The sound of gunfire ripples through the woods, the pop and pock of pistols, the boom of shotguns blasting. The noise reverberates about Blue Mountain, resounds across frost-covered clearings, frozen ponds, tapping the windows of Payne's house. The bullets fly and slash, but there is one white target still untattered at the Sportsmen's Center, still whole until a solitary spot of light appears along the upper edge. A bullet drills the earth. Another pop and yet another hole appears, a little closer to the center. Another bullet and another spot, and through the tiny aperture, a hundred yards away, another flash of light, the barrel spits and jumps and steadies as the gunman feels the clicking of his empty magazine.

Payne flicks the release, the magazine drops free, and he slides a new clip into place. He squeezes gently on the trigger. The small black gun spits flame. Expanding gasses drive, another bullet spins into the daylight with a bang.

Laura wakes with a start to the sound of a car backfiring, construction in the street, to a dull incessant pounding in her head. She pulls her pillow up over her face and groans.

"Wake up, sleepyhead," her roommate, Carol, says. "You're going to be late . . . again."

Laura simply moans. It's too warm in here, she thinks, too warm and safe and comfortable. She hugs her pillow.

"Laura, get up," says Carol. "What's gotten into you lately?"

Laura opens her eyes. She sits up with a start, reaching for her glasses on the night table by the bed, and the room falls into focus —the sagging sofa bed, the vanity, the mottled leather La-Z-Boy. "What time is it?" She licks the inside of her mouth.

"Almost nine-thirty. I thought you had a film class on Wednesdays?"

"Oh, shit," says Laura, flopping out of bed. "I forgot."

"You forgot! All week long you've been cutting classes, moping around. I swear, Laura."

"Leave me alone."

Carol is a lanky twenty-one-year-old in black tights and a Greenpeace T-shirt. She shakes her short blond bangs. "You're a real drag these days, you know that, Laura? You're going to flunk out if you keep this up. It's going to be exams soon. You used to study all night, and now look at you. We've only got a few months left."

"All right, I'm going to class, okay? I promise. Jesus Christ, Carol, you're worse than my mom."

"That's not saying much." Carol picks up her pink ski parka from the La-Z-Boy and slips it on. "Why don't you come out for dinner with Andy and me? Tonight. We can get Italian if you want."

"No, thanks," says Laura. She slips her feet into a pair of ragged wool-lined slippers and shuffles over to her vanity. She is wearing a long white cotton nightgown with a small lace collar.

"Come on, Laura. It'll do you good. Bring a date."

"I don't think so."

"Oh, come on. You can't stay locked up in here forever."

"Who would I go with, anyway?"

"Ask Brian."

"Brian's a jerk. I'm not seeing him anymore."

"What about Ben? You know he's got the hots for you."

"Ben's just a kid."

"He's older than you are."

"He doesn't act like it. Look, I just don't feel like going out, okay?"

"Well, think about it, will you?"

Laura sits down at the vanity and looks at her face in the mirror. It is worse than she expected. There are dark circles under her eyes, painfully obvious despite her large tortoiseshell glasses. Her hair is tangled. Her skin looks shiny and pale.

"Laura? Will you at least think about it? Laura, I'm talking to you."

"Okay, okay. I'll think about it."

Carol snatches her backpack from the floor. "I'll see you at lunch," she says, and starts for the apartment door.

Laura does not say good-bye. She is already far away. She does not even hear the door slam, or the key turn, or the distant echo of retreating feet. She is too busy poking at the bags beneath her eyes, too busy brushing her hair. But it is just no use. She looks like a wreck. She's barely slept in three days and it shows. As she tosses her brush back on the table, something catches her eye—there, in the top right corner of the mirror, jammed underneath the frame, that wrinkled photo of her mother, Kathleen, folded, black-and-white, beginning to slip out, beginning to open slightly, revealing the presence of another half. She pulls the photo from the frame and folds it back. There is her father. He looks so young. He's wearing his policeman's uniform. And there she is, aged six, in her cotton summer dress, his right hand resting on her shoulder, pulling her close to him, always pulling her against him, the large black shadow in the doorway. She folds the photo with her nail and jams it back between the mirror and the frame.

Her stomach feels queasy. She leans against the dressing table. The surface is covered with makeup and perfume and powder and buttons and loose change and nail files and combs. She pokes a finger through the ashtray on the far side of the table, hunting for a roach. Her fingers are shaking. There's one. She picks it up. Not much left. She lights the end of the roach with a green Bic lighter and brings it to her lips, drawing the smoke deep in her lungs. She looks at herself in the mirror, beyond the bags beneath her eyes, the shiny skin, and sees the outline of her own pale wavering form, alone and naked, dancing in a corner of the grimy room, shaking with fear and the dull rhythms of a Donna Summer disco tune before the young man at the desk.

"Who sent you?" he says, barely looking up. He has the nose of an Italian. And that dark brown wavy hair.

"Manny Fishkin. At The Kitten Club. On Forty-seventh and Third."

"I know where The Kitten Club is. How you know Manny?"

"I work there. As a bartender."

He looks up for a moment from his newspaper. He has a thin black mustache that looks, somehow, strangely unreal, and a mole on his right eyebrow. Then he smiles, barely opening his mouth, as if he is embarrassed of his teeth. "Why'd you quit?"

Laura shrugs, trying to look imperious, trying to ignore his frank appraisal of her breasts. "I didn't say I quit. I just got fed up seeing my friends get rich. I dance as good as they do."

"Okay, you're blessed. Put your blouse on." He pulls a piece of paper from a drawer in his desk. He starts to scribble on the page. "We'll call you when something comes up. What's your number?"

And she had told him, just as she'd taken off her blouse, without a moment's hesitation, without even thinking about it really, from that place inside her head where nothing ever mattered. Nothing.

Her vision clears and there she is again, the circles underneath her eyes, the messy hair. She pulls her nightgown tight around her neck, but she can't stop shivering. The roach grows smaller in her fingertips. She reaches forward to stamp it out, and accidentally knocks a bottle of nail polish over on the table. The crimson liquid spills, a dark scarlet pool, lapping her eyelash curler, thickening. Damn Carol! She'd been using her polish again. Laura tries to wipe the spill up with a tissue, trying to keep the memory at bay, seeing it come upon her from the darkness, but intentionally forgetting, until the memory congeals, the sight of Candy lifting up the mattress, the greedy smile, the unexpected horror on her face. Laura turns the tissue over, and it is all there, in her hand—the stain, leeched through the red-brown mattress, the great dark circle and the sudden understanding. Blood! Yolanda's blood. So much of it, and everywhere!

Laura pushes herself to her feet. She staggers to the bathroom and is sick.

Laura loved the movies. Everything about them. Ever since she was a little girl. The stories and the stars. The glamor. The fantasy and the escape. The physics of light which when combined with colored cells created worlds and peopled them. Sometimes she'd go to the local cinema off Prospect Park and just sit back and watch the light dance overhead, like an aurora in the smoke-filled balcony, without paying much attention to the screen, protected by the darkness and the anonymity of her surroundings, a shadow in the dark.

Laura watches the screen intently. The woman is doing a striptease. Marcello Mastroianni is observing. *The Sweet Life*, Professor Cohen had called it—*La Dolce Vita*. But it is nothing like the Italian *It's A Wonderful Life* that she had first expected it to be. Susan can dance better than that, she thinks. A hundred times better. And then she feels the stare. Who is it now? She tries to probe for the direction. Casually, without alarm, she turns her head and scans the lecture hall. Every face is focused on the screen, but she can feel it still. She turns the other way and it is gone. She looks back at the movie screen. Marcello Mastroianni is outside now, on a beach. Some great bloated fish has washed up on the sand. People stand around it, and there it is again. The stare. She can feel it crawling on her. She turns her head and there, in the third row of that section, beside Professor Cohen, before he swings his eyes away. But she has seen him now. He looks familiar, but she cannot place the face. It's dark in the lecture hall. He knows she's staring at him now, and it makes him nervous. Good, she thinks, until his features come together—the dark brown hair, the thin peak of a nose, the deep-set eyes, the generous mouth. Who is he? He turns, and this time there is nothing reticent about his gaze. She feels embarrassed. She shouldn't be, she thinks. Susan wouldn't be.

Laura looks back at the screen. Marcello Mastroianni is talking to a young girl on the beach. She is standing on a little spit of land, separated from him by a narrow causeway. She is urging him to join her, but he cannot cross. He is stranded on his side, marooned.

The music swells and falls, the projector stops, and someone has turned on the lights.

Laura blinks and sits up in her chair. She glances over to the left side of the lecture hall, but the man has disappeared. She stands and glides into the moving crowd. She lets herself be carried by the press of bodies toward the door. The bell begins to ring. It is right above the doorway. Why has she never noticed it before? Bright red, it rings and rings, so loudly that she has to press her hands about her ears to keep the noise out, and then she's through.

Laura makes her way out of West Hall onto Lexington Avenue. It is a cold, wet day. Snow-gorged clouds huddle in the sky like frightened sheep. The air is full of chestnut smoke, the smell of pretzels. She puts on her prescription sunglasses and starts downtown along the avenue, window-shopping, looking for camouflage in the details, the New Year sales, that pair of purple boots marked down fifty percent. *La Dolce Vita*. But it doesn't work. She needs another joint, another pill, another tumbler of amnesia. One month, perhaps two, and she'd be living in LA. Carol's father was a banker there. He'd promised to find her a job, a real job, and then she could forget the past. She'd be safe. Like Candy. Go underground. She'd vanish off the face of the earth.

Laura stops short. There it is again. The stare. She can feel it crawling on her. All her life she has felt it crawling on her. She looks into the storefront window. Reflected in the glass, she sees a fat man walking a boxer across the street. He is checking out her ass. She is wearing ski pants and a pair of high-heel boots. Her short leather jacket is drawn tight about her waist despite her bulky sweater. Her hair is up, her earlobes glistening with rings. Laura whirls suddenly to face him, but the man with the boxer is gone.

She's just imagining things. She's jumpy, that's all.

She looks back at the storefront and is startled by her own reflection in the glass, startled twice to realize that the root of her remembrance is that photograph of her mother, in the mirror of her vanity—the familiar nose, the tiny even teeth. "Just like your mother," her father had always said. "Like two peas in a pod."

Laura continues down the sidewalk. In a moment she has spied the landmark of the College Deli, and a feeling of relief descends upon her. It is the forgetfulness of ritual which she loves, the exquisite banality of the humdrum. She relishes the echo of the bell above the door, the busy chink and clink of washing dishes. Harold is behind the counter, with his paper hat cocked to the side —as usual—with his spatula cutting up a western omelette on the greasy grill.

"Hey, Laura. Over here." Carol is already sitting in the booth by the ice machine.

"Waitin' long?" says Laura.

"Years. Robby Becker came by. I considered suicide, but he only wanted to share some fries, and suicide's a mortal sin. How was film class?"

"Fine, I guess." She shrugs her jacket off.

"Did you go?"

"What do you mean, did I go? Of course I went. Didn't I just say it was fine?"

"What did you see?"

"La Dolce Vita, by Federico Fellini."

"Is that the one with the giant crucifix hanging from a helicopter in the beginning?"

"That's the one."

"What are you having?"

"I don't know. I had a big breakfast."

"Are you on some kind of crash diet or something?"

Laura throws back her head and laughs. "Yeah, it's a special New York diet."

"My god!"

"What?"

"You laughed. Am I dreaming? Pinch me. Can it be? After all these years, the therapy is paying off. She can laugh. The girl can laugh."

Laura picks up a menu.

"What are you doing?" Carol asks.

"What does it look like I'm doing?"

"Laura, you've been here a thousand times. What do you expect to find in there that you haven't seen a hundred times before?"

"Nothing. That's just the point."

"You're really weird, Laura, you know that? You're—Hold it! Don't look now."

Laura stiffens in her seat. "What? What is it?"

"There's a really cute guy checking you out from the counter."

"Where?"

"Don't turn around, you moron! He's over by the door. With the dark hair and leather jacket. See?"

Laura turns casually around. It's the man from the lecture hall, the one sitting by Professor Cohen. He looks straight at her and smiles.

"He's cute," says Carol.

"He's okay. I saw him earlier, in my film class."

"Maybe he's a new professor. Sign me up."

"He's a little old, isn't he?"

"I thought you liked them older. More experienced. More mature. Plus, it usually means they have more money. He's definitely checking you out."

"Professors don't have money. Besides, I'm not interested."

"Since when?"

"I'm just not."

"Jesus, Laura. Brian must have hit you hard."

"It's got nothing to do with Brian."

"Then what is it?"

Laura glances over at her friend, trying to formulate an answer, something she will believe, but the words don't settle. Carol was from another world. Her parents had divorced when she was ten, and she had grown up in New York, living with her mother in a two-bedroom co-op in Manhattan. She would not understand. Laura had never told her of her night job. As far as Carol knew, she simply worked late at the library. What was the point of telling?

That was just Susan, anyway. Just Susan dancing. Just Susan making money, putting Laura through school. Why jeopardize the move to California for a moment of confession? Nothing she could do would ever bring Yolanda back.

"It's nothing," Laura says. "Nothing. I'm just tired."

"Oh, my God, he's coming over. Get ready."

Laura looks up. The man in the leather jacket sidles by.

"Hi," he says.

"Hi," says Carol.

"Hi," says Laura.

He says, "Didn't I just see you in Paul Cohen's class?"

He has hazel, deep-set eyes. They look sad but harmless. They look uncertain, Laura thinks. "Maybe."

"I thought it was you. Your name's Laura Molloy, right?"

"How do you know?"

"Paul Cohen told me. He pointed you out. He says you're one of his best students."

"You're full of shit!"

"Laura!" Carol kicks her under the table.

"He said that, really?" Laura says. "Seriously?"

"Honest," he says, scratching at his chin. He hovers by their table, shifting his weight from one foot to the other. His eyes *are* nice.

"How do you know Professor Cohen?" Laura asks.

"Oh, we're old friends. We went to school together, years ago." He smiles. "Sorry," he says. "I'm Sam. Sam Penn."

"Pleased to meet you," Carol says. "I'm Carol Miller."

The waitress trundles into view. "Ready to order?"

"You want to join us, or something?" Carol says.

He looks down at his watch. "Sure, why not?" He slides into the booth beside her.

"Well, I'm glad that's settled," says the waitress, pulling out her pad. "What'll it be?"

They order. Carol has a chef's salad. Laura asks for a cheeseburger, well-to-burned, and a side of fries. And he has a bowl of chicken soup. The waitress checks the order three times before stuffing the pad back in her apron and moving off.

He says, "Do you always wear your sunglasses indoors?"

Laura leans back with a smile. "Sometimes."

"She likes to travel incognito. Like a movie star," says Carol.

"Afraid of being seen?"

"It's easier to watch when you're not being seen."

"What are you watching, Laura?"

"Today? The world go by. The world just spinning like it always has. The same gray clouds. The same traffic jams and chestnut stands and Christmas sales and the homeless dressed in paper. The same lousy service for the same bad food. How about you? What are you watching, Professor?"

He leans back in the booth and laughs. "Me, a professor? I'm not a professor. What made you think that?"

"What do you do, then?" Carol asks.

"I'm an analyst. Stocks, mostly. You know. I do research on the entertainment industry."

"Sounds interesting."

"It is," he says, encouraged. "I travel around the country interviewing CEO's who lie to me about their companies, about how much money they have, how much debt. Then I learn the truth from people who have no business telling me, so I have to lie if anyone ever asks me where I got the information. Then, every fortnight or so, I write up my analysis—a thin tissue of half-truths—and our clients end up so filthy rich, they're forced to lie to the I.R.S."

"Sounds to me like you don't like your job," says Laura.

"Oh, but I do. I do. Except I work too hard. I never do anything else."

"What are you doing here, then?"

He takes his jacket off and hooks it on the coat stand at the end of the booth. "That's a good question, Laura. A friend of mine suggested I was getting stale, that I needed to take a break, get out of the office, smell the flowers, you know. So I came up to see Paul, catch a film."

"Pick up a coed."

"Laura!"

"Have you always been so frightfully honest?" He is watching her.

"Is that what that was?"

"Don't pay any attention to her. She's been acting funny all week."

"Have you? How come? Why have you been acting funny, Laura?"

"Must be exams."

"You two don't look like college girls."

"Really? What do we look like then?" says Laura.

"I mean you look older, more sophisticated."

"Does that line actually work?"

"Laura!" Carol says. "I'm sorry, mister. She's not always like this."

"Call me Sam."

"Okay, Sam."

"What's she normally like?"

"Normally she's a bitch," says Carol.

He laughs.

"Speak for yourself," says Laura.

"Okay, I admit it. You were right," he says. "Paul promised to introduce me to a friend of his in the classics department. But then I saw you watching the movie. I guess I got distracted."

"That's sweet," says Carol. "Isn't that sweet, Laura?"

Laura rifles through her purse for cigarettes. Why does his face look so familiar? The dark brown hair. The hazel, deep-set eyes. The voice. She puts a cigarette in her mouth. Or am I just imagining things? I'm jumpy, that's all. Because of Yolanda. Just a few more months, she thinks. A few more months, then California . . . and a million miles from the lounge.

She flinches as he reaches out, a lighter flashing in his hand. "Yeah, real sweet," she says, sucking in the flame. Then she sits back, blowing smoke, playing with the cigarette between her fingers.

"I didn't mean to interrupt," he says, plucking a pack of Marlboros from his jacket. He lights up. "Like I said, I was waiting to meet Paul's friend. We were going to go over right after the movie, but it was like waiting to go to the dentist. I don't know. I gave Paul some lame excuse and just ran out. Then when I saw you in the street, when you came in here, I suddenly felt like chicken soup, and it was cold, so here I am." He smiles at Laura. "What are you staring at?"

"You."

"I can see that."

"Your voice."

"What about my voice?"

"It's so familiar."

"Is it?"

"Yeah, it sounds . . . I don't know. Like I've heard it somewhere before. On the radio."

He shrugs and looks away. "People are always telling me that. I must have one of those voices. So," he says, "what do you girls do, anyway? Study, I mean."

Carol giggles. "I'm a marketing major. Laura's in communications."

"Fascinating."

Laura shrugs.

"What do you plan to do with that?"

"We're going to live in California," says Carol, "after graduation, in a few months. That's where my family's from. I already have a job with an ad agency in Venice Beach. A lot of cool high-tech stuff. Laura likes the movies."

"Don't tell me. You want to be an actress."

"Maybe. I don't know. What's wrong with that? I like to dance. Maybe production. I don't know."

"I bet you could be an actress, with your looks."

Laura smiles. "You really lay it on, don't you?" she says, but she feels flattered nonetheless.

"No, I'm serious. A lot of agents I know would snap you up in a minute."

"Laura's a real ham," Carol says.

"Believe me," he continues, stamping out his cigarette. "I know what I'm talking about. It's my business. I've been covering the film industry for more than ten years. I must spend, oh, three or four months every year in LA. I deal with producers, studio execs. And talent too. Sometimes you have to make sure they're commit-

ted to a project. One lousy film can devastate a studio. It can mean
the difference between a buy or sell."

"You must have lots of friends in Hollywood," says Carol.

"I have my share," he says. "I also cover gaming. Mostly Las
Vegas and Atlantic City. I just made a killing on the Shangri-la."

Laura watches him speak. She feels her mind begin to wander.
She sees him talking but the sound is out of sync. She watches his
mouth, the way his smile curls in the corner. He gestures as he
speaks. He slouches on the table. He leans back with a laugh. His
eyes crinkle in the corners, crinkle hazel with a little green, and
brighten as he laughs.

They talk about the movies, about travel, about Hollywood.
Despite herself, Laura finds herself relaxing in his company. He
seems nice enough. And class was fun today, she thinks. Perhaps
Carol was right. School would be over soon. Finals were right
around the corner. Soon they'd be living in California. A whole new
life, she thinks. A whole new Laura Molloy.

"You should come visit me," he says. "When you get out to
LA. I'm flying to the coast on Monday." He lights another cigarette.

"That's great." Carol leans closer. "Where are you staying?"

"I have a house in Malibu. Right on the beach. I'm serious.
You should come over. I've got plenty of room. And if you're looking for work in the film business . . ."

"We'd love to, wouldn't we, Laura? Laura?"

"Yeah, sounds great."

"Hey," he says. "I have an idea. What are you girls doing
tonight? I'm only in town a few more days, and I've got nothing
planned for the evening."

"Nothing special," says Carol.

"What about Andy?" Laura says. "I thought you two were having dinner?"

"And you, Laura?" he continues. "What are you doing?"

"I have plans."

"She's coming with us," says Carol. "For dinner. And then my
boyfriend's band is playing at the Iron Pig. You know that club?"

He smiles. "I think so. Sounds like fun."

"You want to come? He's a great musician."

"Carol!"

"If it's all right with Laura," he says. "But only if you let me buy dinner. I was in college, too, once, and it wasn't that long ago. Can I buy you dinner, Laura?"

"I didn't say I was going."

"Oh, come on," says Carol. "It'll be fun. You and Sam can talk about the movies."

"Look, you seem like a nice guy," says Laura. "Nicer than most of the creeps around here. But I just don't feel like dating anyone right now."

"Who said anything about dating? I just asked you out for dinner."

"Come on, Laura. You haven't gone out for weeks."

Laura rolls her eyes. "Thanks, Carol."

"You know what I mean. It'll do you good."

"I don't think so."

"Oh, come on, Laura. Think about California."

Laura takes another drag off her cigarette. "You and Andy will come?"

"Sure, sure. Then, after dinner, we can all head over to the Iron Pig. The band goes on at eleven."

Laura looks up. He is smoking his cigarette carefully. He is staring at her, waiting, blowing smoke at the ceiling. He puts the cigarette in his mouth, tugs at his sleeve, and looks down at the watch on his wrist. It is an extravagant gesture, completely artificial in its casualness, like a perfectly executed dance move on the stage.

"I don't think so. I should study," says Laura. "I've got a paper due."

He stamps his cigarette out in the ashtray. He rises to his feet. "Well, I guess I'd better be going. It was nice to meet you, Carol. Maybe I'll see you in LA." He slips his leather jacket on.

Laura lifts her feet up on the banquette. "Hey, Sam," she says, but he does not look at her. "Sam," she repeats.

He glances at her legs, the high-heel boots, the ski pants. She watches as his eyes crawl up her thighs, her hips, her waist, the contours of her breasts, barely hidden by the bulky sweater. They crawl and crawl but it is not the stare that she expected, not the perennial grin or leer or suave dissembling smile.

A look of terrible sadness plays across his face, a look more resigned than determined. A look of fear. "What is it, Laura?" he replies.

Now I know why I know that face, she thinks. That's my face. "What about your chicken soup?" she says.

He reaches into his jacket, takes out his wallet, and removes a twenty-dollar bill. "You have it, Laura," he says. "Maybe it'll warm you up."

A flat ironic smile plays on his lips, and it cuts right through her, tears like a piece of fabric. He stands there struggling with his gloves.

"Wait a minute," she says. "Look, I'm sorry. I didn't mean to be such a bitch. I guess my paper can wait."

"You mean it?" Carol exclaims. "That's really great, Laura. Are you sure?"

"I guess so."

"Where do you want to eat?"

And he says, "We can meet for drinks first at the Metro Diner, on Twenty-second and Tenth. At eight o'clock. I know a great Italian restaurant nearby."

"Cool," says Carol. "Eight o'clock. The Metro Diner."

"I've got to go," he says. "I'm sorry. I forgot, I have an errand to run. I'll see you at eight. Good-bye. I'll see you tonight." Then he turns and walks away.

Laura watches him slip through the crowd. He stops for a second at the entrance to the deli. The door opens and he's gone.

The waitress finally arrives. Carol takes her requisite chef's salad, Laura her cheeseburger and fries. "I think he's cute," says Carol, munching. "He's got a sexy voice, and a house in Malibu."

"Big deal."

"Maybe he can get you a job. Dad says things are kind of funny at his bank right now."

"What about the soup?" the waitress asks. "Where'd your friend go?"

"He had to run." Laura stares down at the bowl of chicken soup, the way it simply sits there, steaming. "It's okay. You can leave it." She picks up a spoon and starts to stir the soup halfheartedly.

White meat, Laura thinks, carrots and noodles too. She brings a spoonful to her lips. It tastes salty and delicious. It tastes rich, and warm, and safe, and at least he isn't like those other jerks, all those men from the Party Girl Lounge.

Cold. Colder than yesterday, that's for damn sure. Jimmy hobbles over, hobbles over, hobbles over to the Dumpster in the alley. A whole helluvalot colder. He reaches into the Dumpster and removes a stack of newspapers. He starts to fold them over carefully, one by one. Fold and put aside. Fold and put aside. Then he opens the front of his coat. He lifts the sweater and the jacket too, and begins to slip the newspapers up around his undershirt, folded just so, methodically, just right so they don't slip out when he walks, or sits or lies down in the cold. . . . There is a bottle in the Dumpster. But it is empty, he can see that now. It is all gone, but still he picks it up, still twists the cap off with a crusty hand and brings it to his lips. He can still taste it, dammit. He can still sense the spirits on the very tip of his wet, pink tongue as he strains to reach inside, inside the bottle. He wants to be a ship inside a bottle. Safe and warm. And never hungry. Like at the big house on the corner. But that is all gone now, all past, all long, long, long ago.

Jimmy turns, and there he is, just like he sensed he was—the man. "Who's there?" He brings a hand up to his brow to shield his eyes.

"Jimmy?"

It's him. Jimmy smiles and bobs his head. "Hey, mister, got a cigarette?" He runs his tongue along his lips. He lifts a hand up, reaching out, reaching out as if to snatch the bullet from the air.

There is a small white flower of flame, a muffled pop, and Jimmy finds himself down on the alley floor. The world is spinning round, the stranger's face revolving, round and round, like the round hole in his right hand, and he is gone, and it grows dark and cloudy, but at least the cold is gone, at least there is a great warmth welling all around him, soaking the newspapers, soaking him through, tucking him in the warm dry sheets, to sleep.

XVI

The jukebox plays the Human League. A blue-haired dancer with a leather corset and tattoos throws herself to the floor. "Don't you want me?" She writhes and wriggles to her knees. She shakes her thin white buttocks. She runs a hand between her legs. She feels herself. She grinds, she pumps, she watches as she moves, watches herself in the mirror, the blue-black lips, the leather straps, the dark guy with the pea coat and the cowboy boots. Capozzi turns away.

A tiny Asian girl with hair down to her ass is standing behind the bar. She smells a tiny vial. She squints and shakes her head. "Too sweet," she says, and hands it to the black man standing by Capozzi. He has an entire box of vials before him on the bar. A sample case, Capozzi thinks. A salesman.

The bar girl plucks another vial. She is wearing a turquoise spandex dress that looks like it's been glazed on at high temperature. "Hey, it's empty," she complains.

"All the girls love Calèche. They've smelled it up," he says. "Try this, it's just like Opium."

"How much?"

"Twelve dollars."

She removes the cap and smells the tiny bottle. "Okay. Ten dollar."

"They're twelve dollars, Silvie."

"Ten dollar. I have right now. Ten dollar."

"Here," says Capozzi, reaching out. A ten-dollar bill pokes from his fingers. The salesman eyes the money.

"Okay," the salesman says. "Okay, for Silvie." He takes the bill.

The bar girl grins at Capozzi. She is about five feet tall, with large dark eyes and a jutting jaw. Her smile is loose and open. Her ears poke out from her head. "Thanks a lot," she says. "You really nice. What's your name, mister?"

"Anthony." He turns toward the salesman beside him. "Beat it," he says.

The salesman frowns. He starts to say something, but then thinks better of it. He closes his case, and slides along the bar.

"See you later, Challie." Silvie laughs. It is a bright infectious laugh. "How about a drink?" she says.

"Not now. Maybe later. Maybe a Coke."

"You on a wagon?"

"Something like that. Listen, Silvie. Is that your name? Silvie?"

She leans against the bar, smelling her bottle of perfume. "It make me so hot." She scratches herself between her legs. "You wanto smell?"

"No, thanks. I'd like to ask you a few questions."

She looks skeptical. "What kind questions?"

"About Carolynn Simms. Candy Simms. She used to work here, didn't she?"

"You know Candy?"

"I know of her."

"How come everyone want to know 'bout Candy?"

"What do you mean, everyone?"

"Yesterday. Same thing. This guy come in asking 'bout Candy. 'Bout Susan too."

"Who's Susan?"

She hesitates. Her eyes narrow. She picks up a glass and drags it through the ice behind the bar. Then she fills the glass with soda. "Here your Coke," she says. "Three dollar."

Capozzi reaches into his pea coat for his wallet.

"You a cop?" the bar girl says. "I know you are. I can tell. Why you askin' question? Candy in trouble?"

"Deep trouble," says Capozzi. He drops another ten-dollar bill on the bar. "Tell me about the other man. The one who came by yesterday. What did he look like?"

"Tall. Good-looking, like you. Dark brown hair. Brown eye. He say he was her uncle." She laughs, thrusting her jaw out. "Good-looking, tip real nice."

"I bet he did. What about the other girl?"

"What girl?"

"Susan. Is she a dancer too?"

"She use to dance. She and Yolanda live together round the corner for a while. Candy, too."

"Where can I find them—Susan and Yolanda?"

"I don't know. They don't work this week."

"What are their last names then? Do you know their names?"

"Rodriguez. Yolanda Rodriguez. But she left town last week."

"Where to?"

"I don't know. Florida, maybe."

"How about Susan? What's her last name?"

"Susan Molloy."

"Where does she live?"

Silvie shrugs. "Brooklyn Heights, maybe. That's where she grow up. She quit the lounge a week ago to finish school."

"Which school?"

"That's what he ask. 'Which school?' Somewhere uptown, I told him. I don't know."

"What does she look like?"

Silvie turns away. "Hey, Anthony, you want another drink?" she says.

Capozzi follows her gaze. A black man is standing at the end of the bar. He is staring at them. "Okay," Capozzi says. "Get me a . . . I don't know."

"Bourbon."

"Okay, bourbon."

She turns and lifts and tips a bottle of Wild Turkey. A shot glass rises through the stream, it fills; she drops it on the bar. "Five dollar."

Capozzi pulls his wallet from his pea coat. "What does she look like, Silvie?"

He drops a twenty on the bar. She reaches out and it is gone. "Okay," she says. "You wait. I be right back." Capozzi watches her as she walks along the bar, her spandex outfit clinging to her for dear life. She turns the corner, disappears. Capozzi sips his Coke. He looks around the bar.

The walls of the Party Girl Lounge are painted red with pitch black trim and fake wood beams. Ropes of flashing Christmas lights are strung up on the walls and ceiling. The girl on the front stage has removed her leather corset. Her body is covered with blue and red tattoos. They wriggle on her shoulders, her arms, they gambol on her buttocks. She has a small rose painted on each breast, below each tiny nipple. She runs her hands back through her spiked blue hair and lies down on the stage. She sees Capozzi watching her and starts to pinch her nipples as she undulates. She smiles at him and licks her lips. She writhes and throbs, she wriggles to the rock-and-roll, some old Deep Purple tune, but he cannot remember the name.

"Hey, Anthony."

The bartender has returned. She is holding three photos in her hand. He takes them from her. Promotional shots, she tells him. From this year's Christmas party. Each features a different girl.

The first is a Hispanic, with a small flat nose, large almond-shaped eyes, full mouth. Yolanda. She is wearing a bra the color of a peacock's tail. Her breasts swell over the material.

The second girl is a brunette, with intelligent brown eyes and silken hair streaming down her naked shoulders. Her ears are bristling with rings. Her skin is powder white, with a hint of freckles. Her lips are glossy pink, hiding a row of small white even teeth. He feels a stirring inside him. Susan. There is something about her, he thinks. She is the kind of girl that men approach, and she is used to it.

Capozzi turns the glossy over, and there is Carolynn Simms, a.k.a. Candy Simms, the girl with only half a face. Except that here she's suddenly whole, painfully complete. Despite the folded tank top and the naked breasts, this could be her high school graduation shot. She is trying to be seductive, but it comes off false, as false as her bobbed hair and eyelashes. There is a nervousness about her, as if she's flinching from the flash, or some foreknowledge of the shot which would remove her jaw, transform her into crab food. "Thanks," he says.

"Sure. Sure. You come back sometime when you off duty. Come back Monday. Special dance for you. Remember. Just for you."

"I may just do that. But before I go, Silvie. Just one more thing." He smiles and leans a little closer. He draws her into him. He whispers, "Are you absolutely sure you don't remember where she lives? Susan Molloy, I mean. It could be very important. It could be a matter of life and death. Do you understand what I'm saying, Silvie? Life and death."

Silvie steps back. She shrugs and plays with her hair. "I told you. She go to college uptown. That's what I say." She looks away. "But she won't talk to you."

"Why not?"

"Susan . . ." She laughs. It is the same balloon-light laugh, but this time there is something on the outer edge, something cold and unexpected—like plucking a beautiful flower, and pulling up a clot of twisted roots beneath.

"Susan, she hate cops," Silvie says. "Her father use to be a cop. Just like you."

He looks down at his watch. It's already five o'clock. "Maybe you're right. Maybe she won't," he answers sadly. "But if I don't try, she may never talk to anyone again."

Capozzi drives his battered gold Dodge Aries through the streets of Little Italy toward Brooklyn. He knows each alleyway and shortcut, the timing of each light. He is in a hurry, and he hunches over his steering wheel at every stop, anxious to lunge across the intersection, looking for holes in the traffic.

It is a little before six. He has spent the last forty minutes at the station, filling out forms, tapping into the imbroglio of on-line information pulsing at the heart of the New York City Police system. It wasn't very hard to find Sergeant John F. Molloy of Brooklyn Heights. Sergeant Molloy, retired. And Molloy has a wife named Kathleen, two sons, and a daughter named Laura, twenty-one and living with her parents still, according to the files. Laura. Susan. The names were different, but the age was right, and Capozzi knew that few girls used their real names when they started dancing.

Molloy had spent the better part of thirty years on the force, rising steadily through the ranks, rising slowly but surely, despite allegations of drinking, despite fourteen complaints of brutality and excessive force. It seemed that people were constantly provoking him, according to the reports. They resisted arrest. They reached for his gun. Even that fourteen-year-old car thief, whom he had chased across the roofs of Chelsea, climbing up and down until he'd slipped and fallen and landed on his hip and that soft pension.

The Job just makes you mean sometimes, Capozzi's father had once told him, long before the affair with Uncle Mario. You see too much. You start to understand it. You have to know the way the street thinks, but all you are is what you think, and you become the street—you have to—and all the shit that runs along it.

Capozzi swings up on the ramp to Brooklyn Bridge. The East River glimmers in electric light, shimmers like a dying candle and spills out in the bay. He can see a line of freighters and container ships tied up on the Brooklyn side. Great cranes are lifting freight into the hungry holds. The sky is a pearl gray, pitching toward night. Already lights are gleaming in the borough—the pale magnesium of the streets, the sulphur glow of living rooms, the cacophony of Christmas decorations.

It takes him another fifteen minutes to find the apartment building just off Prospect Park. It is a grimy postwar brick monstrosity, lit up by blinking Christmas lights still clinging to the orange fire escapes, like ivy past the season. There is a little snow still on the corner near the mailbox. Capozzi parks the Aries on the street. He looks up at the building. She is like an old whore wearing too much makeup, but the Christmas lights can't hide the plaster cracks, the sagging fire escapes, the paint job fading by the minute. He gets out and locks the door. Inky clouds foam overhead. The air is almost balmy now, compared to the last few frigid nights. It looks like snow. He walks up the concrete steps. The building is home to more than thirty tenants and it takes him a minute or so to find the small curled label with the name *Molloy*. He buzzes and it buzzes back, as if someone is hanging by the button.

The lobby is just what he expected—worn imitation marble tiles, that ubiquitous mosaic of smeared gilt mirrors, the dusty potted palms. The elevator takes forever but when it finally arrives he's glad that it can only go so fast. It seems to dangle upward to the seventh floor and stops.

Sergeant Molloy is fifty-one and not a damn bit happy about it. He is scowling as the door swings open. He is scowling as he waves Capozzi in. He is scowling as he points down at the mat beneath their feet, and starts to wipe his shoes, one after the other, in a grim determined way, like a bulldog trying to hold his ground. "Detective Capozzi," he says, mincing the words between his teeth.

"Pleased to meet you."

"Likewise."

Capozzi takes a good look at Molloy as they head into the living room. He is about five feet eight, wearing a cable-knit sweater, brown polyester pants, and brown shoes. His face is generous and round. In fact, his whole head seems a little too large for his body. He is bald except for a few gray locks, combed over the red pate, the shape of some great mackerel tail. The sweater fails to hide the bulging stomach, the generous hips and thighs. "Sit down." Molloy points to a yellow sofa.

Capozzi sits. There is a collection of needlepoint pillows at the other end of the sofa. Green, white, the palest blue. There is a rattan coffee table, a pair of standing lamps with matching lemon lamp shades. The carpeting is cream, and there—he hadn't noticed —is Mrs. Kathleen C. Molloy, sitting bolt upright by the dining table. Capozzi rolls to his feet. "I'm sorry. I didn't see you. Detective Capozzi." He offers her his hand. "Pleased to meet you."

She reaches out. Her fingers are ice cold, bone thin, like icicles.

"Kathleen," she says, and turns to look up at Molloy. She seems much older than her husband, with blue-white hair and pale, translucent skin. She is so thin that he can barely see any similarity until she smiles a little and he spies the small, white, even teeth, the nose. Like Susan. Just like Laura Molloy.

Molloy sits down in a large plaid easy chair, facing his twenty-inch screen. There is a football game on TV. Someone goes deep, deeper, but the ball is batted away. "Okay, you wanted to talk, so talk," Molloy says gruffly, eyes on the screen. "My wife says it's got something to do with Laura."

Capozzi nods and turns to Mrs. Molloy. "Like I said on the phone. Your daughter may have some information which could be helpful in a case I'm working on. I'd like to talk to her, if that's okay with you. Is she at home?"

"What about?" says Molloy.

"It's an ongoing investigation. She may know the identity of a suspect. We just want to talk to her, that's all."

"A murder investigation? You're in Homicide, aren't you?"

"That's right."

"We don't know where she is. She hasn't lived here in four years."

Capozzi sighs. "I see. Look, I think you ought to know—"

"What's she been saying? If she's been saying anything about me again, I swear . . ."

"John, please!" Mrs. Molloy turns toward Capozzi. "Can I get you some coffee, Detective? A beer?"

"Oh, no, thank you, Mrs. Molloy." Capozzi unbuttons his pea coat. He leans his elbows on his knees, looks at Molloy. "I haven't spoken to your daughter. I don't even know where she is. I heard she was attending Parnell College, but the offices were closed tonight when I called. That's why I'm here."

"She's living in Manhattan now," says Mrs. Molloy.

"Whereabouts?"

"We don't know and, frankly, we don't care." Molloy reaches for the TV remote. "Not anymore. She's put us through enough, that girl. We have two boys, and they turned out just fine. They're on the force. But Laura. No, thank you."

"Look, Sergeant. Do you mind if I call you Sergeant?"

"You can call me anything you like."

"Okay, Sergeant. Look, I have reason to believe that Laura may be in some kind of danger if I don't speak to her."

"She could have stayed here and gone to college. We would have helped her pay. She didn't have to move to Manhattan," Molloy continues, as if he hadn't spoken. "We have a fine college right here in Brooklyn, you know. There's nothing wrong with our schools. She didn't have to get that kind of job."

"Sergeant, I said I think your daughter may be in some kind of danger."

"It's a dangerous world, Detective."

"Do you know where she is?"

"No, I don't."

"What about friends?"

"She has too many friends. That's the problem. Anyone can be her friend. All you have to do is ask."

"How about a photograph?"

"You want a photograph?"

"If you have one. Something I can use for the wire."

"I'll give you a photograph," Molloy says, pushing out of his chair. "I've got the perfect thing." He vanishes down a dark hall near the entrance.

"Detective Capozzi?"

Capozzi turns. Kathleen Molloy is sitting on the edge of her seat. She is leaning forward, beckoning with her frail hand. "I'm sorry, Detective," she says. "I'm sorry. They used to be so close . . . when she was younger. I know he loves her. I don't want you to think badly of him."

"It's okay, Mrs. Molloy. I don't think badly of anyone. I'm just trying to find your girl, that's all. I just want to talk to her."

At that moment, Molloy swims up out of the hallway by the entrance. He is smiling now. He is happy at last. "Here," he says to Capozzi, holding out his hand. "Is this what you're looking for?"

A photograph shakes in his fingers. It is the same promotional shot, the same damn Christmas photograph Capozzi picked up at the Lounge. He can see Laura's pink breasts, her shoulder and that corner of her smile. He snatches the snapshot from Molloy. He stuffs it in his coat. "Thank you, Sergeant," he says.

Molloy steps back. He crosses his arms, he sneers and says, "Why don't you put that on the wire? Why don't you tell the world about it?"

"I think I better be going."

"You have no right to judge me."

Capozzi stops. He turns and says, "I'm not judging you."

"Yes, you are. You believe her, don't you? All those filthy lies. Well, it isn't true. I'm a good Catholic, Detective. And I was a good cop too. So don't stand there looking at me like that. You're no better than I am."

"Take it easy, Sergeant."

"I knew a Mario Capozzi once. In the Tenth Precinct. I heard he was dirty, got suspended for taking payoffs from the mob. You see. I've still got friends in the Department."

"That's none of your business," Capozzi says. "That's got nothing to do with this case."

"That's right. It's none of your God damn business. No matter what she says."

"We have a lot of photographs."

They each look up. Kathleen Molloy is standing by the dining table.

"Shut up," Molloy says to his wife. "You keep out of this."

"Most of them are from high school," she continues.

"I said shut up, Kathleen." He takes a step toward her.

"I'm not going to shut up. She may be in danger, John. You heard the detective. She's still our daughter."

"She's no daughter of mine."

"Then why do you care if I show him?"

"I don't care. Go ahead. Suit yourself." He drops back in his easy chair. He props his feet up on the coffee table. He turns the volume up on the TV.

Mrs. Molloy takes Capozzi by the sleeve. She leads him gently from the living room and down the long dark hall where she stops short beside a door, and nods, and finally enters. She turns the light on and the room shines back, reflecting on the glossy surface of the wall—the framed photographs above the bed, on the bureau, beside the dressing table.

"These are from grade school, when she first started." She points to a pair of black-and-whites. "She was Tinkerbell in *Peter Pan*. And this is her in *Oklahoma!*, freshman year."

Capozzi takes the photos in. Laura looks so different in each shot, and it isn't just the costumes and the makeup. She really seems different.

"Here," Mrs. Molloy says, handing him a strip of photographs. "These are her, senior year. For some reason she got it into her head to get a passport. You know how girls can be. Just in case she had to to go to Europe, she said, as if she was a movie star or something, like a model. It was kind of silly, I guess. But it didn't hurt no one." She hands the photographs to Capozzi. "So she had these taken at the mall."

Capozzi looks down at the photographs. There are four blackand-whites on the strip. Laura is smiling in the first. Laura is laughing in the second. Laura is trying to be sophisticated in the third. And the fourth shot takes her by surprise, looking down for some nameless object out of sight, her mouth half open, her eyes still trying to focus.

"I like that one," she says, and points at the fourth frame.

"It's very natural," says Capozzi.

"She was happy then. I remember. It's funny, isn't it? All these photographs . . ." She waves a thin hand at the walls. "And this is the only one that looks like her. I hope it helps."

She turns the strip of photos over in his hand. There is a phone number on the back, in pencil. And an address. She squeezes his hand and smiles and says, "She's sharing a one-bedroom with a girl named Carol Miller."

Capozzi tries the phone number from the pay phone on the corner, but there is no answer. Only the same damn endless ringing. He hangs up in disgust and gets back in his gold Dodge Aries.

The trip back to Manhattan takes forever. There is only one lane open on the upper level, and he sits in traffic on the Brooklyn Bridge, watching the city glowing, out of reach. A helicopter thrums overhead. Where is she now? he thinks. On her way back from class, or at dinner? On the way back from the library, carrying her books? "Laura," he says aloud. He honks his horn and it starts an avalanche of sound, one horn against the other, like roosters crowing in the dark. The traffic starts to move. Where are you, Laura?

Are you safe? Has he found you yet, like Candy? And Yolanda Rodriguez too. More crab meat, probably. According to her neighbors,
she'd been missing for a week. What do you know that's killing
you? he thinks. He shouts, "Come on," at no one in particular.
"Get a fucking move on." The traffic crawls and picks up speed.
He reaches down onto the floor. Where is it, dammit? He takes the
cherry out. He opens his window and sticks it to the roof. He flips
the switch and it begins to whine, to flash its bright red glow on
everything around him. "All right, let's go," he says out loud, as the
traffic picks up speed. He tucks his arm against his chest to feel the
reassuring bulge, to touch it, as he swings the car down off the
bridge and northward on the FDR.

It takes him another fifteen minutes to reach Laura's apartment building. It is almost eight o'clock. He double-parks outside
the entrance, and turns the siren off. He runs into the foyer and
buzzes every button he can see. Somebody buzzes back and he is
through the door and up the steps and waiting for the elevator. He
watches as the light descends on the brass panel. Three, two, one
and it is open, and out steps a girl with earmuffs, glasses, and a
leather jacket. He checks her briefly as he rushes by. He hits the
close door button and the brass door slams. Third floor, he thinks.
Third floor. The elevator gradually ascends. Finally the door swings
open and he is down the hall and counting off the numbers. 3B. 3C.
3D. He stops. He knocks. There is a deafening echo, and then
silence. He knocks again. The echo is interminable. It seems to
wind its way from room to room, around the entire building, and it
is only then that he recalls the face—the brown hair underneath the
earmuffs, the small nose, and the chin. Laura! How could he have
been so blind? The girl in the lobby! It was her glasses threw him
off, and he remembers the strip of photographs which Mrs. Molloy
had shown him earlier in Brooklyn, the fourth frame, and her brown
eyes trying to focus. She was trying to focus because she couldn't
see! He dashes down the corridor, back to the elevator. It seems to
take forever once again. He paces by the door. He pounds the
panel. The elevator finally arrives and he descends back to the
foyer. The door jumps open. He rushes out into the hall, and almost crashes into a couple waiting in the lobby.

"Sorry," he says, and tears away. The girl has short blond hair. The boy is carrying a guitar.

"Hey, look where you're goin', asshole," the boy calls, stepping back. But Capozzi is already in the street, already through the door and on the sidewalk spinning, looking round, stalking the shuffling crowd for one black leather jacket in a world of overcoats, but it is useless. She is long gone, just one more shadow on the avenue.

XVII

Thinking ahead of the craft, thinking ahead, just like this. Trimming the controls, adjusting automatically, but never forgetful. The air is uncontrolled in free space; that's why you can't be. Never out of control. Payne takes another sip of his drink.

The Metro Diner is crowded tonight, for a week night, for a school night, thinks Payne. It has started to snow, and the air is charged with anticipation. People stumble by the windows on the avenue, turning their collars to the wind, hurrying home, scurrying here and there she is . . . Laura! She is staring at the night sky, at the snow exploding through the street lights, rapturous. She is wearing a leather jacket and mink earmuffs. Her long brown shiny hair is pinned up in a knot. He can see the tip of her chin as she looks up, the hollows of her nostrils, the lenses of her glasses steaming.

Then she suddenly looks down, as if she senses him somehow, and smiles and waves a little. She walks up to the diner's deco door. She scrapes her feet and steps inside, and she is down the aisle and by his booth, smiling and unbuttoning her jacket, taking it off.

"Carol's not here yet?" she asks.

"Not yet," says Payne, and she frowns. "She's probably on her way," he says. "Sit down and have a drink. Warm up a little."

Laura folds her jacket and throws it on the seat. She is wearing a black turtleneck top under a heather blue crew-neck sweater, a red plaid skirt, and black tights. She sits down, facing Payne. She settles into place, brushing a strand of hair back from her face, smiling politely as he catches the first hint of her perfume, like a gasp of hot wind off some tropical sea. She is wearing four gold rings in just one ear. Her lips are coral pink, her glasses fogged by heat, the closeness, the humidity rising from the steam table.

The waitress shows up out of nowhere—a fat girl with a ruby nose ring, wearing combat boots. Laura orders a rum and Coke, Payne another gin and tonic. Soon they are chatting about school again, about classes and graduation. Payne tries to keep the conversation going, but it is strained and cumbersome, listing from one sentence to the next. The waitress returns with their drinks, and Laura smiles at her—a genuine, sisterly smile—and leaning forward, slips the straw into her mouth, tucking her hair back behind her ears with a quick flip of her fingers.

"So where do you want to eat?" she asks, the straw still in her mouth.

"I thought we'd go to a little Italian joint I know near here called Mayhem. It's not too fancy, and the food's good."

"Great. What time is it?"

"A little after eight. What's the matter, Laura? You seem distracted."

"I'm worried about Carol. Maybe I should call. I think I will. I think I'll call. Excuse me a second."

Payne nods. "Of course," he says.

"I'll be right back." Laura slips out of the booth. She starts to make her way along the aisle between the booths and bar and Payne is suddenly aware of all the others who are staring at her as she walks, the long legs and the way her buttocks shift inside the plaid skirt with each step. The three suits at the bar. The fellow with the big beard, getting change. Even the black guy sitting with the blonde at the next booth. What is it that they see out of the corner of their eyes, what slight suggestion in the walk, what pheromones are floating by, unseen yet irresistible?

Laura swings around the black Formica bar to the pay phone. Payne watches her fiddle with her purse, a tiny square affair. She takes a coin out and drops it in the telephone. Someone is playing a piano. Payne turns around. A woman in a great cape and red hair is huddled in the corner of the diner. She ducks and bounces as she plays. She starts to sing. The voice is round and full and fearless and it fills him with a sudden rush of hope. Perhaps this isn't Susan after all, he thinks. Perhaps it's only a coincidence. They share a last name, that's all. They're the same age. They both have long brown hair, but so do a million other girls. Ten million girls. And if it isn't her, she doesn't have to die. She's just an innocent by-stander. She can go back to Parnell and graduate and move out to LA, and fall in love, become a movie star. He turns and looks at Laura talking on the telephone. She has a finger in one ear, and the receiver pressed against the other. She is shouting now, frustrated, angry. She tosses her hair back from her face. She stamps her foot impatiently, and in the space of that one movement grows the doubt. But if it is her, he considers. What if it's Susan and she knows, and then I let her go and she talks to someone, anyone, just to relieve the burden of the memory? Just to let it go? And Mor-row's right? And how am I to know?

She rolls her eyes. She says a few more words, she spins around, and hangs the phone up with a bang. Then she looks at Payne across the bar. He smiles at her and she smiles back, but it is lifeless and contrived. She makes her way around the diner, back to the booth.

"What's the matter?" he says. "Did you get ahold of Carol?"

"She said she'd meet us at the restaurant. She's running late." Laura slides back on the seat. She shakes her head and says, "I guess I shouldn't be surprised. It's the first time in a week they've been alone at the apartment." She takes another sip of her drink. "You want to get going? I'm starved," she says.

Payne pays the bill. They slip their leather jackets on and hud-dle for a moment by the door before stepping out into the street, into the cold, into the cold white snow.

Payne is caught up by the silence of the night. The flakes feel new, unsoiled against his face. The snow has started to settle. Just a few blocks west, the Hudson floats by under darkness. Across the street, the abandoned tracks of the elevated train lead nowhere into brick. He turns and looks at Laura walking next to him, the careful placing of her steps, the shimmer of her leather jacket, the way she watches him. It isn't her, he tells himself. This isn't her at all. Susan was taller. She had much lighter hair. But as he calibrates each attribute they step up to the curb and a pair of Puerto Rican kids in baseball caps and cotton jackets pass and turn and stare and mumble something in Spanish that Payne can't for the life of him make out. He looks at Laura to say something, something innocuous to bridge the moment, but he is silenced by her face, the blank impassive eyes, the nostrils slightly flared, the little smile. He looks away. The snow falls quietly. A cab honks at a distant light. There is a thick impenetrable hush that presses down on them, a benthic silence, as if they are walking at the bottom of the sea, until he turns and looks at her again, and she says, "God, I'm cold. Where the hell is this place?"

"Right up the street," says Payne.

Mayhem is a bistro with soft lights, tile tables, and a quirky, hip jazz music track. Colorful frescoes grace the walls, scenes from Etruscan life, a set of hills, a villa, a grapevine in the foreground. A muted dark blue light accents the bar. A feeling of lazy energy pervades the room, like a cat pretending to sleep.

They check their jackets and a pretty blond hostess takes them to their table. It is set in the rear corner of the room, in a recessed area slightly off the main dining floor. They order another round of drinks. The table is intimate, barely room for two, let alone four. A few blushing baby roses stand in a pink vase at the center of the table, next to a white candle.

Laura takes out a cigarette. Payne lights it for her. She smiles and says, "How'd you find this place?"

"A friend of mine took me here a few weeks ago. He says it has the best fried *calamari* in the city. It's pretty good, too."

"What's *calamari*?"

"Squid."

"Oh," she says, drawing on her cigarette.

A waiter appears with their drinks. He is a thin black man, not much older than Laura, with chiseled delicate features. "Our specials today are—for appetizers—fresh bluepoint oysters, a *focaccia* with fresh portobello mushrooms, a cream of leek soup . . ."

Payne watches Laura as the waiter delivers his soliloquy. She is trying to catch each word, intent without being obvious. Focussed. Finally the waiter disappears. Laura is at her drink and soon they are talking and smiling again. She's never had oysters, she says. Do they really have blue points? What's a portobello mushroom, anyway? The waiter returns with menus and they spend the next few minutes poring over them. Eventually they decide on oysters and a steak, and soup and *focaccia* for Payne. A bottle of Amarone rounds it off.

"You remind me," she concedes, as the waiter moves away, "of another guy I used to know. He was a businessman, too. His name was Fred. He was an older guy," she says, and he can hear the missing words—*like you.* "He taught me all about different wines. He said he wanted to educate me, but he just wanted to get me plowed, and I knew it. But he was a sweet guy anyway, and harmless." She casts a sidelong glance at Payne.

"Tell me about you," he says. "Where did you grow up, Laura?"

"In Brooooklyn, can't you tell? Brooklyn Heights." She laughs. "It took years to get rid of the accent. You really didn't know?"

He shakes his head.

She smiles smugly. "Brooklyn born and bred. Near Prospect Park. Brooklyn was different when I was a kid."

"Oh, really. How many years ago was that?"

"You know what I mean. In the seventies. My dad was a cop."

"You're kidding."

"No, really. For thirty years. But he quit. What's the matter?"

"Nothing. Go on."

"I don't see my folks much anymore. I see my mother once in a while, for lunch, you know, here in the city. My mom's great. I really love her."

"What about your dad? Why'd he quit?"

"He had an accident and they asked him to retire. Gave him a pension and everything. Now he works for the Farrel steamship line, on the docks. Security."

"Security?"

"It's a union job. Pays good. Anyway, I don't care. I never see him anymore. He and me don't get along."

"Why not?"

She suddenly looks sullen. She puts her drink back on the table, saying, "We just don't, okay?"

"I know what you mean. I barely see my parents anymore. I had an older brother. He died in Vietnam. John. John was his name. He was a few years older than me, and he was really great at everything. Sports. School. You name it. My dad would always tell me, 'Why can't you be more like S . . . like John? John does so well in school. John's won another letter. John's captain of the debating team.' My father." He shakes his head. He takes another sip of his drink. "I hardly ever saw him when I was growing up. He was always at some meeting or other, always traveling. I remember one time calling his office in New York when I was about ten and they told me he was incommunicado. For years I thought Communicado was a country in South America. And when I did see him, all he did was tell me to be someone else."

"I was glad when my dad wasn't there," she says. "That was fine by me."

"He was always so busy making a living," says Payne, "always so busy trying to protect his children from the world that, in the end, all it was about was the protection. I don't know. I used to hate him, but now . . . now I think I understand him more."

"Like a farmer," says Laura.

"What's that?"

"Like a farmer who builds so many fences round his fields, he doesn't have time to plant them."

"That's right." He smiles at her. She looks so beautiful in the half-light. Her elbows are on the table, and her chin is propped up on her tiny fists. Shadows play across her face. Candlelight illuminates the highlights in her hair. She seems much older than twenty-one. Despite her youthful beauty, despite the radiance of her skin, her shiny hair, there is something dark about her, something in the eyes, a shadow, some ineffable mark. Perhaps it is that which men find so appealing. The mystery, the darkness which winds down to the heart of who she is, exposed a little to the elements. What is your secret, Laura? What are you hiding?

The waiter arrives with their appetizers. Laura looks a little lost until Payne shows her how to dress her oysters. He squeezes them with lemon. He picks one up and scoops the meat out with a fork and sucks the morsel in his mouth. "Delicious," he says, and then she tries, and there is but a moment's hesitation before she smiles and swallows.

"They're good," she says, and reaches for another.

"You're amazing, Laura. Most people have to acquire a taste for oysters."

She continues to eat and drink and talk, and he sits back and watches her, occasionally sipping his soup, sipping his drink, just waiting.

". . . and so I moved into Manhattan and worked in a retail store off Canal. But what I really wanted to do was go back to school, to college," she says. "I'd had a couple of cool teachers in high school, plus I did really well on my SAT"s. But even though I got a scholarship from Parnell, I still needed a lot of money to live on, for rent and stuff. I knew my dad wasn't going to help me out unless I moved back in, and I wasn't going to do that, no way, so I got a job as a waitress at this dive on Varick Street. It was the only thing that paid enough, and didn't interfere with school. But I had a problem with the night manager there—he was a real jerk—and I was running out of money so I found a new job tending bar at a club on Forty-seventh. At least for a while. I quit last week. Carol told you, right? We're planning to move out to LA. Her father's a big banker there and he promised to find me a job."

"Would you excuse me?" Payne gets up from the table. He puts his napkin on his chair. "I forgot. I've got to make a call."

"Sure."

"I'm sorry. I'll be right back. Don't go away." He slips out of his chair. He starts back toward the entrance of the restaurant. The place is absolutely packed. They are even setting up more tables in the aisles. It is a mixture of professionals and the avant-garde, a battleground of corporate suits and minimalist design, Armani and the Gap. Waiters in white jackets float along the aisles, settling like bees at tables for a moment before moving off. Payne makes his way to the telephones near the entrance. The music shifts to John Coltrane. Even in the vestibule he can hear the lilting saxophone, the hypnotic strains of "I Wish I Knew" riding the conversations, the clink of cutlery, piercing the iron blue haze of cigarette smoke. In the distance, across the dining room, he can still see Laura's face between a dozen other faces. She is looking around. She is dipping a piece of bread into his soup. He drops a quarter in the telephone. He dials the number. He reaches into his jacket and removes the photograph of Susan, the one the Thai bartender gave him at the lounge. Even now, after everything, despite the icy hand of fear clutching his heart, squeezing it, he feels excited as he sees her, as she smiles a naked smile and looks up at the lens, exposed and vulnerable. Available. The phone rings. He presses the receiver to his ear. He looks across the vestibule, across the laughing heads, the waving hands and toasting glasses to her face. He stares back at the photograph, comparing. Susan. Laura. Susan.

"Hello."

"Glen? Is that you?"

"It's me. Where are you, John?"

"I can't hear you. Speak up," Payne shouts into the telephone.

"I said, where are you?"

"At the restaurant. Listen, I don't have much time. I think we're making a mistake. This girl isn't Susan."

"There's been no mistake."

"Listen to me, Glen. I've been asking her questions all night. I'm telling you, it's the wrong girl. She doesn't know anything."

"Go back to the table, John. Go back and finish what you started. Because if you don't, I will. And it won't be pretty, John. I'll do what I did to Candy. We'll all do it together. Understand?"

"Glen, you're making a mistake. I'm not sure—"

"Then make sure." There is a sudden click, and the dull tone of a disconnected line. Payne hangs up the receiver. He glances once more at the photograph of Susan and then stuffs it back into his jacket. He feels it slide in place, into the inside pocket, slick as if with blood, and as he pulls his hand away he feels the hard edge of the pistol, the flat uncompromising shape, remembering the way it kicks, the way the powder lingers in the nose. He heads back through the vestibule. He needs to feel the pounding of the crowd, the jostling conversations, the laughter as he weaves and glides and slides back to his table.

Laura smiles up at him as he sits down. "Where you been? They brought the wine. I had to taste it by myself."

He simply shrugs.

"Maybe I should try Carol again. . . ."

"Don't bother. I'm sure they're on their way. And the food will be here any minute. You don't want your steak to get cold, do you?"

"I guess not."

"No, of course not." He takes a long sip from his drink. He tips the glass until the ice falls to his teeth. He gnashes at the shards. He spits them out. "You were saying, Laura." He drops the glass back on the table.

"What?"

"About your job. About working on Forty-seventh street. What kind of club was it?"

She looks confused. "Just a bar. A men's club."

"Oh, a men's club. What kind of men? What made it a men's bar?"

"I don't know. Look, maybe I should make that call. It's probably close to nine, and they go on at eleven."

"Forget the call, Laura."

"What's the matter with you?"

"Nothing, why?" he says, but there is something. He knows what he has to do, and what he has to do to do it. It's time to pull away, to separate. Thinking ahead of the craft. "What's the matter with *you?*" he says.

The waiter arrives, breaking the tension as he lays out first her plate, the blackened steak, and then Payne's blanched *focaccia.* Enjoy, the waiter says. Enjoy, thinks Payne, it's your last meal, as she lifts her knife and fork and starts to cut into her baked potato. He watches as she fills it full of butter, sour cream. He watches as she cuts and lifts and takes a bite, blowing on the hot potato, blowing with her pursed pink lips.

"What kind of men?" he says.

"It was a bar, okay?" She drops her fork back on her plate and lifts her wineglass to her lips. But she does not drink. She simply holds it there like a shield. "Why you askin'?"

"Just curious."

She takes a sip of her wine. "Yeah, well, you know what they say. Curiosity killed the cat."

He starts to laugh. He looks down at his round *focaccia*. He takes his knife and cuts it down the middle. White cheese begins to trail the blade, oozing from the incision. "Call me foolhardy," he says. "I want to know. What men?" He looks up from his plate.

She puts her wineglass on the table. She stares at him, her hardest stare, but Payne has set himself already. He is prepared. He has withdrawn under the Plexiglas, inside the bubble, and her dark round eyes don't penetrate. He can watch, but they can't touch him. He is above, and climbing.

"I think I'll try Carol." She stands. She picks her jacket up and throws it over her arm.

"Don't go, Laura."

"I'll be right back."

He reaches for her wrist but she slips out from behind the table, just out of reach. She doesn't even look back.

He watches her maneuver within the crush of the chattering crowd, the press of tables. Heads turn as she glides by. He sees the plaid curve of her hips and then she's gone, and in the vestibule beyond. He sees her settle by the telephones. She picks up a receiver. She drops a coin in with a gentle arching of the wrist. She turns away.

Payne takes a sip of his wine. It tastes rich and full and fills his head with mist for a moment as he swallows, as the bouquet gradually surrounds him. He takes another sip and turns and for a moment everything stands still, the voices of the seething crowd, the sound of knives and forks, the sax, the steady mastication of a hundred mouths. He bobs and twists, but still he cannot see her. She is gone. The vestibule is empty. She's disappeared.

Payne is up in a flash. He throws a hundred-dollar bill on the table and tears into the crowd. He pushes through the restaurant, mindless of everyone. All he can see is the front door, the front door and the snowflakes falling. He dashes through the vestibule. He hurls his coat on as he pushes through and he is out on Twenty-third, and scanning the crowd, the bowed heads and ducked shoulders. But there are just too many people, too many moving parts. He looks up at the sky in desperation. "Shit," he says. "Shit!" He feels the cold air tearing at his lungs as he breathes in, as he breathes out and turns and hangs his head and looks down at the snow, the cold white snow, and the trail of tiny footprints running east.

Payne takes off at a furious pace. At first the trail is easy to follow, black on white, distinct and separate from the larger footprints closer to the curb. But soon the path is crossed and recrossed by a dozen other paths and it becomes more difficult to distinguish. He nears the corner of Twenty-third and Eighth, when he sees the dark distinctive back, makes out the cheap black jacket and the earmuffs. Laura is standing by an open pay phone, huddled against it really, with her face half hidden by the shadows. He walks up right behind her. She has not seen him, has not felt him even as he presses up against her, takes the receiver from her hand, and puts it to his ear.

"Hello?" a voice says on the other end. It is a girl's voice, out of breath. Carol's voice. "Hello, who's there? Who is that?"

He hangs up the receiver. Laura does not even struggle in his arms. The smell of her envelops him, the warmth, the scent of fear. It is palpable. It fills his head like the wine. "That was stupid, Laura. Or should I call you Susan?"

She turns and looks at him, defiant. The fear is still there, simply masked and camouflaged with anger. "I don't know what you're talking about."

"Don't play games with me, Laura." He reaches into his jacket. He pulls the gun out, presses it against her. He can feel her hot breath on his face.

"What do you want from me?" she says.

"The truth."

She frowns and looks down at the gun. "You're hurting me."

"I know."

"Listen, Sam. I'll do whatever you want. Just don't hurt me, okay? Don't do anything you're going to regret later."

"I have too much to regret already." A couple walks by with a baby carriage. The carriage is covered with clear plastic, and Payne can see a baby sleeping soundlessly within. Blue for a boy. He laughs and draws his arm around her, trapping Laura in his embrace. She seems so tiny now. She seems so small and vulnerable— the soft curves, the warmth, the cold nub of the gun between them. He laughs again, and the couple moves away. "Do exactly what I tell you to do, Laura, and you may get out of this in one piece."

"What do you want from me?"

"We're going up the street to that hotel. Up there, see it? I've already checked in. We're going to go upstairs and have a little conversation, and if you tell me the truth, if you don't lie to me . . . then we'll see. I may just let you go. Okay?"

"Okay," she says. "Whatever you say. Just don't hurt me."

He slips the gun into the outside pocket of his leather jacket and pushes her up the street. He keeps one step behind her as they walk, holding her tightly by the arm. He can feel his fingers digging into her, but he doesn't care. The more he hurts her, the worse he feels. And the worse he feels, the more he has to punish himself by hurting her again. He is caught up in the rhythm of the blades. He begins to whistle quietly. Some nameless classical piece. Some Mozart allegro. He drives her on for two more blocks until they hesitate outside the entrance to a large gray building ribbed with balconies. A red neon sign blinks overhead, staining the falling snow. THE CHELSEA SQUARE HOTEL. NO VACANCIES. "Don't say anything," he says. "I'll do the talking." He pushes her inside.

It is unbearably hot in the lobby. The paneled walls are covered with canvases of modern art, a mural, and a mobile made of high-top sneakers. The hotel is a landmark in the neighborhood, a haven at one time or another for every outcast generation, from beat to punk rock psychedelia. There is a tall wooden cage at the other end of the lobby. Payne pushes Laura closer, closer to the elevators, underneath the cut-glass chandelier, the nude, the Hudson River landscape. The fat man in the cage looks over his glasses at Laura. He looks up and down and up and back at Payne and smiles a toothy smile. Then he turns back to his black-and-white TV.

They take the elevator. Payne holds Laura by the arm as they ascend. The elevator lurches to a stop at the sixth floor, and they are walking down a narrow corridor with dark red carpeting and cheap glass chandeliers. "Sixty-six," says Payne and stops. He looks at Laura. She is shivering in his hand like a live wire. He slips the key into the lock. He turns and pushes and they are in the darkened room, right next to one another. The door slams shut behind them, but neither of them moves. Neither reaches for the light switch. They tarry for a moment in the darkness, afraid to take the next step, unwilling to move on, pressed together, warmth to warmth, each flickering with life. And then, reluctantly, he turns. He reaches for the wall. He runs his hand along the surface for the light switch, and it is on, and she begins to move away. She backs into the room, beyond the two twin beds, the pressed wood armoire, and the large TV, beside the small Formica table and the shabby chairs.

She sits down at the table. She sits bolt upright, links her hands together in her lap and stares at Payne, trying to look right through him.

Payne takes the gun out of his leather jacket. He takes the jacket off. He is wearing a simple gray sweater underneath, and a pair of faded jeans. He walks over to the door and chains it shut. Then he turns and looks at her. She is staring at the empty TV screen. He studies the gun in his hand. He feels the weight of it. He pulls the action back. He puts a finger round the trigger. He admires the elegant black compactness. It is an efficient machine. He reaches into his jacket on the table and takes out the silencer. It is heavier than it looks. It is dense and grim, a serious piece of metal. He starts to screw the silencer onto the barrel of the gun. It spins with the quiet satisfaction of a perfect fit. The silencer sets in place. Now, he is done. Now, there is nothing left to do. He has to look at her. He has to lift his face and ask her and be sure. Above all else, be sure, he thinks, be sure before you . . .

He lays the gun on the bed. He looks at her. He says, "Tell me about the lounge, Laura."

"I don't know what you mean, Sam." She shrugs a tiny shrug. She turns her hand out for a moment, and then brings it back into her lap. "Honest, I don't."

"Don't make me hurt you, Laura."

"Please, Sam."

He picks the gun up again. "The lounge. The Party Girl Lounge," he says. "You used to work there, didn't you?"

"Please, Sam."

"You used the name Susan." He takes a step closer, waving the gun. "Remember? Tell me about the men, Laura, the men that watch you."

"Please, mister. My name's Laura Molloy. I don't know anything."

"Take off your jacket, Laura."

"I'm cold. I—"

"Take it off, I said."

She starts to unzip her jacket. She slips it off.

"And the sweater. Stand up."

She stands. She hesitates and says, "Please, Sam. Please don't do this."

"Stop calling me that."

"I'm sorry. What do you want me to call you?"

"Take it off."

She takes her glasses off and lays them on the table. She pulls the heather blue crew-neck sweater over her head. "There you go," she says. "It's off."

"Now the turtleneck."

"Come on," she says. "Don't do this." Her voice begins to quake. "You don't want to do this." She sways a little at the waist. "Please, mister." She shakes her head. "Please."

"The turtleneck."

She reaches down and rolls the black material up, and lifts it over her head. A tress of hair falls to the side. She tears the material from her arms as though it's scalding hot. She stands there shivering, her arms across her breasts. She is wearing a lacy black bra. She looks down at the floor.

"All of it," he says.

She turns away. She stares up at the French doors leading to the balcony. Twenty-third Street flashes at the night. The snow is heavier. It falls and falls and falls. She turns her back to him as she unsnaps her bra in front, and slips the straps off, one by one. "Oh, God. Oh, God," she says, and he can hear her voice crack as she hunches forward. She puts a hand out to the table for support. He sees the muscles quiver in her back. She reaches up and starts to pull the pins out of her hair. The knot slowly unravels. The hair begins to fall in tresses down her back, until, untied, it shimmers in a great wave as she lifts it up and shakes it suddenly, and free. She stands erect. Her head falls back. A hand slips to her hip. She turns to face him, one hand still holding a strand of dark brown hair between white fingers, holding it almost to her mouth, and he can see her clearly now in the half light, the narrow shoulders, the dark line of her cleavage, leading down, the heavy swelling of her breasts and underneath, that birthmark, heart-shaped and pink, the color of wine, like a stain on a tablecloth, a sheet, a mattress dripping in the dark.

"See what you came to see?" she says, and smiles, and it is Susan smiling, Susan of the small, white, even teeth, of the white skin, slightly freckled, as if the very act, the motion of disrobing has, like an incantation, changed her.

XVIII

"Sit down, Laura." Payne stuffs the gun in his belt.

Laura sits down on one of the shabby wooden chairs by the Formica table. He walks around her, trying not to stare, trying to think.

He picks her bra up from the floor and uses it to lash her wrists together, bending the underwire around the slats of the chair.

"You're hurting me," she says.

"Shut up."

"Please, Sam—"

"Shut up. I told you not to call me that."

He finishes tying her. He stands behind her, looking down, looking at her long brown hair, her shoulders and her breasts, her nipples and her skirt, but not her face. From here he cannot see her face. "Susan?"

"What is it . . . John?"

He feels a chill run up his spine. "Tell me about the lounge, Susan."

"What about it?" Her voice is low and even now.

"You remember. A week ago. The night of the bachelor party. There were four of us. No, five. How many were we? I've forgotten now."

"There were five. You know that, John. There were five of you."

"That's right."

"And you were all happy, and you tipped real nice."

"And then what happened, Susan?"

"What do you mean?"

"What happened to Yolanda?"

"I don't know," she says. "She just stopped coming to work."

"Don't lie to me. What happened, Susan? You and Candy tried to find her. You went to her loft."

"She was gone."

"What about the mattress, Susan? Remember?"

"Please, John. Please! I don't know anything. I don't want to know anything. Call a priest if you want to confess."

He pulls the gun from his belt. He stands in front of her, brandishing the weapon in her face. He grabs her by the hair. "The mattress, remember? What did Candy do?"

"Let go of me." She tries to shake free, but he simply holds her tighter, wrenching her head back, exposing her throat. He points the gun at her face.

"Candy wanted that necklace. The one from the islands, remember? Coral and gold. And she picked up the mattress, and there . . . there it was, remember?" He shakes her by the hair. "Remember?"

"The stain," she says, almost inaudibly. "The blood, Yolanda's blood. All over everything." She looks up at his face. "And then we put it back. We just put the mattress back and left, and locked the door as if nothing had ever happened."

"You're lying. She told you something, didn't she? You and Candy were friends."

"What do you mean? What do you mean, we *were* friends? Told me what?"

"About her plans with Bumper?"

"I don't know what you're talking about. I haven't seen Candy since that day we went to Yolanda's loft. Why don't you ask her? You've obviously been talking with her. Haven't you? You must have. You knew about the necklace. Ask her, why don't you? Why don't you?"

He laughs. It seems to rise up out of nowhere from within. It is completely uncontrolled. His hand begins to shake, his hand, his fingers, and the gun. He holds on to her hair. He draws her close. "You're lying, Susan. You know exactly who we are, don't you? You even know our names."

"Look, I don't know anything. If I knew, why would I have gone out with you? I guessed your name, that's all. And I don't give a shit. I just want to get out of here. I just want to graduate and move to California. That's all. I don't care what you guys did. I don't know what happened to Yolanda. I don't want to know. I don't care. I don't care what Candy said."

"I'll tell you what Candy said. She said, 'Please don't hurt me,' just like you, Susan. Just like you." He puts the silencer to her lips, but his hand keeps shaking. He forces the tip into her mouth.

"Just like you, Susan. Candy tried to blackmail us. And Morrow and Litchfield took her to this trailer, and she told them, 'Let me make it up to you.' And she did, at least she tried to, with the only currency she had. Just like this." He buries the silencer in her mouth. "Just like this, Susan."

She starts to cry. He can feel her head shivering as he tightens his grasp on her hair.

"But they didn't care, because she knew, Susan. She knew," he says. "Just like you do. She knew about us, about all of us. What we're really like. Inside, Susan. Whether we do it or not. Whether it happens or it doesn't. That's why she had to die. That's why Morrow killed her. Just like that. Blew her head off in the sink after they'd fucked her for a while, one after the other. Blew her fucking head off. And I was there. I was right there. And I did nothing to stop them."

She tries to say something but the words are swallowed by the silencer in her mouth. She tries to speak, but it is only formless sound, only the background hum of rotor blades, the constant scratching of cicadas. It can't get through the Plexiglas. The world, it can't get through. Like the baby in Jan's uterus, he is insulated, safe, aware of every side street of the city but never close, always a step away, a layer of skin, a thousand feet. He feels his finger on the trigger. He knows what he has to do. Why doesn't he do it, damn it? Why doesn't he get it over with, right now, just like that?

You move a finger and it's done. It's so easy, John. It's like a drug. She saw the blood. She knows, she knows. She talked to Candy. *Kill her. Kill her. Pull the trigger. You did it before. You're already guilty.* And he pulls her head back with the gun still in her mouth. For Jan. For the unborn baby, too. He looks down at her face, the frightened eyes, the tears. *You're already a killer—kill her, kill her, kill her!* And he rises, trying to balance, trying to keep steady, and the blades come up and he is through, like a moment of transitional lift, and he can see himself reflected in her eyes. The distance melts away. He is no longer watching. He is there. It is like the great weight of an ocean has been lifted from his chest. He feels her breath, her quaking heart. He pulls the gun out of her mouth, and drops it to the floor.

"I'm sorry, Laura," he says. "I'm so sorry." He presses his hands to his eyes. "I can't. I don't care what's happened." He shakes his head. "I just can't. Not anymore."

He moves around her and unties her hands. But as he stands he feels the blood rush from his head, and sways and sits down on the nearest bed. It is all over now, he thinks. The lack of food, the sleepless nights have all caught up with him. He feels the slowing of the blades. He feels her sitting down beside him, the slight depression of the mattress, the warmth. He feels her arm around him, drawing him closer, close until the cold steel of the silencer is puckering his face.

"What are you doing?" he says.

"Letting you feel what Candy felt, just before you shot her." The gun bites the bone at his temple.

"I didn't shoot her. I told you. It was Morrow."

"And Yolanda? Was that Morrow too?"

Payne shakes his head. "No, that was—"

The phone rings. Payne looks over at the nightstand near the bed. It rings again. He turns and looks at Laura. She is staring at the telephone. It rings a third time. He reaches over. He looks at her. He picks up the receiver. He puts it to his ear.

"This is your wake-up call," Morrow says. "We're coming up."

XIX

"Let's get the hell out of here." Payne drops the phone back on the hook.

Laura jumps up from the bed, still pointing the gun at his face. "Where are you going?"

Payne laughs. "Either shoot me or put the gun down, Laura, but whatever you do, do it fast. Morrow's going to be here any minute, and he's not like me. . . . He's going to kill you, Laura."

"Why do you care? If I'm dead, you and your friends can all breathe easy."

Payne shrugs. "I don't know why I care. I didn't think I cared about anything anymore. But this has got to stop, Laura. Right now." He rises to his feet. "Listen, don't be a fool. These guys are after you. I can help you, Laura. I know them. I know how they think. You need me. Let me help you."

"Why should I trust you? Why do you want to help me suddenly?"

"You don't have any other choice. Like it or not, we're both in this together now."

She stands there for a moment without speaking. Payne rushes over to the little pile of clothes on the floor beside the table. He picks up her turtleneck, hands it to her. "Go on," he says. "Put your clothes on."

She presses the turtleneck to her chest.

"Hurry up, for Christ's sake, Laura. They're going to kill you."

"What about you?"

"Don't worry about me. Maybe they'll let me go. Maybe they'll shoot me. I don't know."

"Then why are you helping me?"

"Because I have to, don't you see? It's over for me now. I've got nothing left." He shakes his head. "Unless I do this now, I'll never be able to live with myself again. Never. This is my last chance."

She looks at him for a moment longer. She looks at the clothes in her hand. Then she suddenly throws the handgun on the bed. "Let's go."

Payne takes a quick look through the peephole before slipping out the door. They make their way along the corridor, looking for a fire door, a service stair, looking for any way out. They spy an exit sign, and they are down the stairs, with Laura in the lead, the sound of their flat footsteps echoing around them. By the time they reach the first floor, they are both out of breath. They pause for a moment by the door. Payne cracks it open slightly. It leads into the lobby. He can see the same sad landscape, the same mobile that he had seen on the way in. And there's the cage, and the fat man watching his TV.

"All right," he whispers. "Here's the plan." The stairwell magnifies each sound. "My car is parked in front. It's a bright red Honda. You can't miss it. Here are the keys. Start the car and wait for me." He hands them to her.

"What about you?"

"I'll be right behind you. You go first. They don't know you, but they'll spot me in an instant. Go, damn it. *Go.*" He pushes her out into the lobby. She hesitates, then starts to walk, slowly, nonchalantly, toward the entrance. When she is about halfway there, she turns around and looks back at the elevators. Then she smiles and turns, and vanishes through the door.

Payne holds his breath. He takes a step into the lobby. There is no one about. There is no one but the fat man in the cage. He takes another step. There are a couple of pillars by the elevators, partially blocking his view. He starts to walk a little faster. He is closer to the front door, closer, and he turns and stares back at the elevators, and there—a shadow and then two, they turn and it is Litchfield's round familiar shape, and to his side, the blocky shoulders of Glen Morrow.

Payne turns and runs the last few steps. He dashes through the door. He skids along the snowy sidewalk. The red Accord is panting at the curb. Laura is at the wheel. She is trying to maneuver out of the space.

Payne jumps into the passenger seat. "Let's go," he says. He turns the windshield wipers on. It is still snowing. Great white flakes shatter on the glass.

"I'm trying. Some parking job!"

"They must have pulled in after me."

"Yeah, sure!"

Tires squeal. The car rocks back and forth.

"Just drive," he says, and then he sees them in the hotel door. Morrow is wearing a black cashmere coat, a bright red scarf. Litchfield is straining to look past him, looking not at Payne or the Accord, but at the car behind. Payne turns and looks out the rear window. It is Morrow's BMW, night black and ominous. It is blocking their retreat.

"Gun it," he says. He locks the doors.

"I can't."

"Gun it. Back right into it."

Hands pound against the windows. She slips the car into reverse and guns the engine. There is a great crash, a hair-raising screech of tearing steel, and the car hurtles backward a foot. A burglar alarm powers on. There is the sound of breaking glass as Laura slips back into drive. The Honda catches on the front right bumper, it turns and stops, then suddenly jumps free, and they are in the street and screaming.

"Pull a u-ee," he orders. "Go west."

She spins the steering wheel and the car turns flawlessly around. They skid on the snow, burn rubber, and stop. She guns the engine. The tires spin, and they are traveling the other way.

Somewhere a car honks. Somewhere they hear Glen Morrow's burglar alarm still whining, still honking furiously, and then it stops. A pair of headlights impales them from behind. A squeal of tires, a sudden growl, and their car is shaken by a crash. It is Morrow on their tail. He is trying to drive them off the road.

"Go, go," says Payne. He is screaming now.

The red Accord leaps forward. Another car tries to pull out suddenly ahead of them and they are forced to shift into the other lane, forced to skip and dodge the charge of bright oncoming cars. There is a furious howl of honking. They pull back in their lane. Payne turns. A gold Dodge Aries is double-parked outside of Mayhem, and a man in a pea coat is standing right beside it, yelling, shaking his fist. And just behind him is Glen Morrow's car. The night black BMW almost clips the stranger in the back as it speeds by.

"Go right," Payne shouts, and Laura jerks the wheel. The car begins to skid, then rights itself.

"Make a left on Twenty-ninth." They are tearing up Eighth Avenue, weaving the traffic, winding first right, then left, yet always mindful of the black car in pursuit, hearing the mighty engine growling in their wake. At Twenty-ninth, Laura waits and turns the wheel at the last moment. The car begins to skid and fishtail but a taxi bumps it back on course, and they are traveling down the side street. Payne looks up through the rear view mirror. The BMW went too far. Morrow is forced to stop, to back up fitfully against oncoming traffic, to stop again to make the turn on Twenty-ninth.

"Make a right," says Payne. Laura turns and they are idling at the West Side Highway. "Go straight," he says and points. "Right into the heliport. Right through the fucking gate. What are you waiting for? *Go on!*"

The car jumps across the highway, barely avoiding the passing cars, the median, the line of orange cones. They pick up speed. The car is whining as they move, whining and screaming, shedding metal, picking up speed, picking up speed and flying through the metal gate, the yards of cold barbed wire and the concrete base. There is a great rending of metal and glass and the Accord shudders to a stop.

The horn is honking. The horn is honking, turn it off. Payne wills himself awake. Laura is slumped over the steering wheel. There are glass fragments all over her face. Her face is glowing in the dark. It seems to be on fire. He shakes himself. He shouts, "Come on, let's go. Laura, wake up." He pushes her and she begins to stir. "Let's get out of here. I smell gas."

He jumps out of the car. The horn is blaring. He runs around to Laura's side and yanks her door open. She staggers to her feet. Somewhere he hears a pop, a crackle, and then a cloud of sour black smoke begins to pour out of the crumpled hood. "Come on. It's going to blow," he says.

He grabs her by the waist and drags her toward the heliport. There is another pop, a kind of whistling and the night sky lights up with a bang. Payne feels himself picked up and carried like a snowflake. It seems to take forever as he floats and twists and rolls across the sky, admiring the yellow and the gold, the bright magnesium whiteness of the flash, and then the cold uncompromising hardness of the tarmac. There is a great whoosh as the vacuum blown out by the blast is filled. Pieces of metal rain about them, and Payne finds himself trying to cover Laura with his body. She is screaming in his ear.

"Come on," he shouts. "Let's go."

He rolls in one swift movement to his feet. Adrenaline is coursing through his veins. He can feel it. He can feel it pumping his muscles as he lifts her like a child. "Are you okay?" he says.

She nods and leans on him. Her face is lit up by the burning car. Her hair is streaming out behind her, flickering with snowflakes and shattered glass.

He looks beyond her at the open tarmac. Two helicopters are parked beside the tower. They shimmer in the fire. They almost seem to be alive, the way they glow and glimmer in the light. The wind shifts suddenly, and the air is full of acrid smoke. Payne reaches out. He snatches Laura by the hand and starts to pull her toward the helicopters.

"Get in," he shouts, as he steps up. He opens the passenger door.

"Are you crazy? Do you know how to fly this thing?"

"Get in," he shouts.

She climbs inside. He slams the door behind her. The fire is burning out of control. It is streaming across the tarmac on a wave of gasoline. In a minute it will reach the tower.

Payne runs around the helicopter and climbs into the pilot's seat. The sound of the fire is muffled as he slams the door. He can still see rolling flames, and black smoke billowing into the sky, drifting across the Hudson to the west. But it is as if the fire is in another world now. On TV. Somehow unreal.

He picks up his headset and slips it on. Then he makes sure that Laura has her headset and seat belt on before he starts the cockpit check. He moves his hand down by his left foot to check the center console switches.

"Are you sure you know what you're doing? Don't you need a key, or something?" she says.

He pushes the igniter overhead. His left hand settles on the collective, and his right hand on the cyclic between his legs. He tests the directional controls beneath his feet.

"You don't need a key," he says. "Who would steal one of these things? There are less than two hundred people in the whole damn city who can fly one. And besides . . ." He turns and looks at her, his face suddenly morose. "It's a serious FAA violation."

Then he smiles. He flicks the throttle open, pulls the trigger, and the electric motor whines. The rotors slowly spin. The turbine hisses, coughs, and catches. The needle on the exhaust-gas temperature gauge rushes past the red line as the rotors start to blur.

Thump. Thump. Thump. Payne opens up the throttle. The EGT slips back to green. He checks the rotor disk to see that it responds, and as he does, he stops, and hesitates, and sees the headlights of a car explode across the tarmac, like the eyes of some great cat, the telltale silhouette of Morrow's BMW. "Hold on," he says. The fire inches closer. He pulls up the collective and the nose of the helicopter slowly rises off the ground. He corrects for drift. The helicopter stabilizes and he raises the collective further. The ship lifts higher, higher, higher as the BMW slinks forward to a stop. Morrow gets out, then Litchfield too. Payne can see their faces through the whirling snow, illuminated by the flames. Morrow is reaching into his coat. He is looking up, and then a small white flash of fire is followed by a crash, and wind starts whistling through the Plexiglas.

"That asshole's shooting at me," Laura says.

Payne noses the cyclic forward and the helicopter starts to move. He twists the throttle and the ship accelerates across the Hudson, faster and faster until he feels it jump into a climb. Transitional lift. The rotors whir. They turn and swing across the river, leaving the fire behind, leaving the noise and the bullets and the smoke. Payne climbs and climbs and climbs, into the snowy night.

"He's coming after us."

"He's what?" says Payne.

"Look. The thing is practically on fire."

Payne looks down through the Plexiglas. The tower is billowing with flames. They seem to lap against the spinning rotor blades. There is a flash of light as something blows up in the tower. The concussion seems to lift the other helicopter off the ground. Blades blur and the machine is carried up into the night, above the fireball, the shards of glass, the heat. It rises like a phoenix through the sky.

"Great," says Payne. He pulls on the collective, pushing the left pedal automatically. He flares the disk. "Better tighten your belt. We're in for a bit of a ride."

"John?"

"What is it?"

"I've never been in a helicopter before."

He smiles. "Don't worry," he says. "I've never been in a helicopter with people shooting at me before. Piece 'a cake."

He twists the cyclic, drops the collective, and the helicopter veers away. She dives and glides along the river, ten feet above the water, traveling at a hundred and twenty knots. The engine roars. Laura is screaming. Her stomach is still at a hundred feet.

They skim the whitecaps, traveling south. Manhattan flashes to their left. TriBeCa, where it all began, the Party Girl, the Quonset Hut, the flat gray roofs, then City Hall, the gold dome of the World Financial Center. They climb and climb and Payne can see the other ship begin to swim up in their jetstream, flashing, flashing like a constant drip of red on the black sky. Morrow is gaining on them. He has a faster ship. It seems to cut right through the snow, while Payne's ship jumps and yaws along the frigid air, skipping like a stone.

Payne flares and brings his helicopter in over Manhattan, sliding north across the World Trade towers. Steady, he tells himself. Steady now. He swings the ship in close, less than a rotor from the glass, trying to lose himself against the backdrop, in the reflection of the skyscraper and the whirling snow.

Morrow's helicopter appears. It is running off the river, flying south, its nose swung eastward, searching, probing in between the buildings. Then it is gone. It's passed; he's fooled them. Payne pulls up the collective and the helicopter rises. He swings the ship around.

"Are they gone?" Laura's voice sounds tinny and brittle through the headset.

"I think so. I think we lost them. They couldn't see us against the tower."

"What's that?"

"I said, they couldn't—"

"No—*that!*" But there is no need for an answer. There is a flash of light behind him. A wind picks up their ship. He can hear the other helicopter, he can see it too now, the flashing lights, the two distinctive shapes inside the bubble. There is a crack, a spark, a bullet ricochets through the cabin.

"Jesus Christ!" says Payne. He pushes the controls and the ship dives forward suddenly, falling, falling. They skim around the tower, and up and round the other side, then round again. They weave across the Battery, swing north, and double back. Payne has never flown so recklessly. He feels his skids brush trees, sees upturned faces screaming in the snow-blown streets below. The engine whines, he climbs and climbs, and he is back between the World Trade towers, and there is not another ship in sight.

"Where are they?" Payne says, straining round. "Where the hell are they?"

"I can't see them. I think you've really lost them this time. You did it, John. You did it!"

Payne lets the ship veer slowly to the south. He lets it pick up speed, to skate, to skim across the ferry launch, and they are once again out on the open water of the bay. Payne scans the snowy sky, but there is nothing flying anywhere in sight, save for that lonely ship up by the Maxwell House sign on the Jersey side. The neon coffee drips out of the neon coffee cup. *Good To The Last Drop.* Drips and drips. That lonely ship . . . with the familiar lights. Morrow!

What was he doing? Why was he flying on the Jersey side? He wasn't heading west to Teterboro. He was heading north.

The helicopter tilts and dives. Laura screams as the ship begins to pick up speed, to skim the churning waters of the Hudson. "What's going on?" she cries. "You're flying directly towards them."

"I know."

"You know!"

"Just do exactly what I say, Laura. Do you hear me? Exactly." He takes the gun out of his leather jacket.

"What are you doing?"

"Listen to me, Laura. Morrow wants you. He'll do anything, use anyone to get you. Anyone."

"Where are we going, John?"

"Upriver. Up the Hudson, north." The helicopter howls and slices at the snow-filled sky. "Home."

XX

Jan wakes to a thunderclap, to windows rattling in their frames, the night sky shivering like tent cloth all around her. She rolls. Lancets of light stream through the skylight, pinning her to the sheets. She opens her eyes. *Thump, thump, thump,* the light is gone, and the sound trails off to one ear, fading. She blinks her eyes, rolls awkwardly to her left side. She props herself up on one elbow. The helicopter or airplane, or whatever it was, is gone. The engine has died out. The night descends, muffling the world. Jan reaches over and turns the light on by the bed. The skylight is covered with snow. It must have been a dream, she thinks, stretching her back. Her back has been aching for months. She runs her hands along her pregnant stomach, feeling the full, familiar contour, the presence underneath.

What's that? She turns her head. What was that noise downstairs? Only the wind. She spies the postcard on the bedside table. The thick green palm trees, the golden surf. She reaches for it, caught in the currents of the blue-green waters, drawn to the coral reef. She turns the postcard over in her hand. *Having a great time. Anguilla is beautiful! Thanks for everything. Love, Anna and Tom.* She studies the brightly colored stamp, the spikes of creamy petals and the golden crown, like a lotus blossom, its scent unraveling on the breeze, down to the shimmering surf, the sand and the forgetful sea. What's that?

Jan drops the postcard on the table. She slips out of bed, sup-
porting her back, trying to be as quiet as she can. Her swollen feet
slide into her slippers. She picks her robe up from the window seat
and ties it on. It sounds like a kind of scraping, like metal on wood.
She hesitates at the stairs. She casts an anxious glance into the
nursery. The darkness of the stairwell surges like a wave, lapping at
her feet. There is something down there. She can sense it. It is very
close. She can feel the baby shift inside her, turn a quarter turn.
The scraping stops. For a moment there is silence. Then out of the
darkness she feels a draft rise up around her, a cold relentless
breeze that eddies through her legs, beneath her arms, like the
touch of a ghost.

The moon is hidden by the clouds, but light still glances off the
sloping branches of the evergreens, the sparkling snowflakes, the
glazed expanse of the back lawn. Jan stands beside the sun porch
door. She scans the lawn, searching the shadows, the shrubs, the
melting snowmen to the distant meadow below, but there is nothing out of place. She rubs her arms to warm herself. The house is
strangely quiet in the darkness. The window begins to fog. She
bunches her sleeve in her hand and rubs the condensation from the
glass. The sound, like the squeak of a heel, reverberates around the
room, echos down the empty hall. Clouds roll by. The moon peeks
through, and then the whole bright smiling face reveals itself, and
everything illuminates. Lozenge of love—who called it that? The
meadow glistens in the distance, the writhing branches of the apple
trees, the sagging of the rotor blades, the round face of the helicopter. Helicopter! A headless snowman stands beside it like a senti-
nel. The snow-glazed field reveals a line of footprints running from
the ship. She follows the trail like the fuse of a bomb, along the
field, across the low stone wall, the buried pachysandra and the
tulip beds, drawing closer, closer, across the picket fence, the white
lawn streaming like a clean sheet to the door.

"Hello, Jan."

She freezes in the dark. That voice. She closes her eyes and
presses her face against the glass. It is so cold. "Hello, Glen. What
are you doing here?" She turns around, slowly, unwilling to be cer-

tain. Morrow and Litchfield sidle into view. "And Bobby too. What a surprise." Where is her anger? She looks at Morrow's smiling face. He is wearing a long black coat, a bright red scarf. His trousers are wet from the snow.

"Sit down, Jan." He motions her toward the table in the sun porch. He motions, but his hand stays in his pocket.

She sits down at the table. It is dark in the paneled sun porch. Only the moonlight washes through the windows, illuminating Morrow's face. "What's going on, Glen?"

"We're waiting for John."

"At this time of the . . ." she starts to say, but the words fall off into space. She is silenced by Morrow's stare. He is gazing at her with a blank impassive face. His eyes fall in and out of focus. His blond hair is tousled. He smiles, but it is not the warm engaging smile that she has seen him conjure up a thousand times before. Not the paternal smile, the rueful or the ready grin. There is something desperate about Morrow's face. Something hungry.

"You look cold," he says. "Are you cold, Jan? You've barely got anything on."

"Where's John?" she says, trying to change the subject.

"He's on his way. He'll be here any minute. Don't worry."

The words cut into her like knives. An icy chill cleaves her spine. "I'm not worried. Should I be worried, Glen?" Litchfield shuffles in the corner. He is staring out the window, at the meadow in the back.

"That all depends."

"On what."

"On John. He's got something . . . someone we want. And we've got you."

"What are you saying?"

Morrow sits down beside her at the table. "It's been such a long time since we just sat and talked, hasn't it, Jan? It seems like ages. I never get to see you anymore. I know—I saw you at the wedding. But I mean *really* talked. Like in the old days."

"What do you want from me, Glen?"

He starts to laugh. "I don't want anything *from* you, Jan. I want to give you something."

"What?"

"Something precious," he replies. He hesitates, then smiles. "Something at the heart of every good marriage."

"What are you talking about?" She hears the shrillness in her voice.

"The truth, Jan. The truth about yourself. The truth about John." He takes her by the hand. She tries to pull away, but his icy fingers grip her tighter. "You think you know John, don't you? You think you know him pretty well, better than anyone."

"Let go of me."

"But you don't, Jan. Not like I know him. Let me tell you about John."

"Why are you doing this?"

"Let me tell you about Tom's bachelor party, about what really happened that night. It's about time you got to know the man you're married to." He gives her hand a little squeeze. "The man he *really* is." And he begins to tell her. He tells her about the Quonset Hut, about the laughter and champagne, about the waitress. He tells her about the Party Girl Lounge. He tells her about Yolanda dancing, and the coke. He describes the way that Payne looked as Laura took the stage, the way he stood and reached out with the money in his hand, the way he pressed it in between her breasts.

"He loved that girl. He couldn't take his eyes off her. She looks a little like you, come to think of it. But younger. Maybe twenty-two. The same white skin." He strokes her hand. "The same brown eyes."

Jan sits there without moving. She can barely breathe. Morrow's words seem to linger in the air, seem to wash against her like a fog.

He tells her about Yolanda's loft, about the way Payne struggled to his feet and shuffled down the corridor to take his turn. About the scream.

Jan fights to keep the tears back from her eyes. She can feel Morrow's long thin fingers stroke her arm, the fingernails caress her. They seem to tear the skin right from the bone as he describes the room, the bloody corpse, and Payne's white naked body, shivering.

"We stuffed her in a plastic garment bag, and we took her out to Teterboro, and put her in John's chopper. He flew. We dumped her somewhere out to sea, down past the Verrazano Bridge. And everything looked great there for a while. It looked like we'd made it, when one of the other dancers called, a girl named Candy. She threatened to tell the cops unless we paid her off. . . ."

The story unfurls like a bandage, each word revealing a new horror underneath. Morrow describes the meeting with Candy, how Bumper tried to threaten them, and how Morrow had been forced to kill him and the girl in self-defense. "And John was there the whole time, just watching at the door. Your John. The one you thought you knew. The man you married. The whore fucker. You should have seen his face when he went back there to Yolanda. Man, he could barely control himself. How long had it been for him? What's the matter, Jan? Something missing at home?" He strokes her hand. "Well, he's found it now. Her name is Laura. And she's flying with him here right now. That's right. The one he liked. The young one. He doesn't want to give her up. That's why we're here. Because, unlike you, I know John. I know that even though he'd rather die than hurt her, he's going to hand her over to us. To me." He takes her by the hand. "Poor, poor Jan. If only I could say he's doing it for you. For love, even. But he's not. He needs you, Jan. But not who you really are. He needs what you represent. His old life. His family. The home he thinks he's lost, and longs for."

The words drill into Jan. She feels the tears sting her eyes. She feels them coursing down her cheeks.

"I can give him to you, or I can take him away. It's up to you, Jan. Just like before. All we want is the girl. And you want *him*, I know it. I know you."

He reaches out and takes her by the back of the neck. He draws her close to him. "I remember, Jan. The little Point o' Woods girl who just couldn't wait to grow up, who almost died right on the spot the night I asked her out."

"Don't, Glen." Jan tries to pull away.

"I remember the stroll along the walkway in the Pines. You were so drunk, you just wouldn't take no for an answer. And when you took your top off on the beach, and laid down on the sand for me, did you really expect me to touch you?"

"Don't, Glen. Please don't."

"Just like that. Did you expect me to fuck you when I knew that John was crazy about you? Just because you wanted it?"

"Let me go."

"And so you made up that story about me, which no one believed anyway. Just so you wouldn't be embarrassed. Just so that no one would know what you'd done."

"Glen. Glen, I hear something." Litchfield presses his fat face to the window. "There. Can you hear it?"

A helicopter drones in the distance. Jan can hear the telltale thumping of the engine stutter in the night sky.

"Remember, Jan," Morrow says. "I can give him to you. Or I can take him away. All we want is the girl."

Thump, thump. "I see him, Glen," cries Litchfield. A light sweeps through the sun porch. "He's coming down."

Morrow takes Jan by the hand and lifts her to her feet. They look through the sun porch windows at the distant meadow below. A helicopter is landing in a burst of snow and flashing lights. The engine dies. The rotors start to slow. A figure gets out of the bubble. It's Payne. He runs around to the passenger door. He reaches inside and pulls a girl out of the opening. She is struggling in his hands. Her hair streams out behind her. She is so young, thinks Jan. Even in the moonlight she can see the girl is beautiful. Payne motions her forward. He is holding something in his hand, and she looks terrified.

"Right on time," says Morrow. "You see. I knew he'd come. I knew he'd bring her." He turns and smiles at Jan. "Fetch her a coat and some shoes, Bobby. We're going out."

Payne snatches Laura by the arm and holds her steady. The snow is deep here in the meadow, and she slips climbing over the stone fence. They follow the trail through the shrubs, across the flower bed, across the picket fence and up onto the lawn. Across the wide expanse of snow, they can see the bright white Cape Cod house nestled in a stand of pine, the glow of the sun porch lights, and three dark figures standing by the door.

"You know what we want." Morrow's voice carries like smoke through the snowy air.

Payne pushes Laura forward and she stumbles in the snow.

"Send her over and I'll let Jan go. I don't want to hurt anyone."

"Let Jan go first," shouts Payne.

For a moment no one speaks. Then Morrow says, "At the same time then. An exchange."

Payne pushes Laura in the back. "Go on," he says. She turns and glares at him. *"Go!"* She begins to make her way across the snowy lawn. An eerie silence settles on the night. The moon has disappeared again, and the air is full of huge white flakes. He watches Laura's form recede across the clearing. Beyond her, he can see Jan's silhouette, the narrow shoulders, the labored footsteps in the crisp snow. The figures slowly approach each other. A sweep of moonlight floods the clearing, and he can see Jan's face clearly as they pass by. She turns her head just slightly, stares, and her lips curl in a smile so weighted down with pain, such sadness and concern that he feels his heart freeze in his chest. The cold, the cold. He feels it in his feet, his hands. He can hear the snowflakes falling to the earth, the crystals clinging to each other. Jan turns away. She struggles through the snow, one hand around her pregnant stomach. Laura hesitates for a moment. Then she turns and looks at Payne. Her eyes are filled with tears. They glisten in the moonlight. She shudders and continues down the path.

Jan suddenly draws near. Her face is black. Her jaw is clenched and flinching. "Let's get out of here," she says.

"Not yet," says Payne. He stares beyond her at the silhouette of Laura's dark receding back. She has almost reached the house. Morrow moves to intercept her. For a moment, he hesitates. For an instant only as Laura reaches into her jacket, pulls out the gun and swings it down, but Morrow's gone, and at her side, and wrestling with her for the weapon.

"No!" shouts Payne.

Morrow elbows Laura in the face. She staggers backward, tripping in the snow. She struggles to her feet, but Morrow is already on her. He strikes his gun against her head. There is a loud brittle crack which even the falling snow can't dampen. Laura's head snaps back, and she drops lifeless to the ground.

"No!" Payne tries to run but Jan is holding him by the waist.

"Please, John. Let's go. Let's get help!"

"You go," he cries. He starts to pull away. "But I can't just let him kill her. I can't just turn away, not again." He tears across the lawn, plowing through the snow. He can still see Morrow standing over Laura's motionless form. Litchfield is fishing for something in the snow. It is the gun Payne gave to Laura, the gun she had hidden in her clothes. Morrow's nine-millimeter. Payne feels as though his lungs are freezing shut as he draws closer to the house. "Let her go," he screams. "Leave her alone."

"That was foolish," Morrow says. He turns and trains his pistol on Payne. It looks exactly like the other gun, coal black and deadly. Payne ignores it. He runs over to where Laura is lying in the snow. Her head is bleeding. He kneels beside her, feels for her pulse. It's slow but steady. Then he turns toward Morrow, rising to his feet.

"You fucking bastard. How dare you come into my house, threaten my wife? How fucking dare you?"

"Get out of my way, John."

"Not this time, Glen. This has gone far enough. You think you're above the law, but you're not."

"Above the law! You still don't get it, do you, John? I'm not above the law. You, me and Bobby, all of us. The Club. We *are* the law. We *are* the system, and everything it was built to protect. Success. Affluence—"

"God, listen to yourself, Glen. And whoever gets in your way, they're just expendable, is that it? Like Candy and Bumper."

Morrow laughs. "We're all expendable, John. Each at his own rate. We all burn up in our own time. Yolanda is already dead. But you're alive, John. You're alive! You're still in the game. And so are Bobby and Tom. And so am I!"

"And so is Laura. And she's going to stay that way."

Morrow smiles. "You know that isn't possible," he says.

"If you kill her, you're going to have to kill me too."

"Don't make me do that, John."

"I'm serious, Glen. If you kill her, I'm going straight to the police. I'll tell them everything I know."

"About Yolanda, too?"

Payne grins. "About Yolanda too."

"You're bluffing."

"I've got nothing to lose. I don't care what happens to me anymore. I'm a murderer, remember? I'm a desperate man."

"Get out of my way."

"You'll have to shoot me first."

"All right." He points his gun at Payne's face. "I will. I saved your life once, and I can take it back. You've been asking for it, John, right from the beginning. You've been itching for it."

"Don't do it, Glen," pleads Litchfield. "You promised."

"Shut up, Bobby. He's got it coming."

"No, don't. It isn't worth all this."

"Shut up, Bobby."

"It isn't worth it," Litchfield insists. "Do you hear me?" He turns toward Payne. "You didn't do it, John," he says.

"I told you to shut up."

"What? What did you say?"

"It's over," Morrow says. "It's finished. I thought I could count on you, John. I made you a member of The Club."

"Fuck you," says Payne. "Fuck you and your stupid Hunting Club. I quit. Do you hear me, Glen? I fucking quit." He starts to laugh. "What are you going to do about it?"

"I thought I could trust you."

"I quit. I'm joining the human race. You hear me, Glen?"

"I loved you," Morrow says. "Like my own brother. Better than Sam ever did. He just ran away. He left you behind with your mother and father, left all those trophies, all those expectations, everything he couldn't stand anymore. The only reason he went to Vietnam was because your father was against it."

"Shut up, Glen. Leave Sam out of this."

"No wonder he started shooting up. Vietnam must have seemed like a living hell after Hadley and New Canaan. Too bad he didn't tell his copilot. What was his name? Binghamton. Too bad he was too stoned to see the rocket coming, to see it angle up from the trees and tear into the fuselage. Too bad for Binghamton."

"Shut up. Shut up!"

"But you had the courage to stay behind, John. You finished

school. You got a job. You started a family. You didn't run away. You didn't put a pistol in your mouth and blow your head off."

Payne shakes his head. He starts to weep silently. He stares up at the milky sky. He feels snowflakes settle on his eyes. "Oh, Sam," he whispers quietly.

"Just like that, John. Boom. We all go. And now it's Laura's turn. You know it has to be, John. You've got to be strong. Don't give up like Sam did. You want to go back to your life, don't you? Back to Jan? She loves you more than anything. And she needs you, with the baby coming. She needs you. You've got to be strong."

"You're right." Payne turns and looks at Morrow. Tears shimmer in his eyes. He feels light-headed, drained and empty. He knows what he has to do.

"Of course I'm right, John."

Payne smiles. It is a warm and tender smile. "I'm sorry, Glen. I . . ." He chokes back tears. "I know you're only trying to do what's best. It's just . . . It's been so hard."

"I know. You don't know how happy I am to hear you say that." He lowers the gun.

Payne turns and looks at Laura lying in the snow. "I guess I know what I have to do. I guess I've known it all along." He looks at Morrow, his teeth clenched in a grin. "I got us into this. I have to finish it. Give me the gun, Glen."

Morrow starts to hand it over. Then he hesitates, he stares into Payne's eyes. Payne reaches for the gun, but Morrow pulls his hand away. "I don't know, John. Are you sure you're up to it?"

Payne looks at Morrow, holds his gaze. "Maybe you're right," he says. "Thanks, Glen. I appreciate that. I . . ." He turns and looks at Laura. He feels strangely collected, calm. "I'm tired of killing. Maybe you should do it for me. Will you do it for me, Glen?"

Morrow smiles. "If you want me to."

Payne stares into Morrow's ice blue eyes, shiny as glass. They glisten in the moonlight like mirrors. "Now?"

"Okay, John. Let's get it over with." Morrow turns and looks at Laura. She is breathing fitfully, hunched up in a ball in the snow. Morrow cocks the gun. He leans over and touches it to her head, he starts to squeeze the trigger, but he is just too late, too late to see Payne rush in from the side. The shot explodes into the snow. Payne leaps on top of Morrow, hurling him to the ground. They struggle for the gun. Payne punches Morrow furiously in the face, three, four, five times with his right hand, until he hears the sound of breaking bone. He lunges for the gun, but Morrow pushes him away. The gun slips free in the snow. They roll and roll on top of one another. A flash of pain cuts through Payne's wrist. Morrow is bending it back. He's using his larger size and weight to pin him to the snow. But Payne struggles furiously. He wriggles, feints one way, then slides out on the other. The gun. The gun is only inches out of reach. Payne elbows Morrow in the chin. He kicks and punches, he lunges for the gun. The weapon slips into his hand. He feels his fingers close around the trigger. He brings it down and strikes the heavy butt on Morrow's head. There is a dull, sickening thud. Morrow cries out. Payne wriggles free and struggles to his feet. He still holds the gun in his hand. Gasping, he points it down at Morrow's face.

"All right, Bobby, drop the gun."

Litchfield hesitates.

"Do it *now!*"

"No!" Morrow groans and sits up in the snow. Blood is pouring from a gash in his head. "Don't do it, Bobby. Help me up."

Litchfield doesn't move as Morrow struggles to his feet. Payne steps in front of Laura.

"Give me the gun, Bobby," Morrow says.

"Give him the gun, Bobby, and I'll kill you."

Litchfield backs away.

"He's not going to kill you, Bobby." Morrow laughs. "Give me the gun."

"All right, Glen, tell me."

"Tell you what, John?"

"About Yolanda. I didn't kill her, did I? Did I, Glen? Answer me!"

"Give me the gun, Bobby."

Litchfield does not move. He simply stares down at the snow, ignoring him.

"Give it to me, God dammit!" Morrow shouts.

"No."

"What did you say?"

"I said no, Glen. I'm not going to give you the gun."

Morrow's eyes grow dark. He steps back. He touches his head. He looks down at the blood on his hand. Then he fixes his gaze on Payne and smiles, and despite the blood, despite the snow-packed matted hair and battered nose, it is still the famous Morrow smile. It still transforms his face, enlivens it. He stands a little straighter as he says, "No, John, you didn't kill her." Then he turns and looks at Litchfield. "Bobby did."

"Shut up, Glen. You don't know what you're talking about." Litchfield points his gun at Morrow's face.

Morrow laughs. "What's the matter, Bobby? Why don't you tell him? I think it's time he knew."

"I told you to shut up."

"All right, I'll tell him." His voice is low and even now. "Yolanda was smoking a joint, John. You had passed out. Bobby and I were looking for the bathroom." His eyes seem to glaze in the moonlight. " 'Couldn't keep it up?' I said to her. We were standing by her bedroom door. Then Yolanda said, 'It'll cost you if you're coming back for more.' But I told her, 'How often does a man get married in his life. Two, three times?' I remember it. I remember it all."

"Go on," says Payne. "What happened next?"

"We walked over to the bed and I unzipped my fly." Morrow smiles. "It didn't take her long. Then she turned and looked at Bobby. 'Go on, BB,' I said. 'What's the matter?' So Bobby unzipped his fly, too. Then she said, 'How come they call you BB?' " He imitates Yolanda's singsong voice. "And I told her. We were never going to see her again anyway. She started laughing and laughing, with Bobby's little dick in her hand. She couldn't even put it in her mouth, she was laughing so hard."

"Shut up, Glen," Litchfield cries. "You promised."

" 'You little bitch,' he said. 'You dirty little bitch.' And then he pushed her. Her head went back and hit the metal headboard. There was this light brittle crack, you know, like the sound of someone stepping on a branch. Not even very loud. I remember her eyes rolled up. You were lying right next to her, asleep. Her eyes rolled up. That's when she started to bleed."

"Jesus, it was you?" Payne whispers. He turns on Litchfield suddenly. Litchfield starts backing toward the house, his gun trained on Morrow's mocking face.

"Why didn't you tell me?" says Payne. "Didn't you trust me?"

"I had to protect The Club," Morrow says. He starts to laugh. "You were the only one I did trust, John, the only one who could take what I knew was coming. Bobby and Tom were too weak." He shakes his head. "You were the logical choice. And so is this. We have to end it, John. Give me the gun. Come back to The Club." He takes a step closer to Payne.

"Keep away from me."

"Give me the gun."

"I mean it, Glen. I swear, I'll cut you down right here, you bastard."

"No, you won't."

"Don't count on it."

Morrow wipes his hands on his coat. He straightens his bright red scarf. "But I do, John. I do." Then he laughs. "Face it, John, you just don't have it in you. You've proven that already." He smiles and looks at Laura. He brushes the hair back from his face. "Now, give me the gun."

"I'm warning you. Keep back." Payne points the gun at Morrow's heart.

"What are you going to do, John, kill me?" Morrow takes a step closer, his arms extended, palms up, his hands out like a beggar. "You can't. You know you can't. You owe me, remember? I saved your life. I'm the best friend you ever had." He takes another step. A shot rings out and Morrow spirals backward to the snow.

Payne stands there without breathing. He looks down at the gun in his hand. His hand is shaking. The gun is wet from the snow. It glimmers in the moonlight. It sparkles. Cold as ice. Unfired. He takes a breath and turns. Litchfield is standing behind him.

"Glen!" he cries. Litchfield throws his weapon to the ground.

He rushes forward. He drops to his knees by Morrow's crumpled form. A circle of blood begins to stain the snow near Morrow's head. "Glen," Bobby says, over and over, rocking on his knees. "You promised." He tugs at Morrow's scarf. He runs a hand through Morrow's hair.

Somewhere a siren sounds, echoing through the night.

Payne looks behind him at the house. Jan is standing in a gust of whirling snow. The moon is shining on her face. Her forehead glistens. Her hair, flecked with snowflakes, streams in the wind. She stands with her arms outstretched beyond her pregnant stomach, her feet apart, her elbows bent, and Sam's old .45 still cooling in her hands.